"Sweet and spicy and fabulous. . . . Ivy Fairbanks is a terrific addition to the romance genre!"

—Abby Jimenez, *New York Times* bestselling author of
Yours Truly

"Five stars. *Morbidly Yours* is my favorite kind of rom-com. It's funny, sexy, and smartly written, while also being deeply emotionally resonant. Lark and Callum are characters you've never seen before and that you'll never forget."

—Annabel Monaghan, bestselling author of
Nora Goes Off Script and *Same Time Next Summer*

"A delightful, wonderfully disastrous romp through love. Fans of the marriage-of-convenience trope will swoon—as did I!"

—Ashley Herring Blake, *USA Today* bestselling author of
Delilah Green Doesn't Care

"What a marvelous story about friendship, family, grief and, of course, true love. Kudos to Fairbanks for creating a world where heartache and romance can coexist. I laughed, I cried, I definitely swooned. Emotionally complex, wholly unique, and absolutely wonderful—if you haven't discovered Ivy Fairbanks already, you're in for a treat!"

—Marissa Stapley, *New York Times* bestselling author of
Lucky

Morbidly Yours

Morbidly Yours

IVY FAIRBANKS

G. P. PUTNAM'S SONS
New York

PUTNAM
— EST. 1838 —

G. P. Putnam's Sons
Publishers Since 1838
An imprint of Penguin Random House LLC
penguinrandomhouse.com

Morbidly Yours was originally self-published, in different form, in 2023.

Library of Congress Cataloging-in-Publication Data
Names: Fairbanks, Ivy, author.
Title: Morbidly yours / Ivy Fairbanks.
Description: New York : G. P. Putnam's Sons, 2024.
Identifiers: LCCN 2024003598 (print) | LCCN 2024003599 (ebook) |
ISBN 9780593851869 (trade paperback) | ISBN 9780593851876 (epub)
Subjects: LCGFT: Romance fiction. | Novels.
Classification: LCC PS3606.A348 M67 2024 (print) |
LCC PS3606.A348 (ebook) | DDC 813/.6—dc23/eng/20240209
LC record available at https://lccn.loc.gov/2024003598
LC ebook record available at https://lccn.loc.gov/2024003599

Printed in the United States of America
1st Printing

Book design by Patrice Sheridan

TO MY MOM.

There's a confession I must make:
during middle school, I stole every shirtless-cowboy
romance novel from your nightstand that you warned me
not to read. Miss you every day, and
I hope this makes up for it.

AUTHOR'S NOTE

Morbidly Yours is a celebration of love, healing, and finding a balance between the light and the dark.

While optimistic and humorous, both characters navigate grief throughout, including the (past/off-page) death of a spouse, and the loss of an elderly friend. This story also contains brief but honest depictions of caring for the departed in a funeral home.

If you are sensitive to these themes, please be mindful.

IRISH / GAEILGE
PRONUNCIATION AND TRANSLATION GUIDE

CHARACTER NAMES

Saoirse / Seer-sha

Deirdre / Deer-dra

Pádraig / PAW-drig

Tadhg / TIE-g

Aoife / Ee-fuh

WORDS

fáilte / FALL-cha / welcome

Gaeilge / GWAIL-guh / Irish language

sláinte / SLAWN-cha / cheers (literally "health")

amadán / OMma-dawn / fool

tá tú go hálainn / taw too guh HAWling / you're lovely

tá mé i ngrá leat / Taw may ih ngraw lyat / I love you

For intimate terms, turn to the pronunciation and translation guide on p. 333.

Morbidly
Yours

CHAPTER 1

Lark

FIVE BODY BAGS, ADULT SIZE

I blinked and fumbled the box cutter I'd been using.

What the hell?

I looked around, hoping to find an answer in the haphazard stacks of boxes that surrounded me. But no. Just me and the few belongings I'd deemed irreplaceable enough to make the transatlantic trip. It was amazing, really, how little made up a life— especially when you had to factor in shipping expenses from Texas to Ireland.

My attention returned to the innocuous box and the neat stack of black nylon fabric inside. I'd been using the box cutter as a microphone, swept away by Dolly Parton's shimmering voice and the promise of a new beginning as I unpacked, when the shock of the body bags rudely knocked me out of my groove.

I checked the shipping paperwork for the intended recipient: Willow Haven. The bed-and-breakfast next door.

What. The. Hell?

Galway's reputation for liveliness had drawn me to the city, and now I found a package of death supplies in my living room.

Of course the morbid specter of guilt would follow me from Austin. Grief had been my stowaway across the pond.

I peeked through the blinds of my partially furnished rental apartment. No signs of life from the building across the way. The arched windows and stone facade made it a prime example of local architecture. Google Maps Street View had sold me on this quaint Celtic neighborhood only two weeks ago, thanks to its gorgeous views of the bay and vibrant art scene. I may be spontaneous enough to pick up and move my life for a job in another country on short notice, but I'm savvy enough to brush up on the local crime rate before inadvertently signing a lease in a seedy part of town.

While my new building itself was cute and historical, the apartment's furnishings were nothing to write home about: a thread-bare love seat and water-ringed writing desk that now served as home to my trusty iPad Pro and stylus. My battered steamer trunk stood in for a coffee table. Just the basics for my nine-month stay.

My cousin Cielo's loopy handwriting on the side of a box caught my eye. I missed her already. Forty-five hundred miles now stretched between me and everyone in my old life. For the first time in twenty-nine years, I was alone. By choice . . . but still. Body bags delivered to my new apartment was definitely not on my Fresh Start in Ireland bingo card.

Maybe the person who ordered the bags needed them for some kind of project. People who plan to hide bodies usually avoid associated paper trails. Right? Galway was a haven for creatives, with its college and busker-filled alleys. Surely there was an explanation.

Swaths of ivy clung to the Georgian building next door. Graceful willows shaded the yard. It didn't look evil. Maybe the owner needed these bags right away, for a play or student film. This could be an opportunity to make my first friend here. A friend who definitely *wasn't* a serial killer. Outside of the management and HR staff at my new job, I didn't know a soul in Ireland.

I'd even tried to chat up the delivery driver—in hindsight, that was probably what caused the package mix-up. I needed to meet the neighbor before my imagination spiraled. For heaven's sake, this place was voted the world's friendliest city more than once.

I slipped into my favorite Ariat cowboy boots and a sweater against the November chill. Curiosity tingled as I approached the bed-and-breakfast with the box tucked under my arm.

The reception desk was unattended. Traditional yet homey, the lobby held a somber energy. A minor operation run by a doily-crocheting matronly woman, one could only assume. Sadly, probably not my new BFF. A service bell sat on the desk, round and silver, as shiny as a drop of mercury. A satisfying ring filled the space when I tapped it.

Nada.

"Hello?" I felt like the horror movie character who wanders off alone, calling into the dark instead of running away.

Grateful I didn't meet a murderer, I set the package on the counter. But before I could make my escape, a deep voice answered from somewhere unseen.

CHAPTER 2

Callum

THE DEAD WOMAN'S mouth hung open like an opera diva's in mid-note. Moving the needle through Ms. Murphy's septum, I pushed the curved stainless steel through her right nostril before piercing the roof of her mouth. The suture threaded around the jawbone before I returned to the starting point to close the loop. With a gentle tug on the filament, I drew her mouth closed and tied it off in a bow that got poked down into a nostril. There. Much better.

Poor thing. Thirty-four years old—my age. No spouse, no children. A distant relative handled her arrangements. After choking on an olive pit and missing a shift at work, Ms. Murphy had been fired without any inquiry into the reasons for her absence. Twelve days later, her neighbor complained about the smell. Other than my handful of employees, I'd have no one to notice my absence, either.

The front hall service bell dinged, and a woman's delicate voice called out.

"Hello?"

Walk-ins weren't common, but they happened. The clock read 7:00 p.m. During normal hours, Deirdre welcomed our guests, walking them through the process while assessing the possibility of an upgrade to a mahogany or bronze package. Customer service was not my forte.

Pushing against the door, I shouted toward the entry, "I'll b-b— Just a moment, please."

Social anxiety and stuttering were my personal stumbling blocks. Growing up, I became terrified about having to say *present* at school roll call. Teachers singled me out to read aloud or answer rapid-fire questions at every opportunity ("tough love," they dubbed this cruelty), or ignored me. My classmates were worse. Between living in a funeral home and rarely speaking, I was a secondary school pariah. Even though speech therapy eventually improved my fluency, it didn't stop the bullying.

Grumbling, I stripped off my gloves and the splatter guard that shielded my face and spectacles. Once the embalming process started, it was important to follow through without wasting time, so I was glad I hadn't yet begun. Preservation chemicals set fast, locking limbs and expression in place. It would take only a minute to schedule this visitor a consultation with Deirdre tomorrow. Then I could get back to the task at hand.

Steeling my nerves and adjusting my tie, I made the approach.

Silhouetted by the ruby glow of the stained glass, a petite woman of about thirty with a heart-shaped face held out a large shipping box. Blond hair spilled over her shoulders, and she wore a casual jumper and jeans. Attractive. Not that it mattered.

"Hi. I just moved in next door and was sorting through a mountain of boxes. I think this package is yours?" Her drawling accent wasn't local. Pale pink cowboy boots tapped on the parquet. "The post office delivered this to my place by mistake."

I hadn't noticed the previous tenants move out. Blame it on spending most of my time in the mortuary. As owner of Willow Haven, I delegated work-related calls to colleagues. Avoidance and routine were my comforts.

"Fáilte," I managed, and cleared my throat. "Welcome."

"Thanks. Everyone is so nice here. I can see how the city gets its friendly reputation. I mean, I'm used to Southern hospitality. In America, of course."

"Thank you." I took the proffered, unsealed box. She'd tucked the tabs to keep it closed.

"I was unpacking and didn't notice this one wasn't mine until I opened it. Whoops. It's all there, though. Promise. I didn't snoop on purpose." Words flew as her hands gesticulated. "I'm Lark. As in 'happy as a . . . ' And before you ask about the name, yes, my mom does smell like patchouli and read auras. I don't. Read auras, that is. Or wear patchouli."

Auras? Patchouli? Silence stretched between us as I grappled for a response to the verbal barrage.

"Callum Flannelly." Yes, that was the best I could come up with.

Despite my terse reply, genuine warmth infused her smile as she shook my hand. Then she wrinkled her nose. Formaldehyde and eau de decomposition weren't the most pleasant of scents, no matter how many flower arrangements flanked the front desk. After working in the prep room, I always showered, but I hadn't expected an interruption. I wilted as she withdrew her hand.

"Pleased to make your acquaintance," she said.

She traced a finger along the wainscoting. Cozy chairs clustered around a fireplace where a peat brick provided heat. Tissue boxes rested on each end table. Pertinent catalogs and brochures stayed filed away between appointments to communicate an emphasis on connection, not consumerism—my granda Tadhg always believed it crass to keep them on display during a wake. All in all, the effect created a comforting, homelike environment.

"How long have you worked here?"

Self-conscious, I rubbed at the red groove on my forehead left by the face shield and adjusted my glasses before they could slip down my nose. "Hard to say. I grew up in this house and have helped since I could walk."

"All sorts of interesting people must come through, huh?"

My great-grandfather had purchased and converted the inn to a funeral home almost a century ago. Since then, we'd buried Galwegians of all stripes. A tattooist who requested to have a section of their skin removed and preserved for display in their shop. A film buff laid to rest clutching a screen-accurate replica lightsaber, to the sound of a John Williams score. A painter whose family transformed our chapel into a retrospective art exhibition.

The relentlessly outgoing new neighbor plopped down at the upright piano, tapping out "Chopsticks" on the worn keys, without bothering to ask permission. She thumbed through the hymns in the songbook. Sheet music fluttered under her fingers. "Can you play any of these?" She scooted to one side of the padded bench and patted the seat next to her.

Happy as a Lark. Based on her amicable audacity in strolling into my home and blithely requesting a performance, it fit her.

"Oh, I couldn't—"

"Please? It doesn't have to be Mozart. As a nonmusical person, anything more complex than 'Mary Had a Little Lamb' will impress me." She smiled at me. Despite every fiber of my being screaming to hide in the clinical prep room, I crossed to the piano.

I sat and wiped my sweaty hands on my trousers. I didn't owe her anything. She wasn't even a customer. But something about her rambling, energetic presence made me want to oblige.

"Are all of them sad, traditional love songs?"

I supposed they were all love songs, in a way. Grief, rebellion, and faith all stemmed from love. There were a few of the romantic sort. But they weren't all sad.

My fingers moved over the keys as I played the bridge and chorus of "Galway Bay" by memory. Familiar as the mist. Just as imbued with mysterious magic.

The unabashed appreciation on my new neighbor's face flushed me with pride. Lark's eyes drifted shut as warm, rich notes cascaded from the antique instrument. In my peripheral vision, I could see her eyes remain closed for a moment after my hands stilled. I felt paralyzed, all my attention on this brazen stranger.

"I like it." Lark excavated a notebook from under the sheaf of sheet music. "What's this? Some kind of handwritten lyrics—"

Clearing my throat, I pried it away, my hands protectively curled around the worn pages. "That's private."

"Oh. Sorry. Do you sing, too?"

"No." My reply was too firm, too quick.

She frowned as I clutched the notebook, then recovered her easygoing smile. Lark swung her feet under the piano bench. Set up for my considerable height, it kept her boots suspended off the hardwood floor. It reminded me of learning dirges when all I wanted to do was watch the sailboats in the bay as a boy.

"Sooo, I have to ask, even though it's none of my business: What are they for?"

"The sheet music?"

"No, silly!"

Silly? In all the taunts and cruelties thrown at me in my life, no one had ever accused me of being silly. *Slow*, often. *Scary*, occasionally. *Silly* suggested a level of whimsy I'd been too serious to achieve.

"You know . . . the body bags. What are they for?"

"Bodies," I answered, not understanding the question.

Her mouth jerked into an uncomfortable, plastic smile. Not like before. "I understand what they're made for. But why do you need them?"

Lark's query wasn't outright accusatory, but cautious. Apprehensive. I wet my lip with my tongue. "Occasionally, we have a disinterment. It can get messy."

It was her turn to blink. "What?"

"Thanks for popping over. Sorry about the mix-up with the

package," I said, remembering Ms. Murphy still laid out on the table, waiting to be embalmed.

"I'm being nosy." She exhaled a nervous titter. "I was a little freaked out when I noticed what they were. It gave me this wild idea you were about to slaughter all your guests or something. Ridiculous, right?"

"No need to worry. They're all already d-dead."

She paled. "I should go. I'll be going now. Um, good night."

Lark hopped off the bench and retreated toward the door without taking her eyes off me. I stood and took a deliberate step back so she wouldn't feel crowded. What had I said?

"I have to go, too. The guests don't embalm themselves."

She stilled. Her focus darted around the foyer as if seeing it for the first time. Then she turned the same unnerving scrutiny on me.

"Hold up. This is a funeral parlor?"

Afraid I'd frighten her again, I nodded. Shock flashed across her face, and she seemed to shrink in on herself, as if body fluids tainted the upholstery and jack-in-the-box corpses sprung from caskets.

"Oh. Oh, damn! So you're—you were embalming somebody before you answered the bell?"

"What did you think?"

"A Norman Bates situation. I don't know, I suffer from an overactive imagination. Like I said—ridiculous."

The vaguely familiar name ricocheted through my brain. I tilted my head.

"You know." Lark pantomimed stabbing me with an invisible knife while making a screeching sound. "Hitchcock."

Oh. *Psycho.* But why would she . . .

"You assumed I was a homicidal innkeeper?"

From her reaction, my actual vocation wasn't a far step up from murderer.

"Yes!" Vindication blazed in her gray eyes. "You can't blame me for imagining you in your mother's dress."

Squeezing myself into a flowery frock would make a ghastly sight, indeed.

"I thought this might be an artist's colony, with the bags ordered for a performance or maybe an installation. Maybe a political demonstration. I try to give folks the benefit of the doubt. I didn't know you were a . . . mortician." As if it were dirty, she lowered her voice on the last word. "I hate to get off on the wrong foot. You must think I'm a fool as well as a package thief."

Well, yes. A little. I offered her what I hoped was a sympathetic smile. "Only wondering how one moves next d-d-door to a funeral home without knowing." I braced myself for her to make a face at the stammer, but she didn't.

"In my defense, Willow Haven sounds like a retirement community or a bed-and-breakfast. And your sign is in Gaelic."

I'd never understood why Americans used that term for Irish. Here, it was synonymous with the Scots. Regardless, the plaque had stood outside for decades, translating to "Mortuary—family owned and operated since 1931." Countless layers of fresh paint kept it intact through relentless weather. Tradition mattered—I had no interest in adding English. An update wasn't happening.

"We just call it Irish. Or Gaeilge."

She shot me a skeptical look. "Quail-geh? Like the bird with the . . ." Lark curled a finger and brought it to her forehead to mimic a dangling feather.

No. Not even close, considering it was a hard *G* sound. I thought about repeating myself but held my tongue.

"Nothing grates us more than our language being called Gaelic, except hearing Yanks boast what percentage of Irish blood they have, according to some website."

Amused, Lark fiddled with the hem of her jumper. She could barely seem to hold still. "You're kind of a grump, aren't you?"

"You ask a lot of questions." I had a waiting body to return to.

"I thought y'all were super hospitable to foreigners. 'Land of a Thousand Welcomes,' right?"

I snorted. "I'm in the business of goodbyes, not hellos."

"Well, the location would explain why the apartment was available. I have to admit, you wouldn't be my first choice of neighbor—oh God—not you personally, I mean a funeral parlor. That came out all wrong. I'm gonna get out of your hair, now that I've insulted you twice. Sorry."

After Lark left, I stood in bewilderment. Both at the woman herself and at my odd, relatively genial reaction to her. I locked the door and retreated to the familiar sterility of the prep room, donning my protective gear like armor. I liked the tidy order of it. The quiet.

I sliced into Ms. Murphy's neck and probed with the aneurysm hook until I found the artery. Since she had been healthy before the fateful olive pit, her carotid's texture was that of al dente macaroni, easily accommodating the arterial tube that snaked to the embalming machine hose. Formalin gurgled in the clear reservoir like a threat, and I tapped at a pink bubble. Damn thing was on the fritz. One more complication my life didn't need. It hummed into action, creating pressure in the circulatory system to displace the stale blood with preservation chemicals.

I reflected on the unexpected interaction with the blonde next door. Playing piano for Lark had been . . . pleasant. Mostly. I couldn't remember the last time I'd had a conversation with a stranger unrelated to work. Especially one I enjoyed.

Suppose a grumpy undertaker could do worse for a thieving neighbor.

CHAPTER 3

Lark

TEN MINUTES HAD passed since my bus was scheduled to arrive. My visa hinged on keeping this job, and I wasn't about to return to Austin with my tail tucked between my legs. I pulled my phone from my purse, jabbing at the screen to call a taxi.

Inching toward the road, I craned to the right to watch for the bus. A cyclist whizzed past, water spraying from her back tire and drenching my face and hair. Sputtering from the shock of icy gutter water, my grip loosened and the phone fell through the slats of a sewer grate. *No!*

I peered into the murky drain, hoping the device was within arm's reach, but my phone was surfing the sewer now. Fantastic. My first day of work, and the universe was not cooperating.

Thankfully I'd studied the route to the studio when I was figuring out which bus to take. As the autumn breeze strewed fallen leaves in my path, I tucked my trench coat closer around me and set off on foot.

Before my morning went to crap, I'd sauntered in front of the mirror like Jessica Rabbit to give myself a confidence boost for my first day at the new job. Oversize cherry earrings completed my outfit of a bright pink pencil skirt, a red turtleneck under my trench, and my favorite red heels. It wasn't as crazy as it sounded: the founder of Pixar was famous for a rotation of Hawaiian shirts. Animators could resemble cartoon characters at work. Some people even expected it.

My heels skidded to a halt at the sight of massive cemetery gates spanning both sides of the road. A dead end, literally and figuratively. Celtic crosses dotted the neatly mown grass. I shut my eyes, remembering a basketball engraved in granite.

Reese Thompson. Husband. Son. Brother. Coach.

If I cut across the misty, hallowed ground, I might make it on time. A backhoe rumbled somewhere in the distance. Nope. Not worth it. Reese and I may have skydived and windsurfed, both daredevils who reveled in the rush of joyful adrenaline, yet since I was a kid nothing made my pulse race like the somber quiet of graveyards. They'd always freaked me out, and now I couldn't see one without remembering the man I'd lost so suddenly. No shortcut for me. Besides, with my luck this morning, I'd probably trip and chip a tooth on a headstone.

Doubling back, I passed the bus stop as I marched down the street. Few shops were open at this hour, though a cart of roses blocked the sidewalk in front of a florist, brilliant red contrasting with the morning fog. I paused in front of the florist's window to examine my waterlogged reflection. My curls had wilted into soggy kelp, and my "waterproof" mascara ran down my cheeks.

The door swung open.

"Sorry—" A broad-shouldered man dodged me, and the words evaporated on his tongue. Sensual, full lips hung open, offsetting the sharp architecture of his cheekbones. Intelligent arsenic-green eyes surveyed me from behind round tortoiseshell frames. "Oh. It's *you*."

"Hey . . ." *Guy I accused of being a serial killer? Guy I'd offended in his own home?* I settled on: "Neighbor."

Dressed in a black wool waistcoat over a crisp white shirt and slim trousers that made his legs look like sequoias, he clutched an arrangement of calla lilies. No coat, despite the crisp November morning. If the studio asked me to design an "undertaker" character, he'd wear a pin-striped suit and have dark under-eye circles worthy of Gomez Addams. This starchy man's fashion sense fit the stereotype, even if his face and body didn't.

"It's Callum, right?" I thrust out my hand. "Lark."

"You've got a right puss on."

I rounded on him. "Excuse me?"

"Your puss." He gestured at his face, mimicking my frown. Oh. Sourpuss. I had to get used to their weird slang.

"It's been a mess of a morning. My bus never showed up, so I went to call a cab, but this cyclist sprayed me with street sludge and I dropped my phone. Bloop! Right into the sewer grate. Hence looking like the Swamp Thing and rushing to work on foot like a maniac so I don't get fired from my new job."

Callum's nose crinkled. Whether at my mention of street sludge or my rapid-fire discharge of my problems, I didn't know. For an instant, his gaze dropped to my impractical (but gorgeous) footwear. "No cowboy b-boots today."

"Nope. Traded them for a pair of heels that are no fun to walk in." I rubbed the raccoon mask around my eyes. "Hey, could I use your cell to call a taxi? Waiting for the next bus will make me late."

He stayed silent a beat too long, and just when I opened my mouth to say *never mind*, he jerked his head to show I should accompany him. "I'll run you over."

"Are you threatening me or offering me a lift?"

He shrugged like it was a toss-up, face remaining neutral. In all fairness, he had cause to want me under his tires after I'd assumed he was a serial killer.

Did I have a choice? Not really. Unless I wanted to call KinetiColor and let them know I was running late the morning of the first staff meeting for the new feature. This meeting was huge—my introduction to the animators and designers I'd be supervising.

My eyes narrowed at Callum. "Are you sure? Looks like you're busy."

Callum kept walking without answering, until he led me to a gleaming, vintage ebony hearse on the next corner. An actual hearse. My heels came to a skidding halt a second time.

"I don't know what I expected," I mumbled to myself.

"The late Mrs. Higgins will accompany us, if that's all right with you."

"Ha-ha. Almost got me." With a wave of my hand, I batted away the idea. Of course it was unoccupied if he was offering me a lift.

"I'm codding ya. It's empty."

Codding?

After a beat, he smiled. Cautiously, like wearing a piece of trendy clothing he wasn't fully comfortable in. It seemed genuine, if not natural. Nice to discover that the guy possessed a sense of humor after all.

Then, through the windows framed by those strange little curtains, I noticed the passenger. "There's a coffin in the back!"

"It would get scratched in the transport van. No one's in it. Yet."

"Pardon my French, but that's bullshit," I shot back, surprising myself a little. The unwanted reminders of the past had me on edge.

"Care to open it and find out?" One of his thick brows arched, daring me to call his bluff.

"No, thanks! Really, I can't take up your time but I appreciate the offer. I'll just see if the florist has a phone I can use."

"I thought you were in a rush."

"It's fine. Don't worry about me." I pivoted toward the flower shop as he unlocked the hearse and laid the floral spray down in the back. "Nice running into you."

I stopped myself. Nothing bad was going to happen from riding in a hearse for a few minutes. And I didn't want to offend Callum after he offered to drive. Without my phone's navigation, I wasn't even 100 percent sure where I was going anyway. He was my best option, and, well, beggars can't be choosers.

He folded his six-foot-whatever height into the driver's seat and adjusted his tie's complicated knot in the mirror. "Coming?"

I allowed myself an incredulous snort, hoping none of my new colleagues would see my arrival. "This is super weird."

"Just get in," he replied flatly.

Get in the death buggy unless you wanna be late on the first—and arguably most important—day of your new job. With a groan, I jumped into the passenger's side before I changed my mind. God, what would Cielo say when I replaced my phone and told her about this?

"Where to?"

"KinetiColor Studios."

He wasn't familiar, but found it on Google Maps soon enough.

After traveling a few blocks, my heart rate and claustrophobia still hadn't calmed. I took a cleansing breath and, regrettably, sucked in a lungful of chemical air freshener. Or was that lingering formaldehyde? Piña colada was the scent I'd preferred in my beloved old Volkswagen. My chest ached with the memory of Reese presenting me with the decal that read *Normalize Hitting the Curb*. He'd put it on slightly crooked, like his smile. My husband had always teased me about my attachment to that beater. Missing the car that ferried me through the Austin traffic was much easier than missing Reese. Far safer to distract myself lamenting over Loretta the Jetta if I wanted to keep my mascara from running again.

Driver's licenses were an expensive and time-restricted privilege in Ireland, it turned out. As a new immigrant, it would be months before I'd qualify to sit for the test. My boss had assured me that public transport would suffice in Galway. Although, once I thought about it, I doubted that Mr. Sullivan ever rode the bus.

"New job, then?" Callum asked, pulling me back to the present. Today wasn't about fixating on the past; it was a fresh start.

"Yes. I'm the animation art director."

He cut me a surprised look. "You make cartoons?"

"Uh-huh. They brought me on board for their first feature project."

"Worked on anything I might know?"

"The biggest thing was a streaming release about an outcast fourth grader. *Shoelace*?" I listed other small projects, rambling as if small talk could distract me from the fact that countless bodies had been transported in this vehicle. All the tragedy it had seen. The quiet man kept his attention on the narrow streets.

"In a half hour, I'm presenting my ideas in a conceptual meeting with the senior design team. Who I've never met before."

Callum winced. Efficient, almost mechanical movements eased the car into a right turn. "Nervous, are ya?"

I let out a telling, tittering laugh. Nothing like an impromptu ride in a death coach to calm one's nerves. "A little. We're working from a beautiful, quintessentially Irish screenplay. Striking the right tone in our visuals is going to be crucial."

He nodded in sympathy.

Water was still dripping from my hair onto my lap. "You know, I've never been inside one of these before."

"I've never had a passenger so talkative."

"Quit saying things like that so I can pretend it's a limousine and we're chauffeuring to a fancy wedding."

"Know the difference between a wedding and a funeral in Ireland?" he asked.

I waited for the punch line.

"One less drunk at the party." Half of his mouth ticked up, then fell flat. "Sorry. It's a terrible joke."

It was, but I laughed anyway. I rolled down my window,

stealing a sidelong peek at my driver. Callum's reluctant smile was like lightning in a thunderstorm. Brief yet brilliant. Was he so used to tamping down his joy around other people's grief that he subconsciously dimmed his positive emotions?

The navigation app announced that we were a block away from our destination, and I recognized the KinetiColor Studios building from their website. A few of my colleagues loitered out front.

Great. Just the first impression I'd wanted to make.

I noticed Wendy from HR, who'd conducted my Skype interviews. Sculpted brows shot toward her hairline when she recognized me and walked toward my open window.

A bearded man called to someone in the group. "That's convenient. The undertaker's come to pick up the remains of your career!"

The animator he'd targeted didn't smile, and he scurried inside without so much as a backward glance as the other man chuckled at his own quip.

"Lark?" Wendy said, grinning. Once she got a closer look at me, she flinched at my sullied hair and makeup.

Forcing myself to play it cool, I smiled. "Wendy, hi!"

A cluster of young professionals gawked at my ride. I cast a look at Callum, expecting a conspiratorial sparkle to glisten in his eyes, but found none. The defrosting connection between us refroze under Wendy's curiosity.

"Who's yer man?"

"What? No, no, no. Wendy, this is Callum. He's— Callum is my neighbor. Only a neighbor. It's not . . ." I gulped and clapped my hands. "Well! I'll be right up. Big day today, I'm so excited."

Someone poked their head out the door and waved at Wendy, so she excused herself with a promise to meet me inside for orientation and introductions.

"Your entrance will be the talk of the town," Callum said, his eyes averted.

My fumbling declaration that he was just my neighbor must

have suggested embarrassment. But I wasn't ashamed to be seen with him. My discomfort was rooted in the hearse itself and the hungrily empty coffin waiting to be someone's resting place for eternity. The painful memories it all conjured. After the kindness Callum had shown, I was grateful.

"This is the weirdest Uber I've ever taken. Thank you."

"You're welcome. Anytime."

Without overthinking, I leaned across the center console and pecked him on the cheek. Callum's subtle aftershave reminded me of rain.

Nuclear fuchsia blazed on his face and ears once I withdrew. His fingers clamped around the steering wheel, like he was driving over a rickety one-lane bridge with no guardrails. I brushed a thumb over the pink lipstick I'd left and made it worse. Callum swallowed heavily. *Crap.* Would he read the friendly peck as a sign of interest? It wasn't. Back when I had friends, I kissed them on the cheek often, but of course Callum and I weren't on that level. Way to crank the awkward dial to eleven.

"You'll save a few minutes of walking if you cut through the cemetery next time," he said.

I opened the door and teetered on the curb.

"Appreciate the tip, but I'll take the long, not-haunted route."

Before I entered the building, I turned to find Callum's hand raised to his flushed cheek. Our eyes met, and he jerked it away. Okay. He was sort of cute. Before pulling away from the curb he mouthed, "Good luck." I'd need it.

CHAPTER 4

Callum

I STARED AT the chess set, untouched in the year since my granda's first stroke had transformed him. Overnight, that shrewd but empathetic businessman had lost his ability to function independently, so I'd assumed both his day-to-day work duties and his personal care. Loneliness permeated the house even more deeply in the quiet days after his second stroke, which sent him to hospital. He never returned.

"I was always meant to inherit Willow Haven." Pádraig's gruff voice issued from my mobile's speaker. Regardless of shared DNA, I refused to think of him as "Dad."

"It's supposed to stay in the family. The family you left," I shot back. My fist tightened, knuckles blanching around the device. He had no right. My granda's will said otherwise. Willow Haven would be held in trust. If I were still single by the deadline—my thirty-fifth birthday in July—Pádraig would take ownership. However, if I could provide a valid marriage certificate, it would become mine.

Eight months to find a wife. Rather, *six* months, with the requisite three-month wait for a marriage license.

All because my granda was fixated on the idea of an heir to the family business. He made a deathbed effort to reconcile with his estranged son, and it had gotten me into this mess.

"No sense in drawing out the inevitable. Just sign the agreement."

"No! This is my home. My life. I'm not handing it over to anyone. Least of all you."

"Look, O'Reilly and Sons gave me an offer. I don't want to give them time to change their minds."

"You've been shopping for a b-b-buyout from our competitors?"

He cited a number that seemed astronomical to me. "That's what they're willing to pay. It includes the business itself, the house, cemetery, hearse, transport van. Any product on hand. It's a fair valuation."

So that was the real reason he'd traveled from Edinburgh. He'd stealthily taken inventory, scheming while I'd been mourning and preparing Granda for burial.

The Georgian house boasted a prime, picturesque location, and the fact that we owned the cemetery gave us an edge over the competition. The property's high value meant I had slim chance of securing a sufficient loan, and recent renovations had drained our liquid funds. I had no personal collateral to offer except my own Peugeot, no meaningful professional experience outside my duties at Willow Haven. There was no chance I could afford to purchase it from Pádraig.

"O'Reilly promised to consider keeping you on staff. And I'd give you a cut."

I scoffed.

"We should strike while there's a lucrative offer on the table. This isn't personal. Just business."

"I amn't a sellout," I spat into the phone. "This isn't what Granda wanted."

"Stubborn as the old goat himself, are you not? Well, he's not here, so it doesn't matter." Pádraig lowered his voice. "Be realistic. We both know you won't be married by July."

"Watch me."

I hung up.

What was I saying? Lonely as I was, dating was still a nightmare. I was barely able to speak to women. Connection was elusive and always came slowly for me, which resulted in frustrating dates that went nowhere. I moved at a different pace than most people. Even the dates who insisted they wanted to take things slow still expected a kiss good night. I'd tried to force myself more than once, and it backfired when I'd offended them with a dry peck on the lips. Romance is about feeling desired, and I couldn't bring myself to fake that.

After I'd first found out about the will's marriage clause, I panic-downloaded a dating app. I matched with a wholesome-looking schoolteacher. We met, and my stutter created a roadblock that worsened when she asked about my job. I made the mistake of delicately describing the facial reconstruction of a death-by-industrial-accident over dinner. The teacher left for the restroom and never returned.

My fingers brushed my cheekbone where Lark had pecked me earlier this morning; I'd nearly had a heart attack when her lips touched my skin. . . . But I could talk to her. Maybe her nonstop commentary helped. Maybe it was the exuberant way she skipped through her day, even when soaked in gutter water.

In a letter accompanying the will, shaky penmanship revealed Granda's motivations. The stipulation was designed to light a fire under my arse to start a family. And he hoped that my father and I could have a relationship. Fat chance. Pádraig was selfish at sixteen when he and my mother left me to run away to Scotland, leaving me to the guardianship of my grandparents. Our conversation proved he hadn't changed. With a frustrated growl, I tore off my glasses and pressed the heels of my palms to my eyes until they hurt.

Good intentions aside, how could Granda do this? After I'd cared for him in the aftermath of his strokes and poured every ounce of remaining energy into the business to keep it afloat. Willow Haven didn't just need me—I needed it. Caring for the dead and shepherding families through grief gave my life purpose. Not only did I like it and was good at it, but who was I if not another Flannelly in a suit playing a hymn for the deceased?

Grimacing, I opened the dating app. Six months. Consider the fire lit.

CHAPTER 5

Lark

OVERSIZE POP ART greeted me in the KinetiColor lobby. Wendy welcomed me alongside the studio owner, Mr. Sullivan. They looked me up and down and immediately told me where I could wash up.

Once I looked more "competent professional" than "drowned raccoon," I made my way through the labyrinth of desks to the conference room. Each animator's desk was a riot of inspiration, from curated vision boards to vintage toys battling on shelves above computer monitors. Waiting for the team to arrive, I cycled through a PowerPoint of key scenes. An intern set out doughnuts. Fact: when giving a presentation, it's easier to find confidence when your audience has rainbow sprinkles stuck to their chins. Less awkward than imagining coworkers naked.

Mr. Sullivan smiled warmly and gestured to me. "I'd like to introduce our newest art director, Lark Thompson."

My hand shot up in a peppy wave.

"Lark worked on *Shoelace* at Blue Star Studios," he continued as a few people murmured in excitement. "I was so impressed, I invited her to come all the way from the States to join our little team for this project. Let's do our best to make her feel welcome."

The bearded fellow who'd jeered at a coworker outside crossed his arms and skewered me with his eye contact as I stepped forward.

"Thanks so much, Mr. Sullivan." I scanned the room, committing each new face to memory. "Good mornin'. I look forward to meeting y'all one-on-one as we begin work on *The Pirate Queen*. Filmmaking is a collaborative effort, and I want everyone to know my door is open if you have ideas or concerns about the production."

That kicked off a lively round of introductions before we settled into storyboarding. Anvi, a full-figured Indian woman with an elaborate braid that spilled down to the waist of her fashionable dress, shared a handful of sample storyboard layouts she'd drawn at home. Gorgeous and dynamic, they brimmed with drama as they showcased the main story beats.

"Sorry," she said, "I couldn't help but get a jump on it once I read the script. Of course, these are just a rough starting point."

"They're incredible! I couldn't help but get to work when I read it, either," I said. "I'm glad we can hit the ground running."

Anvi was a kindred soul. Overall, KinetiColor's staff was as friendly as they were talented. The background artists with their immersive settings, the character artists with their concept sketches. How I'd missed the camaraderie of fellow creatives.

Bringing joy to people through art had always been my goal, ever since I was a little kid. I'd sit on the floor of my mother's jewelry studio as she blasted an eclectic mix of Fleetwood Mac, Donna Summer, and Kenny Rogers, making simple flip-books to pass the time that I'd give to kids at school. Soon, I was accepting lunch money commissions. People came together over the magic of a moving picture, and I liked being the one who brought them that sense of wonder. Art served as both my escape from the monotony of daily life and my connection to others.

I'd risen through the ranks at Blue Star quickly, starting as a character designer for the ragtag startup founded by classmates.

Working with my college best friend and then sister-in-law, Rachel, was a blast. What our small group lacked in budget or experience, we'd made up for with dedication and enthusiasm. She and I bounced ideas off each other with the rest of the tight-knit team, and the studio became a second home . . . until she couldn't bear to look at me and the once-welcoming group of colleagues quieted whenever I entered a room. I couldn't stay, despite desperately needing something to focus on during my grief. Anything to bring the color back into my life, when everything felt gray with Reese gone. The way I lost him meant I lost Rachel, too, and by extension the team I'd practically considered family. Freelance design paid the bills after I resigned, but eighteen months of loneliness ensured I wouldn't take the opportunity at KinetiColor for granted. My new coworkers wouldn't know about my past. Ireland would be my clean slate, unless they went digging. But I wasn't going to be handing out shovels.

After my introductory presentation, I gathered up my materials, salivating as I eyed the last doughnut. Before I could reach it, the auburn-bearded man plucked it up. "Howya. Seán Fitzgerald."

"Howdy." It wasn't a normal part of my vocabulary—I was from Austin, not the sticks—but it felt like the natural response. So far, it was the minor differences about this place that charmed me, like the variations in language.

Seán took a bite. My stomach growled; I'd been far too nervous to eat before leaving home. "So you're the new boss."

"You're a senior animator, right?"

He preened. Hazel eyes perused me from head to gutter-splashed high-heeled toe, pausing on my kitschy cherry earrings. "Our last art director wasn't nearly so young."

"I'll take that as a compliment. How long have you been here?"

White teeth flashed in warning. "Since day one. Anything you're unsure of, feel free to call me directly." Voice dropped to a discreet volume, he added, "You know, so the rest of the team won't think any less of you."

My smile faltered, but I slapped it back on quickly. "I appreciate that."

"Those ship renderings you want by Wednesday? I don't know if I can swing it." He looked at the carpet regretfully. "My daughter has an appointment Tuesday, so I'll be away the whole day . . . horrible timing."

"Your family comes first. Always." I'd learned that lesson too late. No way would I expect my staff to prioritize work over their children's medical needs. "I guess it should be all right as long as I get them by Friday morning."

"I'll do my best." He cast one more glance at me before disappearing down the hall. "Welcome to KinetiColor."

Sprinkles rolled around the empty doughnut box as I tossed it into the trash. Had he just weaseled a deadline extension from me during our first conversation, or was he being honest? A prickle in my gut told me not to trust Seán Fitzgerald.

FROM BEHIND THE curtains, I peered into my neighbor's yard. My living room window opened right into the garden behind Willow Haven, where Callum was pruning and adding mulch. Suspenders crossed his wide shoulders, and fitted trousers stopped just before his ankles, giving him a look somewhere between debonair and antiquated. Lush crimson roses bloomed on precisely manicured bushes.

Some people want to have their ashes scattered under rosebushes or oak trees: Is that why Callum's garden is so vibrant? Regardless, the notion of my neighbor tending his flowers was more comforting than how I imagined he spent the rest of his workdays.

My single previous experience with a mortician involved aggressive sales techniques, guilting me into the expensive brushed-copper casket. They pushed upgrades and premium granite for the headstone after I'd stared at identical serif fonts for ten bleary-eyed minutes. My late husband deserved the best, didn't he? His headstone was the last gift he would ever receive, they said, so I agreed to a basketball etched onto the granite. *Husband. Brother. Son. Coach.* Reese's memorial didn't bring him back. Nothing could.

The public funeral only made matters worse. The entire high school attended. Shock and shame had me practically catatonic afterward. Cielo took me in when I couldn't take any more of my mom's hollow platitudes. Always stable during a crisis, Cielo force-fed me between her premed classes and made me bathe on a semi-regular basis. Lo was the only person in all of Texas who I felt bad about leaving.

Of course I recognized the necessity of the service Callum performed. Sewers need treating. Root canals need drilling. Bodies need burying. Despite the painful echoes his profession caused, he was interesting. Soft-spoken, with a rich baritone. Mysterious and stoic, though when his elegant hands touched the piano, they'd revealed a depth of emotion. Heart went into that kind of playing.

God. I couldn't believe I'd kissed Callum on the cheek like an old friend. Between the morning from hell and the new-job jitters, I hadn't been thinking straight. We lived next door to each other, and misleading him would be more than awkward. I didn't want to kiss anyone. The guy probably thought I was a complete airhead, anyway, after thinking he was a serial killer.

A tall woman approached the garden. Black hair poured like a midnight waterfall down her back, complemented by a timeless, sapphire A-line dress and opaque tights. A florist van waited on the curb between our houses. Daffodils formed a familiar logo—same as on the shop where Callum gave me the lift to work.

Flannelly, you scoundrel.

The idea of the dour man flirting with someone piqued my curiosity. From the furtiveness of his gaze during their conversation, he read more nervous than charming. After a couple of minutes, the pretty florist gestured at the van. He brushed dirt off his hands and didn't move to touch her, but he watched her go.

As if sensing my presence, Callum flicked his attention toward my window.

Shit.

Caught, I staggered back and tripped over the curtain hem. I snatched a handful of fabric to balance myself and managed to pull the rod from the wall, landing on my ass with a hearty *ooomph.*

I wanted to die. Conveniently, I now lived next door to a funeral parlor.

Before I could pick myself and the curtain rod off the hardwood, a torrent of knocks rattled my door. Of course. I considered hiding under the pool of fabric until my would-be rescuer left, but forced myself to answer.

With a guilty grin, I craned up at him as the door creaked open. He had to be a foot taller than me. "Not here to borrow a cup of sugar, are you?"

"Are you okay?" Callum lifted his chin toward the heap of window treatments behind me. His broad chest heaved like he'd run over.

"I was just hanging some new curtains and the screws must've come loose."

"There's a screw loose, all right."

I rubbed my tailbone. "You're awfully gallant, but I'm fine."

"Our windows are right across from each other." Callum looked down at his hands. Soil ringed his fingernails and knuckles.

"And you accused me of being the creepy one."

Amusement glimmered on his face. We had an inside joke. Kinda at my expense, but it was a start.

I took a centering breath. "There's this comedy café I read about, This Tastes Funny. Wanna check it out?"

"Together?" Callum sputtered. "Like a date?"

"Like friends. To say thanks for giving me a ride the other day."

I clocked his attention on the pale outline left by my wedding band. I had taken off my ring the morning I boarded the flight to Galway. Four years with Reese. Twenty-one months since I'd heard his rambunctious laugh and the clink of the whistle around his neck on game day. The naked sensation took some getting used to.

"Married?"

"I was." Let him assume divorce. I couldn't take pity from one more person. "Is the florist your girlfriend?"

"No." The tips of his ears glowed pink. "How long were you watching?"

"I don't know what you're talking about. I was minding my own business, hanging curtains."

"Mm-hmm."

I watched long enough to see the woman playing with her hair as she watched you tend the garden, I didn't say. "Look, it wouldn't be a date, but if you think it'll ruin your chances if it gets back to her . . ."

Callum tilted his head.

"She's into you."

He huffed a mild scoff in self-deprecation.

"So . . . What do you say?"

"You want to be mates," he said skeptically.

"Is there a long wait list?" I sensed he could use a friend. And I'd enjoy a comedy club a hundred times more with company. Win-win.

"Oh, yeah. People are d-dying to hang out with me." His delivery was drier than the Mojave.

I groaned. "Are you trying to prove that you hate comedy or something?"

"Is it working?"

"If anything, you've only proven you need a night of decent stand-up. Although, if this is the caliber of humor I can expect in your presence, maybe I ought to withdraw the offer."

"No, I'll go."

CHAPTER 6

Callum

"'THIS TASTES FUNNY,'" Lark read from the sign as her pink boots skipped along the footpath. "Clever name, right?"

"Ringing endorsement for a café."

Sweat slicked my palms as the queue moved forward, even though it was a brisk November afternoon. Rehearsing the words in my head over and over, I practiced my order. Interactions with strangers always spiked my blood pressure.

A bored barista manned the counter. She barely hid her annoyance when I stumbled over my words trying to order tea. Impatient customers grumbled behind us. Lark paid them no mind and rattled off her drink and pastry order, along with a compliment on the barista's style.

The barista's Sharpie skated across the cup. "Iced lavender latte for Clark. . . ."

"*Lark*. There is no *C*."

"Got it."

"~~Clark~~ Klark" was scrawled in a messy hand on the cardboard cup when our order appeared at the counter.

"Every. Time."

"No *C*, at least," I pointed out.

"Whose side are you on, anyway, *Colm*?" She smirked, deliberately pronouncing the name on my cup wrong.

As a child, I'd wished my parents had spelled my name the proper Irish way—Colm—but departure from tradition was the point. To rub it in my grandparents' faces, they chose the Scottish spelling.

Lark selected a table near the stage. I'd have preferred to sit farther back. Hell, I'd have preferred to be at home, but I had promised myself that I'd make an effort. Interact with a woman outside of work. That shouldn't be so hard. Dating had never been my forte, but I desperately needed the practice. I pulled out her chair, and Lark's hand flew over her mouth; the seat was topped with a whoopee cushion.

"Classy," Lark said, patting her chair before she sat to ensure it wasn't musical. She shucked off her purple coat to reveal a rainbow-printed dress. The woman looked like an overturned crayon box. I motioned to the wall-mounted chalkboard.

"Well, their menu is . . ." Dead air hung between us as my sentence ground to a halt. To my surprise, Lark waited for the words to come. Most people weren't so patient. "Written in Comic Sans."

She smiled and tore into her cherry pastry.

"Sorry. It's a traffic jam in my brain. I know where to go, how to get there, but I get stuck on the way sometimes. Especially if I'm feeling uncomfortable or stressed."

"No need to apologize. Sounds frustrating. Are you feeling uncomfortable because of me?"

Scattered voices rose and fell around us. "My throat closes up in a crowd."

Lark washed her bite down with coffee. "To stepping out of comfort zones, then."

"*Sláinte*." Our paper cups knocked together. Hot, soothing tea helped loosen the knot in my chest. "I watched your film."

"Fill-im?" Her mouth quirked up as she mimicked my accent. "What did you think?"

"I didn't know whether to laugh or cry. You came up with that?"

"No, I didn't create it, but I was the one with final say over the visuals. *Shoelace* was all about the oversaturated palette without outlines."

"When they pushed the kid into the pool and the water's surface became the same pattern as his broken kaleidoscope . . . It gave me chills."

Her grin burned brighter than the spotlight on the still-empty stage. "That's my favorite scene."

Neither the film's climactic moment nor the obvious choice, the scene had still captured the alienation of my youth. I hadn't watched an animated movie in years, subconsciously relegating them to children's entertainment, but *Shoelace* was poignant. Imaginative. Well-deserving of its slew of awards.

"You googled me? One more checkmark in the 'creeper' column."

"Just the film. What's the new project about?"

"Grace O'Malley. A family-friendly retelling of her life. I'd never heard of her before applying for this job, but she was amazing! Daughter of a chieftain turned pirate queen, commanding a fleet of galleys against the British? Come on, that kicks ass."

"She even refused to bow to Queen Elizabeth the First and somehow didn't get arrested or executed," I added. History was one subject I could discuss, and of course I was familiar with the seafaring warrior from the 1500s.

"I read a few of Grace O'Malley's biographies and studied local art from the time period to develop the film's trademark look." For being such a whimsical person, Lark took her work seriously. "You said Willow Haven is a family operation?"

"My great-grandfather was the first undertaker in Galway to provide a venue for families unable to hold wakes at home." Traditional all-nighters had since become an uncommon request, but business remained steady. "Passed it to my granda, and he taught me."

"A death dynasty. Your folks didn't follow in their footsteps?" Lark noticed I'd skipped a generation.

"My grandparents raised me."

"Oh. You must be very close, then."

"They were strict but fair. My nan passed a few years back. She hailed from South Connemara, where Irish is the first language. Moved to Galway to teach and met my granda. He passed away three months ago and left me the b-business."

If only the inheritance was that straightforward. A bachelor with no prospects on the horizon, the tradition could end with me. My granda had assumed that's what would happen, without his meddling. Though I would never pressure a hypothetical adult child into this grueling line of work. Undertaking is a calling; I couldn't imagine doing anything else. Family legacy aside, it was rewarding to offer a small measure of comfort and closure to the grieving.

"I'm sorry. Sounds like you've had a lot on your plate." Lark tucked her hair behind an ear. "You strike me as a perfectionist. Meticulous. I bet you're excellent at your job."

"My receptionist, Deirdre, handles the phones, consultations, and arrangements. I handle the practical end. I'd rather get myself fitted for a wooden onesie than give a eulogy."

Lark smiled. "I don't think you hate humor as much as you claim."

I wasn't used to socializing. My average evening was usually spent sequestered in the preparation room, in the company of a corpse. But here was this American woman with enough extroversion for both of us, coaxing me out of the mortuary and into the land of the living. It was equal parts terrifying and enjoyable.

"So, what's your favorite animated movie?" Lark asked.

I propped my elbows on the table. "I don't watch cartoons."

"Goodbye!" She cast me a smile that warmed me more than the tea.

I couldn't help but chuckle. "I liked *Shoelace* a lot, actually."

"Kiss-ass." Lark rolled her eyes. "You're really missing out, though. Animated stuff isn't just for kids."

"Give me a recommendation then, please."

"*Spirited Away*. An anime masterpiece. That's the movie that made me say, 'I have to be an animator.' Basically, I want to be like Hayao Miyazaki and create immersive dream worlds, too."

"Ah. You've convinced me."

With a triumphant grin, she plucked a sketchbook and pen from her handbag. Her free hand shielded the budding image as she drew. When Lark finished, she ripped the page from the binding and slid it across the table. Long legs poked out of a black school uniform as a young lad forlornly clutched a skull-shaped balloon.

"Me?" I asked around a sudden heaviness in my throat.

"Your cartoon-deprived inner child. Keep it."

"No one's ever drawn me." I reverently traced the image with my index finger.

Feedback hissed from the PA system, effectively cutting off her response. An obnoxious emcee strutted onto the stage, announcing that the performance was about to begin.

CHAPTER 7

Callum

"LOOK AT THESE two." The comedian jerked a thumb in our direction. Whistles and hoots came from the audience. "We've got Barbie right there . . . but someone switched out Ken for Dracula. I would love to know which dating app made this match."

Okay. So we were an odd couple, with her Technicolor dress and my monochrome attire.

In a terrible Bela Lugosi impression, he sang, "Come on Varvie, let's go party! Ah! Ah! Ah!" Although he sounded closer to the Count from *Sesame Street*, the audience laughed at the iconic nineties song.

As he wound through the assemblage of tables, he took a few more jabs at random audience members, then circled back to us like a bothersome fly at a picnic.

"Just curious, love. Did he pick you up amid a flurry of bats?"

"We drove here in Barbie's Dream Hearse," Lark answered with disarming sweetness.

His brows, and mine, jumped at her snappy retort.

"It's, like, totally pink."

Well now.

"Suppose it has plenty of room in the back, if Vlad gets lucky," he replied.

My cheeks and ears burned with the rush of blood; any embarrassment or anger had me resembling a tomato.

"A blush! Perhaps the Count has a beating heart after all."

Enough. Chair leg scraping, I bolted upright. My heart thudded as the room's attention fell on me. Unsure what to do, I adjusted my tie and plopped back down. Violently loud flatulence erupted from the seat. Which went on over several agonizing seconds. The establishment exploded into laughter. Fecking whoopee cushion chairs. Eyes pinched closed, I said a silent prayer in remembrance of my dignity.

"On that note," the announcer said. "Let's begin the improv show."

The audience shifted their focus as the players entered the stage, but Lark's attention stayed on me.

"Let's go somewhere quiet," she said, pouty mouth tipped in a frown.

I nodded and nestled her sketch, accurate down to my round glasses and deadpan expression, safely in my wallet. She collected her purse and coat, then took my arm as we navigated the tightly packed tables. We slipped away before the announcer could offer us more unwanted attention.

She laughed uncomfortably as we spilled out of the comedy club and into the street, but I was too worked up to join in. Within moments, the revelry of the Latin Quarter surrounded us. International flags fluttered in the chilly evening breeze, crisscrossing between the narrow brick buildings like a game of cat's cradle. I watched Lark take in the scene, from the colorful storefronts to a street performer walking a marionette. These were the same buildings we passed when we arrived, and she remained just as mesmerized by them.

"I haven't wanted to kick anyone's arse in a long time, b-b-but when he started in on you . . ."

"It's not a big deal. Being compared to Barbie? I've heard much worse."

The thought of what she might mean made the tea curdle in my stomach, but she shrugged.

"You do look like a vampire, though. And you keep coffins conveniently on hand for naps. I haven't ruled out the possibility you're a bloodsucker."

I shook my head at her affectionate teasing. "Sun's about to go down. Let's walk the canal and watch the hookers." Nerves frayed, I desperately wanted to be somewhere familiar, away from the crowds. But I wasn't ready for the night to end yet. *Huh.*

Her jaw dropped. "Sorry. I thought you said . . . Watch the *what*?"

"Hookers. The sailboats?"

"You can't help but mess with the American, can you?"

"It's not my fault you've never heard of a Galway hooker."

"Chalk it up to culture shock. Lead the way."

The worn cobblestones clattered under her boots as we set out for the River Corrib.

"How are you liking it here? Creepy neighbor notwith-standing."

"I like it, but I still can't believe I moved next door to a fu-neral home." She tossed a few notes into a bucket as we passed a crooning busker. "When I go I don't want a funeral. Hold a movie marathon in my memory. With a dessert bar. My family knows that if they planned some depressing event in my memory, I'd haunt them for the rest of their days. And if they dared to play that '*in the arms of the angels*' song, I'd make sure they have the worst internet signal ever by possessing a groundhog and making it chew through their wires."

"Vindictive. Creative, but vindictive."

"You know, 'Stairway to Heaven' would be a fun musical choice."

My mouth twitched. "Better than 'Highway to Hell.'"

Lark snickered as we passed a mural-covered wall.

"Where are you from?"

"Austin, Texas—Home of the Weird."

"You don't know anyone here, do you?" I asked.

"Nope. An up-and-coming studio offered me a job, and I couldn't turn down the opportunity to check out someplace new."

"How could you move thousands of miles from home, just like that?"

"For the adventure! I love new experiences, new places." Lark fiddled with the sleeve of her coat, not meeting my eyes. "Despite a couple of notable instances of a slight language barrier, it's been an interesting education so far."

She tipped each street musician along the route and gratefully accepted every flier for an upcoming festival handed to her. I dodged anyone shoving brightly colored paper in my face. As we passed a lively trad band, my smile ticked up. Bodhrán drums, low whistle, and fiddle combined in an infectious beat. My nan Gráinne had taught me steps when I was preparing for the Debs at seventeen. I'd never put them to use. Couldn't bear the thought of being rejected, so I'd never asked anyone and stayed home while the rest of my class enjoyed the dance. Lark attempted to cajole me to move, but I'd had enough public humiliation for one night without demonstrating my two left feet. She gave me an understanding nod, but I detected a trace of disappointment. I could imagine Lark done up like a right debutante, the prom queen in every American coming-of-age film.

Five minutes later, we arrived at the river. Fishing boats with triple sails retreated toward the docks in a race against the dwindling light. Rust-red canvases fluttered in the briny wind, and black pitch covered the boats' hulls in the traditional fashion.

"Those are some good-looking hookers. We're talking *Pretty Woman* level." Lark leaned on the railing. The golden setting sun reflected off the water, painting the sea and sky. Every strand of her hair glowed in its warmth.

"My granda and I liked to play chess here."

"You really miss him, don't you?" She didn't turn from the peaceful view. "The first time we met, it seemed like you were afraid to smile. I chose the comedy place 'cause I thought you could use a laugh. Sorry it backfired spectacularly."

I bristled. My family thought I needed social intervention, as evidenced by the terms of my granda's will. Of course Lark agreed. The truth smarted fierce.

"Lark, spare me the pity, can ya?"

"Pity? No. Not pity." She touched my arm, gravity in her eyes; my stomach tumbled. "I thought we could find a little company together. Kill two birds and all." She could walk into any pub and strike up a conversation with anyone, but she chose me.

"I've no idea what to make of you."

Lark shrugged. "Make me your friend."

Taken aback, I softened. I had coworkers. Acquaintances. Matronly Deirdre . . . the young lad who accompanied me for body removals . . . the medical examiner . . . the cemetery groundskeeper . . . a couple of classmates from mortuary school with whom I kept in touch via sporadic, mostly work-related emails . . . Saoirse, the florist. But friends?

"I think I'd like that." The pale evidence of a wedding band on her left hand flashed through my mind. "Divorce must be lonely, too."

Her smile dropped. Shite. No one would appreciate a near-stranger prying into their failed marriage.

"I'm sorry. I—"

"It's okay." Lark turned toward the water. "Thanks for coming with me tonight."

We walked back to my car in companionable silence.

"Guess you're picking where we go next time. Since this one was such a resounding success, you're stuck with me now. I'm the human equivalent of loose glitter." She pretended to sprinkle some around me, like a possessive pixie.

Glad to see her carefree demeanor recovered, I allowed myself a modest smile. "Or a popcorn kernel impossibly wedged b-b-between my molars." My stomach clenched as I repeated the consonant, but she strode on next to me, unfazed.

"You mean your fangs, Count Flannelly?" Lark swept a challenging look up and down, and put on a fake Transylvanian accent. "Ze night is still young. Or you can go home and floss."

"A morning graveside service needs me at my best." Pragmatism came naturally, but I still felt a little torn over the idea of wrapping up the evening.

"I appreciate you not picking me up in the hearse again," she said as I drove us home in my black Peugeot.

"Last time you left claw marks on the seat, like a nervous cat. I can't afford to reupholster the front bench again."

When we pulled into my driveway, I turned to say good night. Lark bit her lip, and I couldn't help but remember the whisper of her mouth on my cheek. Even though it hadn't been a date, our outing had gone better than any I'd arranged through an app. I wondered if she would kiss me again. What was the etiquette for a goodbye between friends?

Instead, she gave me a quick hug. Other than Deirdre crushing me to her ample bosom after Granda's wake, I couldn't remember the last time I'd been hugged. Subtle citrus and vanilla flooded my senses, reminiscent of an orange scone. It left me biting back a smile as I watched her unlock her flat.

Maybe I could feel something more than friendship for Lark Thompson. Eventually. Perhaps she could even be the answer to the inheritance problem.

CHAPTER 8

Lark

THE WOMAN BEHIND the Willow Haven reception desk lit up when she realized I'd come for Callum personally rather than professionally. In her late sixties with a cloud of puffy silver hair, she studied me with a keen eye.

"Sorry, dear. He's neck-deep in"—*Oh lady, please don't say a corpse*—"bookkeeping at the moment."

Phew. I introduced myself.

"I'm Deirdre. So you're the new neighbor. Heard quite a bit about you."

"Flattering, I hope."

"He wouldn't give the time of day to someone he didn't like." In a singsong voice, Deirdre called, "Callum! Someone is here to see you."

Wiping his glasses on his waistcoat, he stopped short in the hall on hearing my hello and jerked his head up. He shoved his glasses back on his face. "Hi."

Peanut butter scent wafted through the air as I lifted the plate of cookies. "Brought you a treat."

"Really?"

"Ever had a cowboy cookie?"

Callum shook his head and crossed in front of the desk. Deirdre pretended to be engrossed in her computer monitor.

I leaned closer. "The secret ingredient is cornflakes. Gives them the perfect crunch to offset the chewiness of the coconut."

"That's . . . very kind. Thank you. They smell d—they smell great." He blinked when he stuttered, even with a successful detour around the problematic word. He accepted the plate and offered me a bashful smile.

"I have a favor to ask. Remember when you gave me a lift to work, and when I thanked you, you said *anytime*?"

"Yes?"

"There's this dresser I want to buy. The lady selling it lives near here. I was hoping maybe you could help me pick it up? GPS says it's a five-minute drive. Please? Of course, I'd pay you for your time."

Callum looked like he swallowed his tongue, silent with eyes wide.

I kicked myself for being presumptuous. He'd just been being polite. Once again, I couldn't leave this funeral home quickly enough. "Never mind! I'm sure you're busy. Don't worry about it. Enjoy the cookies." I acknowledged Deirdre with a flappy wave. "Nice to meet you."

"But he's not doing anything, are you, Callum? Of course he'd love to."

He cut her a glare, then set the plate on the counter.

"I wouldn't mind at all."

"Really. You don't have to. . . ."

The annoyance he'd flashed at his employee was gone. "I do need a rest from the accounting. Now?"

"I can see if she's available. It won't fit in a taxi, and I can't get a license here yet to rent a truck," I said. "There's only one person I know with an oversize vehicle, and luckily, he's really sweet."

"Sweet?" He reared back as if it were a slur.

"Salty, spicy, savory, sour. Pick the culinary descriptor you like best. Hell, pick umami."

Callum crossed his arms as his reserved smile appeared. "So you approve of the hearse now?"

———

"HI, MAEVE? WE met at the grocery store?"

"Of course. Lark, was it?" Standing in the doorway, her eyes narrowed on the parked hearse, then flitted over to my companion. "I'm not ready to go with the undertaker just yet. Even such a handsome one."

"Oh! This is just my friend Callum."

"Good evening." He doffed his flat cap, revealing a mass of glossy black hair. He was so old-fashioned. Between the cap and the waistcoat, he could've wandered off the set of *Peaky Blinders*.

She waved a hand. "I've already got a plot next to my dear Charlie, and no precious time to waste with a bloody door-to-door salesman."

"Ma'am—"

Undeterred, she continued, "Trust you'll be putting me down for my final rest soon enough, and getting paid well for it, so you can kindly feck right off for the time being. Thank you!"

"That's not— We're here for the dresser. Only this car could fit it."

Her wary eyes scanned his dark suit. "So you're *not* an undertaker?"

"I am. Over at Willow Haven Memorial."

"Ah. Thought you looked familiar. They took care of my dear Charlie. A fine job, they did."

"I'm glad to hear you were pleased." Callum straightened his shoulders with pride, making him even taller.

Maeve put her hand on her hip and cocked an expectant brow at me.

"Oh, I have nothing to do with it," I assured her. "I'm just a gal buying furniture."

Maeve and I had struck up a conversation at the grocery store a day earlier, wherein I mentioned my recent move to the area and my woefully under-decorated apartment. She asked if I'd like to take a look at a cache of old furniture she needed to clear out of her home and gave me her phone number.

Maeve shuffled back inside and disappeared behind a china hutch. When it became clear she would say no more, Callum wiped his shoes on the mat with a wry smile. "Feisty."

"When I grow up, I want to be just like her," I said, following suit to clean my boots. "I can't chew anyone out. All I can do is smile and suffer inside because confrontations give me hives."

We entered the cottage, and my jaw dropped. Antiques filled the modest home like a treasure trove. Vintage signs and framed newspaper clippings lined the walls. File boxes stacked to a precarious height wobbled as Callum squeezed through. Boxy cameras with flash attachments the size of satellite dishes sat atop dusty cartons. A giant carved tiki head grimaced from atop a stack.

"Glad someone will make use of it," Maeve said. "It's been out in the garden shed for a decade."

"It's like a time capsule in here," I said with wonder, ogling the sixties- and seventies-era decor.

In the garage, cobwebs swayed from the ceiling as Callum shifted items and Maeve gave directions. He inadvertently pulled the tarp from a baby blue vintage scooter. Shiny chrome cowls, a tall windshield, and a half dozen mirrors had been added to the customized bike. "Whoa."

Memory lent Maeve's eyes a faraway glaze. "It's how I met the love of my life."

"It was his?"

"His?" Maeve's wry smile appeared. "It's mine."

Hell yes. A woman after my own heart. I felt an immediate

sense of kinship. "'Dublin Lambretta Society,'" I murmured, reading the faded decal under the square headlight.

"A 'sixty-eight Lammy SX," the elderly woman said. "Between my pension and the life insurance, I've everything I need. Charlie was a borderline hoarder. Held on to all kinds of rubbish for decades. Time to let it go." She gave a mournful little smile as her attention returned to the Lambretta. "But she is *not* for sale."

Who could blame her? It was beautiful. Timeless Italian design, curvy and sexy. Even without accounting for the sentimental value, it was an amazing piece in perfect condition.

Heavy lump forming in my throat, I remembered how I'd donated my household belongings to secondhand shops only two months prior. Relics of the past comforted some people, haunted others. I was in the latter camp, unable to look at Reese's sports memorabilia, an aesthetic nightmare I'd cheerfully tolerated during our life together because it brought him joy. When it went into his parents' garage, the absence of the tacky basketball player bobbleheads served as a reminder of a bigger loss.

"I'll wet some leaves while you get to it. You take sugar?"

"Yes, please. Thanks, Maeve."

Her knowing gaze lingered on me before she lumbered off to the kitchen. I cleared my throat and batted at the floating dust motes. Lonely recognizes lonely.

Callum and I loaded the dresser into the hearse and returned to find Maeve seated on a sofa with a teapot, three steaming cups, a stack of scones studded with currants, and a leather picture album.

How had she moved so fast? The woman was at least seventy. I sensed her hospitality was not only due to innate Irish friendliness but also a reluctance to return to the quiet stillness of her home. I sat down, plumping a cross-stitched pillow that read *Making This Took Fecking Forever.*

The plastic-paged photo album smelled musty as Maeve

cracked it open to reveal faded sepia and vintage Polaroids. Beneath a hand-tinted image of a cherubic baby, loopy cursive spelled out *Maeve, June 1945.* A few pages displayed disaffected teens in mod fashion. Girls with Twiggy lashes, boys in suits and parkas atop gleaming scooters.

"It was there I met Charlie," Maeve said. "Beautiful, wasn't she? That summer, we rode from Dublin to the Cliffs of Moher."

She handed us a photo of the two women straddling the same scooter we'd just seen—brand-new at the time—with matching grins so shiny they rivaled the chrome. One was a ginger spitfire. Both wore men's suits, and young Maeve's hand was slipped into the other woman's pocket. Unmistakable affection shone on their faces. Charlie was her wife.

"Those *suits*!" I cried. "You two are absolute badasses!"

"Absolutely." Maeve plied Callum with three more scones stacked on a saucer. "Ever ridden one?"

Callum's eyes widened. "Me? Never."

Reminiscing over a mouthful of buttery scone, I said, "A boy I dated in high school rode motocross. He took me for rides. Then I stole his bike and hit a fence trying on my own. Afterward, he taught me to ride, in self-defense."

From the look on Callum's face, you'd think I'd jumped across the Grand Canyon with Evel Knievel. In reality, Jose was just a seventeen-year-old with X Games ambitions and a backyard mud track.

"What? I wore a helmet. Sometimes. It made my hair flat, okay? He was cute."

Maeve and I shared a wicked laugh. She thumbed through the album and regaled us with stories about her coming-of-age as a lesbian in postwar Dublin. She and Charlie were survivors. Kids with chips placed on their shoulders by a cruel world.

"How many years did you have together?" Callum asked Maeve. He rested his teacup on a saucer.

"Forty, all said and done. Too long I questioned if she was the person meant for me, and there was so much wasted time. We grew apart, lived separate lives for decades, then found our way back to each other. We married in 2015 as soon as it became legal. Charlie said we'd waited long enough."

"How romantic!" Dreamily, I hugged the cross-stitched pillow that took fecking forever to make against my chest. Just because I'd sworn off relationships didn't mean I couldn't appreciate a good love story.

"You were seventy on your wedding day?"

"That's your takeaway? And you *cannot* point that out. It's impolite to mention a woman's age." My mom instilled in me a strong sense of decorum around the subject. Mostly from a superstition that acknowledging her age would make her face melt off like the villain in that Indiana Jones movie, because "what we speak we manifest." Setting the pillow aside, I took another bite of scone.

"What?" Callum asked. "Nothing wrong with being old."

I sputtered and thumped my sternum so I wouldn't choke.

"*Or* a lesbian," he added when I'd recovered. Wincing, I took a sip of tea.

"Callum, darlin', you *cannot* call our gorgeous host old!" I cast an apologetic look at an unfazed Maeve.

"It's all right. Accurate." Somehow, she remained charmed even after the borderline insult.

"You'd really let me choke, wouldn't you?" I said, brushing crumbs off my chest.

"You weren't choking."

Her eyes crinkled as she watched our exchange. "He *is* an undertaker, dear," she said. "You can't expect the lad to go around saving lives and undermining his own business."

"Thank you." He looked utterly unrepentant.

"Which is why I don't trust him," she finished, tongue in

cheek. "As for your observation, Charlie was even older. Seventy-four!"

Callum gave Maeve a tender look.

"It's a wonderful story," I said.

I ached to confide my loss, but I'd already let Callum assume that I was divorced. It was still difficult to say the truth aloud: *My husband is dead.* Keeping those words out of my mouth allowed me my denial a little longer. Sometimes, I almost let myself believe Reese was waiting for me back in Austin.

To tell my widow's story now would be to risk Callum's judgment. If he knew the truth, knew it was my fault, would he wash his hands of our budding friendship? Part of me wanted to tell the truth. The rest wanted to leave that painful chapter of my personal history on American soil.

"Hey. Would you adopt me, Maeve?" I joked.

"If you need a green card, marry him."

Tea spewed from Callum's lips. Most of it landed on his tie, which I blotted with a napkin as Maeve cackled. My palm brushed his firm chest . . . there might as well be a brick wall under that dress shirt. Posture stiff, he stared as I scrubbed the silk.

"No! No! My job sponsors my residence permit. It's just, all my family is back in Texas, and I could use an Irish auntie." Tea seeped through the napkin as I continued dabbing. "I could come over, listen to your stories."

"What do you get out of it?"

"Entertainment, advice, companionship? More currant scones."

She leveled an incredulous look. "After yer man was measuring you for a coffin because of one of my quick breads just minutes ago?"

"Better make it lemon curd, then," I said, and Callum chuckled.

We rose to leave.

"Hope I'll see you again soon," Maeve told me. She cast her gaze at Callum. "Afraid I can't say the same for you, young man."

He bit back a smile and replied in kind.

Once we returned to my apartment, Callum and I dragged the dresser inside.

"Maeve might be the coolest lady I've ever met. I'm going to become her protégé."

"She's gas." He scratched the back of his neck. "I can't b-believe she suggested a green card marriage."

"That was kind of funny. She was only kidding, of course."

"It's embarrassing."

"You're embarrassed?" I asked, gesturing to the sparse apartment. "It looks like an eighteen-year-old beer pong champion lives here. I promise I'm a much better decorator, but I'm only planning to stay for this film until postproduction wraps. I'll be here a year, tops." I pushed the dresser an inch to the left. "Marriage isn't in the cards for me again anyway. Green card or otherwise."

Although I'd loved my husband and was faithful, I hadn't been the best wife. Not the wife Reese deserved, anyway. And after he died and my life imploded, I promised Reese I'd never fail anyone else the way I failed him. Remaining single was the only way of keeping my promise and protecting myself from that kind of pain again.

Callum pressed his lips together until they all but disappeared. Right. Of course. I'd monopolized enough of his time, and here I was, babbling on. My cheeks reddened, and I lunged for my purse.

"Thank you for helping me today. I'm happy to compensate you for the trouble. The cookies were only to butter you up."

He declined the euro notes with a raised palm. "Payment isn't necessary. Though I won't complain about more homemade biscuits." He hesitated a moment, wringing his hands together. "Have you seen much of the city?"

"Just the Spanish Arch, the shops on Kirwan's Lane. Been busy trying to get settled. I can only imagine seeing it via scooter in the sixties."

Shifting his weight back and forth on his feet, he took a moment to gather his words, or perhaps his confidence. "I've a mind to visit the Cliffs of Moher, myself. If you'd like to come along."

"Yes! Let's do it!" I bounced up and down with a series of little claps. "As, um, friends."

THE DOOR TO my office swung open on Monday morning, and my jaw dropped. My five-foot-wide desk, generous enough to display my chaotic array of sketches and jumbo monitor, was gone. My computer, phone, keyboard, everything. All missing.

Instead, there was a plastic Fisher-Price desk sitting in its place, complete with a tiny yellow chair, a plastic computer, and a bright blue phone with a rainbow sticker on the side. Crayon-scrawled memos on a doodled KinetiColor letterhead had replaced real ones on the bulletin board above the child-size desk. Somewhere, a speaker played a simple, playful tune on a toy piano: the theme from *Rugrats*.

I burst out laughing and walked back to the main area, shaking my head in disbelief. The staff's dedication to the bit was impressive. Office hazing at its most cute.

Planting my hands on my hips, I mustered a stern, authoritative demeanor. "Okay. Who replaced my office with the Little Tikes version?"

Anvi, the fashionista storyboard leader, wore a wicked smile and an oversize blazer. Leaning on Anvi's desk, Rory, known for their penchant for frogs and shock of platinum hair, giggled. Hannah fought to smother a laugh.

I quickly broke character and grinned. Pranks meant they'd begun to accept me.

Anvi lifted a hand. "I take credit."

"Hey! We helped," Rory protested, nodding at Hannah. "You couldn't have carried that desk by yourself."

"So . . . where is my real desk?"

ON THE PROJECTION screen in KinetiColor's conference room was Grace O'Malley, fierce and fine-featured, wielding a gleaming saber. Stylized waves curled around the hull of her ship, and wind tousled her auburn hair. Dressed in practical, men's-style clothes that hugged her feminine figure, she was the image of rebellion.

Our team had imagined a half dozen different ways to depict her, but ultimately the director and I settled on one inspired by illuminated manuscripts of the 1500s. Thin yellow outlines provided a way to bridge the gap between modern animation sensibilities and ancient religious art. The gold-plated effect lent each character a regal luminance, despite many of them being actual pirates, so a bit less than kingly (or queenly).

"See the thinner line weight in the face but thicker in her clothes?" I pointed to the concept art.

The group of animators nodded along, sipping their coffee and tea. "Let's keep them dynamic. I want them to almost shimmer as the characters move."

The conference room filled with murmurs of agreement. Behind her funky glasses, Hannah's eyes lit up. She didn't speak much, but her approval didn't need to be vocalized.

Rory scribbled in their day planner, clearly taken by a fit of inspiration at the image. "Really unique."

"Bold outlines would be better," Seán said.

Free exchange of ideas was encouraged among the staff . . .

but this was the third time he'd contradicted me for the *sake* of contradiction during this meeting. Heat flared through my chest.

"I like the gold." Anvi shot Seán an impeccably winged side-eye. "Gilded pirates and mercenaries are unexpected—"

Seán snatched the PowerPoint remote from the table. "Gold is too dainty on Grace." He clicked through the slides until he reached an alternate mock-up with heavy black outlines. A striking illustration, no doubt, but it was a far cry from the distinctive aesthetic I'd developed. "We need something like this."

My heart thrashed like a trapped animal. Grace O'Malley was bold, whereas I was not.

I cleared my throat, willing my voice not to waver as I hid my hands so no one would notice them tremble. "I understand your argument, but this style helps anchor *The Pirate Queen* in the correct time period."

"Yes, yes. We've all heard your reasoning."

His dismissive tone cut deep. I'd handled creative disagreements before but never encountered such rudeness. I looked around the oblong table into the faces of our team. Hannah stared into her tumbler of tea. Rory shook their head, scowling at Seán before glancing my way with—was that pity? Or empathy? Either way, no one wanted to go toe-to-toe with the senior animator.

No one except Anvi, who looked one comment away from yanking the chic hoops from her ears and throwing down right there in the conference room. A low bullshit-tolerance threshold was one of my favorite things about her.

I shaped my mouth into a counterfeit smile, struggling to remain poised in the face of his constant, contrarian rebuttals. "Please, um, sit back down, Seán. It's already been decided, and we have a lot to discuss today."

With a huff, Seán dropped back into his seat and flung the projection remote onto the table.

CHAPTER 9

Lark

BEFORE CALLUM COULD choose a melancholy soundtrack for the journey to the Cliffs of Moher, I commandeered the Bluetooth and connected to my musical library. Steel guitar filled his sardine tin–size car. Black, of course, and so clean on the inside that I was surprised it didn't have that new-car smell. Beyond the city, our adventure awaited. It had been so long since I'd enjoyed a road trip. Reese, Rachel, and I used to drive down to South Padre Island to go windsurfing every spring, but I hadn't been on an outdoor excursion in two years.

"What are we listening to?" he asked.

If he wasn't familiar, I had an educational multimedia marathon to prepare. "Please tell me you know Dolly Parton."

"This is Ireland, not Mars." Callum glanced at my phone, where the album cover for *Honky Tonk Angels* was displayed. "What's a honky-tonk, though?"

"A bar that plays this style of music. Fun for a dance called the two-step."

We took the Wild Atlantic Way down. The colorful shops and commercial bustle of Galway gave way to pastoral scenes as sunlight cracked through the overcast November sky. Verdant hills rose and fell like undulating waves, and the morning light caressed every blade of grass that glinted in the sharply cold breeze.

Thatched roof cottages rested in a quaint hamlet. Each one looked centuries old, the homes of witches and fairy folk instead of living, modern people. I couldn't help but imagine cauldrons simmering over stone hearths and bundles of dried herbs hanging in the kitchens. All along our drive, mortarless walls of stacked stone twisted through a lush landscape. Callum told me the farmers rearrange the rocks at will to make fences for their livestock. Cattle grazed along the side of the road, reminding me of the longhorns ubiquitous to my home state.

"Dolly built a career on being underestimated. People judged her for her big hair and loud makeup and her body, but she has the brains and talent to back it up. She got the last laugh even when they treated her like a joke." I wished I didn't care whether folks liked me or not. "People make assumptions about my intelligence, too. There's this guy at work, Seán? He puts on a helping act so he can plant a seed of doubt in my mind. This week, he did his best to undermine me in front of the animation team during a meeting."

"What did you say?"

"Nothing, really. I don't wanna rock the boat." I was the outsider, as Seán delighted to point out. "Everyone else is great. Just wish he wouldn't steamroll me in front of the staff."

"There's a reason I choose to primarily work with people who can't speak." Callum considered my dilemma to the tune of a weepy steel guitar. "Maybe this Seán fella can take an 'extended holiday.'"

"Holy crap. Did you just reference 'Nine to Five'?" I shoved his arm softly. Only it wasn't soft. Under the cable knit were taut muscles I shouldn't have noticed. "I appreciate where your head's at. However, kidnapping my office nemesis might create a new host of issues."

"Remember, I move corpses all the time, and cremation gets rid of any evidence."

A brief detour brought us to the ruins of a remote, twelfth-century abbey. Graceful arches rose toward the heavens, while vines and moss anchored the fallen architecture to the earth. We were the only ones there, enjoying the reverent quiet of the sacred grounds. When I closed my eyes, I could almost hear the reverberation of ancient prayers.

"It is a lovely place. Five architects constructed it for a king," Callum said. A chunky gray sweater stretched across his broad shoulders, complemented by black jeans and hiking boots. Cozy rugged, but still in character. He wore it well.

"Five?"

"He executed every one after the construction was complete." Callum stepped over a blanket of wildflowers, hands anchored in his pockets. How many locals even knew the macabre history without reading it from a plaque or visitor's guide?

"Some reward for a job well done."

"He wanted to stop them from making something prettier elsewhere."

"Men and their egos." I couldn't help but think of Seán's toxic pride.

A ruined arch in the background framed Callum perfectly. Celtic crosses studded the attached churchyard, and even I could appreciate the Gothic romance of the overgrown estate. "Hold still. I want a photo of you in your natural habitat."

I lifted my phone to catch a rare, bashful smile. Crinkles formed at the corners of his eyes. He didn't look carved out of stone anymore, but approachable. Handsome. A little happiness made him endearing.

"Now lean on that gravestone, drop your hip, and give me a

saucy wink over your shoulder like this," I joked, demonstrating a Bettie Page–worthy pose. "Come on. We can start our own website, call it MournHub."

"We'll be rich."

I snapped another while his teeth flashed. Coaxing out Callum's laugh felt like a worthy achievement.

DRAMATIC, GRASSY CLIFFS bordered the coastline, the ground plummeting straight into the restless sea. While the drop-off was sharp, the coastline was irregular, forming an almost scalloped edge that stretched far into the distance above the frothy Atlantic.

At the bottom of the cliffs, every cresting wave was crowned with a halo of sunlight. A few oaks with wind-twisted branches stood in the area, and a lone stone tower rose in the distance. My hands itched to draw the landscape. Maybe I'd get the Moleskine book out of my purse for a plein air sketching session, but I hadn't brought a watercolor set. Capturing the full glory of this place in ballpoint pen didn't seem possible when it was an explosion of blues and greens, from rich hunter to avocado to chartreuse and cerulean.

"Aren't we going to the visitor center?" I jerked my thumb out the window as we passed a sign that read *Cliffs of Moher Experience.* "The sign said turn left."

"No need to elbow tourists out of the way. We'll take Guerin's Path."

Callum brought his car to rest in a secluded area of the cliffs, and I hopped out, restraining myself from dashing toward the drop-off and winding dirt path. We walked to within a few feet of the cliff's abrupt edge. There was no barrier of any kind between us and a spectacular fall into the frigid water.

"Reese, you'd love this," I mumbled, wrapping my jacket closer around my frame. Talking aloud to him wasn't as much of a habit anymore, but the wild beauty of this place had surprised his name from my lips.

"What?"

I kept my eyes on the horizon. "Nothing. Just thinking out loud."

Callum regarded me silently and, to my gratitude, didn't push. I needed to change the subject.

"People lay down to look over the edge, right? Is it scary?"

"I'm afraid of heights," he admitted. "Chunks of the ledges have fallen off, you know."

"Haven't you ever leaned back to kiss the Blarney Stone?"

His features contorted as if he'd stepped into something squishy. Fair enough. Being surrounded by throngs of sightseers must be his vision of hell, and I didn't imagine the tourist site held appeal for locals.

"My grandparents took me to the castle once when I was young. Said it would help the stutter. I couldn't." He picked at a stray thread at the hem of his sweater.

I supposed it made sense they wanted the gift of eloquence for their painfully quiet grandson. "So you've never seen the cliffs and ocean from that perspective?"

Callum shook his head. You'd think I'd suggested bungee jumping, not baby steps. "You're away with the fairies."

I grabbed his hand and dragged him toward the ground, surprising myself with how things had changed. I didn't pause to think about what his slightly callused hands had touched before, the work they'd been doing. His long fingers just warmed mine.

Just off the path, a peninsula of stone jutted out over the water like a fishing dock. Perfect.

"Let's belly-scoot to the edge. Our weight will be distributed."

"Oh Jaysus! Not sure I can. I'm not a chancer like you."

"Well, you don't have to. But I'll be right here with you. It'll be a rush!"

He hesitated, chewing his lip, then dropped to his hands and knees. A grimace soured his face when the cold morning dew soaked his jeans.

"Come on, Callum. Remember the Alamo!"

"Who?"

Rather than explain the historic rallying call, I channeled my best warrior voice while elbowing forward. *"Chaaarge!"*

We advanced on our stomachs, creeping toward the edge like soldiers caught in no-man's-land.

"My heart's racing," he said.

Mine too.

To reassure him, I squeezed his hand. So large and warm. A little sweaty. "Come on. Snail mode the rest of the way. Inch by inch till we can look straight down at the sea."

Grass stained the front of my coat as we crawled to the edge. Finally, we poked our heads over. It was a dizzying seven hundred feet straight down to the icy Atlantic. Waves churned under the shale plateau, foamy water and wind relentlessly pummeling the island. Breathtaking, in the truest sense of the word.

I filled my lungs with salty air and let out a primal scream. Callum startled, but then he understood. *Catharsis, not fear.*

White blanched my knuckles as I clamped down on Callum's hand and shouted into the ocean. About joy, pain, struggle. Life and death, and unfairness. Loneliness. Guilt. My throat shook, lungs burned. He released a guttural roar, while the hand that wasn't on mine held his glasses onto his face. Above the waves, our necks strained as we held them up against gravity. We were silent now except for the pounding of our pulses.

Uncontrolled laughter broke from my mouth. Yep. Away with the fairies. Crinkles spread from the corners of Callum's eyes and soon a tide of laughter engulfed him, too. Our chests shook as we lay on our stomachs, dangling precariously. I felt . . . revived. The sea and the laughter and the surge of adrenaline made me feel like myself again.

Between his tousled black hair, smile-rounded cheeks, and strong frame wrapped in a cuddly sweater, Callum looked downright sexy. A kaleidoscope of greens reflected in his eyes, which were luminous when he allowed himself joy. Looking into them made me dizzier than the cliff's height.

He rocked back on his knees until he was on solid ground, then flopped onto his back. "Jaysus, Mary, and Joseph!"

I performed the same maneuver. Laid side by side, we panted like two spent lovers. Silver clouds drifted above as we shared an easy silence. Well, not entirely so; I imagined being flushed from a different thrill . . . and he was recovering from a panic-induced coronary.

"Sorry I startled you when I screamed," I said.

"I think we b-both needed it." His palms pressed flat on his chest to settle his heart.

His words invoked something else I needed. Something equally primal and cathartic that involved an enjoyable sort of screaming. A different reason for his hair being tousled. For a split second, it was as if the ledge had broken away, leaving me floating in cartoon space with a sign that read *OOPS*. Suspended before the inevitable drop, just like Wile E. Coyote.

"If this ledge gives, think we'd hover in the air until we look down and realize where we are?"

Closer to his usual deadpan self, he squinted at me. Maybe he didn't appreciate the joking reminder of the ledge-collapse possibility and my using animation logic in the real world.

"It's a philosophical commentary about how observation changes the phenomenon. I know how inertia works," I said. Thinking about lying in bed with Callum had changed the moment. Blame my sex-deprived brain. "Think I'll stand."

"Careful. Crawl farther away first."

A wicked grin tugged at my mouth. "Should I jump up and down?"

Still incandescent with adrenaline, he regarded me as he lay on his back in the grass.

I planted my feet and spread my arms wide. Western winds blew my hair into a frenzy. Farther down the coast, small black shapes milled around among the rocks.

"Am I hallucinating, or are those puffins?!"

Callum watched me without annoyance or judgment. "There's a colony on the Aran Islands, a short ferry trip from here."

"Ahh! So cute." We watched the seabirds dive into the water, filling their colorful beaks with writhing fish.

Still nervous about standing so close to the edge, he crab-walked closer to the trail. I snorted. He looked pretty ridiculous. He knew it, too, rolling his eyes as he scuttled away. Once we made it back to the trail about twenty-five feet away, he stood.

Focused on the view and still disoriented by the unexpected surge of animal attraction, my boot sunk into a soft patch of soil. With a yelp, I flapped my arms for balance. At once, I was in Callum's arms. Clean wool mingled with woodsy spice as I breathed in the scent of his grass-stained sweater.

"Are you all right?"

"Yeah, my foot got caught in a rabbit hole or something."

His embrace was grounding—until he lifted me up off the grass to get my ankle out of the hole. My stomach swooped like a seabird. Lowering me, he brushed his fingers along my arm. My traitorous limb tingled as he stepped back with an embarrassed, upside-down smile. Not a frown—definitely a smile.

Acrobatic organs and alluring scents aside, I wasn't interested in anything beyond friendship. Besides, Callum's proximity to my apartment made a hookup a terrible idea. Smart women don't go to bed with their neighbors. Not that I planned on sleeping with anyone, but a reminder felt pertinent.

"Texas looks nothing like this. We have beaches but not . . ." I nodded at the grandeur of the Atlantic.

"Is there someone waiting for you there?"

Overhead, a gull cried, *kittiwake-kittiwake.* "My mom and my cousin Cielo."

"What about the person you mentioned? Reese?"

The story was on the tip of my tongue, but Callum's ignorance made his company feel safe. I couldn't bring myself to sacrifice that sanctuary. My eyes tipped down, and my voice shrank. "We were married for four years. It didn't end well. I don't want to talk about him."

Callum ran a hand through his dark, windswept hair. "Sorry."

"What about you?" I asked, desperate to divert his curiosity. "Any evil ex-wives? Little deathlings running around somewhere?"

"Deathlings?" he repeated, slightly bewildered. "No. You?"

"Never had kids. And I don't date. Period. More than content to stay single." Nights were lonely, but I could stick to my resolution to stay unattached. I'd made a promise to Reese as we put him in the ground, and I wouldn't let him down again. This wasn't only about risking my own heart; it was about protecting someone else's. My flaws had cost me everything, including my husband's life.

"I've had little luck on the apps. My last date wanted to tour my embalming room."

"And you didn't put a ring on it?"

Callum softly scoffed. "Not after she asked me 'What's the worst thing you've ever seen?' I study my client's photos as I piece faces back together or re-create their favorite hairstyle. I write their obituaries. They're more than gruesome anecdotes." Where some would exploit the shock value of the job for the sake of edginess, it wasn't in Callum's constitution. These people mattered to him.

"Decency is lacking these days," I said. "Especially on dating apps."

With a deep breath, he fixed his attention on the spectacular setting. "When I was growing up, I thought something was wrong with me. All the other lads thought of sex constantly and I . . . couldn't relate. I know when a woman is b-b-beautiful." His eyes met mine. "But I don't fancy them or have the urge to take them home."

A dozen questions ricocheted around my mind. This alluring man was celibate? And most concerning: Why did I feel a stab of disappointment at this revelation?

"Had my testosterone levels checked to make sure it wasn't hormonal. It's just . . . rare to feel desire."

"Nothing wrong with that, even if you never feel it. Sexuality is complicated. But I'm curious—if you're on dating apps, does that mean you want a relationship? Or the whole idea is 'meh'?"

Callum laughed without mirth. "It's always 'meh' in the beginning. Attraction might happen after I know a woman well. Sometimes I develop feelings, after a long while. But pair it with a phobia of meeting people and you'll see why it's a struggle."

"The physical doesn't come first for you." Admittedly, I knew little about it. Dating without a flirtatious spark sounded like torture, though.

"Developing feelings is the hard part. After that, getting, um, physical is grand." Red glowed on the tips of his ears, matching his cheeks.

Intimacy with Callum would be precious and earned. I didn't want to romanticize his frustration with dating, but his sincerity had my heart swelling. "You need to fall in love first."

"No, I don't have to. But, um, I do want that. I wish I could skip to the part where I'm already happily married."

"And miss all the moments that send the butterflies loose in your stomach? No way. First date, first kiss, first slow dance. The falling matters, too. Not just the ever after."

A carousel of memories turned in my mind. Reese linking his pinkie with mine when we watched thousands of bats fly out from under Congress Avenue Bridge on our first date. His arm slung around my shoulders during a Spurs game, his lips on my ear making me forget the crowd. I jerked the emergency stop lever before the memories sent me spiraling. We were talking about Callum here, not me.

"But I get it," I added. "Meeting new people isn't fun for everyone. Especially if you've already had some bad experiences."

Callum sighed. "I need to get married or I will lose Willow Haven. My granda left it to me with the stipulation that I would marry before I'm thirty-five. If I'm still single by then, I will have to forfeit the business."

"But that's asinine! You can't force—"

"My granda wanted it to stay in the family. Tradition was important to him. Even though they hadn't spoken in years, my father may get it. Because I have no one to pass it down to . . ."

"And your dad wouldn't let you remain a part of it?"

"He's already sought a buyout from my competitor. I don't have the funds to make a proper counteroffer."

"Maybe you can find someone who needs a green card. Then you'd be helping each other. Get a divorce later?"

"I'm not getting fake-married to a stranger. And I won't risk everything by committing immigration fraud."

Maeve's joking words seemed to echo between us. *If you need a green card, marry him.* Reese's sister, Rachel, had told me that I deserved to be alone, and she was right, after all that happened. I couldn't imagine repeating those vows again, even if it was only a means to an end. A sham marriage would still be breaking my promise not to get involved with anyone. Good thing KinetiColor sponsored my resident status.

"Your grandparents blackmailed you to rush a relationship that involves sacred vows. *Sacred!* Not to mention the legal entanglement. It's so wrong."

Unreasonable as it was to put a timetable on marriage, I could almost understand their motivation. They knew he'd need a push. Did they want an heir to their death dynasty, or was this about ensuring their grandson wouldn't stay alone after they were gone?

"How much time do you have left?"

"Eight months. Well, more like six because of the paperwork."

"Shit," I muttered. Only thirty-four, with sole responsibility for the family business dropped into his lap along with a deadline to find The One or else lose everything, all while he grieved the man who raised him?

"Indeed. This month alone, I've forced myself to go on five dates, each one worse than the last. Deirdre tells me I should just choose someone who sounds good on paper. Hope deeper feelings will come after I get to know her. Perhaps she's right."

That sounded like a risk to both hearts. And he deserved someone who gave him butterflies.

"What about the florist?"

"Saoirse?" He offered a shrug. "I can't really talk to her. To anyone. That's . . . usually the biggest problem."

"Hate to break it to you, but you're doing just fine talking to me." The butterflies in my own stomach fluttered as Callum met my eyes. I needed to take scissors to those wings.

"That's an anomaly."

"Why, thank you," I laughed, and willed the pesky internal insects to be still. "Tell you what. My coworkers go out every Friday. You should come. Get more comfortable mingling, and you can even see if you hit it off with anyone. Stranger things have happened. I'll keep an eye out for someone nice at the studio, if you want me to fix you up."

"No! That would be worse than shaking the cliff's edge," he said, throwing his hands in the air.

I feigned offense. "What, afraid to date an artist?"

"Artists are only scary. Noisy pubs full of strangers are terrifying."

"So are cliffs, but you did that. I'd never throw you to the wolves. Super-casual group setting to dip your toe in and practice socializing," I said. "You trusted me enough to get you to the edge of the cliff, and you won't trust me in a pub? Come on. What did you call me? A chancer? Maybe it's time you took a chance."

CHAPTER 10

Callum

A WEEK AFTER the trip to the cliffs, Lark sat cross-legged among bright cushions on her tiny sofa. Otherwise, the sparsely furnished flat served as a reminder that her accommodations were temporary. Hazy winter light streamed in through the windows that faced my house.

When we'd first gone out, I reasoned with myself that she was a friendly, beautiful woman with whom I could actually hold a conversation and she checked many of the proverbial boxes Deirdre had pestered me about, such as being driven in her own career. I'd wondered if I could fall for someone like her, given the time. But Lark had since made her boundaries abundantly clear. Our relationship wouldn't extend past friendship.

Although the holiday season was terribly busy in my line of work, I'd accompanied Lark during a visit to Maeve a few days earlier to help erect her scrawny, false tree. Mid-century records played as Lark dug out a cache of blown glass ornaments from the shed while I attempted to unravel a knot of twinkle lights. It was the perfect pick-me-up during a grueling season with three weeks still to go until Christmas.

Now, in her flat, she explained that she'd found a niche dating site while she was learning more about the asexual spectrum. I admit, it was nice to see someone work to understand me. Lark swiveled the laptop to display my new DemiDate profile. In the photo taken at the ruined abbey, I was showing teeth. I hardly recognized myself, which made sense: I'd been happy that day. Lark had insisted it replace the blurry selfie I'd used on a more mainstream app. For good measure, she updated that profile as well. Lots of fish out there, she'd said, best to cast a wide net.

Lark had been excited upon finding a resource for people on the asexual and aromantic spectrum, but I remained skeptical. Because of the time constraints, we were upfront about my job. And while I didn't think my work was embarrassing, disclosing it online hadn't boded well for me in the past. It either turned off prospective matches or attracted red flags.

"Seeking . . . serious relationship? Life partner?" She read from a list of choices on the site. "Marriage? Check them all?"

"Um, sure."

"How do you feel about kids?"

"I want a family before I'm too old and out of touch."

"Nothing you can do about that—all children see their parents that way."

I'd never admitted wanting children to anyone. Not to Deirdre and not to my grandparents. Somehow Lark made it okay to be vulnerable and honest.

"Look—fifteen potential matches in the area. This one plays piano . . ." The screen displayed a pretty but severe-featured brunette administrative assistant in a black turtleneck.

"She looks like she condescends to restaurant servers."

Lark clicked on the next profile. "What about her? She's a 'sustainable fashion designer.'"

I pointed to a photo of her surrounded by felines. "'Must love cats is not enough. Must adore cats!' Oh God. This says she knits using hair shed by her twelve 'fur babies.' *Twelve*."

"This could be the future Mrs. Flannelly. You'd let something as trivial as a dozen cats stand between you and a lifetime of happiness? There's a link to her website—"

We burst into laughter when a photo of the fashionista modeling an ill-fitting felted dress and matching cat-eared hat appeared on the screen. According to the caption, it was created with "ethically harvested tabby fur."

"Just hear me out: She's cute. She has a hobby and, um, talent. Obviously cares about the environment," Lark said, ticking off the qualities on her fingers. "She'd outfit you in a bespoke Siamese waistcoat for the wedding ceremony, for sure. I'd have to eat a pound's worth of Claritin, but I wouldn't miss *that* for the world."

My nipples itched at the mere suggestion. "It would be less weird to marry the cat."

"The ring bearer and wedding party would be cats in bow ties and dresses! Think about it. That would be adorable."

"Lark. No."

"Okay. Okay. Moving on." Lark wiped the mirth from her eyes. For the next half hour, we exhausted the local matches. Nothing especially promising yet.

"I can't look at another profile." I rose from the couch and stretched, already regretting the money sunk into a membership to the app. "Want to get some air?"

Within twenty minutes, we were standing in the heart of the Eyre Square Christmas Market. I tended to avoid the crowded square, but Lark's response to the festive lights, delicious-smelling food stalls, and glittering Ferris wheel won me over.

"It reminds me of Austin." She wound a bright yellow scarf tighter around her throat. "We have this art festival called the Armadillo Christmas Bazaar."

"I don't come here often."

"But you like the music, don't you? No one plays piano as well as you without being a music lover."

I did. Even if her compliment made me instinctively avoid looking at her face. A swarm of tourists crawled past like locusts, crowding to get a look at a juggler blasting awful dubstep carols and tossing pins into the air. The "music" made my teeth buzz.

"I'd rather watch the ships come into the bay." An especially *jolly* university student knocked into me, belched, and stumbled along without apology. "Or tie a stone around my waist and jump in."

"Next time we'll watch the ships." She gave my shoulder an affectionate nudge. "Classic. Contemplative Cancer."

How the hell? "Run a background check on me, didya, then?"

"Pfft. I just did the math. Besides, this"—Lark gestured to my entire form—"screams crustacean. I had you pegged as a water sign from the first time we met."

"I don't believe in that. And refrain from suggesting you've pegged me, please."

"Would you let me run your natal chart? You're a Scorpio moon, I bet."

My nan had believed astrology to be the devil's work. Personally, I took it for a load of nonsense, albeit nonsense that never hurt anyone. If Lark took solace in the idea of the stars governing her life, who was I to contradict it?

"People who have a moon in Scorpio keep a drawbridge around themselves, but when they let someone in, it awakens a sense of deep loyalty." Lark dropped her attention to the cobblestones under her trademark boots. She cleared her throat. "And passion."

My heart performed an anxious jig.

Squeals broke through the noise as a little girl stopped in front of us. Stripes of orange and black decorated her plump cheeks. She held up both hands like claws, then let out a high-pitched "*Rwar!*"

Staggering backward with Shakespearean flair, Lark grabbed my arm. "A fearsome tiger!"

Valiantly, I puffed out my chest and stepped forward to shield her from the tiny threat. "I'll save you!"

"I don't eat girls." Both front teeth were missing from her grin. "I'm a man-eating tiger."

"Oh no!" Lark cried.

I put on a show and cowered from the small beast as her family caught up to her. Her mother herded the girl along, who waved at us before they disappeared into the crowd. Lark watched after them for a moment, something inscrutable on her face. No surprise she was a natural with children, with her innate sense of wonder and vivid imagination. But I'd surprised myself. It renewed the familiar pang to start a family.

"I thought I was a goner for certain."

"You *are* a snack." Was she flirting or was it just her brand of humor? She tugged me toward the face-painting cart set up near the Santa's Express train. "Are you thinking what I'm thinking?"

Face painting? Me? "Where's a boulder and a rope when you need them?"

"No one's drowning themselves today." Lark shook her head. "How about this: pick a design for me, and I'll pick one for you. Then we walk around like that the rest of the day. No matter what."

I narrowed my gaze.

"Don't you trust me?" She batted her lashes.

Defeated, I sighed. Lark pranced in triumph.

She shoved me down onto the folding stool in front of the face painter. "He said I could pick his design," she explained to the artist.

A gaggle of women in party hats strode past. The leader wore a sash emblazoned *Birthday Bitch*. Lark leaned forward to guide my glasses off my ears and everything blurred into noisy oblivion. She whispered her choice into the woman's ear and didn't hand back my confiscated eyewear.

"I'm going to regret this."

Mirth sparkled on Lark's face as the artist worked. I couldn't help but feel the tingle of anticipation at the outcome. I reached for a handheld mirror next to the sponges, stencils, and paints.

Lark swatted my fingers away. "Uh-uh. No peeking! You agreed to wear whatever I chose. Now close your eyes."

They made small talk about the "Lone Star State." I cracked an eyelid open as cool paint swept over my skin. At some point, Lark had put on my frames, and they'd slid down her nose. It didn't seem to bother her that people turned their heads to gawk, attracted first by the subtle twang in her voice or her striking face, then lingering for her infectious energy. Being noticed at all was mortifying for me; I couldn't imagine being so unaffected by the attention. Or thriving off it.

Lark held up a finger in a "one minute" gesture and jogged off toward the crowd. She returned straightaway with something behind her back. "Close your eyes."

I did, and she affixed something over my nose and stretched a string around my head. What was she up to?

"Voilà!"

Allowed at last to take in my reflection, I blinked in stupefaction. The artist twiddled a paintbrush, gauging my approval. Black. White. Two red circles over my cheeks. Orange cone-shaped party hat held in place by elastic as a beak. Charmed, I said, "I'm a puffin?"

"The world's cutest bird." Still wearing my glasses, she turned to the artist. "It's perfect."

"No one's asked for a puffin before," the artist said.

"Thanks for doing it, even though it's not on your menu. The texture turned out so realistic. You're really talented."

Lark was the singular filterless person who blurted out more niceties than insults. Since we'd wandered into the humming street market she'd commented on several buskers' skills, passing out coins and compliments like snuff at a wake. Positivity radiated from this woman.

When her turn came, I considered a number of colorful designs but ultimately chose the same one because Lark loved puffins. The artist remarked with a grin that the birds mate for life. I didn't have the heart to tell her that we wouldn't, and stuffed a tip in her cup as we ambled away.

"You know," I said to Lark, "at one time, we used to consider puffins and their eggs delicacies."

Without warning, she grabbed my forearm, removed her paper beak, and bit down with an exaggerated chomping sound. It took me so much by surprise that I shouted when her teeth grazed the fabric of my jumper. I gathered myself instantly. "Food critic says?"

She spit out some wool fibers. "Bitter. Dry. Needs a splash of hot sauce."

"Let's go b-b-back to the cliffs, and I'll whip us up a nice omelet."

"No!" She howled as though I'd scramble a full nest, the sound strangely amplified as she put her beak back on. "If you're hungry, we can get something that isn't adorable or endangered."

The place where her warm mouth had clamped around my forearm still prickled with goose bumps. I didn't dare touch it.

We made a beeline for a garland-decorated soft pretzel cart Lark had noticed. Amused by our painted faces, the proprietor let out a good-natured chuckle. Somehow, caught up in the unexpected rush of playful contact, I'd forgotten my transformation into a puffin. Surreal. Every moment with Lark had that quality.

"You sort of surprised me with the answer to the question about kids," she said, with her salty prize in hand. "But you were good with that little girl back there. I can see it."

"Some stutters are genetic. There's a high likelihood my child will inherit that as well."

"So? If anything, you would know how to support them."

I carefully removed the paper beak. "I hated being an only child. Living in a funeral home and having a speech impediment made things rough. I always wanted an older brother. The nuclear family I didn't have, I guess."

No one had been around to defend me from bullies before puberty hit, and I gained six inches of height on my classmates. Being raised by strict grandparents a full generation older than my peers' parents didn't help me pick up on modern social norms, either. I'd felt painfully alienated.

"That makes sense," she said. "The inheritance thing is weird, but you're taking it seriously and I respect that."

"I'm not happy about it, but I never could lie to my grandparents, nor could I bear disappointing them."

Even though they were gone, it was my duty to fulfill the obligation. I'd pored over the will again and again, looking for another way. I wanted a family, but this pressure felt like a noose tightening at my throat. I couldn't breathe when every day brought me closer to personal and professional displacement.

"You're a good guy. You have your own house and your own business. Ladies will line up for a chance to call you 'Daddy' and have your babies."

Luckily the paint camouflaged my flushed cheeks. "Willow Haven isn't mine yet."

"It'll happen."

"You'll make a fun mam. If you want."

"Kids are amazing! Reese and I . . ." She broke eye contact, as she always did when she said his name. I'd seen that expression on so many faces. She still grieved their relationship. "I work long hours, and I enjoy my freedom and spontaneity. You can't move to another continent on impulse, as a parent."

"You'd get creative." Nothing could stop Lark from sucking the sweetest marrow out of life. She'd be the type of mam who builds elaborate cushion forts for home showings of Disney staples. Creates pretend holidays to wear homemade costumes. Volunteers to read at the school in funny voices. "Your ex didn't want a baby?"

"He did, but I'm not equipped for that level of responsibility." The finality in her tone signaled the end of the subject. She handed the pretzel to me and licked salt crystals off her finger before restoring her beak.

Her declaration seemed at odds with her job. An animation studio trusted her to oversee their production. Wasn't that a show of responsibility?

"Sorry for prying."

"It's just a sore subject, but it's my fault for bringing him up. You're fine, Cal."

Cal. No one had ever shortened my name, not even when I was a child. Most people except for Deirdre called me Mr. Flannelly, which still conjured images of my granda. But it fell from Lark's mouth with such ease. Maybe I could be Cal, too. A bit silly and vulnerable. A braver version of myself.

"You've got a smear—"

Without thinking, I reached out and gingerly brushed a rogue streak of paint on her chin. Wide gray eyes stared up at me, and my mouth went dry as my thumb slid across her soft skin. Even covered in black and white paint with rosy puffin cheeks and a paper beak, Lark was beautiful.

And not only objectively, based on facial geometry or social consensus. Beautiful *to me.* Utterly captivating. Shite. My feelings had sped past platonic, careening dangerously toward something deeper before I'd even noticed. I jerked my hand away and buried it in my pocket the rest of the afternoon.

CHAPTER 11

Lark

ON CHRISTMAS DAY, I FaceTimed with my mom. I'd never spent the holiday away from family before. Of course, Reese's absence was conspicuously avoided during a conversation full of forced cheer. I was grateful for it to end when Cielo called. Still a little hungover, she lifted my spirits by telling me all about the boisterous Nochebuena celebration hosted by her dad's side of the family.

Callum and I delivered a tray of sloppily decorated sugar cookies to Maeve, who teared up when she opened the Vespa Christmas ornament we'd found at the holiday market. I'd nearly lost it and cried with her. Callum gave me a Saint Dolly devotional candle, which now sat proudly on my desk, and I gave him a 3D printed model of the modified Jaguar hearse from *Harold and Maude*. Without them, I don't think I'd have managed to have found the holiday spirit at all.

Now a week into January, Christmas lights were still woven around the Kilkenny and Smithwick's signage and wrapped around the detailed millwork of the Hare's Breath pub. My gaze drifted through the cluster of KinetiColor coworkers blowing off steam.

Friday gatherings here were Seán's domain. He'd been giving me the side-eye from the bar since Callum and I arrived, but he'd issued an open invitation to all the staff. Callum had finally agreed to accompany me, and it was the perfect opportunity to introduce him to Hannah, the nerdy-cute ginger. He'd been speaking to a few ladies on the app but hadn't met anyone in person yet. I'd appointed myself his modern matchmaker, and he'd readily agreed to a little coaching.

Rory, Anvi, and I had tucked into a cozy booth, waxing poetic about *Avatar: The Last Airbender* and laughing over the best iconic quotes.

Anvi interrupted her rhapsody on the perfection of Dante Basco's voice-acting as Prince Zuko (as if I'd disagree) and rose from her side of the booth. "You keep watching them. Switch spots with me. Otherwise your jealousy will cause a sore neck."

Me, jealous? Preposterous. Need I remind her I introduced Callum and Hannah and then fled? I'd been analyzing the pair since, complete with internal David Attenborough–style narration about the hesitant male venturing to a dangerous watering hole, courting a female unimpressed by his dark plumage. It was all I could do not to intervene.

"I was just watching the soccer match playing over the bar." My eyes bounced to the television there. "Madrid is dominating." Madrid was a soccer team, right?

"Mm-hmmm. Speaking of which, I better give you the number of my massage therapist," Rory said, fiddling with a *They/Them* pronoun button on their Keroppi-print button-down. "He's from Barcelona. Total babe. You'll need his services if you keep twisting to watch your friend flirt with Hannah. Besides, that's Gaelic football, so we know you're lying."

"Callum's flirting?" I whipped around so quickly, I hissed in pain. Okay. So the idea of fixing him up with someone from work had me tense, even though I'd told him there were zero expectations. Back in Austin, I'd been responsible for multiple successful introductions among friends. Long-term relationships, even one engagement. Now the pressure was on, and I was woefully out of practice in the matchmaking game—and I'd never before set up anyone who didn't feel immediate attraction.

Across the pub, Callum chewed his lip. He'd been gnawing at it from the moment we arrived. Both hands cupped his drink with the commitment of someone thawing frostbitten fingers over a fire. When I'd asked what Callum thought of Hannah's social media profile photo, he answered, "She's conventionally attractive." Considering the source, the lukewarm comment was as close as we'd get to a declaration of interest.

"There's a beautiful man with magic hands I can introduce you to, and *Callum's flirting?* is yer takeaway?" As far as Rory was concerned, I'd proven Anvi's point. I relinquished to reason and switched spots, now positioned for a clear view of the bar.

"I ain't jealous, I'm invested. I dragged him along tonight because I hoped they'd hit it off."

Out of nowhere, Seán leaned into our booth and snorted. "*Ain't* isn't a word."

Talk about a jump scare. How long had he been eavesdropping? I'd lost track of where he was slithering through the pub.

My mouth refused to form an intelligent rebuttal. Callum had described the bottlenecked feeling of having a word block. I typically suffered from the opposite problem, words spewing from me like foam from a shaken IPA. Except for in a confrontation, when the perfect snappy retort always came far after the moment had passed. Usually while I was shampooing my hair.

Anvi cleared her throat. "It's slang, and it's in the dictionary. Similar to *amn't*. Try to keep up."

He rolled his eyes. "I'll need two more drinks to think as slow as she talks."

What. An. Ass.

Satisfied with having the last word, Seán slid away to the bar to congratulate himself with another pint.

"You just became my favorite coworker," I told Anvi, wiping beer froth off my nose.

Rory clutched their chest. "You wound me, Lark Thompson!"

"Remember this moment when it's time for raises and overtime," Anvi laughed. She stuck her tongue out at us, like a teasing sibling.

"Afraid I have little pull there. But I've got next round, and you've got my gratitude."

"Seán's such a dryshite." Rory glared at him from across the room. "Nepotism lets people like him get away with murder."

Anvi flagged a server to claim the offer for another round. "Sullivan's his uncle, you know."

Well. That explained volumes of office politics I hadn't grasped before. It made sense given his entitled attitude. "I had no idea."

"That's why most of us are reluctant to say anything, except for Brass Balls McGee here." Rory jabbed a thumb in Anvi's direction.

"He's not used to having *his* balls busted," she replied. "You need to stick up for yourself or he'll walk all over you."

"I've never busted a pair of balls in my life. I wouldn't know how if I wanted to!" I wanted nothing to do with Seán's balls. In any capacity. "Can we talk about anything else?"

I absently drew a smiley face in the condensation of my very full beer, watching Callum and Hannah. Rory drew a pair of grumpy testicles on theirs.

"What's the deal with the quiet one you introduced to Hannah? He's hot in a 'Damien Rice song' kinda way." Rory noticed my attention was still divided. "Let me guess: he's got a crush but won't quit trying to break out of the friend zone, and you're trying to introduce him to a distraction before it gets too awkward."

I shook my head. "Not even close."

Anvi's impeccably threaded brow tilted. "So you hooked up but now you're dating someone else. If he paired up, it would make it less weird to stay friends?"

"No. Believe me. Callum sees me as a dorky kid sister. He is not lusting after this."

They traded dubious looks, and Anvi pursed her lips. "Got a fella, then? A girlfriend?"

"Nope," I said, popping the *p* before taking a hearty swig of my drink. The more nonchalant I sounded about it, the less people pried.

I stole another glance at the bar.

Turns out, two people with social anxiety don't cling to each other like rafts in a Guinness sea. They'd both prefer to sit alone on their respective desert islands until rescue rather than start up an actual conversation. Although Callum *was* trying, bless him. Twice I saw him muster a lopsided smile and mutter a few words. But after a couple of terse exchanges, they each sat on their stools staring into pints, in matching postures of discomfort.

Callum sent me a pleading look. I gave him an apologetic pout. He shot back a stern face that translated to *Never again.*

Mine replied, *We'll see.*

Hannah took notice of our wordless conversation, so I blew the game whistle and walked over. Relief flooded Callum's features when I sidled between them at the bar. It warmed me far more than the drink I'd been nursing. Seán looked on, scrutinizing my every move.

"So I finally get the name of this place." I motioned to the circular sign above the bar depicting three rabbits tangled in Celtic knotwork. "The Hare's Breath. As in 'The bartender will get you a hair's breadth from blackout drunk in only two mixed drinks.'"

Cal's brows knit. "How many have you had?"

"I'm not a big drinker. However, the guys from background texture rendering are already torn on."

Seán narrowed his eyes beside Hannah. "What's that?"

"On a tear," Callum murmured under his breath, leaning close to me.

The deep rumble of his voice, so close to my ear, sent the fine hairs rising off my neck. I brushed at my arms absently, willing away the goose bumps. Faint notes of his cologne added an unwelcome layer of distraction.

"*On* a tear," I said, correcting myself with manufactured confidence. Even though Callum had been shooting ocular daggers at me from the bar a moment ago, he didn't hesitate to come to my aid. Obviously, he could empathize with tripping over one's words and being judged for it. "At least tomorrow is Saturday. Any plans?"

Callum recognized the invisible let's-make-an-exit sign I'd just constructed. He knocked back the dregs of his pint. "I've work early in the morning, actually."

Hannah, already zeroed in on a hipster loitering by the jukebox, murmured a polite goodbye.

"Good night." I blew a kiss to the group. "See all y'all on Monday."

"Y'all? Sorry we don't speak *banjo* here." Pleased with himself, Seán nudged Hannah, who flinched at his touch. Seán didn't seem to notice.

"Everyone. See everyone Monday," I said, quieter. I'd hoped that morale-boosting visits to the Hare's Breath would bridge the divide and cement a sense of camaraderie, but no matter what I did, I couldn't win his respect.

Callum touched my elbow, and his jaw tightened. "If you came to Texas, Lark would welcome you. She wouldn't mock your accent or your imperfect grasp of regional slang."

Seán scoffed. "I wouldn't be caught dead in Texas. Some of us have standards."

All I could do was mumble a farewell. I waved weakly at Rory and Anvi, who were already knee-deep in another debate. Callum grabbed my hand and thrust his shoulder forward to guide us out of the throng.

A blast of frigid air assaulted us the second we were free of the pulsing bass, the mass of bodies, and the sour smell of spilled beer. I drew my arms tight across my chest, regretting not layering a sweater under my flimsy trench to protect against the January cold. My favorite peep-toe heels dunked into a freezing puddle I was too distracted to avoid, and I hissed a curse.

"Are you all right?" Callum leaned down to search my face. "Seán is a piece of work."

"I was the one trying to rescue you." Droplets of water flew as I shook off my foot. "But thanks for sticking up for me."

"Stop."

Seán's unprovoked venom still burned in my ears. "Stop what?"

Callum removed his coat and handed it to me. He peeled off his sweater, revealing a stripe of toned stomach for a moment. My eyes widened, greedy for more.

Would he be ticklish if my fingernails gently grazed his happy trail? Or would he suck in a breath and mutter something dirty? What would he do if I kissed the plane of pale skin, going lower . . . lower . . .

I schooled my features once I realized why he was stripping in the street. Clearly, he was a gentleman. And given my thoughts, I was no lady.

Underneath the sweater, a snug charcoal tee left his toned arms on display, hinting at a similarly fit chest. Not that I was looking. Nope. I handed his coat back, and he pushed his arms through the sleeves again. Then he held my trench as I slipped his sweater over my head. The cable knit enveloped me in Callum's woodsy and rich scent.

"Stop trying to sound like someone you're not. There's nothing you've got to prove to them."

I bristled as I put my coat back on over his sweater. "I know who I am. But Seán resents that the job he wanted went to a foreigner. He hates any reminder that I'm American."

"Who cares? Seán's not in charge."

"I care! And I don't have to tell you what it's like. You avoid certain words on purpose, too. Don't do that with me, okay? Just say what you think, even if it takes a while to get it out."

"Only if you stop suppressing your *y'all*s and *ain't*s with me."

"Deal."

Before he took my hand, he flashed a tiny smile. "D-d-deal."

Overcome with gratitude, I hooked my arm under his. Colorful bunting crisscrossed the lane overhead, swaying in the cold evening breeze. "So . . . my apologies for introducing you to the only woman immune to tall, broody, deep-voiced men. Hannah wasn't giving you much to work with."

As my fingers curled over his biceps, I tried not to think about their firmness. Tried not to inhale any pheromones and intoxicate myself from his sweater. Callum looked so handsome in the moonlight. My thumb ached to trace his stubble-shadowed jawline. Feel the rasp against my fingertips. Despite the time he'd spent with Hannah tonight, walking home together felt like the conclusion of a date.

"I promise, the next time will be easier."

He groaned, sounding closer to an irate bear than a man.

An elderly woman with a basket of roses waved her bundle at us. "Rose for the lady?"

Callum surprised me by saying, "Yes, please, ma'am."

"I've all the colors," she said, grinning. "Pink for admiration, yellow for friendship, ivory for charm . . . Red for passionate love, of course."

He cast a look over his shoulder. "Which one?"

"Any color. I adore them all." I toyed with the long ends of his sweater sleeves covering my fingertips.

"Of course." He cleared his throat and twirled a finger. "Turn around, then."

I obeyed. When he called my name, I turned to find him holding no less than a dozen in an assortment of yellows and pinks and ivories. And reds. I said any color; he got me *every* color. It wasn't symbolic—but my stomach still dropped. The same plummeting feeling as at the Cliffs of Moher.

"Hold on tight." She motioned to the posy but was obviously referring to Callum. We did look the part of a loving couple, strolling arm in arm.

"I will," I answered. Hold on to what exactly? I wasn't sure. To my sense of optimism in helping him find a partner, maybe. To not feeling alone in this country anymore?

"Thank you. These'll cheer up my sad little apartment." I brought the bouquet to my nose. He followed suit, eyelids fluttering shut as he breathed in.

"It's late, and she had a lot of unsold stock." The hour wasn't terribly late, not when we were the first ones to depart the Hare's Breath. Callum's voice lowered. "And I wanted to thank you for forcing me out."

"You were practically melting off the barstool in your misery."

"I'm not miserable now." Meaning: alone. With me.

"You ought to be proud of yourself for pushing out of your comfort zone tonight."

We walked on, a strange energy settling between us. Streetlights shimmered off the Corrib and off the lenses of his glasses. Callum was quiet for a long while until he said, "Meeting new people is the worst. The dating site's a bust."

"It's a little premature to call the game, isn't it? These things take time, and you have to keep putting yourself out there."

"Right. Clock's ticking."

I couldn't imagine the pressure.

"I can't blame you for wanting to give up. I'd be one of those spinster cat ladies already if I wasn't horrifically allergic. A pet would be nice, though."

"No bridesmaid dress woven of tabby fur, then?"

I shivered at the memory and nudged Callum's shoulder with a laugh.

We reached my apartment and stood in front of my door.

"So . . . this is me." I rocked back and forth on the balls of my feet, clutching my roses in one hand. The shy curve of Callum's sensual mouth drew my attention like a magnet. How soft would it be if I lifted up on my toes and sunk into it?

He tilted his head toward Willow Haven. "And this is me."

Perched on the second step, I was at his eye level. My free hand reached out seemingly on its own accord to pet the top of his head. Lush, dark hair tickled my palm, and he leaned into my touch like an affectionate stray. His eyes searched mine. I wondered what he saw there. For a moment, I thought Callum would rest his massive hands on my hips, but he slipped them into his coat pockets . . . as if they weren't trustworthy.

I slung my arms around his neck, careful not to accidentally whack him with the roses. It was a mistake. Wide shoulders, that solid chest. *Mmmm.* I was proud of him. Thankful. All too aware of his crisp scent. I moved to peck him on the cheek, but he turned, brushing his nose against mine.

I froze, millimeters from his lips. *A hair's breadth, indeed.* My grip tightened around the flower stems.

His awkward laugh diffused some of the ionic charge. "Sorry. I, uh—"

"No worries."

His hands hovered in the air, framing my waist, but he patted me on the back instead. Relief and disappointment collided inside me. He hadn't meant to almost meet my lips. Had he?

"Good night, Lark."

"Sweet dreams, Flannelly."

We retreated to our respective houses.

With the bouquet placed in a makeshift vase of a water pitcher, I went to undress for bed and realized I was still wearing

Callum's sweater. He hadn't asked for it back. Against my better judgment, I wore nothing but that . . . and a pair of thermal pajama bottoms to bed. Inhaling the residual scent, I drifted off, imagining his protective arms around me instead of the cable knit.

CHAPTER 12

Lark

"THESE UNDERWATER COLOR gradients are gorgeous." I waved a hand over the computer monitor and drew a steadying breath. "But the opacity needs to be set to sixty percent to match the rest of the sequence. These are far too dark."

The Pirate Queen opened on an eleven-year-old Grace O'Malley stowed away aboard her father's ship. When she was discovered, a crew member informed her that young ladies were unfit for sea, as her long hair would become tangled in the ropes. Young Grace defiantly snatched the knife from his belt, lopping off her locks right there on the starboard bow and tossing them overboard. Our screenplay took a few liberties with history, but that had reportedly really happened.

"All of them?" Seán squeezed his stylus so hard I thought the tool would snap. "I've already done three scenes like this."

Whose fault was that? It was in the style guide, a comprehensive shared file that detailed specific brushes for distinct elements, color palette, and other visual hallmarks of each film. As a veteran animator, he should've known to double-check. Production was accelerated because Mr. Sullivan wanted the forty-five-minute movie screened at the Galway Film Fleadh in July, leaving no time to waste. As far as animation went, that was practically break-neck speed.

I forced warmth into my voice. "I know it's tedious to do again, but if we don't fix it now, we'll just have to redo those scenes later." Retakes were largely my personal responsibility. And sure, every production needed at least a few retakes, but I wouldn't have Seán create extra work for me in the future, when it was his responsibility now. It almost felt like he was trying to sabotage me.

"You said yourself it looked *gorgeous*." He subtly mimicked my inflection on the last word.

Anvi called from her desk, and I made a *one minute* gesture before turning back to Seán. "Please. It's all there in the style guide. That's the way everyone is doing the shadows."

"No way I'll have it by Friday."

"*Seán.*"

"Fine, I'll ask an intern to help."

"This is your responsibility."

Swiveling in his chair away from me, he clicked on a selection without another word. I suppressed the urge to apologize. After all, I hadn't created extra work for him. He'd done it himself. "Ummm, okay. Other than that, it looks excellent so far."

This compliment sandwich was already less than appetizing, but it was best practice, regardless.

"She's got notions," Seán grumbled as I walked away.

During lunch, Anvi and Rory cornered me in the break room. The spoon in Anvi's chai clinked against the mug shaped like Betty Boop's head. Wedges of afternoon light streamed in through the wide steel-framed windows, giving an industrial vibe to the break room.

"Don't let Seán get to you. We all know he's a dosser," Anvi said. I'd heard of a *tosser*, but never a dosser. "It's why you're in a leadership position and he isn't. He's lazy."

So he'd already complained about me for expecting the bare minimum. Fantastic. Before the falling-out at Blue Star, the worst

I'd had to endure had been a background painter who used the break room to microwave salmon teriyaki.

Cinnamon and clove scented the air as I fixed myself a cup. "He's a brilliant artist. So long as he gets his work done, he doesn't have to like me."

If that was true, why had I brought doughnuts every Monday? Why had I made repeated efforts to find common ground with Seán? I'd asked about the photos of his children arranged on his desk and complimented his work to an almost aggressive degree to ingratiate myself to him. Nothing worked.

"As far as Seán is concerned, you're a bully singling him out for undeserved punishment," Anvi said. "Thank you, by the way. Your predecessor didn't value fairness nearly as much. He knew Seán foisted off his responsibilities onto unwitting newbies and still let him take the credit."

Rory shook their head. "Be careful. The last time someone crossed him, they got fired. Reason undisclosed."

"He wants everyone to believe he had something to do with the previous art director being let go, but I don't believe it." Anvi took another sip from her mug, looking unimpressed.

"I'm not taking any chances," Rory argued. "He has Wendy from HR eating from the palm of his hand. On top of his uncle running the studio."

If he'd received preferential treatment from the last art director, it made sense that Anvi didn't believe he had anything to do with the man's termination. Unless he wanted the art director's job . . . the job I ended up landing. How far would Seán go to claim what he thought was rightfully his?

"He can't expect others to clean up his mistakes," I said. "It's not right to exploit rookies or anyone else just because they're afraid to say no to the boss's nephew."

As a chronic people pleaser, I knew something about that. The thought of confronting Seán again made me sick, but my sense of fairness overruled my apprehension for the sake of the team. What I would endure personally and what I would tolerate on behalf of others were two different things.

Glancing at my watch, I bid goodbye to Rory and Anvi and retreated to my office. A batch of scenes needed approval, and emails needed answering. My inbox was stuffed after the weekend, and I cracked my knuckles as I settled at my desk.

Blood turned to ice in my veins when I scanned the list of senders and saw a name that completely unnerved me: Rachel Thompson.

Guilt curdled the chai in my stomach. Trepidation squeezed my throat to a pinpoint. I forced myself to take deep breaths and deleted the email without opening it. Instinct had me clutching my phone, ready to dial Cielo, but she had an important exam today. I'd sent her a series of encouraging emojis this morning. Unloading this on her wouldn't be right; she needed focus, not emotional texts from her cousin. Over the past year, I'd distanced myself from nearly everyone who knew the situation between Rachel and me, but right now I needed to speak to someone who understood. The image of my mom smiled back from my list of contacts. It would be fine; all I needed was a familiar voice. Praying I didn't live to regret it, I hit call. It felt like shattering a Break in Case of Emergency glass.

"Hello? Lark?" She sounded distracted. Only a couple of weeks had passed since we last spoke, but it felt much longer.

"Hey, Mama." Forced levity in my voice, I pulled the corners of my mouth taut, but the smile didn't reach my eyes.

"How's Ireland lately? Magical, right?"

Not the adjective I'd pick at the moment, considering the interoffice friction and the email that fractured my sanity enough to dial her. "It is."

"You always were a little tumbleweed," she said fondly. My mom called me that because I'd never stuck to one thing, except for animation. I'd assured her the temporary move would bolster my career, but she was unaware of how much my mental health hinged on it. Austin was fraught with land mines of memory, threatening to detonate my grief at a moment's notice. I'd lived in avoidance of everyday things: Reese's favorite taco joint. The park where I'd staged our anniversary scavenger hunt. The cemetery I could bear to visit only once.

"You're . . . quiet today." I could hear her nails clicking on the amethyst amulet around her neck, a subconscious habit whenever she was uncomfortable. "Something the matter?"

Static hung between us, spanning the Atlantic as I debated telling her.

"I received an email from Rachel today."

"Oh! How is Rachel?"

"I deleted it without reading."

She tsked in disappointment. An invisible knife slipped between my ribs and twisted. Another failure.

"You two were so close. You ought to let bygones be bygones. Holding a grudge is poison for your soul."

"I wish it was that easy," I said through gritted teeth. A grudge? That's what my mom thought was going on?

Frustrated, I stared out the window at the River Corrib. I didn't want to hear anything Rachel had to say; hearing it once was enough. Her furious words of judgment still reverberated in my mind like a curse, nearly two years later.

My brother would still be here if not for you.

My mom's honeyed drawl broke through the bitter memory. "You'll never guess who I ran into at the H-E-B deli counter yesterday." She rattled on as if I cared about an old acquaintance in her social circle, anything to avoid mention of the schism between me and Rachel and what had caused it.

Not that I wanted to get into it, but I expected something warmer than a non sequitur about a stranger's sliced ham. I'd learned how to avoid tough conversations from the best. Calling my mom looking for comfort was a bad idea.

My mom and I had never been great at handling negative

emotions. She subscribed to that whole no-bad-vibes mindset. Insisted we clear them from the house with various appropriated energy-cleansing rituals. The scent of sage and the deep tones of Tibetan singing bowls wafted through our residence daily. Growing up, my mom never let me cry without feeling weak.

Sadness and depression were an active choice, according to her; she would only engage enough to distract the person suffering. That's how she'd handled sadness when I was a kid. A Popsicle when the neighbor kids banned me from their kiddie pool. Empowering chick flicks when I experienced a high school breakup.

At one time, Rachel had been the person who encouraged me to open up about those ugly feelings. She'd introduced me to Reese—the last person I truly opened up to. Now he was dead, and she blamed me for it, and there was no one I could tell when the darkness was at my door.

"My lunch break is nearly over," I said, grateful for an honest excuse to hang up.

"Nice to hear you're well, darlin'. I worry about you, over there all by yourself." My mom laughed breezily, relief clear in her tone that the call would end before I could dissolve into sobs and ruin her afternoon. "Guess I shouldn't, though. Making friends is your superpower."

One friend entered my mind. I pictured myself at home tonight, queuing up a comfort movie and raw cookie dough—with Callum by my side. A quiet, steady presence—like he belonged there. *Whoa*. Where did *that* image come from?

"Don't worry 'bout me." My nails dug into my palm as we said our farewells.

Before I could second-guess myself, I tapped out a text to Callum inviting him over for a movie. That is, if he wasn't busy meeting someone from DemiDate. Within minutes, he replied to accept. I immediately felt lighter.

CHAPTER 13

Callum

GASPS BROKE OUT. Every guest swiveled in the pews, looking for the source of the paper airplanes bombarding the chapel. My piano hit a discordant note as I rose from the bench to put an end to the pandemonium.

The grandson of the deceased must've collected every spare program, furiously folding them while the adults were preoccupied. One landed in the teased wig of a shriveled old woman. Another whizzed past a portrait of the deceased decked out in a top hat and flanked by sequined magician's assistants. An especially agile plane sailed straight into the open coffin.

A woman screamed. "Rat!"

Rat?! Please don't let it be inside the coffin. Nothing worse for a funeral business than rodents dining on bodies.

"For heaven's sake, Barbara! So dramatic," a man grumbled.

"Don't be a hero, now," she shot back. "By all means, save yourself."

Deirdre thundered into the room, fist drawn like she planned to fight someone. Whether rodent or mourner, I couldn't be sure. Her face contorted when she noticed the distress on mine, and I took the opportunity to ask for her help. "Play a tune, will you?"

She nodded. A moment later, "The Parting Glass" began as if chaos weren't unfolding in the chapel.

"Long! Live! Houdini!" A mischievous boy smirked triumphantly. The little shite had released the vermin deliberately while his parents were distracted. Theatrical flair must run in the entire family.

Black-clad mourners parted like a midnight sea, revealing a tiny white mouse scurrying along the parquet. A fellow in a tweed flat cap stabbed at it with a blackthorn shillelagh to even more shrieks. Rolling up my sleeves, I bent down on hands and knees and reached for it as it ducked between the ankles of a geriatric lady in sagging stockings. "Beg your pardon."

"Dear Lord!"

Closing one hand around the creature's tail, I grabbed the frightened mouse. Without thinking, I held it aloft by its tail. It dangled from my hand like a squeaking Christmas ornament. The woman with the paper kamikaze in her wig looked as if she were about to faint. I cupped my hands around the animal. Tiny feet gently scratched at my palm. "Carry on."

"He got it!"

A cheer went up, and my skin grew itchy at all the attention. I needed a breather in the rose garden.

I'll never forget the time a man's fingers had been gnawed away after a rat slipped through the mortuary window my granda left open to enjoy a bit of fresh air. I was fifteen. Only minutes before the wake, we'd noticed bone peeking through the ripped flesh of his rosary-clutching digits. I'd frantically filled in the gaps with mortician's wax and dabbed makeup to color-match while my granda distracted the family. Thankfully, they were none the wiser. I'd bought the local market out of glue traps, cyanide, and cake icing during the service, vowing "never again."

After the kerfuffle, the guests had sequestered the juvenile offender in an armchair in the foyer. Petulance in his eyes, his shiny wingtips scuffed the floor as he kicked his feet.

"Don't hurt her," he said, arms crossed, as I opened the door to release the mouse. His eyes softened on my hands, still enclosing the rodent. "She's nice. She doesn't even bite."

"You can't play pranks here. Funerals are serious b-b-business." Knowing how cruel children could be about my imped-iment, I braced myself for the inevitable.

"Are you going to hurt her?"

"I'm going to set it free."

Defiance faded from his red-rimmed eyes, replaced with res-ignation. More castigation would bring no comfort, and he would be punished by his family soon enough. "Can I hold her? Say goodbye?"

"Poor thing's scared, with the screaming and the near tram-pling." I sat and held out my cupped palms so he could verify she was unscathed. A docile creature, considering all the stress. "One of your uncles wanted to make a kebab out of her."

He sucked in a shaky breath.

"Keep a hold," I said. The boy tenderly stroked the mouse's back with one finger. "Sometimes we get upset when someone passes on. Raging mad. That's normal, being angry when we lose someone we care about, not just sad."

"I'm not angry at him. I'm angry at my da. He said we're turning Houdini loose before we leave town. I wanted to keep her."

"Sorry about your granda. It was very hard on me, losing mine." I lifted my chin. "The mouse is Houdini?"

The kid clicked his tongue at the animal to calm it. "Harriet Houdini."

"Excellent name."

"I know," he replied. "My parents aren't letting me keep her. She's being turned out in the garden before we fly home. What if a cat gets her?"

My heart went out to the lad. Losing a grandparent, then feeling guilt over his beloved pet. And he had a point. How long would a domesticated white mouse survive in a city filled with alley cats and foxes? The chance of its survival outdoors was low. I couldn't help but empathize with his outrage and desire to send off the creature with one final hurrah.

"What's your favorite memory of your granda?"

"We taught her a trick together over Easter. She knows lots of games and tricks. She used to be his assistant for his magic act. He could make her disappear. Look—" He lowered the mouse to the floor and made his fingers into an arch for her to pass through in a zigzag pattern.

"Clever mouse. And a clever grandson. He must've loved you very much."

The boy's chin began to quiver.

"Maybe we can find a new home for Houdini, yeah?"

"The people have to be nice."

Solemnly, I placed a hand over my chest. "I've just the person in mind. She's the nicest one I know. Now go on and apologize to your family for the scene you caused. There's a lad."

With the boy's blessing, I deposited the mouse in an old jam jar from the kitchen with air holes poked in the lid. My mobile buzzed in my pocket. The contact photo Lark had chosen for herself, posing with a peace sign at the Cliffs of Moher, brought a smile to my face. I quickly tapped out an answer to her invitation before I rejoined the service to relieve Deirdre. A movie would be the perfect way to wind down after this chaotic day.

Afterward, the boy's father approached me.

"The auld man looks good. We almost expected him to sit up and ask us what the hell we're all sniveling about."

"Thank you, sir."

"My apologies about the boy. I told everyone he released the mouse and that you don't have a pest problem," he said, looking embarrassed. His wife had been so distraught at the loss of her father, they'd both nipped outside for a calming fag while their son terrorized the chapel. I hoped he wouldn't be punished too severely.

"He's having a tough go of it, and there was no real harm. He mentioned being concerned for the mouse."

"One more thing I have to deal with, him getting attached." Surviving families complained about the decedent's pets often.

"You d-d-don't have any place to take it?" Where did one take an unwanted mouse? An animal shelter?

"I can't be bothered with that. There's a hutch and another load of rubbish to clean out of the house. Fodder for the charity shop."

"I'll keep the mouse, if it's all the same to you. Would you consider selling the rest of the supplies to me?"

"Come pick it up tonight, so I don't have to chuck it in the bin, and it's yours. For the trouble today."

LARK OPENED HER flat with a tired smile and beckoned me inside. Bright-painted toenails peeked out from under her pajama bottoms, contrasting with her bare face. The intimacy of her un-embellished skin made my addled heart squeeze. A faded Alamo Drafthouse Cinema tee stretched across her chest, faint semicircles had settled under her eyes, and blond strands poked haphazardly out of her messy bun. In my work trousers and button-down, I was overdressed.

Lark gestured to the habitat in my hand. Under my arm I carried a half bag of shredded bedding and alfalfa pellets. "What's all this?"

"It's for Houdini. Well, for you." Heavenly scents wafted through the air. Following Lark into the kitchen, I caught myself watching her hips sway with each step. I cleared my throat. "You said you wanted a pet, and she needs a home."

She wiped a dusting of flour off the counter. "Umm, Callum, I don't know if this is a good idea."

"You don't like mice? I can keep her—"

"No, no. I do. It's just . . . When I go back home, you'll probably have to take her back. I don't think airlines allow pocket pets on international flights."

I deflated at the reminder of her eventual return to the States. "All right."

"I do want her," she insisted, peeking into the habitat. "She's adorable. It just . . . might not be permanent. You understand."

"Of course. She belonged to the magician I buried today. His grandson told me the family planned on turning her loose in the garden . . . so he turned her loose in the chapel for one last performance."

"He did not!"

"Right after he flew a paper airplane straight into the casket." I detailed how I dove between the ankles of a senior citizen to catch the mouse, and the boy ignored by his family after broadcasting his need for attention. "The lad's just hurting and acting out."

"You're more of a softy than you realize."

"I am not—"

"You're a great listener and observer. You shut others out to protect yourself, but when you let yourself connect . . . it means something. It meant something to that kid."

"Anyone would have done the same."

"You're the one who brought him comfort on a day filled with sadness." Lark took the whisk out of a mixing bowl on the counter and gave it a lick. "Batter?"

My brain malfunctioned, but I managed a weak, "Huh?"

She plucked a spoon from the drawer. "Have a taste before I wash this bowl. You won't regret it."

I still held the alfalfa pellets and the see-through exercise ball, wondering what had come over me. Without waiting for an answer, she brought the spoon to my mouth. Sugar and vanilla.

Chocolate chips. *Lark's mouth tastes like that right now*, my un-helpful libido whispered. "Mmm." I didn't trust my voice not to croak.

It had been so long since I'd actually *liked* someone enough to physically react to them. Lark had taken up residence not only in my life, but she'd also carved out a niche in my heart. I felt a little guilty about these new, unwholesome thoughts about my friend . . . and worried about what this meant in the greater scheme of our relationship.

"So you saved her from homelessness?" She went about tidy-ing the kitchen, unaware of the effect she had on me. Spoon-feeding me biscuit batter didn't mean anything. Lark was just comfortable with people.

"I couldn't let her run around the parlor, and it felt inhumane to throw her to the neighborhood cats. She's so d-d-docile, she wouldn't stand a chance. And she knows tricks. She can jump through a roll of packing tape and run an obstacle course."

"Let's build her one."

"Right now? Didn't you just bake biscuits?"

"I like to make things when I'm stressed. These cookies are for Anvi. You remember her from the pub, hair like Princess Jasmine from *Aladdin*? Her parents were giving her a hard time about her job not being 'noble' or whatever, because her sister just became a human rights lawyer. So I thought I'd try to lift her spirits."

Lark was kind. To everyone. She brought Maeve groceries so the old woman didn't have to go to market herself. All she wanted in return was friendship.

"Anyway, I'm done baking now. Up for a Rodent Ninja Warrior showcase?"

"Wanna . . . talk about why you're stressed?"

At the irony of *me* asking if she wanted to talk, the divot be-tween her brows faded. "Nah. I'm just glad to have you here with me tonight. Thank you for being so thoughtful."

Was she homesick? Missing her ex? It dawned on me that I

knew next to nothing about Lark's previous relationship—not even the reason for their separation. I'd mentioned Aoife, the last girlfriend I had, six years ago, who I met in mortuary college. Aoife had remained tight-lipped about an ex I later learned emotionally abused her. What was so dramatic about Lark's divorce to warrant permanent singledom in the aftermath? She was such an optimist otherwise; there must be more to the story.

Fueled by the sugar high, we huddled on her floor and built a miniature gauntlet out of cardboard boxes and packing tape. I told Lark about Emma, a woman I'd matched with on the app. Our first date was planned for Sunday, and I tried to muster some hope. Unrequited feelings for Lark would get me nowhere, and my deadline for a marriage license was fast approaching.

Lark detailed her work issues and showed me some concept art. Every frame of a cartoon was the result of hundreds of decisions, I learned, often taken for granted by the viewer. Not only that, but she wrangled cohesion from a large team of stubborn creatives. More than just a visionary, a leader. And a saint, to deal with Seán without violence. Every day she impressed me more.

"I can't blow it." Lark didn't take her attention from her scissors slicing through an Amazon box. "It's KinetiColor's debut. They've done only commercials before. It's a lot of pressure."

An understandable anxiety. *Shoelace* created buzz around Lark as a young, first-time art director.

Before I could overthink it, I set my hand on hers, which were still clutching the scissors. "I hate seeing you question yourself. They're lucky to have you."

"I was lucky to move next door to you."

Not knowing what else to do, I patted her hand awkwardly. If only I could draw Lark into my arms. Hold her until her doubt abated. Trace comforting fingertips over soft skin. Press a kiss to that haunting mouth. I wet my lips, more in wishful thinking than preparation. Her eyes dipped to follow the movement, and a tingle of excitement electrified my body.

"My ass is numb from sitting on the floor," she said.

Just like that, the moment was over. She stood to admire our handiwork, and I forced myself not to steal a glimpse of said ass in pajamas. Grand—now I was objectifying her.

"Voilà! Moment of truth."

With the maze completed, I reached into the habitat, cooing to Houdini before cupping her in my palm and lifting her out. As I turned my attention back to Lark, I caught a soft look in her eye.

"Wait, wait . . . Houdini needs the right mood," she said. A moment later, the opening strains of "Rat Race" came through her phone speakers.

"I expected the *Rocky* theme."

Houdini scurried through the cardboard labyrinth with ease, so we made it progressively more convoluted with the addition of yogurt-cup obstacles salvaged from the rubbish bin.

"Forty seconds! Let's see punk-ass Stuart Little top that!" Lark whooped.

Awash in affection, I laughed as she narrated a recording on her phone, à la a Formula 1 commentator. Laughter never came as naturally as when I spent time with Lark.

CHAPTER 14

Callum

"CAN YOU SAY 'Daddy'?" Emma asked in a singsong voice, as her little girl scowled at me from her high chair. "Say 'Daddy,' Carrie!"

The baby threw her head back, summoning an ear-bursting shriek that would put a banshee to shame.

My eyes flicked toward the ceiling of the restaurant. *Please let this date be over soon.*

Lark had told me women would line up to call me Daddy . . . somehow, though, I didn't think she meant like this.

"I'd prefer she call me Callum," I said, avoiding the glares of our fellow diners. The only one not giving us murderous glances was the lady at the next table who turned off her hearing aid. I'd envied the ability, before realizing that I might suffer from my own hearing loss before the night's end. "Does she talk yet?"

"No. But for most babies, their first word is *dada*, and wouldn't it be precious if you were here for it? A real bonding moment."

I made a noncommittal noise and shoveled some colcannon into my mouth. The kale and potatoes would be far more appetizing, however, if it hadn't also been smeared all over the table, high chair, and baby's face.

"I was so excited to find a family man on the app," Emma said. "Dating as a single mother is dreadful."

Worse than an eight-month-old third wheel at the table, repeatedly hurling her mushy peas at my head? Doubt it. The banshee spawn might be preverbal, but she had strong opinions on her mother trying to coax the title "daddy" out of her toothless mouth only twenty minutes into our first meeting. Same, kid.

Another handful of peas splattered onto my glasses. I removed them and wiped off the mess with a napkin.

"Aww! Carrion likes you!"

Did I hear that correctly? Her full name was *Carrion*? As in roadkill? No wonder she was so angry. Across the table, the unfortunately named baby narrowed her eyes. Her face said she thought less of me than of the contents of her nappy.

Emma had seemed normal, based on her dating profile. Her being a parent wouldn't have been a deal-breaker, but she hadn't even mentioned it . . . much less the idea of bringing her bouncing baby girl along. She'd asked how I felt about kids, and I told her I hoped to have a family of my own in the near future. I did not mean *this* near. I could almost hear my granda cackling from on high at the irony.

Wait till Lark hears about this one.

———

DEMIDATE'S ALERT INTERRUPTED the quiet of the prep room, signaling another potential match.

"Is that a dating app?" Deirdre asked. She grabbed my phone from the counter. I felt nothing but dread at the prospect of another meetup so soon after the demon baby. "Ooh, she's cute. When are you taking her out?"

"I don't know. We just matched."

"Met anyone you like lately?"

Just one. The wrong one.

"No."

I peeled up Mr. Doherty's papery eyelids to fit the eye caps, giving his sunken sockets a lifelike appearance. The convex plastic, shaped like a large, spiky contact lens, also prevented the lids from popping open mid wake. I'd previously opened the elderly man's maw and pushed a mouth former inside to compensate for his lack of dentures, before sewing his jaw shut and arranging his lips into a placid smile. His gaunt face already better resembled the obituary photo, and I hadn't even turned on the embalming machine yet.

"You have been making an effort, right?" Deirdre asked gently.

"I've seen four different women this month. Each worse than the last. The one I took to dinner on Sunday brought her screaming baby."

"Will you finally ask Saoirse, then?"

"Maybe." Truth be told, I harbored concerns about soured relations with our biggest floral vendor if it didn't work out.

"She's class. The sort you need. She's a business owner, too. Responsible. Beautiful."

As a close friend of the family, and my employee, Deirdre wanted to see me and the inheritance question settled, but her enthusiasm could be overwhelming. To keep her from badgering me about Lark, I'd told her a relationship with her wasn't a possibility. Now Lark herself pushed me out of my hermetically sealed comfort zone. Two against one, with my back against the wall thanks to the stipulations of the inheritance.

The betrayal burned every time I thought about it. The fact my father would take the helm if I failed made it infinitely worse. He'd left us behind decades ago, along with the family trade. He'd left *me* behind. Pádraig hadn't even bothered to keep in touch. The gobshite hadn't come to the funeral of his own mother a number of years back, when his remaining family really needed him. Then when he came to my granda's deathbed, somehow he garnered enough forgiveness to be factored into the old man's inheritance decision. Nothing mattered unless it could benefit him.

"We both stand to lose our livelihoods if you don't find someone soon." Deirdre leaned against the prep table as I began flexing Mr. Doherty's limbs to break up the rigor mortis.

"Neither of us is losing anything. I promise."

She'd worked at Willow Haven for twenty years, give or take. Her maternal demeanor put families at ease. With her experience, she could find a job elsewhere, but I didn't want to put her in that position. A woman with her loyalty wouldn't be in the unemployment line because of me.

"I gave Lark the mouse from the magician's service." I didn't want to talk about dating anymore. "She told me she wanted a pet."

"It's an odd name for a woman. Lark. Like a whim. Suppose it fits."

The old man's hip cracked loudly as I forced his thigh back. Deirdre grimaced.

"She's named after the songbird. She's talented. Hardworking. Courageous to move to a country where she d-d-didn't know a soul."

And she's introduced more joy into my life than I could imagine.

Deirdre frowned. "You need to find someone serious. Are you willing to risk your business—your birthright—to waste time with her?"

"We're just friends. It's been nice to have a friend."

She nodded, face kind but steeped in concern. "Don't lose focus, Callum. What you really need is a wife."

———

SOAP BUBBLES SPLASHED across the bonnet of the hearse as Lark sprayed the garden hose. When she saw me pull it into the driveway for a wash, she'd run out to offer to help—a thank-you for the occasional rides to and from work. When I declined, she insisted she found washing cars to be therapeutic. Somehow, she brought light to even the most mundane chores.

The florist van pulled up to the curb. Lark's brows waggled as Saoirse approached. "Need me to hose you down, or are you gonna be okay?"

I tossed the wet sponge at her. With a karate-chop motion, she batted it away before it could leave a dark blotch on her jumper.

"Hi, Callum."

"Hello. Hi." This would usually be my cue to stumble red-faced back to the embalming room. "This is . . . my . . ."

"Hi! I'm Lark." Grinning, she thrust out a soapy hand. "The neighbor."

"Saoirse. Nice to meet you." Sleek black hair spilled over her shoulders, and she cradled an armful of dewy tulips that I took from her and brought inside.

"What a beautiful coat," Lark said to her as I returned to the driveway. "Blue is totally your color."

"Massive," I muttered. It was rather nice, I supposed.

Lark elbowed me in the rib. Whatever for, I hadn't a clue. "Callum! What are you talking about?"

I stepped closer to Saoirse, who wore a befuddled face.

Oh. This was another instance of Lark misunderstanding a local turn of phrase.

"That d-doesn't mean what you think it means," I assured her to smooth out the awkwardness. But being stabbed in the rib for complimenting another woman in front of her didn't have fantastic optics if I was going to land a date. It did feel weird, though.

"This coat? Clearance rack at Penneys." The compliment must've felt just as strange on the receiving end. Bashful eyes met mine, then her attention landed on my hearse-washing helper. "Cute cowboy boots."

"She's from Texas," I said to Saoirse, accidentally interrupting Lark's thanks. Nope. Despite my best efforts, this was full-tilt awkward.

"Did you know Callum has been taking a more active role in the services? Just this week he caught a live mouse that a little boy released during a wake! He's a natural with children and animals."

Where's lightning when you need it? Merciful creator, strike me dead.

More intrigued than disgusted, Saoirse's nose scrunched. "A mouse?"

Lark powered on. "He jumped right in and scooped it up with his bare hands. He'll be a great dad one day."

I considered jumping into the mortuary cooler to hide, but it would be riskier to leave Lark unattended.

"Pet mouse," I clarified so she wouldn't imagine an infestation of flea-covered pests leaving droppings throughout the parlor.

"Not to worry." Lark rested a casual hand on Saoirse's arm. How could she be so natural with everyone? "She's safe now. Callum rescued her, and I adopted her. He also helped me build a little exercise maze."

Saoirse kneaded her delicate hands. "Are you two . . . ?"

"No. Nothing like that." Lark busied herself with coiling the hose. "I was actually wondering if you know of any cute single guys? I kind of feel like going on a date, and I like to get a woman's endorsement."

Wait—Lark wanted to date?

"One of my bandmates is single," Saoirse answered after giving it a moment's consideration. "If you wanted an introduction. He's a solicitor in his day job."

"Maybe."

Saoirse fished her mobile from her apron, holding it up for Lark. "That's Aidan. Cute, right?"

Her brows bounced in what appeared to be genuine interest. "Yeah. He certainly is."

I leaned in, attempting to take advantage of my height for a peek at the screen, but Saoirse was already handing it to Lark, asking her to program her number in.

"I heard you're a fiddler," Lark said. It launched an amicable conversation between them on parallels between trad and American country-western. "Did you know Callum plays the piano? And he took years of singing lessons and choir, but he still hasn't let me hear a note. Have you had the pleasure?"

Saoirse looked up at me as she answered. "I didn't know that. But I've heard him play."

Although the verbal and musical parts of the brain occupied different hemispheres, my nan had hoped singing lessons would cure my stutter. I grew up performing traditional songs at funerals. As the bullying at school worsened, even Nan's pride in my voice wasn't enough to overcome the swell of anxiety at being the center of attention. My last performance was memorable: after locking my knees, I fell into an open grave when I fainted halfway through a rendition of "Danny Boy." There would be no encore.

"I only play piano. Not particularly well."

"Don't be modest," Lark said before she redirected her attention to Saoirse. "Where does your band perform?"

"Do you know the Hare's Breath? We're playing on Saturday."

"Oh! That's my company's spot, I'm surprised I've never run into you there. We'll all have to get together there sometime," Lark said. What the ever loving hell had gotten into her?

A skeptical look crossed Saoirse's face again as her dark eyes flitted between us.

"Sounds grand." Hell, maybe I could even enjoy myself with her the way I enjoyed Lark's company. "You and I can get to know each other b-b-better."

"I'd love to." She beamed. "I get thirsty after our sets, and you

can buy me a drink." Her phone buzzed. "I have to go. Work call.
You have my number, Callum. I'm, um, looking forward to seeing
you Saturday." Saoirse strode back to the van and gave me a sweet
little wave before she pulled away. "It's a double date."

Double?

"I'm a little out of practice, I admit, but that was a success."
Lark held up a fist to bump.

Reluctantly, I struck her knuckles with my own. She wiggled
her fingers like an explosion, complete with a sound effect. "It
got us a double date. Was that the plan?" I asked. It stung to see
Lark's reaction to the photo Saoirse had shown her. She'd said
she was content to stay single, but was it really that she had no
interest in *me*?

"Yeah, that was . . . not exactly what I meant. I didn't mean
to make it sound like I wanted to get together as a group on
Saturday, but hey, I promised not to throw you to the wolves."

"You don't have to go out with some mandolin player on my
behalf."

"It's no big deal. And don't worry, I won't hover over your first
date like an Apache helicopter. That would all but guarantee
you don't get a second one. I'll just pave the way for easier conversation."

"Like you did just now?"

"Yeah, just now, when you called the woman 'massive'? You'd
get punched in the mouth for that where I'm from, by the way."

"I told you, it's a compliment here. And you said I'd make a
good da. You can't *say* that. Especially after I met Baby Carrion."

Lark had nearly wet herself laughing when I recounted the
ordeal, which almost made it worthwhile.

"Have to let her know what you want. Thank me after you
make beautiful music together, Casanova."

CHAPTER 15

Callum

ON SATURDAY NIGHT, Lark stopped me as I locked up Willow Haven before the date. "Is that what you're wearing?"

I nodded. Before I could stop her, she'd thrown open my front door and was marching up the stairs to the *home* part of the funeral home. I scrambled after her. "Where are you going?"

"Your closet. This is a sartorial intervention."

"Excuse me—"

Ignoring my protest, she opened my bedroom door and emptied half the contents of my closet onto the bed. She was in my bedroom. Uninvited, but not necessarily unwelcome. It had been years since I'd brought someone there.

"You need a woman's ruthless opinion." Lark relished the opportunity to act as an expert. She laid hangers on my bed, piled with fabric in shades of gray and black.

"Why do I need fashion advice?"

Lark gestured to my tweed suit. "Was this room your grandpa's and you kept the closet intact when you moved in?"

"It's vintage," I said sorely.

"Exactly like looking into a void. Don't you have any color?

What about a burgundy button-down? Play up your eyes with malachite or jade?"

Artists. Couldn't she just say *green*? She held a finger poised under her chin, tsking at the dark mountain on my bed.

"I have this," I said, picking some things up from the pile.

She wrinkled her nose at the navy shirt and coordinating necktie that had seen hundreds of memorials.

Honestly, fashion was just another subject I didn't understand. Everyone else seemed privy to a set of baffling rules codified by society without so much as an announcement. Easier to stick to the classics: three-piece wool suits for work, a couple of dark jumpers, black peacoat.

Flinging the offending tie on the bed, Lark surveyed the abyss of the rest of my closet. "What about a Henley? It's sexy, and it's not obvious funeral attire."

"It's black." My thoughts snagged on the adjective of choice. She was a supportive friend trying to boost my confidence even as she slagged me for my taste, or lack thereof. Still, it rang in my ears. *Sexy.*

"I noticed the trend. You look good in black, though." After a brief search, she plucked it from the closet. "Push up the sleeves, don't you dare wear them to the wrist."

"Why not?"

She squeezed my arm, and goose bumps spilled across my skin. That tiny bit of contact would be the highlight of my day. *Pathetic.*

"You want to show off your best assets. Just below the elbow so she gets a peek. Here. Try this on with those tight jeans you wore to the cliffs."

Retreating to the bathroom to change my shirt, I cursed the flush warming my ears. She noticed how tight my jeans were? How mortifying. I'd never given much thought to my looks. Lifting weights as a teen started as a way to get strong enough for self-defense, and as I got older, I wanted to stay on top of my health.

I caught Lark perusing my bookshelf when I returned, hands on a photo of my granda Tadhg, nan Gráinne, and me. "You have the weirdest library. *Smoke Gets in Your Eyes: And Other Lessons from the Crematory*? *In the Wake of the Plague*? Not one, not two, but three books about bog mummies?"

"I like history."

She smiled. "Nerd." She looked to the photo. "I know your folks had good intentions with your inheritance, but I'm also kinda pissed they put you in this position."

I sighed. "Meeting women isn't easy for me. They knew that. I'm terrified I'll freeze up tonight."

"Saoirse understands you're the quiet type."

She bit her bottom lip as she watched me comply with the earlier edict to show off my "assets." I changed the angle of my arm to get a better view as I pushed my sleeves to my elbows. But Lark wouldn't stop staring.

"Is there a stain on my shirt?"

"What? No, it's fine. You look very handsome. She'll love it."

Citrus and vanilla engulfed me as Lark gave me a quick, encouraging hug. Tension thickened between us as she stood in my personal space. All I could think about was tugging her down onto the bed, tumbling over the heap of clothing, and kissing her dizzy.

FIFTEEN MINUTES AFTER I settled in at the Hare's Breath, Lark entered. Snug jeans hugged her hips. Cleavage peeked from her clingy, low-cut blouse. She'd insisted we shouldn't arrive together, and her kohl-rimmed eyes lit when she found me. My mouth went dry.

She sidled up to me as the band played and nudged my shoulder playfully.

"Hey," I said, tempering the relief in my voice.

Aidan, the tenor with muscular arms covered in Celtic knotwork ink, immediately noticed Lark. To be fair, a man would have to be dead a decade not to notice her. The singer's mouth curled into a slow grin as she swayed to the sound of his mandolin, sending a strange prickle through my chest. Naturally, she'd be attracted to someone confident and handsome, rather than a lanky, stuttering loner who raided his granda's wardrobe for vintage suspenders.

"They're amazing! Wow, Saoirse is tearing it up."

Saoirse locked eyes with me as the opening strains of "Finnegan's Wake" sent the crowd into a frenzy. A ballad about a man who cracked his skull falling off a ladder. When mourners grew rowdy at his wake, whiskey spilled on the body, and he roused to join the party in his honor. Had she chosen it for me? By the smirk on her face, I guessed so.

Lark bounced in place, enjoying the lively tune. "I've always been a sucker for a singer."

My mind was suddenly blacker than the Guinness in my hand. I stared into the foamy head, kicking myself for my self-imposed silence as she watched the charismatic vocalist. Inspired by the buoyant feeling I had around Lark, I'd been tooling around with compositions and lyrics, but I couldn't bear to sing them. Least of all to her.

"I'll dip once you're situated," she shouted above the music. "Just don't talk about the history of embalming and it'll be fine."

"I wouldn't."

"Remember that time you educated me on the trocar? While I was eating? You ruined strawberry Danish forever."

"So I'm *not* supposed to expound on cavity aspiration?" Wide-eyed, I acted confused. "How else am I going to impress Saoirse?"

"Talk music. Books. Literally anything but gas in bloated corpses' stomachs."

Aidan thanked the enamored crowd in his Cork accent, and they stepped off the stage. Saoirse hugged me and made the introductions. Jamie on the bodhrán shook our hands and departed, explaining he needed to get home to the wife and kids. Aidan brought Lark's knuckles to his lips and pressed a quick kiss to them, rewarded by her giant smile.

I wanted to shove a trocar down his—

"Look, there's a free booth. Quick!"

The four of us slid into the dim seating, with Saoirse claiming the seat next to me. Her stocking-encased leg brushed mine under the table as she recounted the events of her workday.

"So I deliver the arrangements, one for each of the twenty tables, and the bride squawks, 'What's the matter with them?'"

Lark leaned forward.

"She told me she wanted pink geraniums, right? Insisted on them. So I gave her pink geraniums. Not my first choice for a wedding, but I aim to please."

"What was the problem?" Lark asked.

"She meant pink *hydrangeas*. She got confused."

"Seriously?"

"Yep, just like I'd suggested months ago. She said she knew what she wanted and told me I had no clue. Now she's crying that I ruined her wedding."

Lark snickered. "I'm sorry. She sounds awful."

"Just another Bridezilla," Saoirse laughed. "I'm sure she'll leave a scathing review. Nothing I can't handle, though."

I nodded mutely as their conversation volleyed around me. Lark periodically shot me encouraging smiles over her glass. She was already on her second drink, purchased by Aidan while they became better acquainted. He'd moved here from a rural part of County Cork to try his hand at music but switched gears for the stability of working at a law firm. Aidan helped support his family since their mother left the workforce to homeschool his ill teenage sister. Lark awed in admiration and offered to get them tickets for a screening of the Grace O'Malley movie. Another band took the helm with an infectious, stomping beat. With a wry dimpled smile, Aidan held out his hand, and he and Lark skipped out to the dance floor. Alone with Saoirse, I fidgeted with my sleeve, where it was pushed up over my forearm, wondering what Lark had been staring at earlier. It had been easier with a buffer at the table, but now I was forced to converse like a normal person did on a date. So we talked about her busy upcoming Valentine's Day season and how she became a florist. And how my granda always got chocolates for his wife instead of bouquets, since she associated flowers with wakes. It was nice, not having to explain the context of my life or see my date squirm when I mentioned the funeral home.

"You seem different lately. Deirdre said it's thanks to Lark." Saoirse leaned close to be heard over the noise. Her warm breath caressed my neck, and I leaned back.

"I suppose so."

For years, Saoirse would deliver a wreath or a flower basket and I'd go mute when Deirdre would call me to assist, pretending she was too busy to help. Never in those times had I mustered the nerve to do anything more than mumble a few sentences.

"Lark's . . . perky. Pretty, too." A beat passed where I got the sense she'd like me to refute it in some polite way. "Aidan likes her. So do I."

He doesn't even know her. Probably brings a new girl home from the pub every weekend.

Not that Lark wanted a relationship; she was only on this date for my benefit. My attention drifted to the dance floor, where Aidan twirled Lark. Blond locks cascaded over her shoulder as she let out a boisterous laugh. Maybe she would *want* him to know her.

"Would you like to d-d-dance?" I asked too loudly in the space between one song ending and a slower ballad beginning.

On the dance floor, my eyes met Lark's in a silent check-in. She gave a thumbs-up behind Aidan's neck. They turned, and I couldn't help but focus on his hand resting on the small of her back. My shaky hands found the same spot on Saoirse, and I shuffled awkwardly, trying to remember the steps and how much contact was appropriate. Too many people, too many sounds. Clinking glasses and snippets of conversation shouted over music. "Sorry I'm not very good at it."

"No matter. I'm glad we're getting to know each other better. It's nice to see you cut loose. With such a serious job, it's a matter of mental health."

Floral perfume wafted around me as my hand grazed the small of her back, but all I could think was that it wasn't as alluring as Lark's citrusy vanilla. Saoirse's hand caressed the front of my shirt as my eyes met Lark's again. But I wasn't thinking about Saoirse; my thoughts were with Lark. How I imagined it would feel if she touched me. No, that wouldn't do. Emboldened by the alcohol and adrenaline coursing through my veins, I encircled Saoirse's waist and stepped closer. Deirdre was right. I should try harder.

"Honestly, I didn't expect you to dance. You *are* full of surprises tonight, aren't you? If I didn't know any better, I'd say you're trying to prove something," Saoirse said.

"Maybe I am." To myself, mostly. To my father, who didn't believe I'd meet someone, even with the dire motivation. Maybe also to Lark.

Someone tapped my shoulder as a new song began. "Mind if I borrow Callum for a song?" Lark asked Saoirse. Had watching me clumsily dance with my date affected her? Just the tiniest bit?

With a shrug, Saoirse took Aidan's hand, and the two drifted off into the sea of bodies. "You keep staring at me. I thought it was a cry for help. How's it going with her?"

"It's grand. You keep staring at *me*."

Illicit excitement seized me by the throat as Lark's arm rested on mine, her fingertips brushing my shoulder. She raised her other hand, small and soft in my grasp. Her perfume smelled like temptation and grapefruit. I was unprepared for this.

"I'll show you how to two-step. Don't worry. It's easy."

After some initial fumbling and shared tipsy laughter, I caught on to the rhythm. Tin whistles and concertina filled the air. My focus whittled down to the music and her face, and my nerves abated slightly. Lark centered me, even when slightly off-kilter herself. I hoped she couldn't feel my hand tremble. She was both too close and not close enough.

"Quick, quick, slow . . . quick, quick, slow. That's it. Just step toward me as you normally would, you don't have to be bow-legged. You look like you just got off a horse!"

"I'm afraid of crushing your toes." A grin stretched across my face. "Am I honky-tonking yet?"

With a laugh, she assured me I was doing great. Lark's fingers wrapped around the swell of my deltoid muscle and her mirth-filled eyes bore into mine. Something unsaid seemed to sit on the tip of her tongue, but she simply studied my face as we danced.

My granda always said the best embalmers were invisible. Stealth was the goal. If we performed our work well, it looked as though we hadn't done anything except dress someone in fancy clothes for a nap. Outside of the mortuary, we melted into the periphery, centering the bereaved. Never one to crave attention, it suited me . . . but Lark made me exposed as a body on the prep table. And I *wanted* her to see me.

Neon splashed red and blue across her freckled nose. Feck, this was bad. Moments like these only deepened the well of feeling. It wasn't often I felt anything for a woman, and she was the wrong one.

She's leaving. She doesn't date. She doesn't want more.

"You and Aidan are getting on."

She blinked away some of her buoyancy. "He's a nice guy."

Nice? Half the audience drooled over him onstage, the other

half focused on Saoirse. . . . Like *I* should be doing, I remembered with a jolt of guilt. The concertina stopped abruptly, and the Hare's Breath thundered with cheers. Electric tingles shot through my arm when Lark dragged down the length of it before letting go.

"Thanks for the lesson. I ought to find Saoirse."

Lark nodded tightly.

Within a few moments, Aidan relinquished his dance partner with a flourish. "She's all yours."

As we danced, Saoirse smiled up at me, but my thoughts—and gaze—drifted back to Lark. And Aidan offering her his jacket by the entrance. *No.* They were leaving together. The thought of her spending the night with Aidan sent my stomach straight to the beer-sticky floor. Our eyes locked across the mass of swaying bodies, and she mouthed, "Goodbye." I muttered an apology and tore away from Saoirse's embrace.

I ran to the restroom and stared at the wallpaper above the sink. Vintage advertisements starred pinup girls leering suggestively. I fought against the mental image of Lark giving Aidan a similarly sultry invitation. This was a mistake. I pulled out my phone. Lark hadn't even said a proper goodbye, and she was buzzed. Saoirse insisted her bandmate was trustworthy, but it did little to assuage my anxiety.

> **Do you need a lift home?**

After an agonizing minute, her response came.

> **LARK:** No, Aidan is taking me. I
> didn't want to interrupt

My right eye twitched as I reread the sentence. Someone knocked. The voice of the perfectly lovely woman I'd abandoned mid song came muffled through the restroom door. "Callum? Are you ill?"

"I'll be right out!" My voice echoed off the tile, and my ears rang from the loud music.

> **LARK:** She likes you. Play your cards right and you're definitely getting a kiss tonight

Unbidden, the picture of Aidan leaning into Lark on the steps of her flat came into my mind. His tattooed arms drawing her close. The two of them falling into bed.

> **LARK:** Put your phone away and pay attention to your date

Well, that was an obvious dismissal. Fortifying myself, I splashed some water on my face and wiped it with a scratchy paper towel. My heart sank at the sight of Saoirse in the booth by herself with her hands in her lap, wistfully watching couples dance.

"Hey . . . ," she said, rising to her feet as I approached.

"Something came up. Work." I rubbed the back of my neck. "I have to go."

Smile fading, she replied, "Oh. You need to leave?"

"Yes. Need a lift?"

She gathered her coat. "I'm fit to drive. Walk me out."

At her car, Saoirse stepped closer. Maybe I needed to give this another chance, with no distractions. Saoirse was intelligent and attractive. Interested in me, for some reason. I'd be a fool not to give it time to develop.

"Can we try again next week?" I asked. "Someplace quieter, just the two of us?"

"All right." Dark eyes shining in the streetlamps, she looked so hopeful. Her hand skimmed over my chest as she leaned in, placing a soft kiss to my cheek. I kept my arms down, squeezing my hands into fists. If I only turned, I could press my lips to her mouth. The fact that it was almost tempting made me second-guess everything. Was it a mistake to leave? I needed this to work. Saoirse did her best to make me comfortable, and the fact that we already knew each other certainly helped. Maybe I would enjoy kissing her if I tried? No. I doubted that, when my mind kept returning to the way Lark looked at me tonight. I needed to be alone and sort through these messy thoughts.

As I approached home, I made a quick turn. If Aidan's car was in Lark's driveway, I didn't want to see. Social battery thoroughly drained, I found myself at the canal, sitting at a picnic table and staring into the frigid water. When it was well past 1:00 a.m. and slushy rain began to fall, I finally mustered the courage to drive home. The driveway was empty, to my great relief, but so was my heart.

CHAPTER 16

Lark

SEX AFTER REESE felt like a bandage to rip off. The thought of being so vulnerable wasn't exactly appealing, but I'd begun having a strictly physical interest in it just before I left Austin for Galway. A night of hard seltzers and aching loneliness led to an ill-advised trip home with a stranger. Anonymity was supposed to make my first time with someone else easier. It made the experience disorienting instead. I had a panic attack before anything happened and caught a Lyft home. Before the double date with Callum, I'd actually purchased condoms, in case I really hit it off with Aidan. But I still wasn't ready. In another life, I'd have pulled that sexy, tattooed singer into my bedroom without a second thought, but the idea of even kissing him made my stomach slosh in a nauseating wave. We politely bid each other good night after he dropped me off.

Aidan had probably noticed I'd stared at Callum like the bug-eyed, whistling wolf in a Tex Avery cartoon all night. From the moment I saw him at the Hare's Breath, dressed down with his hair flopped over his brow as he swayed to the band, I'd fought the urge to throw my head back and howl. The tipsier I got, the more I shamelessly salivated over his exposed forearms. When he laughed and held me close as I taught him the two-step, I knew I had to leave before I did something stupid like confess my growing attraction to him while we were on a double date with *other people.*

Despite the biting February cold, I'd purposely taken the bus to and from work in the week since, still avoiding the frost-covered cemetery. Callum's standing offer to chauffeur me was sweet, but if he was getting closer to Saoirse, it would be wise to distance myself. He told me they were taking it slow and that another date was on the calendar.

The second anniversary of Reese's death hit me hard, nine days after the double date. Cathartic tears came only under the right conditions, but once they did, I felt uncorked. Knowing I wouldn't be very useful to anyone, I'd helped Maeve with her groceries the day before and called in sick to work. Distraction helped me cope, but there was no way I could put on a brave face for work or for socializing. I didn't bother to change out of my pajamas, since I left my bed only long enough to grab a bag of chips from the pantry. Without regard for oily crumbs in my sheets, I shoveled them into my mouth and dissociated. Lo checked in via FaceTime, the only person I'd allow to see my puffy eyes and red-tipped nose. And I deleted another unopened email from Rachel. Of all the days to contact me . . . this one?

My mom was fond of the expression "If you fall off the horse, dust yourself off and get back on." Well, I hadn't just fallen. Life had trampled me. Some days I galloped again. Others were closer to the scene where Artax succumbed to the Swamp of Sadness in *The NeverEnding Story.* I'd been too invested in my own story to appreciate what I had until it was gone. Too defensive when the man I loved told me he was unhappy. Maybe if I'd simply listened instead of reacting so harshly, he wouldn't have left home to cool down. Regretting how I'd mishandled his honesty, I'd called him to apologize and promise to do better, but Reese never answered his phone. He died believing that I had prioritized my job over him . . . and he wasn't wrong. I had.

It was our argument that had driven him to get into his Jeep. Skid marks burned into asphalt. Bits of glass and metal surrounding the gashed oak tree. Balloons tied to the fence, teddy bears in basketball jerseys left by his students and team. He crashed because he was too distraught to drive . . . or he'd purposely run into the tree. Either way, my husband would be alive if not for the explosive fight we had that night.

Even as I acknowledged I was developing feelings for Callum, I could never forget that the last time I'd found a good man, I destroyed him.

The evening after the anniversary, movement in the rose garden next door caught my eye. Through my window, I saw Callum pacing agitatedly. Wrapping a robe around myself, I slid my shoes on and headed downstairs. I still hadn't dressed properly or brushed my hair since Friday, and it was now Monday evening.

"You're lurking more than usual." After sobbing for two days, my voice sounded like a garbage disposal. My breath formed little clouds in the cold.

Exhaustion weighed down Callum's face as he pulled his glasses off and pinched the bridge of his nose. I took his hand and squeezed.

"Tell me what's the matter."

"It's never easy working with babies," he said in a brittle voice.

My heart plummeted at the unfathomable loss. At the thought of Callum tenderly dressing a tiny body.

"I don't charge those families. Even when they insist, I won't accept their money. But god, they're the hardest."

For so long, I'd mistakenly believed every undertaker was emotionally detached at best, or an opportunist eager to capitalize on tragedy, at worst. But Callum put the needs of the bereaved before his own comfort. Every single day. Although his job bothered me when we first met, I had grown to admire him for it. Where I ran from grief, or hid from it under a ratty robe and old episodes of *Adventure Time*, he lived alongside it by choice. But that didn't mean it didn't weigh on his broad shoulders.

I drew him into a hug. Even though he was significantly taller, he curled into me. This stoic man sank into the embrace. I nuzzled into him, breathing in the rich, masculine scent of his waistcoat. Warmth spread through my hollow chest like a lantern lit against a consuming, dark night. Callum had become my haven . . . and I had become his. It snuck up on me, unplanned and unforeseen, but that didn't make it any less true.

He pulled back and fixed pink-rimmed eyes on me. "Were you crying? What happened?"

"Removing my mascara." Not a lie, since I had sobbed it off.

His features contorted in disbelief.

"Wanna watch a movie? Take your mind off things?" The distraction would help me, too.

"I have to clean the parlor after tonight's viewing."

I swallowed hard. "Umm, you can come over after."

JUST AFTER SEVEN, there was a gentle tap at my door. At least I'd had a few minutes to brush the potato chip crumbs out of my hair and pull it into a ponytail, change into fresh pajamas, and tidy my living room. Uncharacteristically haggard and even quieter than usual, Callum slipped inside and removed his shoes. He'd changed out of his suit into a hoodie and joggers. Houdini's exercise ball bumped against his feet, and Callum cracked a fragile smile. Today's first, I could tell.

Brushing some hair from his forehead, I said, "I see you've come prepared to get cozy."

He sniffed the air and followed me into the kitchen, liberating Houdini from her plastic bubble. Callum cupped the little white mouse in one hand and gently stroked her back, murmuring in Irish. Something melted inside me. Gooey like an undercooked brownie. I held a bowl aloft. Ribbons of caramel and chocolate oozed down a mountain of fluffy popcorn kernels topped with coconut flakes.

"This is popcorn?"

"Somewhere under there. It's what my cousin Cielo used to make when I was sad. We called it the kitchen-sink mix. Comfort food isn't supposed to be healthy."

"Are you homesick?"

"Sometimes. I miss going roller-skating with Lo and being able to get authentic barbacoa tacos anytime, but I do like it here."

"I know you had a hard time with your ex—"

God, he didn't know. I couldn't get into it tonight. Not over popcorn and a mindless comedy. Not with the weight on Callum's mind and the guilt on my heart. Instead of divulging the truth, I cut him off. "Heartbreak gets the best of us. But don't worry about me. I'm fine."

He accepted the candy-drizzled treat and dropped the topic, though he tracked me with knowing eyes. Sometimes I wondered if he'd seen enough grief to recognize it in me.

"We need something to wash down all that salt and sugar. Tea? Coffee?"

Lying by omission makes a person thirsty. Houdini had taken up residence on Callum's shoulder, whiskers twitching as I brewed two cups of oolong. Deposited back into her exercise ball, she tumbled away. My love seat was small, forcing us close. I rested my head against his shoulder and sighed contentedly.

"This okay?"

"Wait." He pulled the hoodie over his head, then eased back against the cushion. "There."

Before he could object, I swiped his sweatshirt from the arm of the love seat and had it halfway over my head. I shivered at the intimacy of his faint body heat retained in the soft fabric, and breathed in the rainlike scent. He ran a hand through his tousled hair, his toned arm distracting in that plain shirt.

"Cheeky little thief." Callum pouted as he took another sip of tea.

Warm and sleepy, I burrowed into him. Ten minutes in, and I'd barely noticed what was playing on-screen. Rather, I enjoyed the feel of my cheek against Callum's sturdy chest.

Why couldn't he have chronic halitosis? Or sketchy political leanings? Anything to squelch my growing attraction and complicated feelings.

"Know what I like about you?"

"My jumper," he replied dryly.

"What?"

"If you want to keep my jumper, just say so."

After he'd wrapped me in his cable-knit Aran sweater the night of the failed matchmaking with Hannah at the Hare's Breath, it took me a full week to bite the bullet and return it. Laundered, because I'd slept in it all seven nights. "I wasn't— Fine. I needed a hoodie anyway."

His smile was audible. "What were you going to say?"

"No, no, you nailed it. Compliment you to weasel into your clothing. You figured out my master plan."

His chest jostled slightly with a silent laugh, but when he spoke it was introspective and gentle. "This is . . . really nice."

Far better than it had the right to be, in fact. "I feel safe with you, Cal."

"I like when you call me that."

I thought about the tenderness in his voice as he cooed to Houdini. How would it sound whispered into my ear? I wanted his dulcet brogue telling me all about what he liked. Whispering praise as I situated myself between his knees and stroked him through his soft joggers. I was acutely aware of his drumming heartbeat and the way his long legs bent lazily across my tiny sofa. Of course I'd end up with a crush on my closest friend when he was desperately seeking The One. How selfish of me to want something casual with Callum, of all people?

"Know what else I like?" he said, derailing my guilt again.

"My grotesquely sweet snacks. Admit it."

"The way you make the world more colorful. I don't think I realized how much I needed it until we met. Not just your job, *you*. There's so much sadness in this world, and you seem to always be spreading joy through it."

My heart squeezed at his words. "You're the grotesquely sweet one."

"Thank you for coming to the Hare's Breath with me the other night."

"Happy to," I said.

Based on the way the pupils of Saoirse's eyes morphed into hearts in his presence, she'd been nursing a crush on Callum since she began delivering their floral arrangements. They were a good fit. Loudmouthed Texans wouldn't be his type, even if I hadn't promised to stay single.

"Saoirse's a knockout with that black hair down to her waist. Plays a mean fiddle. Total wife material." Silence settled over us for a minute, and the scene on the TV flickered. "So . . . You only go to bed with someone if you love them?"

He tensed and swallowed. God. I had made it *weird*.

"Not that I'm suggesting you do that if you're not ready," I hurried to add. "I've just been curious how it works. Shit. Don't answer that. Tell me to mind my own business."

"No. It's nothing so noble as waiting for true love. Or love at all. I just need to feel close to see someone that way, to want them."

I could only imagine. I *had* imagined.

"You, um, like one-night stands?" he asked, almost whispering. Were we talking about Aidan now? Did Cal assume I'd slept with him?

"I had my share in college. Sometimes it's easier with no emotion attached. You can satisfy some needs while being far less vulnerable."

"It's hard to understand the appeal. The two are entirely linked in my head."

"There's a certain thrill in anonymity. Spontaneity. Novelty. It can be a potent combination. Casual is fun when you're both on the same page."

"Figures you're excited by novelty." His eyes sparkled in a way that made my stomach flip.

"That's fair. I'll try most things at least once."

"I'm not entirely unadventurous."

"Oooh!" My eyes flashed, and I took a deliberate sip from my mug. Consider my curiosity piqued. "Care to elaborate?"

He bit his lip, not daring to pry the lid off that can of worms. My intention in inviting Callum over had been wholesome; it wasn't to seduce him or make things awkward between us. I filed that juicy morsel under Follow Up Later.

He studied me silently for a few moments. "Saoirse's bandmate was nice."

"I'm not interested in Aidan like that. Like I said, I just came along as a favor."

Callum traced a finger along the paisley pattern on my couch cushion. "What happened with your marriage?"

Over the course of the conversation, we'd somehow arrived at this gaping sinkhole in my chest. Callum stood on the precipice and shouted into it. It echoed through the empty space where my heart was supposed to beat. The space I was terrified to fill again. Part of me wanted to tell him. Keeping him in the dark was becoming harder and harder.

His phone buzzed, and he mumbled an apology before stepping outside. Time collapsed inside our intimate bubble. It was 9:17. Who was calling him so late? Picking through the snacks on the coffee table, I attempted to recalibrate. At this hour it was so quiet on our street that Callum's deep timbre filtered through the door. I didn't have to strain to pick up his side of the conversation.

Repeating an address. A soft promise to be there as soon as he could. Give him a half hour.

Was he meeting someone for a late drink? Trad music usually didn't begin at the pub until at least nine thirty. Was it Saoirse? They liked each other, after all. It was one thing to discuss a hypothetical, quite another to hear his phone ring and watch him rush through the door in his socks to answer. In *February*. I wished the soles of his feet would freeze to the landing so he couldn't leave.

No. Mentally, I doused the burn of jealousy with a bucket of water, and my blackened pride sizzled like a fajita platter. *You're not allowed to get territorial over the guy you're trying to help pair up.*

Two minutes later he reentered, face shuttered like he'd had the same thought.

When he caught me standing on the other side of the door with his empty mug, he frowned. "Sorry, I have work."

"This late? What could be the rush? They're not going anywhere." I forced myself to be glib on the subject if he was going to pretend he didn't just receive a call from a woman.

Callum crammed a hand into his hair, leaving it even more rumpled. "That is why I rush. The family needs me to remove their grandmother from their home. D-death doesn't keep polite hours, I'm afraid."

"That's the coroner's job, though. Come on. Be honest. Who really called you, someone from DemiDate? Saoirse?"

"The Gardaí called." *Police.* "It is my job, depending on the circumstances. Elderly cases. Nonviolent accidents. Unless the Gardaí need a postmortem exam, the bodies come directly to me."

Oh. Of course. I'd been so preoccupied imagining Callum with someone else, I hadn't considered the obvious explanation. Not that he needed to explain himself.

"This could be the worst night of someone's life. I won't make it worse by making them wait all hours for someone to pick up their loved one."

"God, I'm so sorry. I didn't even think . . ."

I didn't deserve someone like him.

"It's okay. This was just what I needed." Callum gave me a quick, one-armed hug. "Thanks for the movie. And my dentist should thank you for that popcorn."

CHAPTER 17

Callum

EVENING TEA WITH Saoirse that weekend was pleasant enough. Surface-level conversation meandered over a secluded, candlelit meal. Her foot grazed mine under the table, but I pulled away. When she asked about my day, I certainly couldn't tell her I'd spent it fixated on my neighbor. Something had shifted between Lark and me; my distraction must've been obvious as I picked at the food, barely tasting it.

"A friend of mine is playing at the Hare's Breath tonight," Saoirse said as we walked to my car afterward. "Care to pop in?"

All I wanted was to crawl into bed. Alone. But the July deadline loomed five months away, just over two months to put in for a marriage license, so I agreed.

Raucous laughter and the sounds of clinking glasses filled the tightly packed establishment. Onstage, anchored by a melodic accordion, Saoirse's friend sang traditional ballads. I couldn't help but remember crushing Lark's toes during the two-step. My foolish heart flopped.

"Hey!" Seán, resident douchebag of KinetiColor, approached our booth, motioning to me. "I know you. The Yank's man."

Saoirse gulped her wine.

"Oh, sorry," he stage-whispered as he noticed—and mentally undressed—my date. "The fiddler? Fair play. Didn't think you had it in you."

"What was your name again? Séamus? We're trying to have a conversation, Séamus."

His nostrils flared. "Think I'll take a lash at Lark, if you're all done with her. I've always had a thing for blondes."

Fire burned in my eyes as I leaned close, every muscle in my body quivering for a go at him. "That's. Really. Enough."

"I haven't had enough by a gallon yet, Lurch." He nonchalantly took another pull from his pint.

"If you were even half as smart as Lark, you'd go home without another word."

Hooking his thumb in his belt loop, Seán mimicked Lark's foreign drawl. "Yes, sir. This here cowboy's gonna break that wild filly."

I imagined breaking the pint glass over his head. Disemboweling him with the jagged end. "D-d-don't speak about her that way."

His insufferable smirk wavered as I stepped closer.

"Leave Lark alone. If I hear you've uttered one inappropriate word—"

Saoirse interrupted my murderous fantasy. "Callum, you promised me a dance."

She was giving me an out that didn't involve him bleeding. The latter would be more satisfying. Saoirse took my proffered arm.

"D-d-don't worry," Seán sneered. "I won't tell Lark you're *d-d-d-double-dipping* if you let me have the next *d-d-dance* with the fiddler."

"I've no interest in dancing with a knob like you," she sniped. "Get lost."

With a filthy wink, Seán turned on his heel, reabsorbed into the crowd. Bastard. I burned with humiliation.

"What an ogre." Saoirse wrinkled her nose. "Lark really has to deal with that guy at work? He's a sentient HR violation."

Unresolved anger still shook my hands. They wanted to be around his goddamn neck. "He'd b-b-better leave her alone or I swear . . ."

"Did you two ever date? I don't want to get in the middle if you have history."

Not for lack of wanting on my part. "No, but I couldn't let him carry on that way. Lark is a great person but . . . we have different needs."

"Such as?"

"I want to settle down. Have kids. She doesn't."

Hope sparkled in Saoirse's dark eyes. "I've waited for you to ask me out for so long, I gave up. What were you waiting on?"

"I'm still learning how to communicate what I want. This isn't easy for me."

"Well, I know what *I* want." Saoirse raised up on her toes, and her mouth pressed against mine. Soft at first, then a wet glide of her tongue along the seam of my lips.

Out of instinct, I jerked back and swiped at my moistened bottom lip, effectively wiping her kiss off. Her coy smile evaporated. Wrong. All wrong.

We froze on the dance floor. All I wanted was to curl up on the couch with Lark, hear her laugh when Houdini's whiskers tickled her palm, give in to my urge to tilt her chin up and kiss her deeply. Kissing another woman wouldn't erase my off-limits attraction.

"I know you're shy, Callum, and I got tired of waiting for you to make your move," Saoirse said.

"Sorry, but I can't. I thought—" Never had I imagined rejecting a woman who ticked every proverbial box, but kissing Saoirse was as exciting as making out with a loaf of soda bread. Simply standing close to Lark sent my heart into palpitations. "You're sound, but I already—"

"It's Lark, isn't it?"

I backtracked. "That's not what I said."

"You couldn't take your eyes off her the other night, and your forehead vein pulsed like a homing beacon when that guy insulted her." Her scowl deepened. "Why would you lie?"

"If she knows I like her, it'll ruin everything. Please, I hope you can keep this between us."

Saoirse deserved someone fully invested. Someone who felt about her the way I felt about Lark.

"I apologize for leading you on. You're brilliant and I figured if we gave it an honest go . . ."

"Callum." She touched my cheek, obviously conflicted. "I wish you'd asked me out before she came to town."

My mouth ticked up in a regretful smile. For so long, I'd let opportunities pass me by, countless wasted chances for happiness. By focusing on a career revolving around death, I had a life half-lived. Until Lark appeared.

"If you could tell how I felt, why did you kiss me?"

"I thought I could get you to forget about her for the night. Start from there. Decent men are scarce. I thought, 'If she won't claim him, then I will.' Can you blame me?"

"No one could make me forget about Lark, not in a million years." The words came out before I'd wrapped my brain around the realization. I was in so. Much. Fecking. Trouble.

"Instead of confessing it to another woman, you ought to tell her."

CHAPTER 18

Lark

"YOU'RE ALL SET. I just forwarded the plane ticket to your email."

"I can't wait to see you," Cielo answered. "Thanks for this, Lark. Seriously."

"Hey, it's not every day my favorite cousin graduates with a bachelor's in biology. It's worth celebrating!"

Cielo and I scheduled video calls in the slim overlap of our work and school demands and time differences. Six hours stretched between us. In Texas, it was one in the morning. She'd called me at the tail end of a late-night study session before I went to work. Somehow, she still had energy, her brunette bob swinging through the FaceTime window while I sipped my coffee. Cielo had cared for me during the lowest point in my life, and I wanted to give her something to commemorate her upcoming graduation from my alma mater, UT Austin. There was so much I wanted to show her before I left Ireland.

"I, uh, applied for the Atlantic Bridge program at NUI Galway," she added quietly. "For their medical program."

"Seriously?!"

"God, my mom is gonna lose it when I tell her I'm visiting you on an overseas flight." She laughed. "I've never been on a plane before. Can you imagine her reaction if I get accepted to study abroad?"

Where my mom took a laissez-faire approach to parenting and kept me at an emotional arm's length, her sister was fiercely overprotective of my cousin. Broadening her horizons would be good for Lo after such a sheltered upbringing.

"You remember I'm not staying for long, right? I'll probably be gone by the time the fall semester starts."

"I know. You're still a terrible influence for inspiring me to try, though." She added, "When I visit I'll finally get to meet your mysterious friend, who may or may not be a vampire. You need to FaceTime me with him."

"Callum's really shy, Lo. I'll just send a photo."

"No! Come on, I need the complete package."

"*Package?* Are you really objectifying a man you've never even seen?"

"Whenever you mention him," she said, clamping on to the subject tighter than a pit bull, "there's this goofy look on your face. He's definitely hot."

To demonstrate, she gazed into the middle distance with a sappy expression. It reminded me of the springtime scene in *Bambi*, where Thumper gets horny before bouncing off to make lots of little bunnies with his bunny wife off-screen.

"Callum's not my usual type, but he's sexy in his own way."

I fired off the picture from the ruined abbey, Callum looking aloof and pensive. For the sake of balance, I sent another with his eyes crinkled in laughter, then propped my phone so I could apply makeup in the bathroom mirror.

"*This* is your neighbor? I'd let him take me to the boneyard."

I aggressively blended concealer into my under-eye circles. Rest hadn't come easy on Saturday night, thinking of his date.

"Honestly, it's been nice to just have a chill person to hang with outside of work. If I listened to you, I would've banged my way through Galway, Dublin, and half the countryside by now."

"If it were me, I'd already be working my way across Scotland one kilt at a time."

We stared at each other for a beat before we both cracked up. I still couldn't bear to tell her I'd purchased condoms, then chickened out when given an opportunity to use them with a handsome singer.

"Do you really expect me to trust you on a video call with Cal when you won't behave? You'd eat him alive."

"Why are you being so skittish?"

"He, um . . . he doesn't know about Reese. He assumed I got divorced, and I never corrected him."

My cousin understood what the move to Galway meant. Radical change. For two months after losing Reese, I stayed with her because my mom was a fount of toxic positivity and platitudes. She'd barely been able to look at me, wrapped as I was in guilt and sorrow. Cielo also played mediator when Rachel demanded a few items that belonged to Reese. I'd had neither the inclination nor the energy to argue. I'd been too raw to even be in my home alone—the home I shared with Reese. Lo had packed three boxes for Rachel and left them on the porch. She refused to forgive Rachel for what she'd hissed at the memorial in front of our families, friends, and coworkers.

"But I thought you braided each other's hair and told each other all your secrets every night."

"At the time we didn't know each other well. I didn't want to change how he saw me. Now I'm in too deep. Promise me you won't say anything."

"Why would I bring that up? I'm trying to get you laid."

I groaned. "He's giving me a ride to work in five minutes. I gotta go."

While Callum had been enjoying his second date with Saoirse,

I'd busied myself with sketching. Before long, a large black rat had appeared on the page alongside Houdini, the tiny white mouse. Skeptical of magic, but kind-hearted, I'd dubbed him Plague Rat, knowing Callum would appreciate the reference. Intending to work on it during lunch, I tossed the sketchbook into my tote and slipped on my coat to face the drizzle and mist typical of an Irish February.

SILENCE ENVELOPED US for the first half of the ride. "Gonna keep me in suspense? How did the date go?"

"It was fine."

Rain pelted the roof of Callum's Peugeot. Peaceful under normal conditions, the rhythm only added to my anxiety today. My video call with Lo had highlighted how strong this ridiculous crush on Callum had grown. Hell, the first night I wore his sweater to bed, I had a sex dream (not under penalty of death would I admit that to Cielo, because she'd never let it go). For the good of our friendship, I needed to squash my attraction.

"Did you kiss her? Score a third date?" *Ugh, why did I have to say* score *and* third date *in the same sentence?*

"No."

"You'll need to be more specific," I prodded. Maybe this was another case of Callum taking things slow. Glacial.

"No third date."

So there *was* a kiss. "Well, I'm glad you had fun. Saoirse's, um, nice."

I sounded so patronizing; I wanted to slap myself. The other woman had done nothing wrong, and I'd spent the last two nights telling myself not to resent her.

Callum frowned. The wipers swished at a frantic pace but did little to clear the sheets of rain. Unless his schedule made it impossible, he insisted on driving me to work in poor weather. It didn't matter that I owned a cute umbrella and had become proficient in reading bus schedules.

We arrived at KinetiColor Studios, and Callum's hands twisted around the steering wheel.

"Has Seán ever come on to you?"

"You mean has he ever sexually harassed me? No. He bothers me in other ways."

"We ran into each other on Saturday."

Seán arranged happy hour Fridays, and it stood to reason the Hare's Breath was his preferred watering hole. Objectively handsome, he garnered attention there often, wife apparently forgotten. Misogyny and xenophobia ran like a dark undertow just beneath the surface of his weaponized good looks. "I want you to stay away from him."

"I can't avoid him any more than I already do. Believe me, our interactions are kept at a minimum."

"I'll be back to give you a lift home."

"That's all right—"

"Grand. I'll see you then."

Unbuckling my seat belt, I pivoted. "Cal. What's gotten into you?"

"You're being weird," Callum said. *Pot, meet kettle.*

Mercifully, the dashboard clock drew my attention while I avoided eye contact. "It's this quarterly staff meeting. I have to present our progress to Sullivan and the Suits. That's what Rory and I call the owner and the producers."

"What you showed me is amazing." He rested a hand over mine, gently atop my knee. "Just breathe."

How could I, with his fingertips grazing my thigh? I didn't want to face Sullivan, and I certainly didn't want to deal with a certain smug colleague. I didn't want to leave the car.

Callum said, "About Saturday night . . ."

Scratch that. Before he could say another word, I threw open the door. What I really didn't want was to dissolve into a puddle of emotion. "We'll talk after work."

"Good luck," Callum shouted as I jumped out.

Shielding my hair from the rain, I sprinted to the lobby door. I needed a few minutes alone in my office before the meeting. Last quarter, I'd had to defend my stance on more laborious techniques, but if everyone pulled their weight and kept to the timeline, staying on budget was possible.

I closed the door to my office, sat at my desk, and popped in headphones, Dolly Parton centering me. A soft knock disrupted the soothing vibrato and guitar.

Cursing, I pulled out my earbuds. "Come in."

"Enjoy your weekend?" Speak of his infernal majesty. Trust him to launch an ambush during my stolen moment of peace.

"Sure did." I'd caked on only a quarter pound of under-eye concealer to compensate for the lack of sleep. "How was yours, Seán?"

His attention snagged on the headphones. "Music fan, huh? I caught some live music at the Hare's Breath. Saw your friend, in fact, the tall one who doesn't speak much. Didn't see you, though. Don't blame you. Depressing, being the third wheel." Seán patted my arm condescendingly, and I recoiled. Creep.

"Please don't touch me."

"That fiddle player, though, she's incredible," he continued, ignoring me. "You ought to come hear her."

I'd rather puncture my eardrum with a pencil than go on another double date.

"She's a fine thing, too. I wanted her number, but your friend got to her first. They were dancing and carrying on. Mauling the faces off each other."

All weekend, my imagination ran amok with scenes of flirtatious touches and little jokes, Callum's wide hands guided by the flow of alcohol and beat of the music.

With every mustered ounce of my professional authority, I said, "We have to start the meeting." I smoothed out my dress as I stood. "Was there something you needed?"

An icy smile frosted over his blinding teeth. "Just came to offer a hand with the presentation. I used to help the last art director, and I know what Sullivan likes."

Right. I didn't trust Seán any further than I could throw him. He'd happily claim credit for the entire production. Anything to paint himself as the rightful art director.

"Got it, thanks."

"Wasn't easy last time, to convince the studio to spend more money," he said.

"It won't cost more to do a few hand-painted environments if everyone meets their deadlines," I snapped. "We shouldn't have to cut corners because of poor time management."

"Just offering my help. I care about this project, too."

"Sorry. Of course, I didn't mean to—"

God, why was my first instinct always to be agreeable, even when my indignation seethed?

CHAPTER 19

Callum

TOMBSTONE-GRAY CLOUDS threatened a downpour as employees filtered out of the KinetiColor lobby, but Lark hadn't yet emerged. Gloomy weather was the perfect excuse to give her a lift home.

I tweaked the radio knob, shuffling past stations until I landed on a folk tune about a flaxen-haired woman with an indomitable spirit. Struck by the aptness, I mouthed the lyrics, startling when Lark opened the passenger door and climbed in.

I turned off the radio. "Hey."

"Were you singing?"

"I don't sing."

"I think you do." Her expression shifted into playful suspicion when I blocked her from pressing the button. For her to know what I'd been singing along to was a different matter. I drove in silence instead of risking the radio.

Questions gnawed at me, but I didn't want to accost her immediately. I hoped a few minutes of decompression would pave the way for a conversation about Saturday.

Lark's mobile vibrated in her purse. "I promised to debrief

with Cielo, and she gets hyper-eager about these things. I apologize in advance."

Before I could ask about her ominous warning, she answered the video chat. "Hey, Lo. Look who I'm with. This is Callum." I froze like a kid caught nicking the last biscuit from the jar when she angled the device toward me. A Latina woman a bit younger than Lark filled the screen. That familiar anticipation was back: the weight of first impressions.

"The Angel of Death. Nice to finally meet you."

On its own, my hand lifted from the steering wheel. "Um, hello, Cielo."

I got the distinct feeling of being cataloged like a specimen of some curiosity.

Lark grabbed my arm and rested her head on my shoulder. Wafting citrus-vanilla proved to be an effective distraction. "*Lo.* I recall a promise that you wouldn't make him uncomfortable."

"Right. Sorry." Cielo's attention returned to Lark. "Tell me, how did your meeting go?"

"Seán tried to psych me out beforehand, and it worked. By the end, I was apologizing to *him.*" Her hair swung as she tossed her head. "The meeting itself was okay. Our timeline has to be extra tight if we want to implement the changes I suggested. Which means relations will get worse with Golden Boy."

They launched into a rapid-fire exchange about the producer's response to her suggestions. I wondered what discouraging seeds Seán had planted in her head. Soon, there was a lull, and Cielo was blinking at me.

"So. Callum."

"How are your studies going? Premed, right?"

"I desperately needed a break. Monday is Presidents' Day, which means three days off, so the family's having a barbecue. They'll just take any excuse for a cookout, even if it's technically winter."

Lark gave a melancholic smile. How many people did she

miss back home? Would she and I have become close if we'd met in Texas instead and I was the expatriate?

"Lo applied to the medical school at NUI Galway for the fall," Lark said.

It snagged in my brain. If Lark's cousin was coming here, would she still want to leave when the Grace O'Malley project was done?

"Best of luck to you," I replied.

"This girl's a genius, Cal. She's a shoo-in," Lark added.

Cielo shook her head modestly and redirected her attention to me. "How are you taking care of my cousin?"

"She takes care of herself."

"Good answer."

Lark squeezed my arm. "He humors me."

"Not everyone can handle Lark. And most people bore her right away."

I cocked my head. She threw a not-so-covert look at her cousin.

"She's worth it, though." Cielo's focus stayed trained on me. "No one is more loyal."

Lark blushed a little and looked out the window. Of course, I'd known from the first time we met she was special.

"Well, it was great talking to y'all . . . Cuz . . . Angel of Death." Cielo nodded at the screen. "Oh, and call your mom. She's been asking me all kinds of questions about Ireland that I can't possibly answer. Release me from this nightmare and update her, would you?"

"Short of a ritualistic sacrifice, I don't think I could summon the energy to deal with her today."

"Did you know she has the month marked on the calendar when you're supposed to come back? Told me all about her daily affirmations. She's trying to manifest a safe return home."

"Not too soon, I hope," Lark said. "I have a lot more work to do here."

I hated the reminder of the expiration date. After they said their goodbyes, Lark picked at her cuticles before dropping her mobile back in her purse.

We pulled into our street, and I parked in my driveway.

"I d-d—" Why did this have to be so hard? I grimaced as Lark waited for me to try again. "Ididn'tkissher," I blurted out in one word.

"What?"

"Saoirse kissed me."

"Well, I can't blame her," Lark said without looking at me. "Are you going to ask her out again?"

"No. Not in that way."

Saoirse ticked all the boxes. Cultured. Talented. Poised but unafraid to speak her mind. Looking for a serious match. Conversations were pleasant enough, and yet I felt nothing. She didn't make me feel alive like Lark did. Challenged and curious and . . . *optimistic* for the first time in decades.

"Is it . . ." Lark seemed to have trouble finding words, too.

My heart pounded.

"Going too fast? Seán said he saw you dancing, so it couldn't have been that bad."

Son of a bitch. "Seán isn't to be trusted."

"You're allowed to have fun."

If Lark's encouragement was real, it meant her feelings were firmly platonic, which was for the best since she was leaving in a few months.

"I would've had more fun staying in with you."

"You'll never find someone if you hide in my living room. Take her someplace low-key next time. How about a walk by the bay?"

I didn't want to take anyone else to watch the hookers. "No. That's special."

"You took me."

Lark and I had played chess by the water twice, and she understood the significance of the spot. It sounded like she wanted me to explain why I'd chosen to take *her* somewhere special. I wasn't ready to confess, but I raised my brows meaningfully.

"Cal, it'll get easier."

Somehow, I doubted that, when she was the only person I looked forward to seeing.

CHAPTER 20

Lark

"THOSE ONES, TOO." Maeve motioned to a stack of boxes in her garden shed. She'd asked me to help sort and donate items to the charity shop. "I'd like to clear the lot of it out."

"Are you sure you don't want to look through them first? Keep the special ones?" There was a time in my life where I'd felt suffocated by the contents of my own house, but even I didn't get rid of it all. A plume of dust rose from a stack of old records when she pulled out a Thin Lizzy LP.

"So, Callum's on another date, then?"

"Uh-huh. There's a woman I think he likes. I went on a double date with them and it was . . . fine."

Maeve thumbed through the faded spines. "You don't approve of her?"

"They seem like they'd be good together. It's just been harder than I thought to see him with someone else."

"So why are you pushing the lad into another woman's arms?"

We'd been over this. To my surprise, Callum had shared the unusual inheritance situation with her during our last dinner visit. She'd been extremely interested in my reaction to it.

"I am not getting married again. Period."

"Chrissakes, child, it's a slip of government paper."

Old cardboard and vinyl filled my nose as I pulled another box from the corner. "Was it just 'a slip of paper' to you and Charlie when you were finally allowed to marry?"

Maeve softened. "Suppose not. But surely this situation warrants considering it."

"You don't understand. I wish it was that simple to do him this favor, but it's not for me."

"What has you so frightened? Is it losing another partner?"

My jaw dropped open. "I— What?"

She nodded. "I've always known you lost your husband."

"But *how*? What are you, a witch?" I sputtered, half joking.

"Always calling me names, aren't you!" Crepe crinkles formed at the corners of Maeve's smile. "I could see it in the way you reacted to the story of how I lost Charlie. It was more than empathy. It was firsthand knowledge. And I've seen enough in my life to recognize a runner standing right in front of me."

"Damn, Maeve. We should set up a psychic business: Madame Maeve's palm readings. I can draw up a logo, and you probably have a crystal ball around here somewhere."

"Does Callum know that's the reason why you won't marry him, even if it's just on paper?"

"You know how people look at you when they find out you're a widow? The pity? I can't stand it. The way they feel guilty and apologize if they mention their own spouse in conversation, that kind of thing."

"Not everyone knows how to react, but Callum deals with death every day. Don't you think he would want to understand the context of your life?"

"He's become my best friend, and I've hidden this from him the whole time. It's been easier to pretend like it never happened. Because the way he looks at me will change if he knows."

"Everything changes in this world. Not always for the worse. Wounds heal, if you let them."

But I deserved every ounce of guilt and grief I felt. Could that wound ever heal?

"During my marriage, I was a workaholic. I even forgot our anniversary one year because I was so wrapped up in a project. If I had only pulled my head out of my ass, I would have noticed how unhappy Reese was becoming. If I'd paid attention to the man I'd promised to love and cherish, I wouldn't have been in denial when he finally told me, and we wouldn't have fought so badly that Reese drove into a tree. . . ." My breath caught on the final sentence as a sob began to rise.

Maeve rested a veiny hand over mine. "I'm sorry you lost him in such a way."

"I'll never know if he was coming home to ask me for a divorce or if he was on his way to try to make up. I just regret arguing with him at all." A tear slid down my cheek. "I have so many regrets, and I promised not to repeat them."

"My biggest regret was not telling Charlie how I felt earlier, and missing out on years we could have spent together because I was afraid to talk. You should tell Callum."

I'd traveled across an ocean, to a place where no one knew me, to control my own narrative. All that running was exhausting, but I still didn't know if I could bring myself to tell him the truth.

CHAPTER 21

Callum

OVER THE NEXT few weeks, I went on a dating spree. *March Madness*, Lark called it. She even created a Bad Date Bracket to keep me in good spirits. The awkwardness only got marginally easier to endure as I exhausted my DemiDate matches and branched out to the mainstream apps. Saoirse was right. The dating landscape was practically dystopian.

On the nights I wasn't meeting someone, Lark and I enjoyed movies at her flat. She chose animated films she thought I'd appreciate. *Coraline*'s surreal horror. The stark, honest humor of *Persepolis*. *Corpse Bride*'s macabre musical. Guillermo del Toro's bittersweet stop-motion *Pinocchio*. She'd convinced me of the validity of the art form long ago.

Not all of the movies we watched were animated, though. One night, Lark made me sit through the roller-disco opera awful enough to inspire the creation of the Razzies. Dated production and musical numbers only added to the campy cult appeal, she maintained. Not that I minded what we saw.

"Sometimes I think I was born in the wrong era," she'd said, lamenting missing the heyday of roller disco by a few decades. I decided I'd bring the seventies to her for her birthday coming up next month.

After some searching, I found the perfect gift: pink roller skates with daisies printed on the wheels. For myself, a pair of battered tan quads with tangerine wheels and front stoppers half worn away. I knew they would surprise the woman who had brought so much surprise into my own life.

On her birthday I insisted on giving her a lift home from KinetiColor. I blamed the March weather, but suspected we both knew it was a flimsy excuse. Listening to her describe her vivid, bizarre dreams in hilarious detail or sing along with the radio—it didn't matter, those stolen ten minutes each morning set an invariably brighter tone for the day. Lark was a counterbalance to the somber mood of Willow Haven. I craved her light like a houseplant languishing in a dark corner.

When she hopped in the car to go home, I held out the coffee I'd picked up for her on the way.

"You shouldn't have."

"Wait." I raised a toast. "On your birthday, we drink to your coffin."

Lark's brows skewed. "Pardon?"

"May it be built from the wood of the hundred-year oak tree I shall plant tomorrow."

She knocked the cups together and intertwined our arms as she took a sip. "Only you could get away with that."

I'd stashed her gift in the boot. When we arrived home, I ran a hand through my hair. "May I come in?"

Lark waved me inside as I grabbed the bag and tucked it under my arm. "Is that my present?"

"Just wait."

"I'm changing out of these work clothes," she said, disappearing into her bedroom. A shiver ran up my spine at the mental image. Lark's blouse dropping to the floor, trousers sliding down the smooth skin of her thighs. Goose bumps rising along the slope of her exposed breasts.

I shook off the fantasy and fled to the bathroom. A rogue

whiff of funk that must have dated from the eighties assaulted me when I opened the bag.

I squeezed into garish, itchy spandex. Sequins traveled down the single sleeve of the royal-blue figure skating costume like feathers. On the other side, my arm and shoulder were left exposed, so I resembled a half-plucked macaw. The garment didn't quite fit, leaving a strip of leg hair visible above my ankles. Synthetic fabric cupped my balls obscenely. I resisted the urge to cover my crotch as I made my way through the carpet to the living room on wheels, bracing the wall.

"Surprise!"

Laugher erupted from Lark's mouth. From the very depths of her soul. Pink-faced, clutching-her-sides, wiping-the-mirth-from-her-eyes-level laughter. Okay. It looked like I got lost on the way to the Winter Olympics . . . in 1978. I tugged at the spandex riding up my ass, and she wolf-whistled in response.

"Oh my God! Seeing you in that outfit is the best gift I could have ever gotten. Are those rental skates?"

"Indeed! How many sweaty feet do you think crammed into them prior to landing in the charity shop?"

"Wise men don't ask questions they don't want answered," she said. I decided not to dwell on what would surely be a disturbing number of strange toes.

"You're fabulous—and the sweetest guy ever." Lark threw her arms around my neck and tugged me down. She pressed up on her tiptoes to kiss my cheek, and I nearly burst into flames.

Calm down. It's just gratitude. She doesn't want to actually kiss you.

I handed her the gift bag. "Misery loves company."

She squealed and changed in record time. When she emerged from her room, my jaw dropped. Ruffles in alternating waves of royal blue and silver accentuated her waist, and the short skirt cut high up her thighs. Only an Aqua Net–fortified perm was missing.

Lark popped one ruffle-covered hip. "How do I look?"

"Olivia Newton-John, eat your heart out."

Her megawatt smile could've caused a power surge. Outside, I checked my laces and made the sign of the cross for show. The day was fresh and clear. Thankfully, privacy hedges protected us from an audience. I looked ridiculous. Newborn giraffes learning how to walk weren't this awkward.

"We need roller derby names," she said. "It's mixing eras. And sports. But I don't care."

Determined not to fall, I focused on putting one wheeled foot in front of the other.

"Loch Ness One-Eyed Monster."

In feigned offense, I slapped a hand over my wounded heart. "D-Deporting you for that."

"To be fair, you said you're part Scottish but never clarified *which* part. What about Shamrock Shake Ya Ass?" Lark beatboxed as she circled me effortlessly. She slapped me on the butt, propelling me forward. I threw my arms out for balance before I sampled a taste of the pavement.

"Whoa—"

"River Dance Dance Revolution?"

"This was a mistake. I'm taking back your gift."

"Got it!" She snapped her fingers. "This Lucky Charming Man." Of course she'd create a mash-up of a post-punk anthem and a marshmallow-laden breakfast cereal.

"I like it."

My legs moved in opposite directions, sending me crashing into Lark, who locked her arms around my waist.

"Hold still."

"I'm on wheels!" I protested, although they were my idea.

She tossed her head back and giggled. I joined in, snickering until my cheeks ached. If making a fool out of myself made her smile, I'd do it every day. To hell with my dignity.

Lark gazed up at me from under heavy lashes. She focused on my mouth, then back up, eyes flitting back down again as the hand fisted in my unitard unfurled and grazed the edge of my rib cage. My heart whacked against my sternum and hit every rib as it fell into my stomach. I wanted to shut my eyes and savor her caress, but damned if I could tear myself away from the ocean of her irises.

Unmistakable desire thrummed between us. Licking my lips, I drifted closer. If this backfired, it could be the end of our friendship. If it worked . . . I couldn't imagine denying her a single thing.

Suddenly, I sent us both shuffling against gravity for a moment before I toppled. Lark came down in a blur of colorful ruffles and a sharp elbow into my stomach.

"Sorry! Are you okay?"

"Only a ruptured spleen." I winced.

"Is this a deliberate attempt to get out of skating to ABBA?"

Her legs straddled my thigh. Warmth flowed through the thin spandex. X-rated thoughts flooded my brain. Wisps of blond hair fell across her face and I shifted to brush them back. I tried to recall my list of surefire boner-killers. Nothing would come to mind except Lark's exquisite scent.

Jaysus, Mary, and Joseph.

Rosy color dusted Lark's cheeks and upturned nose. Rock-hard now, my entire body was attuned to the heat between her thighs. Rigor mortis it was not. I could almost taste her breath as she drifted closer. Closer.

Barks from the neighbor's collie broke the trance. I'd nearly forgotten we were in the garden.

Fast as it had ignited, the embers in her eyes cooled. Sequins clicked against each other as she rested a palm on my sternum. It doused the fire that threatened to burn our friendship down. Of course, Lark lived by carpe diem. If she wanted the same thing as I did, she'd have acted on it already. Abruptly, she lifted herself off me, and humiliation coursed through my veins. A flash of pink fabric peeked out from the short, ruffled figure skating costume. I bit back a groan, imagining peeling her knickers off with my teeth.

"I need a fag," I joked. I'd never picked up the habit, since my granda showed me an actual emphysemic lung after a few boys from our parish were caught smoking when I was ten. Yep. *Think about disgusting, diseased organs until this . . . passes.*

"Should've known better, with Mercury in retrograde." Lark and her astrology. I'd tried to follow along as she explained the impact of the celestial phenomenon once, but I struggled to understand the logic.

Were we going to ignore what just happened? The words were right there, resting on my tongue like a piece of hard toffee. I swallowed them down. Better left unsaid.

Brushing the dirt off my backside, I stood with my back to her. Spandex had wedged into my entire groin, straining against the bulge. Employing the old *walk it off* technique, I skated, cautiously. Motion blur might make my throbbing erection less obvious. Although Lark couldn't read my thoughts, I needed to stop thinking of her knickers.

"So much for the choreographed routine to Peaches and Herb," I said.

"Thanks for dressing like a carnival float to indulge me." She shook her hips, skating backward as more disco played from her mobile. "Try going backward. It's easy."

Graceful as Frankenstein's monster, I attempted to skate in reverse. She was right. "It *is* easy."

My right foot swerved. Before I could catch myself, I felt the horrible whoosh of air. And then darkness.

SUNLIGHT BURNED INTO my brain through slitted eyelids. Smooth blue spandex brushed against my cheek as Lark cradled my head on her lap. "Oh God. Callum, wake up."

Copper taste buzzed in my mouth. Neither my thoughts nor my vision was clear.

"You fell and hit your head." Lark wiped blood off my lip with her thumb. She framed my face in her hands as she examined it. "And I think you bit your tongue pretty hard."

Oh. That makes sense.

"Remember, we were skating?"

Were we? I shook my head and silently vowed to not do that again; it hurt like hell. I sat up on my elbow to get a better look at her. She was in the secondhand leotard I'd bought her, worry etched on her lovely face.

"Why are— You're wearing it?"

Her brows pinched together. "You don't remember? The matching outfits?"

It was all a confusing, pain-tinted blur. Looking down to see that I, too, resembled a mirror ball only made it more disorienting. My bare shoulder bounced in a little shrug in Lark's lap.

She gingerly felt the back of my skull. It stung at her touch. She unlaced my shoes, and I realized they were, in fact, roller skates as she slid them off.

"I think," I mumbled, "I'm going to be sick."

"Come on, we're going to the hospital," she said, slinging my arm around her shoulder. The cool footpath chilled my sock-covered feet.

"I just need a nap."

Lark ran inside and must've found my keys next to my folded clothes. They jingled as she jogged back to me. Before I knew it, I was buckled into the passenger seat of my car and the voice navigation on Lark's phone narrated the route to the hospital.

"This is so weird, driving on the other side," she said, talking to keep me awake.

Nausea returned with a vengeance at the roundabout. Bits and pieces of memory came back, like her hysterical laugh and a roller derby name referencing The Smiths. At the stoplight, Lark's fingers tenderly brushed through my hair.

We hopped out at the valet, and Lark supported me to the

door. Heads turned as we entered the A&E. If I'd had my full wits about me, I'd feel awkward being seen in gaudy spandex, but with the bright lights worsening my headache, I just held a hand over the throbbing gash at the base of my skull.

"Are you family?"

I yawned, trying to say *no* at the same moment Lark answered *yes*.

The receptionist's polite smile flatlined.

"She is," I said.

"I mean, we're not family yet. My fiancé hit his head rehearsing a dance number for our reception—we were roller-skating."

Ultimately apathetic about our foibles, the man handed Lark a clipboard stacked with intake paperwork. She smiled at me once his back was turned.

"Terrible liar." I wondered why she hadn't said we were cousins. We didn't need a ring for that.

"Lower your voice," Lark hissed. No one had ever accused me of loudness before. I poked at the goose egg forming on my occipital ridge. "I needed to lie so they'll let me back with you. Don't you know anything about hospitals?"

I hadn't given it much consideration.

"Let me get you a pair of those grippy socks. I should've run back inside to grab your shoes. Your feet must be freezing."

"Just stay with me. I'm okay."

"This is all my fault. You could barely skate, and I encouraged you to go backward."

"My clumsiness isn't your fault. The only thing I'm upset about is wearing a unitard in public . . . and you spending your birthday in the A and E."

"Our matching emergency room couture is the only thing I *don't* regret."

"I look like I went through the wash on the wrong setting. Every person in the waiting room can see the d-distinct outline of my—"

"Nessie?" Lark waggled her brow at the same moment a nurse called out my name.

"Flannelly!" The privacy curtain pulled back with a screech. The nurse stopped short when she noticed us dressed like a pair of rejected figure skaters but recovered without commentary. I cut a secret smirk to Lark, who bit back her own as the nurse explained the cognitive evaluation. Lapses in short-term memory were common in this type of injury, she assured us. It could come back all at once, in pieces, or not at all.

The impact had been hard enough to split my scalp just over my nape and give me a nasty concussion. When Lark described to the nurse what had happened, she gripped my hand. She thought she'd seen bone, and when the nurse confirmed it, Lark practically turned green. One CT scan and eleven stitches later, they prepared me for discharge.

"Someone will need to agree to monitor you over the next few days. Head injuries can be tricky." She consulted the intake form on the clipboard and said to Lark, "You're the fiancée?"

I liked the sound of that far more than I cared to admit.

CHAPTER 22

Lark

"MY PLACE OR yours?" I asked on the drive back from the hospital.

"I want to go home," Callum said with such longing I couldn't deny him the comfort of his own space.

I assisted him upstairs so he could change into sweatpants and a faded tee. To be honest, I'd miss his sequined unitard. We sat in the family room of the upper level, a showroom of gleaming coffins and urns beneath us. Despite this being a beautiful historic building, he told me his workspace boasted modern amenities with germ-killing ultraviolet lights and sleek equipment. I tried not to think about it.

Callum rested on his side on the couch, to not disturb the angry lump at the base of his skull. Streaks of blood marred his carefully parted hair along the stitched seam.

"There's a mess back here, I can put a towel down if you're too tired to wash it. But at least they didn't have to shave you."

I'd almost fainted when he slammed his head on the raised stone curb of the garden path.

"Can I help you wash it?"

"Please?"

I grabbed shampoo and a towel from his shower. With measured steps, we made our way to the kitchen and the sink's handheld nozzle. Callum sat in a backward dining chair, straddling it to lean into the basin. I collected his glasses and set them on the counter.

"Wait. Your shirt will get wet."

He put his hands to the hem of his shirt and got that shy look again. So endearing, so irresistible. The more he hid, the more I wanted to discover. Muscles bunched as he pulled it off, and *Jesus, take the wheel.* I wasn't strong enough for this. My fingers gripped the towel as I resisted raking them through the patch of hair on his defined chest. I recalled his firm thigh nestled between mine. Hours ago, I'd straddled him like the mechanical bull I rode on my twenty-first birthday. Best believe I'd hold on longer than eight seconds.

Back off, cowgirl.

I wrapped the towel around his shoulders and tipped forward until he stared down into the drain. A strange re-creation of peeking off the edge at the Cliffs of Moher. I'd been so reckless then, encouraging Callum to join me for the sake of a thrill. What if the ledge had sheared off where we lay?

"Dizzy?" I asked.

"A little."

"Sorry. I'll go quickly so you can rest. Quick but gentle."

"I trust you."

That's what got him into this mess. I grabbed the sprayer nozzle. Pink swirls tinted the water as I rinsed. The dull snap of his head on the pavement echoed through my mind. I built a lather, protecting the wound with the washcloth.

Callum sucked in a breath, gripping the edge of the counter when my breasts skimmed his bare back. My nipples tightened through my thin bra and silly leotard. I bit my cheek to stop from moaning at the incidental friction.

Control yourself.

"Feels nice," he murmured as I raked my fingertips across his scalp. God, to feel him relax under my attention. I could lose myself in it if I wasn't careful. "You okay?"

"You scared me earlier."

He reached back blindly to squeeze my forearm, a thumb caressing the suddenly sensitive skin. I imagined him brushing over my pebbled nipples. Descending on them with that sarcastic, plush mouth. Having your hair shampooed by someone else is an intimate act, but I felt like the vulnerable one. I shut off the tap and wiped the splashes from the counter. The injury was a reminder that I could lose him at any time; it simultaneously petrified me and made me want to live each moment to the fullest.

Callum turned to sit properly in the chair. I got a good look at his toned body. Admittedly, I'd wondered what was hidden under those black suits and cozy sweaters, so I let myself drink him in. Chest hair and a tempting trail leading south drew more attention to his already distracting torso. When I made my way back up to his face, I realized he was scanning over my body, hovering at my chest. A burst of heat threatened to incinerate me where I stood. So . . , he felt that, too.

Cue the MournHub intro music.

I ruffled his hair with the towel. He slung his arms around my waist. This didn't feel *friendly*. Not at all.

"Sorry for going Humpty Dumpty on you. I wanted to make your birthday special."

"It was the absolute best surprise. I'll never forget it."

"Then it was worth it."

His words vibrated against my heart, in more ways than one. He rested his chin against my chest, the towel draped around his shoulders as he looked up at me. Rivulets of water trickled down along his hairline. Powerful energy crackled between us as he kept me close. It felt like waiting atop the drop tower at Six Flags . . . bracing for the inevitable fall.

Did Callum remember what had happened? Or was it lost to

the impact? If he didn't retain the memory, I could pretend it never occurred, but that felt wrong. Deceitful. If I was in his shoes, I'd want to know, but if I were to hear it secondhand, I'd feel robbed of the erotic thrill of crossing that boundary. Either way, it was best to move on as if it never happened. Nothing could come of it. He'd been on dozens of dates in the last few weeks, desperately seeking a wife to save Willow Haven. I couldn't jeopardize his mission. I wouldn't. And I couldn't marry him. After losing Reese, I couldn't treat those vows so lightly.

But, *oh*, did it feel right to be wrapped in his arms.

"Right b-b-before it happened, you called me This Lucky Charming Man, right?"

"The doctor said if you'd hit any harder, it would've fractured your skull."

"Exactly. Lucky." Thickheaded man. Literally.

"We have very different definitions of the word, then. I saw your *skull*, Callum, I saw . . . more of you than I ever imagined today."

"I thought the unitard would fit. The eBay listing said 'large.'" He smirked.

Lord. Callum never outright smirked. Once I'd gotten past the vintage outfit's hilarious design, I'd appreciated how it showcased his defined shoulders. And how it clung to the rest of him. No wonder he looked a little smug. I resisted glancing down at his sweatpants. *Friendly thoughts. Friendly thoughts.*

"Not funny." I returned Callum's glasses, and he perched them on his nose without bothering to put his shirt back on. Like some kind of sexy male librarian fantasy. Was he *trying* to seduce me?

His hands returned to my waist, thumbs smoothing circles onto my lower back with just enough pressure to soften the knot underneath my skin. I hated him for it; I wanted him to never stop. "Something else came to me, just now."

My breath hitched.

"Your roller derby persona."

"Dare I ask?"

"D-D-Dolly Pardon My French."

"God, the way your swollen brain works! But we should pause our derby ambitions, considering."

The halos of his irises were all but gone, pupils blown wide. "I am lucky. To have you."

"You couldn't get rid of me if you wanted. I wouldn't leave you alone in this huge, spooky-ass house when you've just scrambled your cerebellum."

"It is a lot for one person."

"You won't be single forever. You'll fill this place with a family. It'll happen." The thought made me ache. I couldn't give Callum that, but eventually he'd find someone who would.

"Before we met, I don't know if I believed that. I forced myself on dates, but I couldn't see it happening. Then you moved in next door and . . . now I feel hopeful. Maybe for the first time. You wrecked my comfort zone. Jammed a stick of TNT in and exploded it. I'll never be the same, Lark."

I brushed some damp hair off his forehead. "Wile E. Coyote reference aside, that's the sweetest thing anyone's ever said to me."

"Last week you called him the underdog of Looney Tunes because he's an eternal optimist." Knowing he paid attention to my animation rants was even more heartwarming. He remembered last Wednesday, but there might still be a chunk missing from his recollection of this afternoon.

More than anything, I wanted to kiss him. Straddle him right there in the kitchen.

Going out on a limb never ended well for the coyote. I admired the poor critter's grit but didn't share his hubris in the obsessive pursuit of what he desired. A happy future with Callum wasn't in the cards for me. Allowing myself more with him would result in an anvil to someone's heart in the end, anyway.

My fingers still rested on Callum's biceps. Warmth from his

bare chest seeped through my clothes. His mouth was so alluring. Subtly upturned at the corners, as if my sunny disposition had rubbed off on him. Had it always been so? Maybe I needed to stop staring.

Callum leaned forward and pecked me on the mouth. Just a teasing brush of his lips . . . but powerful enough to throw Earth off its axis.

He drew back, tentative.

My entire body tingled. Callum's eyes widened as if realizing the full brunt of the intimacy of the simple action. Frozen in place, his gaze traveled back down to my mouth. Ardent yearning filled his eyes. A reflection of my own.

I'd never felt so wanted. I'd never wanted anyone so badly.

Screw it.

I surged toward him, cupping a hand at the nape of his neck just below his stitches. He let out a muffled moan. Fire ignited in my blood. Our noses bumped, but we soon negotiated an angle that allowed me to sink into him. Callum sucked my bottom lip, sending a jolt of electricity through every nerve in my body.

Callum drew me closer, splaying his hands across my back. I didn't dwell on the consequences. Didn't plan or overthink as his trembling fingers slid down my sensitive neck. Tender but insistent, our kiss deepened. Delicious. Perfect. Long overdue. Mint toothpaste juxtaposed with the heat of his tongue. It was all I could do not to melt into a human puddle.

Half convinced it was a dream, I breathed out an incredulous laugh and caressed his stubble-shaded jaw.

Callum laughed, too. Swallowing hard, he stammered, "Happy b-birthday, love."

Hundreds of questions poured into my head as the haze cleared. Why had he kissed me first? Why did he kiss me back when I decided an innocent peck wasn't enough? What did all this mean?

My brain melted into slush from the scorching kiss. Callum

waited a moment, but when my words refused to form, he sealed his mouth over mine again. Slow and sensual and almost painful in its intensity. Solid pecs under my palm. Sweet, gasping breath. I mapped the topography of his body. Callum returned the favor, fingertips grazing my hips.

On instinct, I climbed into his lap. A deep, rumbling moan punctuated the contact and made my clit throb; I'll never be able to excise that erotic sound from my memory. Callum scattered kisses across my exposed collarbone while I ground against the stiff length in his joggers. The sensations shook me to my core.

"Cal," I whispered. My hips moved in urgent need against him.

Callum squeezed me possessively under the frilly spandex skirt, then took my mouth again. This time, an undercurrent of determination seasoned his kiss. No hesitation. Only a single-minded focus. He planted wide hands on my ass to guide the movement, and I arched against his cock with a desperate moan. I was all too happy to surrender.

An upbeat chime broke through the panting breaths and rustling of clothing. Although familiar, my brain didn't process it immediately. DemiDate. Callum's phone had just alerted him to a match on DemiDate. Because he needed to find a serious partner. Get married. Save his family business.

All I could do was derail his future.

Despite the greedy protest of my body—of my heart—I paused. Callum's kiss-swollen mouth broke away from mine.

"Lark?"

"I can't do this, Callum."

My leg wobbled as I swung it back over his lap and connected with the tile floor of the kitchen.

He reached out, enclosing me, but I pulled away. Devastation flashed across his face. But he didn't force it. We both knew why this was a bad idea, and it wasn't only the preservation of our friendship.

"Lark, wait—" Callum grabbed his phone from the kitchen table and silenced it, but the chipper tones of the alert had already served as a stark reminder of reality.

It would be wrong to take him by the hand, drag him out of the kitchen to his bedroom, and unwrap him like a gift. Callum was a Christmas present addressed to someone else. He wasn't *for me*, but I wanted to play with whatever was under the shiny paper. Worse . . . I wanted to keep him for myself.

Once the connection between my brain and my mouth was reestablished, I mumbled, "I'll call you in two hours. To check in. Like the nurse said."

CHAPTER 23

Lark

THE REASONS *NOT* to kiss Callum could fill a movie credits scroll.

We'd just talked about him starting a family, feeling optimistic about meeting the right one, and then he kissed me. *He* kissed *me.* With a kiss that had no right to be that hot. Neither of us had been thinking straight. At least he could blame his lapse of judgment on light brain trauma. I had no excuse.

I scurried back to my apartment under fickle clouds in the Irish sky. How quickly things change. Just an hour ago, it had been sunny. Just an hour ago, my neighbor and I had been only friends.

Yeah, right.

I'd been developing feelings for Callum for months, like a Polaroid photo slowly coming into focus. Before I knew it, I was looking at a vivid portrait of a kind, sensitive, witty man. And being drawn to him, far beyond the physical.

Relieved to finally shed the fabulously sequined spandex monstrosity, I changed into regular lounging clothes, then fed Houdini and responded to work emails that could've waited until the morning. Anything to distract from the way Callum so tenderly traced the curve of my neck. The way his throat rumbled when our tongues slid together. Even the blast of icy water from the shower did little to subdue the desire to march next door and have my way with him on his kitchen table. Then, again, in *his* shower.

When I rang Callum at ten to check in on him, he didn't answer. I tried once more, but the call went to voicemail. Maybe he was fixing himself a cup of tea. Or sleeping. I forced myself to scroll on my phone for three minutes, resolving not to panic. Just because he wasn't answering didn't mean he'd succumbed to his head injury; he'd been well enough to make out with me earlier.

By the third unsuccessful attempt, I'd already slipped on my (well, mine *now*) hoodie and tennis shoes. I had to be sure.

Hood raised to protect from the sudden, bitter rain, I jogged down the sidewalk between our properties. Rain poured from the spouts, occasional bursts of lightning threading through the moody sky. My chilled fists stung as I banged on the stained glass door. "Callum! Cal!"

Another heavy set of knocks, so hard the entire landing shook with each blow. No response. Was it me who was shaking? I dodged puddles on the path through the gate into the garden.

Rain pelted the rosebushes, the willows, and a garden bench. Ivy blanketed the back of the house, framing one narrow window inches above my head. Bingo. With a grunt, I dragged the small iron bench through the muck to reach the window. Locked. I found a large stone and hurled it at the glass. It shattered, but I'd worry about that later. Callum could be in danger. To protect against the broken edges, I slipped my hand into the oversize hoodie sleeve as I undid the latch. The window rose with an ugly screech.

Grateful for my petite size, I squeezed through, feet first, dropping into the dark room with a wet squelch. Glass shards crunched underfoot. Hands extended, I felt around, soon realizing I was higher than the floor. I hopped down cautiously. A pungent chemical aroma filled my nose. Something cold. Something metal. Chills ran through me.

Fumbling for my phone and its flashlight, I yelled, "Cal—"

My voice shriveled into a tiny squeak. Light gleamed off an industrial wheeled cart and stainless-steel table. This was the embalming room.

Instinctively, I backed away. Hard metal pressed into my shoulder blades. When I realized it was the handle on the mortuary cooler, I jumped. Heart pounding, I scrambled to the door, swinging the arc of the flashlight wide and knocked into a cart. Sharp instruments and weird rubber thingamabobs clanked to the tile.

Sudden pain filled my senses as something struck my head.

Harsh fluorescent light flooded the space. Warning alarms and air-raid sirens bellowed in my mind at the sight of Callum in the doorway. Scowling and shirtless, chest heaving, clutching a hurling stick. Was a person allowed to be turned on in an embalming room? Because I was. Not that I wanted him to ravage me on the stainless steel prep table or anything; I'm not a *complete* deviant.

Callum winced and dropped the stick onto the tile with a thud. He lowered himself to one knee to help me up. "Lark? Are you okay? I'm sorry!"

"Son of a . . ."

"Just what are you up to?"

"Ow." I rubbed my head. Furious that he'd scared me so badly, I snatched the stick and whacked his arm with it.

"Hey! I thought you were a kid, sneaking in for the craic."

An easy mistake when I wore his dark hoodie, pulled up. I could pass for a middle schooler looking for a bit of trouble to impress their friends. That explained why he didn't strike with much force, though it still hurt like a mother. He was strong enough to deal *real* damage, had he been trying to harm the intruder.

"I thought"—I whacked his right shoulder—"*you'd* slipped"—

another whack—"into a coma!" It's what he deserved for ignoring me. "For the last fifteen minutes, I've been calling and banging on the door. Why didn't you answer?"

He yanked the hurling stick from my grip and set it on the counter, then gave me an apologetic squeeze. I wanted to stay annoyed, but I was too awash with relief. I just clung to him. Smelled the shampoo I'd massaged into his raven-dark hair a little while ago. Sent up a prayer of thanks and a plea for strength . . . or at least divine mercy.

"My granda always said I slept harder than the corpses. Guess my mobile was on silent." His tone sobered at the reminder of what had snapped us back to reality: the tinkling DemiDate alert. "Sorry to make you fret. And for hitting you."

"Now don't try to beat me with that goofy hockey stick again—"

"You're the one beating *me!*"

"But I did sort of break your window."

"I heard." He offered a cautious, forgiving smile. "My, um, my bedroom is right overhead."

His bedroom. *Don't even think about it.*

I tore my attention from his sinewy frame. Plain cabinets hung over the workspace, and a weird machine sat next to an array of colorful bottles that looked like paint mediums. Toiletries were arranged on a counter, regular brands of shaving cream, shampoos, and perfumes. Photos of an elderly woman were tacked to a bulletin board, no doubt as references for hair and makeup styling. Was that the drawing I'd made at This Tastes Funny, of a little Callum holding a skull-shaped balloon? My sentimental heart swelled. Not only had he saved it, but it was prominently displayed in his workspace.

"You kept my doodle?" How could I not want to kiss him again?

Stifling a guilty grin, Callum lifted a hand. "How many fingers am I holding up?"

"Six?"

His smile collapsed at my ill-timed stab at humor.

"Three. You're holding three. I'm okay," I said. "Were we at the hospital for so long this afternoon that you developed a crush on a nurse and need an excuse to return?"

Concern still creased Callum's forehead, but he smiled wanly. "Giving me shite even after I thumped you. Suppose you're not too hurt."

"Did you think it went *Return of the Living Dead* in here? Just for a second? Be honest."

"That wasn't a documentary. Wash your hands. You touched the prep table."

Horrified, I glanced down at my hands, and he pointed to a sink. Wisps of steam rose from the near-boiling water as I scrubbed, not wanting to think about what the surface had seen. I motioned to the open doorway. "Can we talk literally anywhere else? This place gives me the creeps."

He gathered what I now identified as a makeup airbrush kit off the floor. Between his sudden appearance and my throbbing skull, I'd forgotten it was still there. A reminder he was an artist in his own right.

"Is the airbrush broken?"

"No. I'm more concerned about pests coming in." He grabbed a file folder and held it up to the jagged, fist-size hole in the window. After digging in a cabinet, he retrieved a familiar silver roll.

"Is that what I think it is?"

"I've many uses for duct tape," he said with a roguish smile. Then he tore off a strip and patched the glass.

"I'm afraid to ask."

CHAPTER 24

Callum

WE SAT ON my sofa side by side, each clutching ice packs to our heads. Lark's on the top of her scalp, mine on the back. Because my eyes were still sensitive, I hadn't turned on the lights, but a faint glow from the streetlamp filtered in through the rain-battered window. Just enough to make out her profile.

Were we just going to avoid talking about it? Was our kiss nothing more than a diffusion of the tension and stress of the day?

After Lark fled my kitchen, I'd dozed off, thanks only to the painkillers. Sleep arrived in a swirl of confusion and sexual fantasy. Clearly, she regretted our kiss. I should apologize again for initiating it, but the way she'd arched against me . . . I had a hard time believing she didn't want me.

"I still need to check on you. You're not supposed to let a person with a concussion sleep," Lark said.

"Actually, that's a myth—"

"How's the head?"

The head on my shoulders wasn't where my mind went. A moment later, the innuendo dawned on her. Lark turned away, tucking a strand of loose hair behind her ear. The air between us grew stale. Emotional whiplash was more disorienting than the concussion.

"Feels like a jackhammer in there."

Jackhammer? What in the pornography was I talking about?

Without warning, Lark turned on the light attached to her mobile and obliterated my retinas.

"My head's already b-banjaxed! Is it necessary to blind me, too?"

"Quit being so ornery. Hold still. I refuse to let you slip into a coma on my watch."

"I'm *fine.*"

At the hospital, Lark had asked many worst-case scenario questions. The nurse assured her concussions were most dangerous for those who hadn't sought medical care to rule out greater injury. After my CT, I'd been more or less cleared. They told me to expect a bumpy recovery and sent me home in Lark's care. A duty she took seriously. As a result, my pupils were now scorched as charcoal briquettes.

Satisfied, she turned off the light, and the living room plummeted back into darkness. Phantom spots danced in my field of vision, and I wished I could see more than her silhouette. Wished I knew what to say. Other than her jumpiness in the embalming room and seeing me hurt, she was usually fearless.

"I almost feel like I should spend the night," she said.

My head still pounded, all thoughts reduced to a lustful slurry. I'd been starved for caresses and soft, warm skin. For the steady tide of another's breathing against my chest. I'd been with only two partners before. A girl in my speech therapy who I dated for a year when I was sixteen, and Aoife, a classmate at mortuary college. After three years of patience, she'd admitted that she just wasn't willing to move in together, after what her ex put her through. I hadn't sought out anyone new in the six years since—until I was forced to—but I had missed intimacy with someone I cared about. I wanted Lark to stay the night. To stay forever. I wanted more. Strings very much included. Tangled, woven, knotted strings.

"Perhaps you should, since now we both have head injuries. If you're okay with b-bodies in the house."

I felt her shiver beside me. Once, she admitted she didn't even like haunted houses on Halloween.

"*Plural?* How can you even sleep in here?"

"Easy. None of them have ever shined a torch in my face."

"I should've left you with Nurse Ratched."

The single upside to the ice pack was its ability to distract me from developing a throbbing erection. Enough blood diverted to my also-swollen brain that I could still function. Barely. I mentally recited the anatomy of the lowest extremity to distract myself from the memory of her tongue skimming mine.

Tibialis posterior. Abductor hallucis. Flexor digitorum brevis.

"Cal?" Lark's voice was tinged with faint alarm. "You stopped breathing."

Entirely possible. I forced myself to yawn. Yawning would be a normal response. More normal than hypoxia.

She propped herself up on an elbow and reached for her mobile on the end table. I grabbed her wrist. Fortified by the dark and my earlier flirtation with brain damage, I brushed my thumb over the velvet skin. Lark's pulse thumped wildly.

"Aim that torch my way and you'll get the hurley again."

"Are you threatening to paddle me?" she asked, a smile in her voice.

Gluteus maximus, my brain unhelpfully supplied. *Gluteus minimus. Piriformis.*

My fingers and my pajama bottoms tightened. My body was making up for lost time, the libido I lacked for years rushing in like a flash flood and threatening the annihilation of our friendship.

"Yes."

"Surly as ever. I think that's a sign of health," she murmured, mocking my earlier statement.

"Lark . . . Thank you for taking care of me." I let the whisper of gratitude settle over us like a blanket. Rain pattered against the windows.

"You take care of me. More than you know."

My heart bloomed. If only my penis would deflate, but it was an obstinate fecker. "I liked kissing you. I've wanted to do that for a while."

Lark shifted her weight, giving me a long, incomprehensible look before ghosting her ice-chilled fingers over my cheek. Without daring to close my eyes, I sucked in a breath at the delicate swipe over my bottom lip. Adrenaline coursed through my veins. I was delirious. Lightheaded.

Then her fingers fell away.

"And I liked kissing you, too. Enjoyment wasn't the problem."

"I know."

She played with the tea towel wrapped around her ice pack. "I'll check on you in the morning before I leave for work, okay?"

Everywhere Lark touched me, my nerves burned with a neon afterglow. I wanted to kiss her again. Keep kissing. Grind against her until she panted and begged. I wanted to take my time. The problem was, I was running out of time. We both knew it.

CHAPTER 25

Lark

CALLUM ANSWERED THE door in those sinister gray joggers the next morning. Because the gods had decided that my self-control would not go unchallenged. Although rumpled, he looked good for someone with little sleep and a head injury. I couldn't help but imagine him looking like that as he rolled over in bed beside me.

"Mornin'. How are you feeling?"

"I'll survive," he said. "Come upstairs. I'll put the kettle on."

Bad idea. Deep groans and raspy stubble replayed in my memory, the protective curl of muscular arms holding me tight. I wanted him. Desperately. That couldn't happen—not with his future at stake.

"I really have to get going."

"Just a moment. I have a spare key for you."

I worried my lip between my teeth. Callum zeroed in on it, then diverted his attention. "What, you don't want me smashing any more windows?"

He let out a dry chuckle and led me upstairs. Callum lifted a brass key off a nail in his kitchen. The same kitchen I'd practically given him a lap dance in. He pressed the cool metal into my palm. Weeks ago, I'd given him a spare key to my place after I'd accidentally left mine on my desk at work. Not driving meant I didn't notice until I went to fish them out of my bag on my doorstep.

"I don't want this to change anything b-b—anything between us. We're still friends, right?

Worry creased his forehead. I ran my thumb over the key's edge to refrain from reaching up to wipe the wrinkle away. "Of course we are, Cal."

The way he focused on the floor suggested he was more saddened than reassured by my answer. "It's still raining. Let me give you a lift to work."

"I'm a big girl, and I came prepared." I held up my pink umbrella, complete with a wooden handle shaped like a flamingo's head. "You need rest. Doctor's orders."

"No rest for the wicked."

"Wicked? You're as wicked as a puffin," I said. "But I have to head out now."

Best to leave before I called into work and dragged Callum to his room for some "bed rest." I bolted downstairs before my self-restraint gave out.

The front door creaked open, and Deirdre entered. He hadn't warned me about the possibility of crossing paths during my pseudo walk of shame. All the embarrassment, little of the pleasure.

"Good morning!" she said, looking startled. "What are you doing here?"

Fighting a losing battle with my libido.

I clutched the banister when Saoirse entered. What was *she* doing here? It was early for a delivery, but she lugged in an impressive arrangement of sunflowers.

"Cal hit his head yesterday," I answered Dierdre. "I came to check on him. He's, um, upstairs."

"Oh, dear."

"He'll be fine, but the doctor wanted him to rest for a couple of days."

Maybe after a few days, he and I could go back to normal.

Oh, who was I kidding? Even if he forgot and moved on, I couldn't. Our kiss had been infused with fervent need; it made me feel both cherished and ravenous for more.

"That won't happen. The man's a workaholic," Deirdre said, keys swinging from her pinkie.

I needed to change the subject.

"Hey! Those are beautiful." I motioned to the vibrant blooms Saoirse carried. "Hydrangeas, right?"

She smiled at the inside joke about the wrong flower.

"I've always loved sunflowers. They're my favorite. So happy." What else was I supposed to say? Of course I rambled on about the arrangement.

"A pleasure to see you, though I'm sorry to hear Callum's hurt. I'll just grab the rest of the delivery," she said, making herself scarce.

Deirdre leaned closer. "She comes around twice as often as the last florist, always finding reasons to pop in."

My lungs tightened.

"He's had his eye on that one forever, but he was always too professional to flirt at work. Callum's certainly come out of his shell lately."

Glad I could help. As I kicked myself, the man himself came downstairs. Pulled together in a dark suit, ready for a typical workday. Stubborn, sexy bastard. Saoirse reentered, pushing a cart overloaded with massive blooms. My heart turned leaden as I watched a reserved smile form on Callum's lips as he assisted, and they shuffled into the parlor. Just out of earshot.

Saoirse had already experienced their softness. Now, so had I. My masochistic heart ached for more than a one-time indulgence. I'd always been a dreamer, but it was delusional to entertain that desire.

"Tell ye the truth, when you first moved in next door, I thought the two of you might . . ." Deirdre made a vague gesture, keeping her voice low. "But Callum informed me 'Nope, not happening.' Can't blame me for being a romantic! But it's grand that he has a friend. He can't always come to me for women troubles, can he?"

"If any women trouble him, they'll contend with me." Protectiveness flared in me like a bottle rocket.

"I don't think you'll need to defend his honor anytime soon. She's a good one. I knew they'd hit it off, if they only had a chance."

Of course. Together, the two made their way to the reception desk, and Callum winced as Deirdre flipped a lamp switch.

"The light bothers you?" Saoirse angled the shade away. "I'll bring dinner tonight so you don't have to cook. I'm making cottage pie, and there's always too much for one person."

What? I should be the one taking care of him. Though I wasn't even sure what a cottage pie entailed.

"How sweet!" Deirdre said. "His favorite."

Are you freaking kidding me?

"Thank you." Callum coughed with a pained expression.

"I saw an article in the *Independent* about *Pirate Queen* the other day. People are really looking forward to it. I know I am." Dark eyes fixed on me without a hint of malice. Saoirse's friendliness was genuine, which almost made it worse.

"Glad to hear that. Actually, I've gotta run so I'm not late to work."

No sign of the passion we shared hours ago showed on Callum's face. Two sets of eyes studied us, but he couldn't bring himself to meet mine. We were on the same awkward page: giving in to the pull between us was a mistake.

"I appreciate you checking on me, Lark."

"What are friends for?" The sentiment scraped against my throat like sandpaper.

"LO, I MESSED up." Defeated, I slumped back on the love seat and held my phone to my ear. "I kissed Callum last night."

"At last!" She heaved a dramatic sigh. "Thought you'd combust from the sexual frustration. Rewind. Start at the beginning. Leave nothing out."

After a recap of the near kiss during skating, my panic over the concussion, and washing his hair, I told Cielo about climbing through the window only to land on an embalming table. Cuddling on the couch. I told her about the spontaneous peck that led to Callum drawing me in for a sublime, electric kiss.

"I can't stop thinking about the way he touched me. But I'd hate to ruin our dynamic by making it physical." Maybe I'd already damaged our friendship irrevocably.

Callum's dick between my legs was torture. A tease of what I couldn't have.

"You deserve a little graveyard smash."

"I *can't.*"

"Your vow to Reese wasn't 'I'll never look at another guy if the unimaginable happens,'" Cielo said.

No, but I did make a promise that I wouldn't allow myself to enter another relationship.

"Are you gonna limit yourself to flicking it to *Bridgerton* forever?"

Unbidden images of Callum in leather riding breeches, loosening a cravat around his throat with a promising glint in his eyes flooded my mind. Having a vivid imagination ain't all it's cracked up to be.

"Don't mock my Regency kink. It's gotten me through hard times," I warned. "Thanks to the inheritance situation, Cal needs someone who could one day be his wife. How can he emotionally invest in someone new if we're hooking up?"

"You're not the only one capable of compartmentalizing,"

Cielo said. "Friends-with-benefits arrangements aren't complicated if you lay down ground rules. Make sure he knows you want him to keep dating. I doubt he'd find the proposal unsuitable. All the perks, none of the romantic expectations."

Tempted, I chewed a hangnail. From what I'd learned online, it wasn't unheard of for some demisexual people to have casual sex. Callum himself assured me love wasn't necessary for him to feel turned on. Just connection. I didn't want to toy with his heart, but I did want to *play*—though I couldn't in good conscience distract from his marital goal. His entire future hinged on it.

"Look," Lo said. "He initiated a kiss you described as 'panty melting.' He knows your stay is limited, so he's not expecting commitment. Give the man some credit—he's telling you exactly what he wants. Sleep with him. Get some, and get it out of your system."

Maybe we could just bang out our mutual sexual frustration once and things would go back to normal. Clear boundaries could be set between consenting adults. Callum had a goal. I had my perma-single rule. No reason to expect more than one hot no-strings tumble. Well, hot was an understatement . . . this was at playing-with-matches-while-doused-in-gasoline temperatures.

I finally understood the appeal of arson.

"Maybe just once." I smiled. "Get it out of our systems."

CHAPTER 26

Callum

"DO YOU THINK it worked?" Saoirse shoved a Tupperware container at my chest and stepped through the doorway.

"What are you on about?"

"This," she said, waving a hand at the dish and then herself, "was deliberate."

"Cottage pie?"

"I brought dinner to make Lark jealous, amadán." *Fool.* That sounded about right. Saoirse shook her head. Glossy lipstick accentuated her mouth, and a snug dress revealed most of her legs. A far cry from the demure professional attire she'd worn this morning.

"What? Why?"

"Because you've been circling each other so long, *I'm* dizzy. Sometimes jealousy spurs people to act."

"Lark . . . isn't an option, remember?" My head throbbed. I was still knackered and didn't want to discuss this.

"What happened between you?"

"Nothing!"

What was I supposed to say, that we'd dry humped in front of my kitchen sink? *Ha.*

Hand on her hip, she stared me down. "Liar."

"I kissed her. I kissed her, and she left. She couldn't leave fast enough."

"When?"

"When what?"

"When did you kiss her?" Saoirse enunciated each word in exasperation. "Your head really did take a beating, didn't it?"

"Last night."

"And yet she's back in your house first thing in the morning."

"She only came to check on me b-b-because of this concussion."

"Is it really your injury, or are you this dense? Lark cares about you. I bet she kissed you back."

She did more than that. I could still feel her breath on my neck as she moaned. Still feel her firm ass in my palms. Still taste the faint salt of her skin.

"I—"

Saoirse held up a hand. "Callum, you don't have to answer. It's all over your face. And I could see it written on hers."

She could?

I didn't have time to waste in finding someone. A warp-speed engagement wasn't my idea of romance, and every day a whirlwind relationship seemed less likely. At this rate, Willow Haven would surely end up in my father's hands, and then O'Reilly's.

I wanted to ask Lark, but even if she agreed to marry me to meet the requirements of the inheritance—unlikely at best—I would want more than a marriage of convenience. I wanted the real thing. Real for both of us. No favors.

Unless Deirdre had mentioned it to her, Saoirse was unaware of my predicament, but I had told her about Lark and the fundamental incompatibility that concerned me: for all her warmth and affection, she didn't want kids. Much less a ring on her finger. She'd been explicit about it.

I had to find someone else, and quickly. Less than four short months until my birthday at the end of July. Four weeks until I'd have to apply for a marriage license. The thought nauseated me more with each passing hour, not that I was down to counting those yet.

"One day she's going to leave and you'll realize you've done nothing to make her stay," Saoirse said. The truth of it landed like a harpoon to my chest. The confusion that had flashed across Lark's face as she scrambled off my lap. She'd run away without looking back. And she'd probably do it again when her film finished in the summer.

Resigned, I crossed my arms. "You're right. One day soon, she *will* leave."

I was terrified she'd take my heart with her.

CHAPTER 27

Lark

ANVI LOOKED UP from the closing credits storyboard. Half the staff had already filtered out of the open-plan office space, eager for the weekend to start. "Pints at the Hare's Breath after work?"

"Nah, not this time." I didn't want to go without Callum, and I wouldn't drag him to a noisy pub if his headaches hadn't improved. I just . . . wanted to be alone with him. And, to be honest, I wanted to see if he'd be amenable to a Friends 2.0 situation. It wasn't a conversation to be had in public.

"Uh-oh. Incoming." Anvi jerked her chin to the side. Honestly, the scent of sulfur should've preceded Seán to give folks fair warning. She fled toward the bathroom, and I didn't blame her.

"Hey, Seán. I wanted to ask if you'd like a long shift."

His brow quirked. "Would I?"

"Or if you're available to come in on a Saturday for a few hours. We have to get this done, and your part is behind schedule."

"So, Lark, what I'm hearing is you're trying to give me an extra shift," he exclaimed, casting an amused glance around the room like he'd told a joke. "Or a long shift?"

Styluses paused mid stroke as our coworkers took in the spectacle. Rory watched me with a conflicted expression, gnawing their lip like they wanted to say something.

Seán stepped closer, a challenge in his eye as he invaded my space. "Which would you prefer from me? A long one after a hard day's work or a little one on a Saturday night?"

Discomfort prickled in my gut. "Either. If you don't want to take the extra hours, I'll have to offer them to someone else."

"Giving shifts away to anyone, then?" He smirked, and a red-faced Hannah scowled at him. "Sounds desperate."

"Leave her alone." Rory's voice was hesitant but clear.

I tipped my head to them in gratitude. Seán intimidated most of the crew into unwitting silence when it came to his bad behavior. Rory's and Anvi's courage and camaraderie strengthened me.

"Yes, desperate to complete this film without asking the producers for an extension. I've never needed one before, and I won't start now." My eyes narrowed on him, even as my own voice wavered. "Is that a yes?"

"An extension won't be necessary. I'll get it done."

Bizarre. As Seán stalked away, Rory shook their head and motioned me over, but a call from Mr. Sullivan redirected me to my office. After I'd updated him on the progress made this week, my phone buzzed.

My heart skipped at the sight of Callum. Earlier, I'd asked him how he was feeling, and now he'd replied with a photo of himself in the coffin showroom giving a deadpan thumbs-up. Anticipation surged through my bloodstream as I thought about suggesting we take care of the tension between us, once and for all. About unfastening his stuffy waistcoat button by button while ragged breaths sawed from his chest. About large, capable hands molding to my body. About the desperation in his arsenic eyes when he ground against me.

We needed this.

One night. One night was all, then we could leave this tension behind. But how do you ask your best friend to sleep with you?

CHAPTER 28

Callum

"MAKE YOURSELF COMFY." Lark waved me inside her flat. "Mi casa es su casa."

Chessboard in a box under an arm, I shuffled through the door. She'd wasted no time changing out of her business-casual wardrobe, already in a rainbow camisole and a matching pair of tiny seventies-inspired athletic shorts that hugged her thighs. Within the past two days, the sensation of them wrapped around me had replayed countless times in my mind. Reluctantly, I tore my eyes away.

Two grease-stained bags of Supermac's rested on her steamer trunk coffee table. I'd been so busy with work, I hadn't eaten lunch. The doctor had ordered four full days of rest after the concussion. Of course I'd worked the past two days, despite Lark's and Deirdre's objections. If I wasn't trying to scrape together the funds to buy Willow Haven from Pádraig, I'd have hired some help a while ago.

"I was suffering from a bad case of Whataburger withdrawal," Lark explained around a mouthful of curry-doused fries. "Even though their patties are superior, and I miss the little jalapeño on the side, I have to admit you Irish know your way around a potato."

We shared our meal in relative silence. I noticed Lark didn't ask about yesterday's cottage pie, nor a certain florist. Her gaze kept bouncing back to me, curious, a little uncomfortable but . . . unmistakably hungry. It gave me hope that the kiss replayed in her memory, too. Our typical movie night wasn't an option thanks to the doctor's orders to avoid TV and phone screens for a few days, so after ice cream, we set up the chessboard. True to form, I preferred to play as black.

"Today Seán made fun of me," she said quietly after a couple of moves. "I can't always tell what he means, but I know it's downright rude."

The bloody bellend. My fingers tightened around a pawn. "What happened?"

"Well, I asked if he'd take a longer shift. Or a small shift on the weekend. He needs to step up. But I didn't understand why it made him laugh. So weird. He said I was giving long shifts away to anyone, calling me desperate."

"*Shifting* is slang for 'kissing.'"

"*What?* Ugh."

"Report him," I said, forcing my voice to remain gentle. My anger was directed solely at him, not her. "Seán is a jealous, petty little child."

"He made me sound clueless in front of the team. And I can't even say anything since he's the owner's nephew."

"You're far from clueless. You're hardworking and courageous, and you're his superior. Don't let him forget it."

"I'm paranoid that one day someone is going to say something really gross. Er, manky," Lark corrected. "I'd like to know if I'm the butt of another of Seán's mean jokes or being propositioned at the pub."

"I'll happily knock a man's teeth out for you, if that happens."

The very idea of her being openly mocked made me want to

take my old hurley stick to her coworker's thick skull. Violent instincts aside, Lark needed to hold her own at work or that arsehole would never leave her alone. Maybe I could help arm her with enough knowledge to defend herself next time.

"Would you like some lessons in Irish slang?"

"Would you mind? Back home, we have an expression: *bless your heart.* Taken at face value, it's sweet. In reality, it's often a thinly veiled 'you're a dumbass' or even a 'screw you.' I need to know those, especially."

I smiled as I confiscated another pawn. "God love you. As in: 'God love you, look at the size of you' to a pregnant woman. It's supposed to take the sting out of an insult, but it's ineffective."

We discussed idioms and passive-aggressiveness, until the discussion strayed into other slang terms.

"Talk Irish to me," Lark drawled in an exaggerated accent worthy of a bouffant-haired Texan debutante. Her fingertip fondled the domed top of her bishop just long enough to be suggestive. "Give me some of the more creative ways your people say . . . well, you know, sexual things. For the sake of cultural competence. You won't offend me, I promise."

Feck, this was painful. Now she wanted to discuss sex? Silently, I advanced my knight to corner her rook.

"Never mind. We don't have to—"

"Taking a swim in the mossy b-bog. That's for . . ." I wiped my mouth with the back of my hand sheepishly. She squinted, not understanding. Chess was my game, not charades. "For pleasuring a woman. Orally," I clarified.

Her eyes widened. I imagined what she'd taste like, what she'd look like immediately after I kneeled between her thighs. Lips parted, hair disheveled, eyes hooded.

"Or growling at the b-b-badger, but that's more Scottish."

"Oh my God!" Laughter bubbled out of her, and she clapped in delight. "They are both wonderful and traumatizing."

I plucked up her rook, and it joined the congregation of

pawns on my end of the checkerboard. "What's a euphemism one might say in Texas?"

"I don't know . . . Knocking boots? But that's for the act itself."

"Cute."

Lark's queen crossed the board toward my king. A moment of charged, silent eye contact passed, her sweet smile giving way to something more intense. She carefully asked, "How would you say that seriously? To go down on a woman? In your language?"

My cock twitched. This tangent was a horrible idea if we were really going to keep things platonic. She always liked to take risks. Had she changed her mind since fleeing from my kitchen?

"Gnéas béil." My voice grew gravelly with want.

"I like that version much better. Say it again?"

I repeated it, staring straight into Lark's face as she shivered at the sound. What else could make her shiver and writhe? My mouth, my hands . . .

Pink bathed her cheeks. "Speaking of tongue, how is yours healing?"

"Still tender." A nasty semicircle still marked where I bit myself during the fall. I stuck it out slowly, without taking my eyes off her. She leaned forward to examine it and the low neckline of her camisole put her cleavage on display. I tried not to imagine tasting the lingering vanilla ice cream on her own tongue.

"Ouch," she said, snapping me out of my thoughts. "Um, whose turn is it?"

"Mine. Sorry."

Absently, I utilized my rook in defense of the king. I was losing, and terribly. Blame my incredibly distracting, scantily clad opponent. She deposited my rook among the rest of the casualties. All in black, they looked like mourners in a procession.

"For educational purposes . . ." Lark tucked a lock of blond hair behind her ear. "How do you say *sex*? Like, conversationally, not clinically."

With great effort, I swallowed. "Ag bualadh craicinn."

"That's a mouthful. How does it translate?"

I smiled shyly. "Slapping skin."

"And how would you say *dick*?"

"B-Bod."

Obscene thoughts drifted through my mind. Did she ever think of me, late at night? I'd thought about her. My thoughts always returned to her.

"You live to fluster me," I said. Not quite an admonishment, it was more an acknowledgment of a truth that had always been there between us. At once, Lark was foreign and familiar. Comfort and challenge. A beautiful contradiction.

"Only because it distracts you from the game." She snatched my queen.

I blew out a puff of air and shook my head. "Cheating little shite."

She wiggled her hips playfully at the teasing accusation and pointed toward her seated butt. Her brow arched as she silently sought a translation. That blush glowing on her cheeks was stunning in the early-evening light.

I smiled and looked away, but my eyes couldn't stay off her for long. "Tóin. That's, um, rear end. Not vulgar."

Frenzied electrons crackled in the air between us. She grazed her palms over her chest, hard nipples straining through the thin camisole and bra.

"B-b-brollach," I hissed, telling her how to say breasts. "Tá tú go hálainn . . . you're lovely."

"How would I say . . ." Lark trailed off, invitingly parting her legs. Blue-gray eyes burned into mine, filled with an unspoken dare.

"Um, it's faighin." God, I really was flustered as I stared at her crotch in those criminally tiny shorts. "Or púrsa te if she's . . . áilíosach. Turned on."

And I could tell she was. Lark might've been the seductress, but she wasn't the only one with power in this situation. *She* wanted *me*.

This was happening, smart idea or not. Anxiety ran like an undercurrent to my anticipation. Could I even satisfy her? It had been a while since my relationship with Aoife. Long enough for me to forget whatever skills I'd once enjoyed—but I'd certainly try my best for Lark.

"How do you say *touch yourself*?" Half request, half confession. Pure provocation. Shifting back in her seat, she brushed her fingers back and forth on her bare upper thigh.

"Féintruailligh," I growled, my trousers tented and straining. I leaned into it. The indecent-Irish lessons. The intoxicating tone of Lark's voice. Her left hand strayed between her thighs and skimmed her most sensitive spot for the briefest instant. I *felt* her breath hitch, and I stopped taking in oxygen altogether. Lark's sinful expression brought my entire body roaring to life with furious desire. For the sake of something to do with my hands, I maneuvered my knight without so much as a glance at the board.

"Please?" Was it a translation request or a desperate plea for clemency?

"Le do thoil," I translated, little more than a ragged breath. Literally, "with your will." It sounded more like begging when I said it.

"My turn." Smirking, she withdrew the restless hand from her thigh, wrapping it around my king with teasing slowness to savor the victory. Lark could claim anything; I was hers for the taking. "How do I say *checkmate*?"

I planted both palms on the steamer trunk to lean across the chessboard. "I'd rather teach you something more practical."

"*Sore loser?*"

"Tabhair póg dom." My tongue darted out to moisten my lips and her eyes followed the motion. I couldn't help but grin. "Means 'kiss me.'"

Yielding to the tension, we connected in a fiery smash of mouths over the board, knocking over the pieces. Any logical argument for why we shouldn't do this simply evaporated. The blunt edges of her short, painted fingernails grazed my stubbled jaw, every nerve firing with the bristling sensation. She smelled delectable. I wanted to draw her into my lungs. Inhale her. Consume her.

Lark rose from the floor in front of the steamer trunk and stood in front of me. While I was still sitting, our height difference wasn't so prominent. Not that I minded. She situated herself between my knees, fingers interlaced at my tender nape, just under the stitches. Life was too cruel and unpredictable to live timidly. Too short to live wishing you had gone for it. Deep down, I'd always known that, but she gave me the courage to finally act.

We both huffed out awkward laughs when our eyes met. Partial relief, partial disbelief. A pause settled between us. An opportunity to think this through before we permanently altered our relationship. A shadow briefly passed across Lark's face. Brows pinched, hands still. She was having second thoughts.

I pulled back. "Only if you're sure, love."

In response, Lark whipped off her camisole. Petite breasts were cradled in a lacy pink bra. *Fuck me.* "I'm sure. We'll do it once, and get it out of our systems. We can still be friends. Lots of people do this."

Friends. She'd never asked me how to say "I love you." And why would she? Lark didn't want a relationship. As far as she was concerned, the phrase was irrelevant to this moment—but not to me. I'd never get her out of my system, but I'd take what she was willing to offer.

An expanse of bare skin and lace beckoned for my attention, and I allowed myself to savor that gorgeous sight for a moment before I removed my glasses. What really did me in was her expression, at once vulnerable and erotic.

"I am a little nervous," she admitted softly. "The last time I was with someone, I was married to him."

"Not that it's a competition, but I think it's been longer for me. Six years or so." I shrugged self-deprecatingly.

"Let's not overthink it," Lark said. "We can have fun, release the tension. Embrace spontaneity."

I laid a soft kiss on her lips. Lord, it felt good to finally have permission to do that. "There has been a little tension, hasn't there?"

Her answering smile was a vision. Just like the rest of her. My trembling hands smoothed over her soft stomach, her hips, the sides of her ribs. Pliant under my wide palms, she practically melted.

"How do I say that I want you?" Lark whispered.

I struggled to verbalize, chest rising for two breaths until I managed, "Santaíonn mé thú."

CHAPTER 29

Callum

LARK LED ME to her bedroom by my hand, then placed my hand on her breast. *Shite.* This was really happening. Tremors shook my fingers as the soft, lace-covered palmful yielded to my squeeze. Dilated pupils nearly engulfed her eyes with a hunger that sent a shiver down my spine. With torturous slowness, she pushed me down on her bed and straddled me. I ground against her with increasing desperation. Breathless, she pulled back and tugged my shirt overhead, appreciatively caressing my chest and arms.

"Oh my God," I mumbled, thumbing her nipples. Lark pressed hard on my erection, sending her keening. I delighted in her responsiveness. Each tensing of muscle and resulting exhalation. Heady vanilla-citrus filled my nose, intoxicating as her sultry gaze.

She slid down my body and eased herself to her knees, pulled my zipper down, and tugged at my trousers. I lay there, heart thundering as she undressed me. Every cell in my body wanted her. And Lark wanted me. My cock sprang free from my boxer briefs.

"Who knew the reaper had such a pretty scythe?"

"What did you just call my penis?" Banter and corny jokes helped to remind me this was casual, not profound.

"I'm a tiny bit afraid you'll kill me with that thing."

My laugh gave way, and my eyelids drifted closed when Lark's palm wrapped around me. She increased the pace of her strokes, but I wouldn't last long if she kept that up. I flipped her onto her back, pressed her down against the mattress, my forearms caging her. Heated kisses traced her jaw and neck, my hours-old stubble surely chafing her sensitized flesh. I peeled one strap of her bra down, then another, kissing each shoulder.

Primal need shot through my bloodstream. It had been so long since I'd felt this way, and never with such intensity. Every place our bodies made contact practically sizzled.

"You're perfect." Lowering my head, I lavished attention on her sweet breasts, seizing a tightened bud between my teeth.

"Cal!"

I froze. Had I gone too far? She sank a hand into my hair. "I'm into it. You just surprised me. A little biting is okay."

Relief turned my mouth upward. I dragged it down her torso until I was kneeling on the floor at the foot of her bed, assuming a position of worship. Which was exactly what I planned to do. "Tell me if you want to stop."

"Touch me before I lose my mind."

Grasping her ankles, I tugged Lark down until her shapely calves hung over the bed's edge, flanking my ears.

"Féintruailligh," I countered, in the Irish I'd taught her a few minutes ago. "*Touch yourself.* Show me how you like it. Show me how to touch you. Show me everything."

I slid her shorts and dampened knickers over her legs and tossed them to the floor. Heat flared in Lark's eyes as I spread her knees and breathed in her scent. My mouth literally watered. She was more than ready. Stoking my desire, she obeyed my command, slim fingers massaging her wet pussy. She watched me observe her, biting her lip when she touched a particularly sweet spot. My focus oscillated between her face and her slick, nimble fingers. I'd imagined this, but real life beat fantasy.

Hungry and impatient, I brushed her hand aside. "My turn."

At the first slow, delicious lick, Lark whimpered and clamped her thighs around my ears. *Yes.* Fingers laced in my hair, she murmured my name as I pinned her legs open. I devoured her, alternating delving in with my tongue and pressing sucking kisses to her swollen clit. Pre-cum dribbled from my cock. *Not yet.* It nearly sent me over the top when a juicy burst hit my tongue. Wet sounds mingled with her cries as I quenched myself. As I drowned in her.

When I pulled away, she lifted heavy eyelids, legs still quivering. I made a performance out of licking my lips as I climbed over her. She should know she was delicious. I took Lark's mouth, wanting her to taste. She teased my cock, a slow glide across every ridge and vein. I groaned, half in agony, half in ecstasy.

After months of yearning, I had hit my breaking point. I'd never lied to Lark before, but I wasn't strictly honest when she'd asked how to say "I want you." *Santaíonn mé thú* also meant "I love you." When it came to Lark, want and love were one and the same. Whispering it to her in Irish made the confession safe.

Breathily, she said, "I just remembered: the French term for orgasm is *la petite mort.* How appropriate."

"That's *actually* what I named my dick. The Little Death," I joked between kisses. A realization hit like ice water. "Shite. Rubbers."

"I have some."

Reluctantly, Lark climbed off and retrieved the protection from her bathroom. Pert breasts bouncing, she sprinted back into bed and hopped on the mattress, wearing nothing but a filthy grin. I was one lucky bastard.

"Let me," she said. I watched as she licked the tip of my cock, engulfing the head between her kiss-swollen lips before rolling on the condom.

Please, please let me make this good for her.

With aching slowness, Lark mounted me and sank down. For a moment, we stilled, locked in mutual disbelief. She felt incredible. Staring into my eyes, she accepted every inch. When I filled her, she filled me with awe. Until there was no room for loneliness. Only Lark. Only us. Only this perfect moment.

"Keep talking to me," she begged as we found our rhythm. Nervous and overcome with sensation, I worried about my ability to speak. "How do I tell you this feels amazing?"

"Braitheann sin go d-deas."

Experimentally, she rolled her hips. We both cried out at the intensity.

"Níos moille," I whispered, peppering kisses across her beautiful tits. "Go slower."

Determined not to leave her behind, I snaked a thumb between us to strum her clit and she arched her back. *Holy shite.* Lightheaded, I relinquished myself to it, admiring Lark as she unraveled. I set a slow, sensual pace as she dug into my shoulders. Disheveled blond hair partially obscured her hooded eyes, but her gaze was terrifyingly reverent. Unfallen tears shone in her eyes.

I braced her hips to still her undulations. Had I accidentally hurt her? "Lark?"

"Cal . . . don't stop now. Please. I need you."

My heart nearly burst. She grabbed my wrists, pinning them on either side of my head. Greedy hands ran appreciatively down my forearms, then interlaced with my fingers. So intimate. I tried to hold eye contact, but she squeezed her eyes shut and rode me with renewed aggression. Right. This wasn't lovemaking, it was fucking.

At least, it was supposed to be.

"Give it to me," Lark demanded. "Faster."

Anything she wanted. Anything I could give. Easily breaking her grasp, I planted my hands on her ass. I thrust rougher up into her, until my rhythm became as choppy as our labored breath. Just like that, she was clenching, writhing, moaning. Vision and hearing faded out as touch dominated my senses. Salt buzzed on my tongue as my teeth grazed her skin. I hugged Lark close. Muttering a string of expletives, I dug my heels into the mattress and filled the rubber. I refused to loosen my grip even as our movements slowed and I softened inside her. Even as she captured my swollen lips for languid, sated kisses.

I never wanted Lark to climb off me; I never wanted to go back to being only friends.

CHAPTER 30

Lark

CALLUM PRESENTED A tray laden with plates of eggs, beans, soda bread, grilled tomato slices, and black pudding. Traditional Irish breakfasts: the lament of cardiologists, the friend of morticians. We'd fallen asleep entwined together, but he must've snuck out to grab the ingredients and tray from his own kitchen before I woke and come back to prepare it.

Cal wanted to take care of me. Just like I wanted to take care of him.

I sat up and pulled on a sweater. Nothing I'd experienced in the past two years had brought me peace like his embrace . . . but what would happen in the aftermath?

"Wow. Is this a ploy to impress me? Consider it successful."

"Figured we needed to eat, and I wasn't ready to let you out of b-b—out of bed, yet."

I wasn't ready for him to leave, either. Self-consciously, I attempted to rake my fingers through the blond tumbleweed atop my head.

Callum took up residence beside me, legs extended and crossed at his ankles. I regretted having only a single pillow and propped it between the headboard and his back, but he insisted I take it. Generous and patient, he would make an amazing husband. For someone. Someday soon, if all went according to plan. I couldn't keep my chin from quivering at the thought and turned so he wouldn't notice.

How would I switch off feelings for Cal after experiencing his tender kiss? How would I ever stop wanting him, after hearing him growl as ecstasy flooded his body?

He mopped up some beans with his toast. I got to initiate this conversation. Lucky me.

"Last night was . . ." *Profoundly satisfying on every emotional and physical level.* "A lot of fun."

Ugh. Did I just cheapen that life-changing spiritual experience by dubbing it *a lot of fun*, like some random hookup with a stranger? What was I supposed to say, that it brought me to tears? *No.* I wasn't ready for our bubble of contentment to burst. My reckless heart sank, knowing my feelings had already become helplessly involved.

"Very much so." Callum smiled wanly.

If I could, I'd engrave the shape of his lips onto my heart, so there would be no chance of ever forgetting their softness.

"We should probably, um, talk about it."

"Yes. That's kind of why I brought it up," I said.

"Okay."

"You go first."

My bedroom went silent, save the tines of my fork screeching against the plate as I skewered a grilled tomato.

We'd exchanged few words during our foreplay. Bodies and brains marinated in hormones don't always make sound decisions, but what was done was done. Acknowledging our potent connection was scarier than I'd imagined. The idea that it was merely platonic had been a protection for both of us. Now the illusion was shattered.

Was it a mistake to sleep together? Contradictory emotions swirled in my chest. Seducing him was counterproductive to helping matchmake. No matter how *right* Callum was, I was all wrong for him.

He blushed. "This is awkward."

"So you've seen my boobs now. It's not a big deal. With all the time we spend together, it was bound to happen. We've both been through a long dry spell. We trust each other. We obviously have physical chemistry. Well, like, 'Oops, we accidentally blew up the school science lab' chemistry."

"You want to do this again." Sea-glass-green eyes bore into mine. It wasn't a question.

Now that I'd had a taste, it was obvious once wouldn't be enough. Friends made arrangements like this work all the time. We just needed to define expectations up front. Desperate to buy time to formulate a response, I swallowed a scalding gulp of tea, then fought back tears as magma-temperature Earl Grey seared my esophagus.

"Friends with benefits," I said. "But we'll have rules, to keep us both safe. One: you keep dating. Promise me this won't impact your search."

Callum's focus shifted to the suddenly fascinating beans on his plate. "Yeah, of course. What else?"

"Two: we should probably limit this to once a week. So that you stay focused." Touching Callum was already addictive, so that one was mostly for me to remember my place.

He nodded.

"Three: no more sleepovers. It blurs the lines."

"Okay."

"Feel free to cook me breakfast anytime, though," I said with a laugh.

"Can I add one?" Callum asked.

"Sure. This goes both ways."

"Rule four: we stay friends. No matter what."

"Perfect addition." I lifted my mug. "No matter what."

CHAPTER 31

Callum

BRIANNA'S CRIMSON-PAINTED FINGERNAIL skimmed the rim of her wineglass. "Do I make you nervous?"

No, I'd just rather be with someone else. I didn't say that to my latest match, of course. Time was running out. I'd promised Lark I'd continue to date, keep looking for the woman I'd marry. Suffice it to say, it wasn't Brianna.

Even in the dim lighting, the woman across from me barely resembled her profile photo, which had been photoshopped within an inch of its life. When she waved me down in the restaurant, I didn't recognize her. She wasn't bad-looking at all without all that editing, a perfectly decent face . . . if not for the messy lipstick bleeding around a wolfish grin that made me feel like I was on the menu.

Another contender for Lark's bracket of sketchy dates. God, I wished it was her across the table from me. Same thought I had during every date I forced myself on—even the nice ones.

Brianna snatched her half-empty wineglass. The movement sent the reek of cigarettes my way. "Have a drink."

I declined.

"Umm, d-d-do you know that gentleman?"

Besides the blatant catfishing, something didn't sit right about her. Since we'd sat down, an older man two tables over hadn't taken his eyes off her. It was getting creepy, but Brianna seemed to enjoy the attention.

"I do." She leaned across the table with her elbows together, awkwardly jamming her breasts toward her chin. Her push-up cheetah-print bra peeked out from the low hem of her top. The garment was certainly working overtime, as her breasts threatened to choke her. The thought of resuscitating her put me off my meal; she'd taste like an ashtray. Not that I wanted to stay long enough to actually order something.

"He's my husband."

I sputtered my water. "Your what?" My eyes darted back to the man hiding unsuccessfully behind the wine menu.

With a husky laugh, she grabbed me by the chin and jerked my face back to look at hers. Long red talons caressed my cheek like a bird of prey toying with its quarry. "Don't worry. He likes watching me have fun. Have you ever heard of a cuckold?"

I had *not* signed up for this. My chair scraped against the floor as I wrenched myself from her grasp. "I have to go."

"Are you sure?" Raising one eyebrow, she held a breadstick up before deep-throating it.

I dealt with decaying human remains on a daily basis, but even I had my limits. Brianna pulled the saliva-coated breadstick out of her mouth and regaled me with a hacking cough that sent her poorly contained breasts practically bouncing out of her top.

"Positive."

"WE STILL CAN'T offer you a cash loan in that amount, Mr. Flannelly."

"This is my livelihood. My home. Please." Reduced to begging in a banker's office. Again. I pointed to a graph in the stack of paperwork I'd brought. "Based on the aging b-b-baby boomer population, we're projected to have fifteen percent growth over the next five years without raising prices, outside of inflation."

With a grimace, the loan officer slid my folder back across the desk. Mass die-off of the elderly generation didn't sit well with him, business boon or not.

I'd explained my circumstances, except for the marriage complication. All he needed to know was that my father (I hated acknowledging Pádraig as such) intended to sell, and I wanted to buy. I'd attempted to cobble funds together using smaller loans from multiple banks, but the sum still couldn't compete with the cash offer made by O'Reilly and Sons.

"This is the third time you've come to us, and the third time I've had to decline. Perhaps you could try a private investor."

I'd looked into that already. Turns out, a musty old funeral home didn't compete with trendy new shops in the Westend. I even reached out to old mortuary school classmates to see if anyone wanted a stake in the company, but it didn't pan out. Flannellys had been stewards of that cemetery for generations, shepherding families through grief for nearly a century. If there was one thing I agreed with my granda on, it was that the tradition should continue. I might never have a child to pass the torch to, but I wouldn't allow the flame to die in my hands.

Pádraig would have to pry Willow Haven from my cold fingers. I had to find a way . . . but finding a match grew less likely with each passing hour. There had to be a solution I wasn't seeing. One that didn't involve promising forever to someone I didn't want forever, or asking Lark for something fake when what I wanted from her was real.

After thanking the loan officer for his time, I walked the long way home, following the canal leading to the bay. Salty air filled my lungs. Gulls cackled overhead, swooping low to see if I had any chips to steal. Crimson-sailed hookers drifted in the distance. It was all so familiar, yet it offered little comfort.

As much as I missed my granda Tadhg, I was furious with him, too. Marriage under legal duress only exacerbated the stress of running a business and finding someone special.

Despite it all, I *had* found someone. Lark had an inherent ability to dismantle my defenses without even trying. Disoriented, I stood on uncharted, shaky ground. Not knowing how to take the next step.

CHAPTER 32

Lark

I DRAGGED MY cursor along the cartoon rat's mouth to fix the lip-syncing to my own filtered voice. *The Magical Adventures of Havarti & Plague Rat* was a one-woman production, meaning I was even providing the male character's voice by tweaking the pitch.

So far, it was turning out well. I suppose Callum inspired me. A narrative had naturally sprung up around the sketches I'd made. Almost four minutes were already animated and voiced; it was how I kept myself occupied while Cal was on his dates, since the one time I'd tried to distract myself by visiting Maeve she'd drifted off in her armchair before 8:00 p.m. I couldn't keep the poor woman up late as frequently as Cal was out on dates, which was a lot. Like we'd agreed.

My phone rang, and his face lit up the display. "Want to explore? I have to get out of this house."

"You know," I said, "I still haven't seen those castle ruins in the neighborhood."

"Meet me in five?"

On a daily basis, we drove past the remains of a lone stone tower crumbled on one side, like a half-disassembled game of

Jenga. Tall grasses and purple harebells sprung up around fallen chunks, beckoning to me through the window of Callum's sardine-can car. It seemed a shame to ignore a little slice of medieval history in the city's heart.

As he drove, I leaned across the seat and played with his tie, which was anchored by an artful, intricate knot. Another of his fashion idiosyncrasies.

"Awfully dressed up," I said. Now that it was spring, I was back to enjoying sundresses and denim jackets paired with my boots.

"Honestly, I forgot I was wearing it. I had a meeting with the loan officer at the bank."

I sat up straight. "What did they say?" Had I known, I would've gone with him for moral support.

If Callum could gather the cash to buy the business from his father, he could put this whole inheritance mess behind him. After his encounter with Breadstick Brianna, I didn't blame him for trying that path again.

"They said no."

"I'm sorry. It was worth a shot," I said. "Hey, you know who is a lawyer? Aidan. Maybe he could help."

Aidan would be willing to give Cal a consultation. An estate planner would be able to find money in his business, right? Or maybe there was an answer elsewhere in the inheritance.

Callum had once confessed that the thought of one day admitting his legal situation to someone he was dating was scary, but he knew that full disclosure would be necessary to start any marriage off honestly. Deirdre only found out because she was present when he received the bad news. And me . . . well, he'd said I always had a way of loosening his tongue. Then he demonstrated by kissing me. I hadn't minded.

"I have a solicitor already, my granda used him for years. I just need to get my mind off it for a while."

I brushed my hand up the inside of his thigh, and his hands tightened around the steering wheel. "Distraction. Yeah, I can do that."

The new terms of our leveled-up friendship were complicated, rewarding, and exciting. Every touch was electric, and when contact broke, I found myself desperate for *more*. Each moment together felt borrowed against time as *The Pirate Queen* drew closer to completion. Although I prided myself on keeping to production deadlines, it was tempting to let this one lapse, just to stay here longer.

After a short drive, we pulled up to the remains of the once-noble edifice. Tangled vines laid their claim across rough-hewn stone. Water bubbled from a tributary of the nearby river. History survived there, untouched except by lichen and rain. Callum held my hand, helping me navigate the fallen tower's piles of stone. Foxgloves popped up among them and swayed in the pleasant breeze. Not another soul in sight.

"Remember when you told me you weren't entirely unadventurous?"

He adjusted his glasses. "And you told me you'd try most things at least once."

"Mmm. It's been torture trying to figure out what you meant." I stepped closer and loosened the knot at his throat. "What's your idea of adventure?"

His mouth parted, but no words came. I dragged his tie along his collar in a hypnotic rhythm. Lit by the April sunset, Callum looked damn near edible.

"Well, I've always wondered," he replied, "what it would be like to be carried away and not even care where you are. I've never experienced that."

"It feels like your body is on fire. And nothing but your partner's touch can put it out."

Without preamble, he hoisted me up. I let out a surprised

squeal and drew my legs around his hips. *Frisky* Callum was new. A far cry from the stoic man I'd met months earlier. Dense muscles in his shoulders shifted under my palms.

"How about here?" His rough whisper tightened my nipples under my dress. "Right now."

"Here?" I shot him an impish grin, and my thighs squeezed. It was so brazen. Ancient, moss-coated stone walls provided privacy and protection from the elements, but anyone could stumble upon us. We were still in the city, not the countryside.

"The sun's going down, so I don't expect anyone will come."

"Oh," I snickered, "someone's definitely gonna come."

Callum cast a look around to confirm we were still alone. All clear. He sucked my breast through the thin cotton, his hot mouth leaving a dark blotch over one stiff peak, then the other.

Shocked and more than a little turned on, I demanded, "Who are you, and what have you done with Callum Flannelly?"

"Lark, I'm more myself with you than anywhere else."

Swoon. He couldn't say things like that and expect me not to react. And I felt the same way about him. Accepted. Valued. Understood.

I undid his two top buttons and licked his throat, then wound his silk tie around my palm and slid down his torso. Once on my knees, I looked up with my best doe eyes. Furious desire pulsed between us.

"You'll have to keep watch." I played with his zipper. Halfway down, halfway back up. Halfway down. Pause. Back up as he blew out a pained exhalation. "So we don't get caught."

The outline of his hard shaft strained against the fabric. I pressed my lips to it. Quick, teasing pecks that made him squirm. I looped the undone tie around the back of my neck and offered the loose ends to Callum, to direct me, as if they were reins. I wanted to allow him a small measure of control . . . while I took him apart. "Show me what you want, but don't use your hands."

"Oh, fuck."

Hunger blazed in his eyes as I pulled his cock out. He slid the tie behind my head, fists taut on the silk. I engulfed his length, one deliberate, maddening inch at a time. Callum whispered in Gaeilge, halfway wrecked already.

He couldn't resist pulling to guide me deeper. With a firm yank, he set the pace and depth as his molten eyes stared down. Mine pleaded, *Keep going.* Cheeks hollowed and lips stretched around his girth, I felt myself growing wet and ready.

"Wait," he said.

Gagging, I pulled him from my mouth. Adrenaline shot through me. Was someone else here?

"I won't last if you keep that up." He gently tugged upward to bring me to my feet.

A chorus of frogs and crickets began their nightly performance. Twilight closed around us, with just enough light remaining for me to see Callum's face. I unbuttoned the top of my dress and let the fabric fall open. Wild-eyed, Callum reached a hand in, rolling and pinching my nipples.

"Let me have you here," he said, deep voice full of desperation. His rigid cock pressed against my stomach, fingers tracing over the cotton between my legs, but withholding contact where I throbbed for it most.

I writhed with anticipation at the marvelous tease. "You're a little bit of a sadist."

"I'm not the one who started the *Fifty Shades of Grey* shite."

"With you, would it be Fifty Shades of Grave?"

"Wow." He huffed a laugh. "And you make fun of my jokes."

"You know you love my awful puns."

I got heated, rough kisses in reply. He pulled my panties to the side and went in for the kill. Two fingers massaged my clit. Moans tumbled from my mouth, and biting my bottom lip couldn't stop them. Each time I arched my back and my legs quivered, Callum pulled away at the last second.

Fingers clamped around his arm, I said, "I hate you so much."

Mercifully, he drove his fingers in. A relieved, filthy moan tore from my throat—and then Callum was groaning.

"This is about the buildup, love."

Of course. It was his favorite part. I let the pet name slide, only because I was teetering on the verge of bliss, but that four-letter word echoed in my ears and thrummed in my blood.

Just like that, he extracted his hand from between my legs. I'd murder him. After my orgasm. Callum inserted each glistening digit into his mouth, sucking them clean without breaking eye contact. He withdrew each one with an obscene little pop and a hum of approval. This was him at his most primal, poised to screw the hell out of me . . . in semipublic.

"You make me want. I've never *wanted* anyone quite like this before," he breathed. Dappled evening light fell across his cheek. "What are you doing to me?"

I've never felt quite this way before, either, I wanted to tell him. Instead I said, "Anything you want."

Which was also true. I didn't know if I could tell Callum *no* anymore. My body, my heart chanted *yes, yes, yes* in an eager chorus. To anything he wanted. Even though I knew that he was still dating, I secretly worried he would ask me to marry him to keep Willow Haven. And I didn't know what the hell I could possibly say if he proposed such a thing.

This arrangement had turned me inside out. Almost literally. Earnest, penetrating eyes stared at me like he could see through my nonchalant seduction. Feeling seen was as unnerving as it was comforting. A freaking emotional paradox.

His ragged breath warmed the nape of my neck as he pinned me against a low stone wall. Pants still open, he eased himself behind me. Languorous kisses wandered up my neck, and teeth flirted with my earlobe. With our height difference, he'd have to hold me up the entire time if we remained standing. I had a better idea. Cold stone pressed against my cheek and forearms as I lay my stomach across the top of the wall. I arched my back to present my ass.

I couldn't believe we were doing this. Here. Anyone could stumble upon us. My dress fluttered over my hips as a breeze picked up, and my legs dangled over the edge. I liked feeling so untethered. The tease of his cock nestled between my ass cheeks, dipping into me to brush against my wetness.

Callum pulled away and rolled on a condom from his wallet. I gripped the wall hard in anticipation.

At last, he sank in. Patient. Slow. From over my shoulder, I saw him watch his length enter me with dark determination—I forced my eyes to remain open as the sublime friction threatened to eclipse all else. A sigh broke from my mouth at the exquisite intensity. Possessed by need, I clenched, squeezing him even tighter while our hands and hips moved in harmony.

Inspiring lust in someone who rarely felt it made me feel like some temptress, but Cal wasn't exactly innocent before me. Filthy and aflame with need, he was a man who knew what he wanted and how to ask for it. In the two weeks since our first time, we'd both become better at communicating, but sometimes we didn't have to speak. One look, one touch, one smile, and the spark between us would ignite . . . but damn if I didn't love the subtle edge in his voice that only appeared when he praised me or demanded more. The man who could hardly speak in my presence when we met. The first man I'd wanted in years. The *only* one.

"Mo chuisle . . ."

Translation unknown, his voice was sweetly urgent. The yearning vibration in his baritone triggered an internal shock wave. Callum switched to deep strokes that rendered me mute, pounding me through my climax.

Never would I have imagined this, but it was unspeakably hot. Raw. Tender. Honest. Frantic. Trusting. Merciless. Throwing his head back, his momentum grew erratic. Waves of pleasure carried me even higher, higher. My fingers dug into the mortar groove to keep from being swept away. Callum drove himself in deeper, twitching and writhing as he finished with a guttural noise.

Velvet night enveloped us now, and I was again aware of the natural nighttime symphony. Gradually, I regained my bearings.

"I can't believe we just did that. Not that I'm complaining," I said, still panting.

"You taught me I enjoy a little spontaneity."

I sat up on the wall in a satisfied daze.

"Wait," he said. "Let me take one last look at you like this."

Breath hitching, I stilled.

Seeing each other so unvarnished and unfiltered was a rush. I watched him with a coy smile, legs splayed, dress unbuttoned and rucked up to my hips. Obviously thoroughly fucked, all flushed cheeks and tousled hair. Callum groaned. A deep, erotic rumble that would be sure to plague my dreams. In a reluctant farewell, he kissed each breast before buttoning my dress and lowering the hem.

Our eyes locked, and I rested my forehead against his.

"I've never had a friend like you," he murmured.

"Ditto," I answered as my heart splintered.

CHAPTER 33

Lark

I'D BEEN SUBSISTING on sexual endorphins and self-delusion. And little sleep, as the warmth Callum provided in bed one night a week only made it feel emptier when he wasn't next to me. Turns out, kicking him out post-coitus didn't stop my growing feelings for him. It just left me feeling incomplete. This was the downside of being friends with benefits. I'd do well to remember why I established the "no sleepovers" rule.

An email pinged in my inbox while I was reviewing a clip from *The Pirate Queen*. I clicked. KinetiColor's executives were looking to interview for positions with the next project: a series. They were accepting internal applications for key roles first.

My eyes raced over the memo again. Hope flared. If I secured a permanent spot, I could stay. Ireland had started as a temporary stopover on my grief tour, but it wasn't that anymore. I'd made friends here. Eked out a place among my peers. And except for one coworker, KinetiColor was a great place to work.

Anvi burst into my office, talking before the door even swung shut behind her. "Tell me you're applying for the job."

"That email arrived, like, two minutes ago."

"And the entire office is already buzzing," Rory said, hot on

Anvi's heels. They leaned against my desk. "Your contract was only for *The Pirate Queen*, right?"

"That's right."

"I told you, Rore, she might have plans back home. Her family still lives in the States."

Home. Home wasn't Texas, hadn't been for a while. If offered the position, I could *stay. And I wanted to.*

Not because Galway was a quaint novelty. Not because it simply wasn't Austin, haunted by Reese's ghost. Or even because starting over again alone felt daunting. No other city on earth was home to Callum Flannelly. No place could feel like home without him. The realization hit me over the head like an Acme-brand wooden mallet.

A few nights ago, I'd found myself imagining a permanent life here as Callum played with my hair. A romantic future together was only a dream, of course, but I wanted him in my life—even if I had to watch him build that sort of future with someone else. This was my chance. Perhaps my only one, as animation jobs were hard to come by.

"So, are you?"

"I— Yeah." Once I said it out loud, it seemed scarier. A fragile thing easily crushed. "Yeah, I am applying."

"Of course, Seán will be competing for the same position," Anvi said. She picked up the unlit Saint Dolly devotional candle next to my monitor and smiled at the sacrilegious monument to my favorite singer. "And you'll wipe the floor with him."

Rory shuddered. "Can you imagine him as our boss? He'd probably make us line up to kiss his ring every morning when we enter the building."

How awful would Seán be with even more influence? I didn't want my friends to have to find out. Anvi had never hidden her distaste for him, but since standing up for me, Rory was also a possible target now.

"I'll miss your biscuits too much if you go back to the States."

"What Anvi means is," Rory offered, "we like having you around. I hope we can keep our little gang together."

I grinned. "Me, too."

My first instinct was to tell Callum. I wondered what Maeve would say when I visited her after work. I returned to my office after my lunch break, only to find an unwelcome ass occupying my chair. Seán.

My personal sketchbook lay open on the desk. Usually, I had it in my purse, but thoughts of Callum on his most recent date had distracted me. Some Pilates instructor. I loathed her on principle. Maybe that made me a bad feminist, but it was the truth. As usual, I'd busied myself with my *Havarti & Plague Rat* project. I only realized I'd left the book behind after digging fruitlessly through my purse at lunch.

It was open to a page of Houdini in a top hat, sawing a chunk of cheese in half. More versions of her filled the pages. I'd drawn them to clear my head, but it had flowered into something more. Now, dozens of pages filled the sketchbook as I fleshed out the animated short meant as a birthday gift to Callum. Or rather, a parting gift, as my employment contract ended the same month he turned thirty-five.

The thought of Seán snooping through my desk made my spine rigid.

I cleared my throat, and the phone in his hands immediately dropped to his lap. For a split second he appeared to be apologetic and pocketed the device.

"Can I help you?" Translation: *What do you think you're doing in my office?*

He stood, and my chair swiveled lazily with the movement. "I just wanted to hand in those revamped scenes from the overboard sequence."

To steel my nerves, I smoothed out my skirt and drew in a deep breath. "Next time, please wait at your desk until I'm here. I don't like anyone in my office."

"Sure thing," Seán said, unbothered.

I studied him warily. Usually he'd argue.

"Are you applying for the series job?"

There it was. I knew there was a reason he was acting so casual. Seán would be mistaken if he thought he'd take this from me.

"I am."

"Well. Good to know who the competition will be." Seán cast a look over his shoulder on the way out of my office.

Eager to make up for lost time, I dove back into the clips of an animated Grace O'Malley. My open sketchbook and the office interloper were quickly forgotten.

CONCERN DOGGED MY heels as I walked to Maeve's cottage. She'd tired easily during my recent visits and got off the phone abruptly just a few days ago. Often Callum accompanied me, always up for ribbing the old woman (and indulging in her scones). Today, I went alone. As much as I loved spending time together, I needed a step back from him to maintain my perspective. We weren't a couple, even though the lines had blurred.

A brusquely efficient woman wearing scrubs greeted me at Maeve's door. The nurse introduced herself and let me in; she said that Maeve had just received a dose of medicine that would make her sleepy soon. I was surprised to see a hospital bed covered by a vibrant handmade afghan dominating the living space where we'd sifted through Maeve's yellowed photo album.

"Lark! What an angel you are. I'd almost forgotten about our visit."

"Hey, Maeve. How are you doing?" I asked delicately. The nurse's presence and hospital bed twisted my stomach.

"At the moment, I feel marvelous. They give you quality drugs once you're my age."

I sat in the armchair pulled up next to the bed, clutching a cross-stitched pillow that read *I had my patience tested. I'm negative.*

"How's yer man?" Maeve asked.

"Callum is well. Working tonight. He says hello."

"I imagine he'll be working on me, soon enough. Sorry for surprising you this way." Things clicked into place; her hostility toward him on our first meeting was because she knew she was terminal, even then.

"You know I'd want to be a support to you. I didn't know you were sick."

"Have been since last summer. Remember when we talked about being treated differently after telling people you're a widow?" she said.

"Of course." I understood the instinct to hide pain from those around you, but I'd already lost one person with so much unsaid.

Maeve frowned. "It doesn't get any easier to say goodbye with age."

"No. I don't imagine it would. Though I think it's worse not being able to say it." I took her hand and stroked my thumb over her papery skin, grateful to be here with her.

She hummed sagely. "Did you ever tell Callum why you really left Texas?"

"No," I admitted.

"When was the last time you were completely honest to anyone? Yourself included."

Oof. To think, I'd felt unburdened the first time she and I had talked about our shared widowhood. "Not pulling any punches, are you?"

"We show the people we love the ugliest parts of ourselves, and we tell them the truth even when it hurts, because that's what intimacy is."

I *had* kept part of my history at arm's length from Callum.

Even from myself. I couldn't allow him all the way in. Falling completely would mean that when he finally found the right woman or when I left Ireland—however this thing between us ended—it would hurt even more.

Jagged coughs rattled her body. I fumbled for the tissues at her bedside and offered one as the nurse pushed past.

"Maeve, I'm sorry to have gotten you worked up. I'll let you rest."

"Wait," she croaked, wispy brows drawn into a *V*. She caught her breath and whispered something to the nurse, who headed for the kitchen. "There is one more thing I have for you, but in exchange, I want a promise."

I swallowed. "I've already told you, I'm no good at promises."

"You haven't let me down yet," Maeve said. "Grief is a burden no one should carry alone. And if not Callum, then maybe it's someone else. But you—you, Lark—deserve love. Healing. No matter what happened before, I think your husband would agree with me. Promise me you'll stop running and let someone in."

The nurse had retrieved a key from the kitchen. I stared at it on her proffered palm for a moment before gingerly plucking it up. She left again to keep herself busy in the pantry.

"I don't understand."

"Lark, you are the only one who comes close to understanding the significance of my bike. And you're the one who needs it."

Tears ran down my cheeks, though I don't know when I began crying. She was too generous. This was too important to her. I didn't deserve it. "No—no way, I can't accept the Lambretta."

"Not unless you give me your promise to look after it. And yourself."

"But you're . . . medicated! It's not right—"

"I made the decision in sound mind. Now don't go questioning your elders," she said. "But I do need that promise."

"I . . . I'll try." Fear strained my voice. "I promise I'll try."

Walking home, I reflected on her plea that I trust Callum.

He'd already put his faith in me, an honor since he didn't allow many people into his life. I didn't care about Callum *despite* his job. One of the reasons I cared about him was *because* of his commitment to remembering and honoring those who were gone. The tender dignity he offered them, the way he held space for others. Social withdrawal had never stopped him from being empathetic, deep in his heart and in all his actions. I could trust him not to judge me.

After two years of running from any reminder of mortality, compartmentalizing my memories to avoid falling into the yawning chasm of depression, I ended up close to a man whose very life revolved around death, from his career, to his family legacy, to his home itself. And I became friends with a dying woman. Talk about irony.

CHAPTER 34

Callum

"YOU RODE THAT thing without a helmet?" That was the first thing out of my mouth when Lark pulled the classic Lambretta into the driveway and killed the engine. She didn't even have an Irish driver's license, much less one for motorcycles.

"Maeve gave it to me." Lark absently ran a hand along the chrome handlebars. "A hospice nurse was there. She's dying, Cal."

Poor Maeve. I hoped she wasn't in any pain. Losing her irreverent humor and kind wisdom would hurt, especially so soon after losing my granda. How would Lark process the pain of loss? "I'm very sorry to hear that, love. But there's no need for you to beat her to it."

Lark scowled as she lifted the scooter onto the kickstand.

"You've obviously never d-dealt with a complete decapitation before." Maybe I was being aggressive, but using a wooden dowel to reconnect a severed head to its body left a lasting impression. Not to mention the other motorcycle fatalities I'd seen. If I had my way, she'd walk around swaddled in Bubble Wrap.

"I'm so sorry about Maeve. Does she seem comfortable?" I brushed Lark's arm.

She nodded.

"I worry about you. I can't help it. What I've seen . . . Please be careful." Never mind that soggy weather was as predictable as the sunrise. I shuddered at the thought of Lark caught in poor conditions on the road.

She lifted up on her toes and pecked me on the cheek. "Promise."

Later, Lark asked me for a walk by the river, saying she wanted to be someplace quiet. Something about her request put my nerves on edge. Was she ending this thing between us? Apprehension turned my stomach into a rock tumbler as the River Corrib shimmered in the late-afternoon sun. Bloodred hookers rode the waves, but their presence brought little peace, given the way Lark only showed me some half-hearted smiles.

She tucked her cardigan closer around herself. "I, um, wanted to talk to you about Reese."

The internal rock tumbler jerked to a violent stop. She had never wanted to talk about him. Though I'd seen the persistent dark cloud at the edges of her sunny disposition, visible in the way she'd grow distant with talk of commitment or brush her thumb over her bare ring finger.

Lark wrung the rail in tortured fists as she stared at the turbulent water. The metal findings on the moored ships tinkered in the bay's fresh breeze. "We never split up. We were . . . in a rough patch when he died."

There it was. Confirmation of my hunch.

"I'm so sorry that you've been carrying this on your own. But you don't have to." Curiosity niggled at me. "How long ago was it?"

"February was the second anniversary."

I searched my memory. The evening she'd found me pacing in the garden, her eyes had been vacant and sorrowful. I put my arm around her, wanting to shield her from the pain.

"I've always suspected. I've witnessed grief my entire life."

"I didn't want you to know I screwed up, okay?" Moisture shimmered in her eyes. She turned back toward the river.

"Lark . . ."

"Reese felt so alone, but I was right there beside him. Wearing rose-colored glasses, as usual. When he told me he wasn't happy, I got defensive. We hardly ever argued, but that one turned into a blowout. He went for a drive to let off some steam . . . and wrapped his car around a tree." Lark allowed me to squeeze her hand. "If we hadn't been fighting, he'd still be here. His sister, Rachel, told me at the funeral that it was all my fault. In front of everyone who cared about him. Their dad had to pull her away."

I'd broken up a few heated familial exchanges at memorials. People lash out and assign blame.

"It's not your fault." I swallowed hard. "Tell me about him. Tell me the good times."

Relief passed over Lark's face at the invitation, as if she needed permission to reminisce about her own partner. Watery eyes paired with her soft smile. "Reese coached high school basketball. He'd dance with the mascots to embarrass his players. We met at a Halloween party in college. He'd seen me on his sister's Instagram page and showed up in a Meowth onesie because Rachel told him she and I would be dressed like Team Rocket from Pokémon. God, I loved him. I still do."

That was the reason Lark refused relationships in favor of sex with a friend: her heart belonged to a dead man. I couldn't take his place . . . but I wanted a part of her heart, too.

"Everything imploded after the accident. Rachel was my best friend, and she was a coworker, too. Every interaction at Blue Star afterward carried an undercurrent of judgment. Or sympathy. I resigned after we wrapped on *Shoelace* and went freelance." Wind whipped Lark's hair in front of her face. "I moved here to feel intact again. To pretend, at least."

"You don't need to pretend. I want to share in your happiness *and* in your sorrow." I pulled her slackened body to my chest as the sobs began, and her tears soaked my shirt. "I'm here, love."

Hiccups jostled her in my arms every few moments between

sharp gasps for air. I rubbed soothing circles between her shoulder blades and felt her gradually calm.

Galway, the eight-hundred-year-old cultural heart of the nation, held both the past and the present simultaneously. Medieval walls tucked into modern shopping centers. Museums and monuments among innovative animation studios. I'd always appreciated that sense of remembrance. Integrating painful history into a collective story has been our way for generations. We didn't forget, but we moved forward. Maybe this was the place Lark could grow. Honor her pain and find new joy. Maybe I could be her joy. Her second love.

Somewhere along the line, I'd fallen in love with her. *Fuck*. I *loved* Lark Thompson. There was no use denying it to myself when this woman's every emotion inspired such soul-deep empathy.

"Sorry I never told you. I just wanted you to see the best version of me."

"I want to see all of you." I brushed a tear from her cheek. "You're brave and resilient. Generous. You're patient when I can't get the word out, or when I repeat it. Even when I can't—when I can't say it the *way* I want, you've always made me feel accepted. Thanks to you, I've become a better version of myself. You helped me learn to let myself be vulnerable."

Before I could register it, her lips smashed against mine. My heart drummed so forcefully, she had to feel it. As much as I wanted Lark, I needed her to want me for more than numbing the pain.

"Stay over tonight," she said.

Who was I to deny her? But . . . *no*. It wasn't right to exploit her pain for my pleasure. And we had a rule against sleeping over for a valid reason.

Mustering self-control, I braced her shoulders. "I don't want to be your d-d-d-distraction from real life."

Mascara-smudged eyes scorched me. "This *is* real. Spend the night with me."

This is real. It had been real for me since the beginning, but did that mean the same thing for Lark?

I couldn't believe I was breaking my resolve so quickly. Grief is as nonlinear and convoluted as it is persistent. I wouldn't shut her out completely because she wanted to cope physically tonight. Our *friends* arrangement was a mind-fuck. I wanted commitment and reassurance and . . . stability. Lark couldn't offer that until she trusted herself again.

———————

WE STUMBLED INTO her bedroom in a frenzy, and Lark pushed me onto the bed. Seated on the edge, I fumbled blindly in the drawer of her nightstand, searching for the box of rubbers while Lark stood and kissed me.

She rested a hand over mine. "What if we didn't use one?"

Impossibly, I grew even harder at the thought.

"Umm, well, I d-d—"

Smooth. Real smooth.

She rested her fingertip over my lips. "I had an IUD placed years ago. If you want to, it's okay. If not, that's all right, too."

Did I? Absolutely. But this was huge. I cradled Lark's face and kissed her to show that I wanted this, too.

With painstaking slowness, I slid one strap of her bra down. Then the other. Subtle citrus scent inebriated me. I dragged my nose against her skin, nipped at her through the lace. Rosy peaks stiffened under my gaze as the cups fell away. So beautiful. Greedily, I suckled, rewarded by her fingers dragged across my scalp.

Lark stripped me down with just as much enthusiasm as I'd undressed her. I'd never tire of the feeling of being so bare and open. Of her teeth grazing my collarbone. Of the reverence in her expression when she took in my body, naked and eager for her. Of the familiarity of her touch.

Her knickers were next. I stripped them off and threw the

slick fabric aside. Then I laid on the bed, pulled Lark over my mouth and buried my tongue between her legs. She sighed. Clung to the headboard. Guided my hands to her chest. Watched me as I savored her taste and sensation without breaking eye contact. Sweet and tangy, dripping over my mouth and chin.

She needed to get out of her head for a while. She deserved to feel good.

"Just like that, just like— *Oh!*"

My cock pulsed harder each time she writhed on my face. Palms pressed against the wall, Lark undulated her hips. Faster. I could feel her pleasure build and intensify as she rubbed herself over my nose, my chin. Did I need to breathe? Oxygen was inconsequential compared to her bliss.

Then she whimpered in ecstasy. I held her down and pushed my tongue deeper into her juicy warmth. The whole bed shook. Hell, it probably showed up on the Richter scale.

"Cal . . . How are you so good at that?" she breathlessly asked, scooting back to sit on my chest. I could feel her wetness on my sternum, like she was an animal marking me with her scent. A deliciously primal notion.

"I enjoy making you come. So I pay attention to how to do it."

By now, I knew she liked being licked softly and fucked hard. Eye contact excited her when she went down on me. Speaking Irish always got her insanely aroused. Straddling my body—so much larger than her own—made her feel powerful. I may not be very experienced, but I'm a fast study, and Lark's pleasure was my favorite subject.

"Can I make *you* come now?" Lark asked, all doe eyes and diabolical pout.

"Any way you want."

"Hmmm. How 'bout a cuddlefuck."

"Cuddlefuck?"

"Yeah, you hold me from behind like this." She lay down, pulling my arm around her so that I spooned her. My cock skimmed her wetness. From this position, she could twist her upper body to kiss me. Perfect.

She laughed. "Oh, you like that?"

"I need to be inside you."

After licking her, I was so damn keyed up. Slowly, Lark lined up my tip where we both needed it most, teasing and gliding. She stared into my face as I penetrated her inch by inch. Holy shite. Slick and velvet soft. Everything else fell away. Nothing remained but Lark and the bond we shared.

Something had changed between us since she shared her story. There was a new vulnerability in her eyes.

"Tá tú chomh tais," I growled into the crook of her neck.

"Mmmm . . . You sound so sexy. What's it mean?"

"You're so wet for me."

Again and again, she impaled herself on my bare cock. Shallow, shallow, deep. Shallow, shallow, deep, deep, deep.

Delirious with pleasure, my hand braced her sweat-beaded thigh as I thrust harder. She gasped my name as my other hand slipped over her clit. Concentric circles brought her to the precipice. Lark's fingers pressed into my arm, pinning it in place between her legs.

Twisting back, she kissed me. Messy and imprecise mouths desperate for contact as our bodies moved in sync. Our rhythm had become more intuitive. I trembled out of adrenaline now, not anxiety. Tension built, heightening my awareness of every humid breath and roll of her hips. Moments like this were ours alone. Earned. Cherished. Together we teetered on the edge.

"Yes. Don't stop."

Caught in the moment, I whispered to her words I meant with all my soul. "Grá mo chroí. Mo chuisle mo chroí." *Love of my heart. Pulse of my heart.*

Eyes closed, Lark shuddered as she rode shock waves of pleasure. She loved it when I spoke Irish. But would she feel the same if she knew the translation wasn't dirty talk but a confession?

"*Feelssogood*, Cal," she moaned. Sultry and a little hoarse from all the heavy breathing.

All I needed to launch over the edge.

I gripped her thighs for a final deep plunge into her tight heat. She looked into my eyes—straight into me—and clenched as my cock spasmed. Reveling in it, coaxing every drop out. Her eyes locked on mine. I didn't dare blink.

The intensity made me weak. Wonderstruck.

I'd always been so cautious; it was my first time having sex without a barrier. The fact that I'd just finished inside Lark and the evidence was now glistening on her thighs was surreal. I'd never come so hard. It was more than the physical sensation or the forbidden aspect. It was the trust. The way she'd stared into my face . . . like she loved me, too.

We lay intertwined on our sides. Panting. Sticky. Exhausted. I peeled away a strand of flaxen hair plastered to her neck and kissed her thumping pulse. Heavy-lidded and satisfied, I curled my hands around her breasts, feeling the stubborn muscle pound within. My heart, walking outside my body.

Lark's head rested against my chest, her hair friction-teased and faintly luminous in the dark. She traced invisible mandalas along my bare stomach. We'd never spent a full night together since the first time. I'd turned off notifications for DemiDate earlier, having learned my lesson about interruptions. The cheerful chime gave me a negative Pavlovian response anyway.

"Cal?"

I'd been staring up at the ceiling, awash in the sensation of her smooth length pressed against me. "Hmm?"

"We're wrapping principal animation on *The Pirate Queen* this week."

I knew the end was inevitable. That it would hurt. But this was too much. "That's exciting," I said around the lump in my throat.

"There are still postproduction tasks, but we're close to the end, so the producers announced the next project. A series. Twelve episodes to start, with the possibility of ongoing seasons if the streaming service decides."

Elated by the prospect, I sat up, taking Lark with me. She gasped as the sheet fell away but didn't move to cover herself.

"Are you staying for it? The series?"

"I hope so. I applied."

"Really?"

My arms ensnared her tightly, and she giggled at my enthusiasm.

"Don't jinx me, now."

In the short time we'd known each other, our lives had fused organically. I'd always wanted my own family, but it had been difficult to envision, manifesting as a dull ache rather than a clear mental image. Now the images came easily, when Lark waved at curious toddlers on the street or wistfully sighed at babies in prams. Once, we'd noticed an elderly couple at the bay, watching the sailboats alongside us, and she'd rested her head on my shoulder. I could never replace the man she'd loved and lost, but we could build something new together. Not as some clandestine arrangement but to belong to each other.

If Lark wanted to stay, maybe she felt the same.

"When will you know?"

"Soon. Seán is applying for the position, too. He feels entitled to my job, but I'm not handing it to him without a fight."

My mind flashed to his cruel sneer. She could beat him, of course, but I didn't trust him to play fair. "That's my girl."

She met my eyes, paused, then kissed me. No, she wasn't mine.

How could I ever love anyone else? It felt ridiculous to seek out endless dates, when the one I wanted was just next door.

CHAPTER 35

Lark

CALLUM'S STUBBLE GRATED my palm as I cradled his face after we made love. As much as I was meant to be an animator, Cal was meant to be an undertaker. It gave him purpose. If I didn't do something drastic, there was a real possibility Willow Haven would be sold out from underneath him. After all the support he'd given me, I couldn't let that happen. Marriage vows weren't to be taken lightly, but I couldn't let Callum lose this piece of himself, not if I could help it.

I swallowed heavily. "We should get married."

Shock, relief, and doubt flashed across his face until it landed on something I couldn't quite decipher. Hope? His throat bobbed. For every millisecond of his silence, the pounding of my heart grew louder.

It wasn't technically breaking my promise to Reese if it wasn't a real relationship. Or so I told myself. Reese wouldn't want me to stand by while a good man lost everything.

"How could I call myself your friend if I sat by and watched you lose Willow Haven?"

The odd expression in his eyes faded, and Callum pulled away from my touch. "Thank you for the offer, but I d-d-don't want that."

What?

"You can keep your business. Then you can take your time and find the right woman after everything is squared away and we're divorced. Let me help take the pressure off."

"I don't want that with you." His words hit with blunt force. Passion filled his eyes. "I want to be in love. I want to be loved in return."

After all this strife, his heart remained set on a real marriage. Something authentic existed between us, even if we wouldn't be a truly legitimate husband and wife. We both felt it. This arrangement between us had gone too far. I wasn't good for him, not if whatever this was meant he wouldn't accept my help.

I clutched the sheet covering my chest. "I think this should be the last time we . . . do this."

From the corner of my eye, I saw him nod stiffly and sit up, reaching for his trousers on the floor. Ugh, I really should have waited until we were both dressed to propose, but the last thing I'd expected was a rejection.

"If not me, who will you marry, then?"

"Deirdre offered."

I pretended like it didn't wound me to hear that he'd rather wed his receptionist. "Oh. I didn't realize she was your contingency plan."

The room was silent, except for the *tink* of his belt buckle as he pulled on his trousers. It took every bit of willpower to not beg him to stay, but I simply couldn't reconcile what I wanted and what was right.

"Well, you're going to keep your home," I mumbled. "That's what matters. And I'll still try to help you find The One."

Callum stood in the doorway clenching his shirt in his hand. "Good night, Lark."

———

A DELIVERY BOX sat on my doormat when I came home from work the next day. Remembering the mishap that led to meeting Callum the first time, I double-checked the addressee before tearing it open. A helmet. Immediately after he'd chastised me about the Lambretta, he must have ordered me a helmet. Complete with sunflowers on the sides, it couldn't be more "me" if I'd designed it myself.

I pulled out my phone and called him, but it went to voicemail. I thanked him for the gift in a text, and as I changed from my work clothes into jeans, he replied: Busy working. You're welcome.

Last night had been so raw, so poignant, then I'd gone and ruined it.

I donned the helmet and kick-started the Lambretta.

The hospice nurse answered the door of Maeve's cottage and waved me back to the garden. Rosemary and thyme scented the air. Maeve gingerly sat up from her lounge chair as I gave her a hug and settled into the one beside it. She'd become so frail, but her eyes still shone brightly.

"How are you feeling, Maeve?"

"Ready." She smiled at the helmet tucked under my arm and the mess it had made of my hair. "I see you're enjoying my scooter. Is the clutch sticking?"

"A little."

"How about that promise you made me?"

I sighed and stared at the moss growing through cracks in the quaint stone wall.

"Forgive me," she laughed, "I don't have time to beat around the bush."

"I told Callum about Reese, and he was great about it. So great, in fact, that I took him home and proposed." I paused. "And he said *no*."

Her lips pursed in confusion.

"Did your premonitions predict that?" If I didn't joke about it, I'd cry. "He wants a love match. And if it's not a love match, he has an arrangement with his receptionist."

"Maybe you don't need to marry Callum to help him. Maybe being his friend is enough."

"We're so far past *friends*. I think . . . I think I might love him." My throat wanted to close around that four-letter word.

"Sure, I didn't need a crystal ball to see that."

"I care about Callum, can't stop thinking about him. But I feel guilty for having these feelings, you know? Scared out of my mind that I'll get so wrapped up in what I want that I'll lose sight of what he needs."

"Don't be scared to keep living. For what it's worth, I'm not afraid of dying. Not when Charlie is waiting."

"She waited too long to be your wife to ditch you in the afterlife," I said with a sad smile. Miles and decades had separated them before. If they found their way back to each other once, they could do it again. Their story made me believe that some couples were determined by fate.

Maeve closed her arthritic hand around mine. Quiet settled over the garden. I wasn't ready to lose her. To leave Ireland. To let go of Callum, even though he'd never really been mine. Tumbleweeds break from their roots for a reason, but I wanted to ground myself here.

Vision murky with tears, I stared at our hands. "I'll miss you."

"A terrible thing, that. But all we can control is how we choose to move through life. With honesty. With bravery. With love. I know you can do it."

CHAPTER 36

Callum

JUST AS I was beginning to believe that Lark might have fallen in love with me . . . she brought me back down to earth. Lark loved me; I believed that. She loved me enough to compromise her vow against another wedding. But was she *in* love with me?

Her reaction to my confession—that I didn't want a marriage of convenience with her but the real thing—still had me spinning. She'd doubled down on it being a favor between friends instead of a sacred, lasting commitment. It cut me to the bone after I'd let myself get my hopes up about what it meant for her to choose to apply for the promotion that would extend her visa. Meanwhile, I'd deactivated my dating profiles, knowing that no one could hold a candle to the woman I'd rejected.

We kept our distance from each other for the first time since she'd barged into my life and lit it up. But then three days after that night, I received the call from Maeve's hospice nurse. The news of Maeve's death brought Lark back into my arms, but I'd have given anything to spare her the pain of another loss.

"When is the wake?" she mumbled into my chest when her tears subsided.

I continued stroking her hair. "Saturday. I need tomorrow to put all of her arrangements in place."

She pulled back, and I reluctantly let my arms drop. "We wrapped the principal animation on *The Pirate Queen*. I'm supposed to celebrate with everyone at the Hare's Breath tomorrow, but I don't think I can. Not the night before Maeve's wake."

As a leader, and a contender for the series position, she was all but obligated to make an appearance to the milestone celebration. She needed me, even if she wouldn't say it.

"Then we'll raise a pint to Maeve's memory tomorrow and say our farewells on Saturday."

MOST OF THE KinetiColor staff came out for libations. Voices and music clashed loudly, and a chorus of shouts rose with Lark's entrance. She tugged me by the hand as we made our way toward the group.

"One round, then we're out of here. I'll fake severe intestinal distress if necessary," she said into my ear as I leaned down.

I could kiss her—but we'd ended that.

"Lark!" Anvi parted the crowd, her complicated plait swinging as they hugged. Her eyes flitted back and forth between us. "And Callum. Nice to see you again."

"Same to you. Congratulations on completing your . . . what exactly is it again?"

"Principal animation." Lark touched my arm. Every time she touched me, it threatened my resolve. Pushing her away was the hardest thing I'd ever done, but I couldn't go through with a sham arrangement knowing that I loved her and she didn't feel the same way. She meant well, but I wanted her heart. Not her altruism.

"We would not have stayed sane through this process without

our fearless art director," Anvi said. Others murmured in assent and raised their pints in agreement.

I broke off, waiting at the crowded bar while she mingled. She didn't have the emotional reserves to keep this up for long. Then her smile wilted when Seán approached.

"A drinking game," he announced. Multiple heads turned. "Between Lark and myself."

Alarm paled her cheeks. "I couldn't—"

"Come on, don't say you're afraid of a little friendly competition?"

She reshaped her grimace into a forced smile.

"It's been a long day and I have early-morning plans." She flicked her attention to me. Only I could see the sadness contained within. Maeve's death was still a fresh wound, and she had come only out of professional obligation. "I'm not a big drinker to begin with."

"Hmmm. A round of darts, then?" Seán widened his arms as he raised his voice. "What do you say, KinetiColor? Pool? Darts?"

"Ten euros on Blondie." Anvi slapped a few notes on the counter in solidarity. A few bystanders took notice and placed bets for the sake of gambling.

"Come on," Seán said, baiting her. "Name the game."

Reluctant, Lark shrugged and abandoned her drink at the table. I hated that she felt pressured to play along. "Okay. One game of darts."

Shaking out her hands and shoulders, she approached the board and collected three red darts. Seán claimed blue. Lark looked to me for reassurance, and I nodded.

"I'll let you go first," he said, full of faux chivalry. "Watch out! Step aside and keep clear. Female throwing!"

Half the observers groaned. Hannah rolled her eyes. Some old tool at the bar chuckled, offering Seán just enough validation to keep his ego boosted.

Seán leaned closer to Lark. "May the best one win."

Concentration hardened her features, and she pulled back, throwing the dart. It landed in the double ring. Whistles and shouts filled the air.

Seán attempted to look bored as he lined up his shot. With stunning force and speed, the dart stuck in the bull's-eye, gaining him fifty points and the lead. A few men—Seán's lone ride-or-die supporters—whooped enthusiastically. The fact that his own co-workers didn't root for him spoke volumes.

Lark marched to the line and closed one eye.

"Go, Lark!"

"Come on, Texas!" cried Rory, their lime-green mechanic's jumpsuit garnering attention in the crowd, even before they called out. They certainly had a unique sense of style.

Finally, Lark aimed the dart, and the fire in her eyes told me exactly what she was imagining hitting. The dart struck five. A few onlookers made disappointed chatter.

"Sullivan recognizes the value of seniority and experience for promotions. He won't make the same mistake twice," Seán said. My hand formed a fist as Lark's performative smile dropped. Another effortless bull's-eye. "So would you agree now that experience counts?"

Lark answered through gritted teeth. "I never discounted it. I only agreed to play darts."

"I just believe any position should always go to the best man for the job." Seán spoke over the rim of his glass. "That shouldn't be a controversial statement, but somehow it is these days."

Anvi rolled her eyes.

"Your turn, sweetheart."

Lark was one comment away from sending the dart straight though Seán's eye. I half hoped she would.

"That series job is a big deal," he continued as she lined up the shot. "Better to go to someone deserving this time."

I stepped forward, but Lark's arm jutted out in front of me like a locked metro turnstile. For the sake of office politics, she needed to fight this battle independently. Reining in the urge to intervene, I ground my teeth so hard they squeaked.

"I . . . I worked hard to get where I am." Lark's voice wavered.

"You know, Sullivan only wanted a woman because it's the Grace O'Malley story."

Anvi jumped in. "And this woman is fit to tell it."

"An American wasn't the right choice, at any rate. Are you gonna shoot or not?"

One would be hard-pressed to name a historical figure who better embodied the indomitable spirit of the isle than Grace O'Malley. But their boss—Seán's own uncle—chose Lark to develop the film's visual language. The screenwriter, director, and most of the animators and voice actors were Irish. One American on the team didn't invalidate what would always be a deeply Gaelic tale.

Lark's hands trembled around the final dart. She swallowed hard and dropped it onto the bar top. "I have nothing to prove to you, in this bar or at the studio."

Her voice shook, but she didn't shrink from him. I squeezed her hand, a subtle reassurance. Then she slipped away toward the restroom, shooting me a look that warned *Don't follow*. Every instinct shouted at me to go after her.

High on his perceived victory, Seán loudly said, "That Yank's first day of work, she got dropped off by a hearse. Attention seeker, she is." He cast a look at me. "Her husband offed himself, and she started banging the undertaker!"

Seán's timeline made little sense, but his point was made, regardless. I'd seen that sort of grief destroy people. What did this vicious arsehole know? Nothing. A silent look was exchanged between Hannah and Rory; the two of them knew exactly who I was.

"Didn't even let the body grow cold before she started enjoying the life insurance settlement." No one was laughing along with Seán. "Probably cut his brakes herself."

"Stop," I barked.

"Yeah, you can't say things like that. What is wrong with you?" Anvi's attention shifted toward the bathroom in search of Lark.

"See for yourself. Search for Reese Thompson. I have it on good authority that's why she left Blue Star. Forced resignation is good as fired—"

No way could I sit by and listen to this nonsense. "*Shut your mouth.*"

Some of the group took out their phones, whether to distract themselves from the awkward situation or to verify his rant, I didn't know. I scanned the sea of bodies until I found Lark chatting with a group of her peers.

"Besides, everyone at the office saw her arrive in that hearse. A man *died*, and it's a laugh to her. Shameless."

"D-do-don't call her that," I growled, and deposited my half-full pint glass on the counter. Everyone went quiet.

Not only was he turning Lark's trauma against her, Seán was using me to worsen the blow. I was used to being written off as less intelligent by the closed-minded because of my stammer. They assumed I was perpetually terrified, but the stutter was exacerbated by any heightened emotion. The current reigning emotion was utter rage.

"Why? You offended on behalf of her dead man?"

Without thinking, I was an inch from his face. Words and syllables were free-falling Tetris blocks, and I tried frantically to rearrange them. Easier said than done. "I'm offended on b-b-behalf of my friend and your—and your colleague."

"Widows and morticians: a match made in heaven, right?" A yeasty laugh blew into my face, and he leaned forward to whisper, "Is she as good a ride as she looks, or should I even bother going after her? Apparently she'll go to bed with an eejit, so it shouldn't be too challenging."

I grabbed him by the collar and slammed him against the wall. In my calmest voice, I said, "I will put you in your grave with a smile on my face if you say another word about that woman who is a hundred times your equal."

An infuriating smirk spread under his beard. "I'll take that as a yes."

My next movements were involuntary, and I didn't register them until my knuckles smashed into Seán's nose. He staggered a step back, hands guarding his face. I could've disfigured him so badly, even *I'd* be challenged to put him back together well enough for a proper viewing. I shook the dark thought away as blood poured through his steepled fingers. He muffled a cry of horror. Hannah's mouth formed a shocked *o* shape. An intern stared like I was a food-frenzied grizzly bear wantonly mauling a camper.

"I'll have your little girlfriend's job for that." Pink spittle hit my face with his words. Someone's arm flew between us before I could get in another swing.

"Hey! Hey! Break it up."

"He's not worth it," I heard Anvi say.

No, Seán wasn't. But Lark was.

Fire burned in my chest as his sour breath fanned across my cheeks, but I refused to budge. Until I heard Lark's faint drawl above the music and chatter.

"Callum?"

Seán bared his teeth, a trickle of blood tinting them crimson. I was reluctant to turn away but did so at the second call of my name.

Concern swam in her wide eyes. "What's going on here?"

"This moron broke my nose!"

I threw Seán aside. My hand trembled with barely contained rage as I dug out a few euro for the bartender. Without a word of explanation, I grabbed Lark's hand and plowed through the crowd toward the door.

"What the hell happened? You can't go hitting my coworkers," she sputtered once we pushed outside the Hare's Breath, wrenching her hand out of mine.

"He was out for blood tonight."

"Looks like you were, too." She refused to look at me as she marched to my car with arms crossed. "This is my job! And that makes me look bad. Again: What. The hell. Happened?"

"I couldn't let him get away with it."

Now that some of the blinding anger had dissipated, I recognized the mortification in her expression. Lark hated confrontations.

"He knows about Reese. He must've been digging for dirt online. He's threatened. Trying to throw you off your game by any means necessary," I explained once we were in the car. My restless fingers drummed against the steering wheel. "He told everyone Blue Star forced you to resign from your last position."

"That's not true."

"I know." I didn't tell her there were also accusations of mariticide.

"Seán has always felt entitled to my job. Told everyone it should've been an internal promotion and went on a rampage when he found out it went to an American with only one movie under her belt."

"You still don't want to take the 'Nine to Five' approach?"

"This isn't funny. If I lose my job, that's my ticket back to Texas. I need KinetiColor to stay here. Residence permits are super strict."

It made sense now, how cruel he'd been. The red shark's smile. Seán stood to become their boss if Lark stepped down. The perfect opportunity to showcase his dominance. He'd wanted to get a rise out of me, an excuse for Lark to be reprimanded by association. It was a setup. Guilty of walking directly into the trap, but unwilling to apologize for defending her, I redirected the focus of the conversation.

"Anvi stuck up for you. She's a solid friend."

"Yeah, she's great." Lark swallowed heavily. "But now every one of my coworkers will know. Again."

"Hey," I said. "Knowing what happened didn't change how I see you. It doesn't change how good you are at your job. All it does is show how heartless Seán is, if he can talk about it that way. It'll be all right."

"Your temper could cost me my job, Callum." Lark's eyes brimmed with unfallen tears.

"I'll go into the studio myself to take full responsibility."

"No. Just . . . Don't come to the studio. Please."

"Promise me you'll go to human resources on Monday. This has gone on way too long. It's unacceptable. And if he says anything else—"

"You'll what? Bust his kneecaps? Beat him with your hurling stick?"

I hated Seán for using the greatest tragedy of Lark's life to rattle her professionally. This was beyond a toxic work environment—and I couldn't protect her there. Fists clenched, she muttered imprecations at her coworker. Or at me. Both of us, probably.

We didn't exchange another word the rest of the drive.

CHAPTER 37

Lark

"SEÁN ALWAYS WANTED you to jump ship," Anvi said over speakerphone.

I'd answered her call practically on autopilot. My mind was a jumble of anxiety. Today would be my first time in a cemetery in two years. I already missed Maeve. Her rude pillows and kind wisdom.

"It doesn't surprise me that he's trying to provoke you," Anvi continued. "Sabotaging your relationship with your boyfriend—"

"Callum isn't my boyfriend," I mumbled, raw and overwhelmed. In a haze, I dumped all my dark clothes onto my bed so I could pick through them. Vibrant shades generally comprised my closet, not black.

"Could've fooled me. Wish I'd recorded him breaking Seán's nose. Seán was way out of line, and what he said was bullshit. I'm so sorry about your husband, for what it's worth. I didn't get a chance to say that before because you ran out of the pub so fast, but I really am."

"Thanks. It's . . . it's okay. I just had to get out of there."

Sighing, I decided on a navy dress. Maeve's funeral started in an hour, and a sense of dread was closing in. Despite being upset with Callum, I wanted to run into his arms, but he was busy working on the service. Instead, my favorite coworker had called, and even though I wasn't in the best state for a conversation about Seán, I appreciated her concern.

"Pretending the confrontation didn't happen won't make it go away," Anvi added. By now, it was common knowledge that I treated problems with the ostrich solution and favored burying my head in the sand. "That man is toxic. Half the team lives in constant fear of his wrath."

"You're right. I'll schedule a meeting with Sullivan on Monday. Thanks for checking on me, Anvi."

"Anytime. I know you'd do the same for me."

I slipped into a pair of demure heels and made my way to Willow Haven. Deirdre greeted me, directing me to Callum's office, but I wanted to pay respects to Maeve first. The knot in my stomach wasn't as tight as I expected, but when I approached her casket, a familiar heaviness surrounded my chest.

Memories flashed through my mind. My mother avoiding looking at my face. Reese's devastated parents huddled in the front pew. I had stared at the photo of his smiling face, knowing it was my fault he was in a box. Knowing it was far too late to help him. To apologize. Rachel's scorn when I joined them.

My brother would still be here if it weren't for you.

Shame. I'd sat in my Jetta, bawling in the parking lot while everyone else picked at crudités inside. Lo had tapped on the window and came to sit silently in the passenger seat while I let it out.

But Callum would be here with me today, an anchor in the hurricane of emotion.

Of course, laying Maeve to rest differed from losing Reese. For one, she'd lived a long and authentic life. Still, it wasn't easy to face death again. I hadn't seen a body since Reese's reconstructed face. I hadn't wanted to look, but Cielo told me our argument shouldn't be the last time I saw him. Maybe she was right; this was part of the healing process. And Callum had captured

Maeve's vibrancy along with a sense of tranquility. Hair immaculately curled, a touch of blush. He'd even given her a manicure, I noticed with a pang of bittersweet warmth.

I whispered a thank-you to my friend. For her kindness, her humor, her generosity, and her wisdom. Like Callum, she had seen my grief for what it was all along. Even when I thought I'd hidden it.

A rumble of engines snagged my attention. In the parking lot, a group of mourners arrived on vintage scooters. Clusters of lights and extra mirrors adorned their shiny, curved bodies. I smiled. Maeve would've gotten a real kick out of that. The visitors shuffled in, and Deirdre directed them to the guest book. I took it as my cue to make my way upstairs to Callum. Door ajar, he paced back and forth in the office.

"Maeve requested a singer, but the one she wanted won't be able to make it." Callum grimaced. "Caught in traffic on the M-Six."

"Maybe we can find something to stream. Do you have a wireless speaker? What did she request?"

I opened a music app on my phone, giving myself a job to stop thinking about saying goodbye to Maeve. About the disaster my work had become overnight. About the last memorial I attended.

As if sensing my neurotic edge, Callum's fingers rested on my lower back. I still wasn't happy about that stunt at the pub, but his outburst had come from a place of protectiveness . . . however misguided.

"No," Callum said. "She wanted a final serenade, and I'm going to give her one."

"You're going to sing?" I asked, lighting up.

"The last time I attempted anything like this, I was so nervous, I locked my knees and fainted into an open grave."

I squeezed his hand. "Are you sure? We can stream an acoustic version of the song she wanted."

"Somehow, I feel like Maeve arranged it this way on purpose."

"She was a crafty one."

It seemed odd for Maeve to change her last wishes only months after meeting Callum and me, but we'd chalked it up to the fact that she was in hospice. Had she deliberately requested a flaky musician to create this very situation? No. How could she have known . . . unless his fear of singing came up during one of our visits and I didn't remember?

With a glance at his watch, Callum nodded. It was time.

"I know you can do this." My fingers wrapped around his tie, and I pulled to guide his cheek to my lips, for a chaste kiss. "To keep your knees soft."

He smiled gently. "That'll work."

Internally, I kicked myself. Kissing him felt so natural, but I needed to stop giving Callum mixed signals.

Maeve's Lambretta stood sentinel at the graveside, a floral wreath resting on its headlight. She was missed by many colorful characters. Some were grayed and needed the aid of walkers and wheelchairs. Of course, a few arrived on gleaming scooters of their own, in tribute to the subculture that had sparked their friendships. White roses festooned the Celtic cross headstone next to hers, which marked her beloved Charlie's resting place. Reunited at last.

Callum stepped forward, drawing in a steadying breath. "And now, a final tribute to our friend Maeve Burke. She requested this song specifically, and if you're moved to, she wanted you to sing along."

His nervous gaze met mine for an instant before he closed his eyes with a soft smile and began to hum. I'd often imagined how his baritone voice would lift in song. Nothing could have prepared me for the rich sound that poured from his broad chest.

I didn't recognize it at first. Not until Callum sang the chorus. "Always Look on the Bright Side of Life."

Monty Python. Maeve had him singing the song from Monty Python's *Life of Brian*. I laughed in spite of myself. Of course she wouldn't choose a haunting, mournful ballad.

Guests swayed softly; some clapped along. A chorus of her loved ones joined in with the verse about life being a laugh and death being a joke, and the fact that the last laugh is on you.

All were moved by Callum's unexpected vocal dedication. The notes rained down, a cathartic shower of sound. He'd faced a fear, for someone else. I hoped he'd also done it for himself. Our eyes met as the last verse reverberated through the breeze, sending willow leaves dancing across the grass. Pride and adoration filled me. This wonderful, humble man had been hiding his light under a bushel, but no more. He was dashing and dazzling in his own modest, tweed-suited way.

I mouthed a silent thanks to him before he helped lower Maeve's coffin into the earth.

As the mourners shuffled toward the funeral home for the reception, we hung back by the graveside, next to the Lambretta.

"Callum . . . that was perfect. You were amazing." I wrapped my arms around him in a quick hug, breathing in deeply. Fortified by his embrace.

"Go away outta that."

"Really. Your voice is beautiful, even if you were quoting Monty Python. Maeve would've been very happy. She never heard you sing, did she?"

He shook his head.

"I think she heard today," I said, running a hand along the curves of the Lambretta. Gleaming chrome shone brightly in the late-morning sun, offsetting the soft petals of the floral wreath. "I still can't believe she left this scooter to me."

"You don't take things for granted. She saw that."

"It's a shame you don't know how to ride. I could teach you."

A tiny smile bloomed on Callum's lips. "Someday when I've more courage."

"A cappella singing in front of a group of strangers? That's enough to send most people into a cold sweat, and you nailed it. You did Maeve right today. And I'm proud of you."

"I know it wasn't easy to face another funeral," he said, softly rubbing my back. "I'm proud of you, too."

We could finally acknowledge my loss—and it actually felt good to do so.

Callum's fingers cradled my chin and tilted me toward his lips. Sweet and all too short, but professional duties still required his attention. It seemed he was struggling with self-control today as well. We walked the path between the gravestones, hands entwined.

The song was right: life was quite absurd. Because as he'd sung, I realized I was hopelessly in love with Callum Flannelly. And I had been for a while.

CHAPTER 38

Lark

ON MONDAY, I arrived early and speed-walked through the common areas of KinetiColor, then barricaded myself in my office. Nerves jangled, I called Mr. Sullivan's secretary to arrange an urgent meeting. For all I knew, Seán had already contacted his uncle about the events at the pub, and my pink slip was waiting for me.

While I waited for a meeting, I stared at my Saint Dolly devotional candle. Callum's voice echoing in my head asked, *What would Dolly do?* She sure wouldn't cower under her desk to avoid coworkers and a tantrum-throwing manbaby. Neither would Grace O'Malley. They would strut in, chin held high and dignity intact. Fight for it! That's what I intended to do.

Would Mr. Sullivan deem me unprofessional for being the catalyst in the confrontation between Seán and Callum? For stirring up conflict when we needed to focus on postproduction? Would I be packing up my desk's succulents and my Saint Dolly candle today?

Anxiety percolated in my stomach as I made my way through the halls, like a condemned prisoner walking to the electric chair. If this project flopped or the executives were unhappy with the early cut of the film, I could kiss my career as an art director goodbye, and my residence in Ireland along with it. I smoothed my skirt and adjusted my blouse. I wasn't a fierce pirate queen, but my roller derby name wasn't Dolly Pardon My French for nothing.

All that bravado evaporated when the conference room door swung open. Mr. Sullivan sat at the oblong table with Wendy, opposite Seán. A bandage rested over the bridge of his nose between purple-ringed eyes. *Oh, Callum. Look at the mess you made.* I plastered on a professional air as best I could, extending a handshake to the studio owner first, then Wendy. I didn't dare touch Seán. When they gestured for me to sit beside him, I winced, hoping no one noticed.

Wendy clasped her hands. "It's come to our attention that there has been a . . . rivalry of sorts between you and Seán that came to violence this weekend. Other team members have corroborated the altercation, and that a man involved with you was the aggressor."

Had Seán intimidated everyone to revise the night according to his narrative? I knew Anvi and Rory had my back, but what about the rest of the staff? Everyone believed he'd gotten the last art director canned.

"I'd never tell my, *my friend*, to do something like that. And it wasn't, um, unprovoked." The adrenaline coursing through my veins made me bumbling and ineloquent.

"There was a misunderstanding at the pub when the group went for a round after work," Seán said with a sour expression. "And it led to her boyfriend attacking and threatening me."

With pitiful puppy-dog eyes, Seán picked at the end of the bandage to draw attention to it. Wendy's expression softened, before she turned a hard look on me.

Bile crept up my throat, along with sheer panic. "That's— that's not how it happened—"

"You weren't even there when that brute smashed my nose."

"Is this true?" Wendy asked.

My hands formed impotent fists in my lap. "I was in the ladies' room."

"One minute, she and I were playing darts. The next, he was swinging at me, warning me he'd kill me if I talked to Lark again! I told him we're only colleagues, but he wouldn't hear it. Working with her is creating a hostile environment. It's not conducive to my mental well-being or productivity. I've tried everything in my power to foster a healthy professional relationship here. I am at a loss for what comes next."

If I wasn't insanely terrified, my eyes would've rolled back in my skull. This felt like playing "he said, she said" in the principal's office, trying to avoid expulsion.

"Did you tell your boyfriend to beat up Seán so he'd drop out of the competition for the series job?"

"Of course not!"

Mr. Sullivan stayed silent, observing every tiny response and shift in energy. He'd noticed my fists clenching, and I attempted to keep my hands relaxed on my lap. Now that I'd been called hostile, I wanted to give no confirmation of that label.

"My friend was defending me. But I didn't *tell* him to. Seán said something . . . deeply personal to the team about me."

"See, I thought we were finally becoming mates, Lark," Seán said, then pivoted to his uncle. "Before I was assaulted, she and I were engaged in a friendly round—"

Mercifully, Sullivan interrupted. "Personal?"

Seán aimed eye lasers in my direction. Wendy leaned closer, interest piqued.

Seán crossed his arms. "I found an old tweet from Blue Star Studio, a fundraiser in her late husband's memory. His sister worked for the company, too, so it was a big deal. This was publicly posted information. All I did was mention it to my peers in conversation, but her boyfriend was scuttered and jealous and took it the wrong way."

No use in refuting it; although Callum wasn't impaired, no one would believe alcohol didn't impact the situation. I fought the urge to sink into my seat. I didn't want to explain it. Or relive it.

"My husband was in an accident before I moved here. It's . . . part of the reason I didn't want to stay in the States. Seán didn't lie about that," I rasped through my constricting throat. It was still hard to say.

Shallow breaths made me lightheaded, and my heart tried to claw its way out of my chest. I wanted to tell them all about his concern-trolling, undermining my authority in group settings, and outsourcing his responsibilities to others through brash manipulation.

It was as if I was trapped in a sealed glass jar. Unable to call out. Unable to draw in enough oxygen.

Wendy studied me skeptically. My friends had warned me that she was a friend of Seán's. After I'd put a stop to his behavior of "delegating" tasks, supposedly on my behalf, my relations with Seán and Wendy soured further. But the proof was there: his output diminished substantially. Seán had relied on labor of others for so long, he couldn't keep pace on his own. Shady behavior aside, he didn't deserve the art director job when he couldn't even handle the typical workload of the senior lead animator.

Polar vortices were warmer than Mr. Sullivan's inscrutable stare. And I couldn't *breathe*. Pins and needles crept up my fingertips from clenching again. Was I having an asthma attack—was spontaneous, adult-onset asthma even a thing? I forced my face into a neutral, bland expression. Not like a woman on the verge of a complete breakdown and idiopathic medical emergency.

Keep it together. Be professional. Don't make them think you're hysterical.

"I never intended for it to be hurtful. And I am sorry you felt so offended." Seán laid it on thicker than molasses, with that punchable pout. "I hope you can forgive me, and that we can put this whole dreadful business behind us. For the good of the studio."

Manipulative prick. Seán never attempted to really know me before appointing me Public Enemy Number One. He'd made assumptions, weaponized my trauma against me. Now he played the empathetic victim to the head of the studio? *Please.*

Nothing about it was all right. I wouldn't forgive Seán for disclosing my greatest pain to every one of our colleagues as if it was juicy gossip. Now they'd see me as a pity party or a black widow. That's how it had been at Blue Star. Everything changed.

"Uncle—I mean, Mr. Sullivan, sir, about the series," Seán pivoted. "I've been nothing but loyal to this studio. Since day one, I've proven my worth, and I deserve this promotion. You know I do. Didn't you say you loved my presentation?"

"We haven't made our decision."

Wendy cut Seán another sympathetic half smile. Did that mean he was the top contender?

Seán was taking everything from me and getting rewarded with a promotion. That suffocating feeling whittled my focus down to his smug face. I wanted to shriek at the injustice of it all.

"Human resources will have individual meetings with both of you." Sullivan motioned to the door. "For now, you're excused."

I fantasized about a security guard on the other side, waiting to escort Seán to his desk for packing, then out to the curb where he belonged with the rest of the trash. But it wouldn't go down that way, would it? Men like him were rarely punished for their misdeeds. Especially when those around them were too frightened to speak up.

"I look forward to it," Seán said. "Have a nice day."

Unfallen tears welled in my eyes as I turned to Seán before he left. "Lark," he said. And he *winked* at me. *Winked* at me!

The glass jar burst. Shards of anger and fear cut through my good sense, my self-preservation instinct. My voice came out in an emotional, quivering burst. "What you—what you said was deplorable, and you *deserve* that broken nose!"

Coolheaded at this vindication, Seán muttered, "See what I've had to deal with?"

"Don't you have work to do?" I hissed through clenched teeth.

He shrugged at Sullivan and Wendy as if to say, *This is exactly what I'm talking about.*

An inferno raged in my chest. Broken glass left my ego lacerated and bleeding. But what else could I say?

Wendy and Sullivan exchanged an enigmatic look. Crap. *Crap.* Why had I said that? After months of subtle toxicity, I'd finally found my voice and I used it to tell Seán he deserved it, like a child? What was wrong with me?

Sullivan pulled the silver pocket square from his suit jacket and handed it over. Through the blur of tears and emotion, I couldn't read his face. "Seán. You can go."

Without looking back at me again, he did.

Grateful for the tiny piece of silk, I dabbed at my face. My heart continued to gallop. My lungs felt a quarter-filled. I tried to return the soggy pocket square, but Mr. Sullivan held a hand up in polite refusal.

I wanted to crawl under the conference table and dig my way to Singapore. Start fresh where no one knew my name or my shame. Without formulating a response—my brain the endlessly loading rainbow wheel on a MacBook—I bolted upright to make a beeline for the conference room door.

"Lark, wait." Mr. Sullivan drew his hands together.

"I'm so sorry—"

"The executives screened the early cut of *The Pirate Queen* on Saturday."

Oh.

"Do you have any feedback yet?" I snuffled, swiping at my wet cheeks. Any distraction from that emotional outburst shitshow.

"There are a few notes, mostly for the editors. Handful of

retakes. Overall, it looks excellent. You and your team have done a fine job."

Pride warred with humiliation as I lifted a modest smile at the praise. My knuckles curved around the pocket square as I forced my vocal cords to cooperate. "Thank you, sir. This opportunity has meant so much to me and I hope we can move past this . . . unpleasantness."

Keep smiling. Keep moving. Don't let them know how much it hurts.

CHAPTER 39

Callum

"CALLUM, I KNOW dating has been hard for you, so I took the liberty of finding *alternative* resources." Deirdre swiveled the reception desk's computer monitor toward me.

I squinted at the screen, but it was full of small text. "What am I looking at?"

"It's a forum for women seeking green cards."

Braking tires screeched in my mind. "I can't wed someone I don't know at all. Stop acting the maggot."

"You tried your best—and fair play to you—but you needed to pursue other options *yesterday* if you stand a chance of keeping Willow Haven. Or I'm dragging you to the registry office with me."

I shot her a floppy smile. I'd said as much to Lark, but I still hoped it wouldn't come to that. It would be a mutually beneficial legal arrangement, as Dierdre would receive a stake in the business in return for helping save it.

When I allowed myself to imagine a hypothetical future wife, I could see only one heart-shaped face behind the white veil. Eyes gray as the river meeting mine as I slipped my nan's shining claddagh over a dainty knuckle. An effervescent laugh as I carried her over the threshold of my family home, like the groom in an old black-and-white film.

Before she'd proposed, I'd nearly asked Lark a half dozen times. In the sweet afterglow of lovemaking, when all seemed right in the world. As we walked along the bay and watched herons wading along the shore, or cuddled on her miniature sofa as a movie flickered on the screen. Every time, a mixture of sensibility and fear kept me from it. With her people-pleasing tendencies and a deep awareness of the dire stakes, it was wrong to put her in that position. I'd felt that way even before confirming that her hang-ups about marriage revolved around the way her previous one ended.

If only there was another way. I'd pored over my granda's will, searching for an answer. According to the solicitor who wrote it up for him, it was iron-clad. But it just felt so wrong. Pádraig would assume ownership, only to auction off the family business to the highest bidder. All because of some arbitrary birthday.

"I'm going to ask Lark. Really ask her."

She dropped my arm like it burned her palm, and studied me. "You're in love with her."

"I couldn't stop myself."

"And she loves you?"

I knew what I felt, but that couldn't guarantee that Lark would respond the way I hoped. All I could do was convince her of my sincerity and hope that she'd swoon instead of run.

"Oh, Callum. I warned you."

"I know. And you were right. No one else compares to her." I sighed. "I know I want her. And that I'd want her even if there were no inheritance to fret over. She needs to know."

Compassion filled Deirdre's face. "How are you planning to propose?"

"HEY, SAOIRSE, D'YOU have a minute?" I asked after she'd completed her delivery of roses, jerking my chin toward the chapel for her to follow me.

At the reception desk, Deirdre paused mid keystroke, rub-bernecking like she was crawling past a wreck on the highway. I wished I could afford to send her home for the rest of the day, but we were too busy and she was invested. An occupational hazard when my marital status was tied to her job stability.

I fluffed the baby's breath at the front of the chapel, attempt-ing to muster the nerve to ask for a favor I didn't deserve.

"Lark doesn't want to move back to the States."

Saoirse's brows lifted. "Really?"

"She's applied for a more permanent position at the studio. She's trying to stay."

"That's wonderful. Are you two finally . . . ?"

"I need to hire a musician for Saturday. A fiddler. It's short notice."

Her eyes narrowed. "What for, a service?"

"I'm asking her to be together. Officially. Sunflowers!" I blurted, my mind still scattered. "I also need to place a large order of sunflowers. If you happen to know a florist."

I wanted to love Lark the way she lived: colorfully and full of spontaneity. For my entire life, the scent of flowers had been asso-ciated with mourning, but now, I wanted to give Lark something so huge and cheery, the sun itself would pale in comparison.

A warm smile covered Saoirse's face. "Using me for the perks, are ye?"

"Would it be worse to go to your competition? Supporting a friend is the least I can do," I countered. "This needs to be perfect. I trust you. Please."

"Don't think for a moment you're getting a discount on either service."

"Go ahead and add an arsehole surcharge."

"You're not an arsehole. What's the plan, then?"

"I, um, wrote her a song. Are you free tonight to rehearse?"

CHAPTER 40

Lark

NOW THAT THE pressure was on, I had to prove myself to Mr. Sullivan, which meant perfection on the final edits of *The Pirate Queen*. Although I craved Callum's supportive presence like oxygen itself, I couldn't afford the distraction. Too much was at stake. He seemed almost relieved at the news, saying he had a taxing workday as well.

My desk faced the window toward his home, and I periodically lifted my head to cast a yearning gaze at it. Around seven o'clock, his door opened. Casual in his dark jeans and that damn snug Henley, Callum sent a furtive glance toward my apartment before getting into his car.

Because he hadn't mentioned a date tonight, I assumed he'd gone for takeout. An hour passed. Maybe he was grocery shopping. Maybe he was enjoying a walk by the bay. Two hours.

Saoirse's delivery van was parked at the curb when I arrived home. Maybe he was giving it another try with her. Scenarios played in my mind as I tried to focus on work. Callum telling a joke, his mouth lifting in the wry grin usually reserved just for me. Saoirse squeezing his arm. Leaning in for a kiss? Sharing a *moment*. By the time he pulled back into the driveway, it was past eleven and I'd completely spiraled.

Hidden by the curtains, I watched as he walked to the front door, an unmistakable pep in his step. He hummed a melody, the deep notes drifting through my open window in the darkness. Moonlight highlighted his smiling cheeks, and it was all I could do to not rush downstairs and demand to know where he'd been. Declare my feelings, come what may.

I'd done it to myself, getting attached to the man next door when I knew it couldn't last. It was better this way; Callum moving on before I could hurt him. He'd gone on a date and enjoyed it. Like he was always supposed to.

THE NEXT MORNING had me deeply regretting all my life choices. Cross-eyed from studying animation samples for hours, I stumbled into the break room in search of caffeine.

Anvi leaned on the counter, sipping from her Betty Boop mug. Sensing my unease, she asked, "What's the story?"

"That's a loaded question."

She brushed her thick black hair off her shoulder. "Is the problem personal or professional?"

"My brain will liquefy and pour out my ears if I have to consider all the things wrong in both. So let's leave it at 'professional.'"

"Ah. Don't dodge me. You listened to me when my family gnawed my ear about my sister becoming a solicitor *and* you brought biscuits the next day to cheer me up."

"Lark?" Wendy's knuckles rapped on the break room's open door. "May I have a word?"

Trepidation seized me so hard I couldn't even vocalize the *yes*. I just nodded mutely.

Anvi crossed fingers and mouthed, "You got this." I followed Wendy down the hall, and she entered my office instead of continuing down the labyrinth to human resources, which I appreciated. A conversation on my own turf would be marginally more comfortable.

My heart raced as the door clicked shut behind us. Wendy crossed her arms and leaned on my desk. I stood next to her stiffly. Sitting would only put her above my eye level, and I needed the illusion of even ground.

"Before you hear it from anyone else, I wanted to let you know Seán got the series."

CHAPTER 41

Callum

"I SHOULDN'T. I have a lot to do before our premiere." Lark's dimmed eyes barely met mine. Work pressure was obviously taking a toll, evidenced by her midafternoon Hello Kitty pajamas and messy hair.

"Come on. It's perfect weather for a scooter ride. I'll have you home for supper," I insisted, leaning on the doorway of her flat. "You wouldn't make me go alone?"

"But you don't know how to ride."

"Exactly. I'd stall out at the first traffic light without you."

"Okay." She allowed herself a thin smile. "Only because of that ego stroke."

"Ah yes. Nothing more alluring than an opportunity to bail out an incompetent man."

"You have no idea." She laughed mirthlessly. Part of her mood must be about the job competition. Lark had nothing to worry about. Of course they'd choose her as art director for the series.

I'd made a vow to myself to make her forget all about that this afternoon. I waited in the garage and shot Saoirse a text as Lark changed. Sunflower decals adorned the side of her ballet-pink helmet. My own helmet was black, naturally. I'd ordered them after Lark first arrived on the Lambretta without one.

Lark's vibrance made me fall for her. Stifling it would be akin to plucking a wild, rare bloom, only to watch it wither under a bell jar. While I'd never be fully comfortable with her riding on two wheels without the benefit of side-curtain airbags and seat belts, I'd never inhibit her joy, either. I could only strap on a helmet, mumble a petition to Saint Christopher, and hang on.

To love was to accept risk. In all honesty, the half-century-old scooter was a thousand times safer than giving anyone my heart—and I'd done that months ago.

"Are you certain about this?" she asked, adjusting her helmet strap.

"Yes."

"Where are we going?"

"I'll tell you where to turn. It's a surprise."

My body vibrated with energy as Lark kick-started the scooter. She whooped as the Lambretta rumbled to life with a puff of petrol. I could do this. Maybe. Lark showed me I could face my fears, and I would. For us.

I climbed on and bit back my grin. My arms encircled her waist and her warmth radiated through my clothes like sunshine, infusing my entire body with optimism and possibility.

Inattentive drivers in Galway had me white-knuckled, but once we got on the road to Connemara, it felt like we were airborne. Wind howled around the tall windscreen above the scooter's light. Tiny cottages dotted the landscape of my nan's birthplace, stocky ponies grazed in their fields. As we approached Trá an Dóilín—Coral Strand—my heart thundered.

Lark turned off the engine, shucked her helmet, and shook out her hair. I stored the helmets in the back of the scooter. Aubergine clouds streaked across the afternoon sky above us. Foamy waves licked the shore that was composed not of sand but countless bits of calcified seaweed that resembled coral. Lark scooped up a palmful and examined it before shoving a few chunks in her pocket. Her sentimentality delighted me.

"Look!" Seals frolicked in the water. She grabbed my arm to point at their heads bobbing above the waves.

"We should've packed a picnic. Next time," I assured her. There would be so many *next times*.

My mobile vibrated in my pocket. I chanced a peek as Lark clambered up an outcropping of wave-battered rock. Saoirse had replied. An emoji had never given me so much anxiety. I was already kilometers from my comfort zone. Perched above the rock pool, Lark's arms were outstretched. Wind whipped through her hair, and anemones swayed in the tide pool at her sandaled feet.

"You look like a siren," I said. "Or a goddess. Botticelli's Venus with less shell and more clothes."

She batted her lashes. "A goddess, huh?"

"So gorgeous, I could break into song."

She rolled her eyes. "If I'm a siren, you'd better hope *I* don't start singing. Not unless you have a vendetta against sailors and need the business."

It was a wonder her hand didn't slip out of my sweaty paw when I helped her back to the shore. If she noticed, she said nothing. My mobile buzzed again. Probably Saoirse. No way in hell would I want Lark to see her name on my screen before the big reveal and get the wrong idea. Although she never said it aloud, I could tell she felt threatened by Saoirse. She needn't have. But jealousy was an irrational beast. Its teeth dug into me at the memory of Aidan's flirtatious hold on Lark at the Hare's Breath. I couldn't blame her for feeling the same way.

In fact, maybe this was a terrible plan. A lifetime of formaldehyde fumes had gone to my brain.

At the sound of the text alert, her smile faded to nothing more than a hairline crack in fine china. "Did you go out last night?"

I gulped. "Yes."

"Good. I'm glad." Resignation filled her voice, and Lark turned to the waves again.

The truth was too big for me to hold in anymore. She needed to know how I felt. *Now or never.*

I took a deep breath and started to sing. Pouring all my emotion into the lyrics, I kept my eyes closed. I couldn't look, not yet.

My heart thumps like a drum
With the taste of your lips, the sweet breath in your lungs.
I tried not to fall, but I had to succumb.

Rounding out the first verse, I cracked an eye open. Awe covered Lark's face, her hands clutched over her heart. Just behind her stood Saoirse. Lark was so engrossed, a marching band could've snuck up on her. When the first chord of the fiddle came unseen from behind, she jumped. Confusion flashed on her features when she saw who was playing, but I kept my focus solely on Lark.

There would be no mistaking who was being wooed by this serenade. Every note belonged to her.

Too long I made my feelings discreet
The truth is, without you I was incomplete.
A hollow chest you taught how to beat.
Until the hourglass is drained of sand
I'll cradle your heart in the palm of my hand.
Swear on this life, beside you I'll stand.

Tears sprang to Lark's eyes. Simple as they were, my words moved her. One more thing needed to be done. Sweet notes of the fiddle signified the end of the song, and Saoirse took a bow. I'd never been able to write a proper ballad, until Lark had barged through my door holding my open package, transforming my life into a Technicolor adventure. Thanks to her, I now did things like sing at the beach.

"I . . . What . . . Callum . . ."

I took her delicate hands. "That's, um, named 'Larksong.'"

Fathomless gray eyes gazed into mine, deeper than the ocean behind her. "That was like a dream. Your voice and the song and . . . you wrote that? Oh my God, I can't believe that just happened."

I kissed her knuckles, aching more than ever to slip my nan's gold claddagh onto one. The ring that had so plagued my thoughts was now burning a hole in my pocket. Excitement and trepidation warred inside me.

"We rehearsed it last night. That's where I was." I nodded at the fiddler. "Thanks, Saoirse."

"My pleasure," she answered. "Hi, Lark."

Looking a bit puzzled, Lark said "Hey" as she wiped a tear from under an eye. Nobody was sure what to say as a quiet beat passed. "That was beautiful. Um, thank you."

"I'll catch up with you two later." Saoirse turned on her heel to walk down the beach, smiling like the cat that caught the canary. She'd refused to let me pay her for helping me in the musical ambush.

Lark exhaled. "Cal, that was the most romantic thing anyone has ever done for me."

"If you're staying, I want us to be all in. A real couple."

My breath hitched at her hesitance and quivering chin. Something was wrong.

"I didn't get the job. They chose Seán."

I felt as if I were eleven years old at the schoolyard again, punched in the stomach. Left gasping like the fish out of water I'd always been. Hooked but still stubbornly flailing. Was it my fault? An assault on her competition couldn't have helped.

"What? Why didn't you tell me?"

"I can't stay without the permit, and it's only for approved jobs. And . . . nothing listed online will work. Not even in Dublin. I searched recruitment sites all night."

"We'll make it work. We have to."

Lark looked fragile enough for the sea breeze to whisk her away.

I dropped to one knee in the bits of sharp, wet coral. "Marry me. Lark Thompson, I want to be your husband."

Sunlight gleamed off the iconic design of hands cradling a crowned heart as I held up the ring. This was terrifying, but nothing compared to the fear of losing her forever.

"Is getting married . . . for me or for *you*?"

"For us." My heart pounded.

"Why now? What made you change your mind?"

"I never changed my mind. I want forever with you, mo chuisle. I always have."

Twin hurricanes of uncertainty whirled in her eyes. I'd be her safe harbor if she trusted me.

"What does it mean? You called me that before."

I blinked. Was she not going to respond to my proposal?

"Mo chuisle? It means 'my pulse.' I never quite understood it before, what it meant to have another person be the d-driving force behind the pump of your blood, but it's true. Lark, your smile saved me like an emergency transfusion. Your laugh is the song my every blood cell dances to. Your touch revived me from darkness. You are my pulse. You make me feel alive even when I'm surrounded by death."

Lark looked at me like it was the most touching thing she'd ever heard. And the most painful. Her shoulders dropped, and coral crunched under her feet as she took a step back. One step that felt like a yawning chasm.

"Cal, you mean so much to me. More than I could ever have imagined when we first met, but you know how I feel about being in a real relationship again. You deserve better than I can give you."

Anxiety rose to a fever pitch as my unanswered question hovered between us. I slowly rose to my feet. "I'm not Reese, and you're not the same person you were when that happened."

"Haven't you paid attention to anything I've ever said about relationships? Anything I've said about having kids? Being someone's partner is a responsibility I can't take. I loved him, but it wasn't enough. I couldn't hold my marriage together, and look at what happened as a direct result."

"That wasn't your fault. And I might not have known him, but I'm positive he wouldn't want you to punish yourself forever for something you had no control over. He'd want you to be happy again."

"You're an expert on what Reese would want, huh?"

"Then let's concentrate on what *we* want. You want to stay. I want you to stay. This would make it possible to b-b-be together. We'll have all the time we need to sort the rest."

"Callum, we both knew this wasn't forever. It was only supposed to be one night. I'm just not ready for more than a legal arrangement. Even that was pushing my boundaries for your sake, because I care about you."

No matter what she said, I knew the truth: something special existed between us. Untimely as it may be, it had grown. *We* had grown. Together.

"Misplaced guilt won't get you closure. Keeping me at arm's length won't, either. Stop punishing *us* for your husband's death."

"It isn't misplaced. I didn't notice he was unhappy. I didn't listen to him when he told me, and I'm the reason he got into that car upset. I didn't stop him; I was too selfish. And that hasn't changed— I took what I wanted from you when I *knew* I couldn't give you what you needed. I was a distraction when you were supposed to be finding The *One*."

Loose coral shifted underfoot as I closed the gap between us. "I don't give a fuck about anyone but you. Can't you see that?"

Tears slid down Lark's cheeks. "When we started this, you promised . . ."

"I didn't sleep with you as practice for someone else."

She crossed her arms as frothy waves crept toward her toes.

"I'm not asking you to be my wife because I need to get married; I'm asking because I want you. Not the funeral home. *You.* No one else. I know this is a little mad, but we'll take it one day at a time, hand in hand. It can't be any more dangerous than roller-skating or riding the scooter."

Sorrow filled her eyes. On a shuddering breath, she said, "I can't do this, if you want it to be real. I'm not ready."

"I'll move to the States, then. We don't have to get married at all. Ever." The miserable voice behind my impassioned plea was unrecognizable to my own ears.

"Immigration doesn't work that way, Cal. And you'd lose Willow Haven. You're willing to drop your entire life for me? Turn your back on your family's legacy? No. You'll regret sacrificing everything. You'll resent me."

I shot back, "You *are* everything."

Moisture fogged the lenses of my glasses. Desperation clawed its way up from the depth of my soul, making a last appeal with every iota of conviction I could muster.

"We *work* together. I give you a soft, stable place to recharge. You energize and embolden me," I said. "Give this a chance. Let me make you happy. You d-d—you deserve to be happy."

Lark's head hung low.

"Callum." I've never hated the sound of my name before, but it sounded so defeated. A plea for mercy from a person who believed herself undeserving of clemency. "I can't."

CHAPTER 42

Lark

EMOTIONAL CONFRONTATION HAD never been my strong suit, but this level of avoidance sunk me to a new low. On autopilot, I'd climbed on the Lambretta. Alone. Running again. Abandoning Callum like the worst kind of coward.

After his heartfelt declaration, how could I handle pressing against his body the entire ride back to Galway? Before I knew it, I was revving the engine in a sorry attempt to distance myself from the problem I'd created. It didn't matter how many miles I put between us. Guilt matched my pace like shadow.

Until the moment he proposed, I hadn't completely understood the reason commitment was so terrifying. It meant being vulnerable to the same devastation I'd experienced with Reese. Our life had imploded in one moment, the love we'd shared collapsed in on itself to become something dark and destructive. If I abandoned Callum first, he couldn't abandon me. Tragedy happened to good people; Reese himself was proof of that. Callum's job reminded us of it every day. Pure instinct and self-preservation made me leave him behind. Not logic. Not that it brought me any less shame for the unforgivably selfish choice. If anything, it proved my point far better than I could articulate: I was broken.

Despite what I felt for him, I couldn't even show him basic compassion.

Callum's song and the crestfallen slump of his shoulders haunted my thoughts the entire journey home. As the verdant landscape rolled past, I reminded myself I'd been through worse. I'd lost a best friend. The man I loved. Now I was losing both, in the same person. Dulcet notes echoed in my ears, along with the dull roar of the waves and the honeyed sound of the fiddle. When Callum looked into my eyes and sang of devotion, I believed him. And I believed in us. Admittedly, for a brief instant, I could see a storybook future together with stunning clarity. I was caught up in the moment.

His explanation of *mo chuisle* evaporated the cloud built by his heavenly voice and dropped me straight down to earth without a parachute. His pulse. I couldn't be his pulse, couldn't let him place his heart in my hands. Look at what I had done to Reese's.

Deep down, I'd thought he might love me. I was loath to admit it, because then I'd have to do the responsible thing and cut him off for his own well-being. And, well, I was selfish when it came to Callum.

Giant, cheerful blooms greeted me when I arrived back home. An explosion of yellow, brown, and green filled the living space, vases of sunflowers on the counter and tables. My helmet hit the floor with a soft thud. Tears flowed down my cheeks. He was so thoughtful; further proof I didn't deserve him.

In my guilt, I closed my eyes to block out the flowers, their happiness incongruent with my mood. Earthy sunflower scented the air to remind me of their presence. Each petal was an indictment: *he loves you, he loves you.* And even though I loved him fiercely, I'd essentially stripped every petal off our relationship and shouted in his face, *She loves you not.* What else could I do after he'd said that? Called me that . . . asked me to marry him for real?

Faint buzzing in my pocket interrupted my emotional

nosedive—Callum. I'd left him on the beach to call for a ride. I couldn't speak to him, not yet. I tossed it on the steamer trunk coffee table and collapsed on the couch, listening until it stopped.

After an indeterminable time spent crying, I crossed to my desk, where another bouquet sat. I wanted to bat it off the surface like a house cat. Houdini was strangely quiet. Usually, her wheel provided a squeaky soundtrack for my scribbles by this time of the evening.

"Hey, girl." I lifted the hollow coconut where she napped and brushed aside her bedding. She was gone.

"Houdini? Harriet?" As if a mouse would come at the sound of her name. A narrow strip of space in the latch caught my attention. She must've squeezed through there. I hadn't noticed it was becoming loose. Actually, I hadn't given her much affection at all over the past week, with postproduction and the competition for the series consuming all my time. And Callum acting as a delicious distraction in the interim.

"Dammit," I hissed, furious at myself. For everything. Unless it was a cartoon, anything I touched turned to shit, and I had no one to blame but myself. I couldn't even take care of a rodent . . . and Callum said I was *the pulse keeping him alive*?

Moving through the apartment on my knees, peeking under furniture, proved unfruitful.

I peeked in the closet. My shimmering premiere dress hung like an accusation. When I'd bought it, I'd imagined walking the red carpet with Callum. Studying his profile in the low theater light as we screened *The Pirate Queen* for the first time. Compared to Cannes or Sundance, the Galway Film Fleadh was small, but it still received international attention. Our little film deserved that. Now the garment was a harbinger of my departure from Ireland. I thought of Seán, smug and secure in the promotion, and wanted to tear it apart at the seams. Only because I couldn't do the same to him. Or myself.

Now I certainly couldn't concentrate on the redraws. They

stayed untouched as I padded to the fridge, pulled out some cheese, and shoved a handful in my mouth. I placed a slice on the floor to lure Houdini. Maybe I had a chance of catching the tiny fugitive.

Flowers graced every room in the small apartment, even the bathroom. There was no escape. Their subtle, grassy fragrance permeated the entire space. I retrieved my phone for its flashlight to look under my bed. Missed texts and calls populated the lock screen.

> CALLUM: Let me know you're home safe. Please.

Even after I'd tossed his heart into a meat grinder, he cared about my safety. With a steadying breath, I tapped out a measured response, stopping and starting over again.

> I'm home. Please give me some space.

Immediately, dots to indicate typing bubbled up on my screen . . . only to stop without a message. I wondered if he'd witnessed my false starts, too. Been tortured by the inability to read minds. I added one more. Callum always said I could never communicate a full thought over a single text.

> I'm so sorry.

No dots came in response, and his messages stopped.

CHAPTER 43

Callum

ASKING LARK TO be my girlfriend would've been risky; begging her to be my wife was downright ludicrous. When she left me at the beach with the claddagh pinched between my fingers, I thought about ringing Saoirse for a lift, but I couldn't even respond when she'd texted me asking how the proposal went. For hours, I stared vacantly into the salty waves. I couldn't reconcile the bond I knew Lark and I shared with the way she'd left me behind. Like I was a stranger in her life already. Long after the sun slipped beyond the horizon, I called a taxi home.

Lark shuffled out her door the next morning without so much as a glance toward my house. I knew because I stared out my window until she emerged for one of her final days at KinetiColor. Back to being the creep next door. More than anything, I yearned to feel close again. To share a joke or casual touch. I'd squash my desires down to preserve our friendship, if that was the cost. It was dear, but I'd pay it. She'd probably already purchased a ticket to Amsterdam or New York or Seoul.

Too early to drink. Too late to go back to bed. Fingers poised over the piano's keys, I channeled my lament into music instead. Resonant notes spilled into the parlor. I could hear the melody in my mind, like the ghost of Lark's laugh, but it wasn't so easy to transcribe. Hours I'd been at this. My focus drifted back to the window of the neighboring flat. I'd never be able to look at it again without thinking of her. I tore off my glasses and rubbed at the bridge of my nose.

How had I been so careless, allowing my affection to grow so deep and consuming? Love was a living thing. It spread like wild brambles and took over everything. Somehow, Lark had managed to hack her way through and move on; I remained pinned under vine, skewered and sliced by thorns.

"Good morning!"

Deirdre and Saoirse wore matching sheepish looks. Guilt threaded through my listless mood. I'd been so ready to give up Willow Haven and follow Lark back to Texas, but where would that have left Deirdre?

"Gracious! You look worse than the corpses." Deirdre tsked as she looked over my unshaven cheeks and eye bags. "Have you got a bad dose? I heard something was going 'round."

"I don't think he's sick," Saoirse volunteered, setting a spray of roses on the counter.

Deirdre frowned. "Lark said no?"

I nodded miserably. Most of the time, Deirdre wasn't much for "I told you so," but still, she had warned me. She didn't need to say it.

"Can you give us a minute?" Saoirse asked.

Deirdre declared a cup of tea was in order and made her exit.

"You never answered my text. I hoped that meant it went well." Saoirse put her hand on my shoulder. I scooted over to make room, and we shared the narrow space on the piano bench.

"The first time I met Lark, we sat just like this," I said automatically. The memory was painful now, like when I'd outgrown my favorite shoes as a boy but insisted on wearing them still. Unable to let go of one of the few things that made me feel good about myself.

I needed to let go. Lark wasn't in love with me.

Saoirse frowned at the silent piano. "I'm sorry it didn't work out the way you wanted, Callum. For what it's worth, it was a remarkable gesture."

My shoulders slumped. "I ruined the remaining time we had together."

"The night we rehearsed, you told me Lark inspired you to write again. Sing again. No matter how it ends, she gave you something that helped bring back your voice and your confidence."

"I didn't know it could hurt this much to care about someone."

"You're grieving," Deirdre said as she proffered a steaming mug; I accepted it with gratitude. "Losing your friendship. The future you envisioned. That's a valid form of grief."

"Seems disrespectful to call it as much here."

Deirdre shook her head. "Almost every soul you've laid to rest has felt what you're feeling right now. I'm sure many would disagree."

"Can I give you a hug?" Saoirse asked.

Instinctively, I tensed.

"That's all right. Never mind."

"Um, yeah. Okay."

"Okay?" She gave me a quick, platonic squeeze.

"He never lets me hug him, and I've known him for nearly twenty years!" Deirdre complained. "If *she* gets one . . ."

Thick arms constricted around my neck from behind, like twin lavender-scented anacondas. I sighed in manufactured resignation and patted an arm.

"This never happened," I grumbled.

"Your secret emotions are safe with us," Saoirse said.

Deirdre released me with a chuckle. "Drink your tea. Everything feels more manageable after a cuppa."

"Thanks. I don't know what I'd do without you. You're more family to me than my own blood." I savored the brew. Acknowledgment wouldn't fill the hole in my heart, but it meant something. I turned to Saoirse. "And thank you. For everything. Your friendship means a lot to me."

She gestured at the piano and notebook full of frantic scribblings. "If music helps, you are always welcome to come play with the band. The guys liked you."

"I'll keep it in mind."

CHAPTER 44

Lark

THE CHEESE I'D left in the dish on the floor was gone. I'd waited for the little mouse to come sniffing, but nodded off before she scurried over. Hope flickered in my chest like an old neon sign. Houdini hadn't performed her final disappearing act.

A memory rose: building her maze with Callum. Could I create a trap that wouldn't hurt her?

I gathered delivery boxes, tape, and a mop bucket. Using the cardboard, I crafted a breakaway ramp leading to the center of the bucket, which would tip under her weight. It looked like a diving board. When Houdini went for the food, it would fall, depositing her safely inside. The rest of the boxes served as makeshift stairs, and I used cheese as bait.

Seven days had passed since I detonated the relationship dynamite in a blaze of martyrdom.

Today my mood was lighter. Cielo had just completed her bachelor's in biology with flying colors. As planned, she was coming to visit me to celebrate, so I took a cab to the airport in Shannon.

Last week I was downright giddy at her pending arrival. Now

showing my cousin the best of Ireland felt like a cruel twist of irony.

Lo's radiant smile warmed my heart as I waved to her at the pickup curb. Her caramel-highlighted hair was pulled into two small messy buns, and she slung her carry-on into the back seat and smothered me in a long-overdue hug.

"How are you holding up?"

"Better now that you're here."

Hiding my pain had become an automatic defense mechanism, but how could I hide it from the person who'd seen me at my most vulnerable? I'd already given her the CliffsNotes version on the phone. As the cab entered Galway, I let Cielo enjoy the initial impression of the seaside city. All the independent shops and cafés that lined the streets, the ancient buildings next to splashes of modern art. She rolled down the window, allowing fresh air and blips of music into the back seat. The unabridged version of my nightmarish week could wait.

When the taxi pulled into the hedge-lined street and Willow Haven came into view, Cielo craned her neck for a glimpse of Callum. Of course, he still hadn't updated the wooden sign, which was entirely in Irish except for the name. I didn't bother to turn; he was likely holed up in the mortuary. Even his rose garden had been neglected, unless he was deliberately tending it while I was at work.

"This is it? Callum's place?" Lo peeked over the fence facing the garden. "It's really cute. Everything in this neighborhood is adorable."

"You won't see him, he's a total recluse when he wants to be. It's for the best."

"Says who?" She trailed behind me as I climbed my steps, banging all three with her carry-on. "From what you tell me, he's the feet-on-the-ground type. You're easily carried away by flights of fancy, that's not always a bad thing. I think you two balance each other nicely."

"It doesn't matter. With this film wrapping, I won't be able to stay unless the studio gives me another project."

I'd been oscillating between wanting to hop on a plane to anywhere and wanting to dig my heels into the ground and refuse to leave. My instinct was to run to avoid reminders of pain, the way a shark must continue to swim to avoid drowning. Not that I had much choice in the matter without an extension on my work visa.

"Answer me this: If immigration laws and inheritance clauses were no obstacle, what would you do?"

"I'd . . . want Callum to be happy. Fulfilled. With me, he can't—"

"He told you exactly how he'd be happy," Cielo said. "You didn't wanna hear it."

Undeniably guilty of that, I jabbed my keys into the lock. The door swung open to the sight of the dozens of sunflowers. Not much else marked this place as mine; I hadn't wanted to take real ownership of it until recently.

Cielo gaped at the giant blooms. "It's like a sunflower explosion."

"Yeah. Cal remembered I like them." I eyed them warily, like they might hide teeth between the petals. Even though they hurt to look upon, I couldn't bear to discard what was most likely the last gift he would ever give me. This entire apartment now reminded me of Callum. The colorful cushions on the love seat reminded me of our movie nights. Even my sheets retained his scrumptious scent, but this morning when I'd held my pillow to my nose for a hit, I'd noticed with disappointment that it was already fading.

Drained from her journey, Lo rolled her luggage next to the love seat and kicked off her shoes.

I slumped beside her. "I wanna go home."

"No, you don't. You're just used to running away."

The last time I'd been surrounded by painful memories, I'd

packed them up and dumped them at Goodwill or my mom's garage. I'd ran . . . straight into Callum.

No matter where I went, I'd ache for this place. Music and ruins and the bitter foam of Guinness. Drizzle and rolling hills and the River Corrib racing outside my office window. My coworkers' good-natured pranks. The man I'd come to think of as home.

"I can't marry Callum. I'm a disaster. He deserves better."

"You are the best person I know. Well, except for leaving him at the beach. That was messed up."

I dragged a hand over my face. "God, I know. It was horrible. I haven't even properly apologized yet."

"You don't have to say yes to his proposal, if his employee would do it," Lo said. "Callum told you he'd follow you to the States if you needed to go back?"

I tucked myself into a ball. The conversation had me feeling defensive. "Choosing me would cost him everything. Saving his business was the whole point. I love him. I can't let him sacrifice that. And he also wants kids, remember?"

"What are you talking about? You've always wanted to be a mom. You've kept a list of baby names in your Notes app for years. I saw ovulation testing kits in your bathroom in Austin."

"Wait. You went through my stuff?"

"I was looking for a tampon, thank you very much."

Reese and I put conception on indefinite hold when I got the promotion at Blue Star. "Reese wanted to try, but I was focusing on myself. I thought we had more time."

"He celebrated your success. Maybe he was disappointed to wait, but he understood the enormous opportunity of *Shoelace*. It's okay that you weren't ready yet. Or if you changed your mind about it." Lo clamped onto my shoulders. "But nothing that happened was your fault. Life dealt you a shit hand. Sometimes it happens to the best people. Doesn't mean you're unworthy of love. Reese would tell you that's nonsense. He never would've wanted to be the reason you stop yourself from going after what you want. Or who you want."

Tears pushed at my eyes. "How can I trust that this isn't just me being selfish again?"

"Because it's what Callum wants, too. You've gotta trust him to know what he wants." She drew me into a hug. "You deserve to start a family of your own one day, if that's what *you* still want."

"I want—*wanted*—a baby, too, but I can't even take care of a mouse."

"You've been telling yourself lies for too long, darlin'. It's time to unlearn them."

MY MATTRESS MIGHT as well have been stuffed with rocks, for all the rest I'd gotten in the past week. I stared at my empty wall long after jet lag claimed Lo. A hollow plastic *thunk* roused me, followed by the faintest squeak. Houdini! I scrambled to the bucket in the corner of my bedroom. Sitting up on her hind legs, my mouse was clawing at the bucket's smooth sides.

Not a whisker out of place. Soft fur brushed my skin as I scooped her up and cradled her to my cheek.

My chin quivered. Houdini was just a mouse, sure, but she was mine. This creature trusted me to care for her. She looked up at me, sniffing the air innocently. As if her silent exercise wheel and empty cage hadn't made my crisis even more vivid.

"I've got you. You're safe, girl."

Heaven knows I wasn't ready for a baby, but perhaps I wasn't a total lost cause. Convincing myself I wasn't cut out for nurturing made the disappointment and ache in my soul more bearable. For two years, I'd told myself it was the responsible thing to remain single. For the first time I considered whether maybe that wasn't true.

MY LAST DAY at KinetiColor brought a pang to my chest. While the film festival wasn't until July, my part in the process was complete. Now it was handed off to sound mixing and marketing, and it was time for me to move on. I'd always planned to stay through the premiere, working freelance after my contract was finished, as the visa included a cushion of time after the job. Maybe I'd take a trip to somewhere in Europe, just for a change of scenery and distraction.

I hate goodbyes. Just as I'd miss the foggy mornings and walking along the canals, I'd miss this place. Anvi's humming to Adele songs on her headphones while she worked. Rory's highlighter-inspired fashion sense. Sympathetic looks punctuated my return to work after the announcement that Seán had scored the promotion. How much of that was due to the job, and how much of it was because they now knew I'd become a widow at twenty-eight?

"You can't leave us!" Rory bounded over before I made it to my office, crushing me in a hug. I'd worked from home since I'd gotten the horrible news about Seán days ago. Now I only had to pack up my office.

I swallowed around the boulder suddenly in my throat. "Wish I could stay."

Anvi gave me a sad smile. "We'll miss you, Texas."

Rory pulled her into the hug, too. I didn't want to cry. Reluctantly, I extracted myself from the six-armed embrace. If I got sappy, I'd really humiliate myself.

One more row of desks to pass before I reached my office. I summoned my fiercest Grace O'Malley attitude, threw my shoulders back, and began the trek. Twenty feet of space felt like an epic gauntlet when I knew who sat there.

Seán twirled a stylus between his fingers. "Good morning, boss."

Maybe Callum had the right idea with violence after all. Okay, not really. But when I noticed the lingering traces of bruising under Seán's eyes and the new tilt to his nose, a small part of me couldn't help but wish I'd gotten the satisfaction myself.

Quiet fell over the room. I clutched my purse strap so hard, my nails dug into the leather. "Congratulations," I mustered.

"Thank you. No hard feelings?"

There was an audience, and I already looked unprofessional. One by one, I pried my fingers off the strap and held them out. An olive branch. Anger roiled off my skin as I gave him a tepid handshake.

Seán leaned against the desk with practiced nonchalance. "So, headed back stateside?"

"As I'm sure you're pleased to hear."

"We all have our places."

Not a single person in the large, modern space moved. Anvi planted a hand on her hip, eyes narrowed into hateful slits.

"This job is more than being a skilled artist, Seán. It's about leadership and—and teamwork."

He hummed. "To which category does siccing a mad dog on a coworker belong?"

Avoiding his infuriatingly smug gaze, my eyes flitted over the ephemera covering his desk. Photos of Seán coaching his sons' Gaelic football team and attending his daughter's dance recital. Handmade cards for Father's Day. He sought the promotion to make better lives for his kids. On his monitor, I spied the image of a mouse in a top hat. The colors were oversaturated, detracting from the charming Beatrix Potter–inspired aesthetic.

"What is this?" I asked. Numbness had overcome my senses. All at once, I remembered Seán's furtive evasion when I found him in my office with my sketchbook lying open. Blood boiled in my veins, but all I could do was stare at his bastardized version of my work. Was this what an out-of-body experience felt like?

"It's nothing. Just shorts to play between series episodes." He turned off the computer monitor, and the evidence therein vanished. "But that's none of your concern if your employment here is done."

That slammed me back in control of my motor functions. Not that I had control of my emotions.

My finger jabbed at the black monitor. It came back on to display the same scene of Houdini performing a magic trick. Shrill tones came out of my mouth, but I didn't care. Let me look hysterical. "I knew you were ruthless, but I never guessed you'd resort to stealing!"

"Pilfering from you? I don't need to copy you to succeed."

Hell no. He wouldn't gaslight me into believing the similarities were by chance. I'd dealt with too much to shrink myself to keep the peace again. Besides, art theft was an act of war. I excavated my well-loved Moleskine sketchbook from my purse and slapped it on his desk, spread open to the corresponding sketch. Gasps and murmurs broke out.

"You're not nearly as special as you think you are, sweetheart. You think you're the first person to draw a hat on an animal?"

Voice raised and trembling, I shot back. "It's identical to mine. That's no coincidence. It's based on my pet mouse. I made it for—"

Callum. I'd started the project as a gift for Callum. Just for him, I'd created Plague Rat, who didn't believe in magic. As a history lover, Cal would appreciate the nod to the real Harry Houdini's famous skepticism. It was a thank-you for the pet herself and a celebration of our friendship. A goodbye present. But now—I wasn't ready to say goodbye. Not yet.

What would Dolly do? Or Grace O'Malley? They'd fight.

"You thought I wouldn't find out you plagiarized my art? My entire concept?"

Seán figured I'd be back in the States by the time the project came to fruition and aired on the streaming platform. And Ireland supposedly *didn't* have snakes. Ha. Seán proved that wrong. For so long, it seemed crucial for everyone to like me. Life was too short to seek approval from someone unwilling to give it.

"What the bloody hell is wrong with you, Seán?" Anvi blurted.

Seán squirmed. Through my indignation, I became aware of Wendy among the crowd of rapt coworkers. Then Sullivan stepped forward as the cluster of staff parted to create a path.

He cleared his throat, calculating eyes bouncing between me and his nephew. "Lark, if you're serious about this accusation, we need to talk privately."

Incensed as I was, I hadn't even noticed his presence before that moment.

"Everyone in this office should know that these aren't his drawings. They're mine." With trembling hands, I held up my sketchbook and panned it around for the rest of the office to see. "I made these sketches *months* ago."

One by one, their faces turned from astonished and confused to downright angry.

Red-faced, Seán spat, "Unbelievable. I drew it. I pitched it. I got the job. End of discussion."

"Wendy's office, Ms. Thompson," Sullivan said. "Now."

He nodded toward the HR department. Wendy and I broke off and headed to her office to discuss the matter while he stayed back to speak to Seán. What was there left to lose? My reputation as a black widow who sent a brute to attack her competition? At least I had artistic and ethical principles.

Last time, my fear kept me from speaking, but this time I couldn't remain silent. That didn't mean another panic attack wouldn't happen. Wendy's office door clicked shut, and we stared at each other. What was Seán saying to his uncle out there? He had these people eating from the palm of his hand. From Wendy's disapproving face, I could tell she assumed this was retaliation for Seán being awarded the series. One last feeble attempt at mud-slinging before being pushed out the door.

Sullivan entered the room and silently regarded me for an agonizing moment. Words erupted from my mouth.

"Sir, I know what it looks like. But this is a clear case of theft. I carry this sketchbook every day, and doodle in it during my lunch break. A while back, Seán was in my office alone. I thought he was just being nosy, but he ripped off my work, wholesale. I can bring you my project and prove it."

CHAPTER 45

Callum

LARK HAD ACTED as the rainbow to my storm cloud, the lone sunbeam brightening a dreary landscape. How could I look at her window and not imagine lying entwined in her bed while our steamy breath and bare skin fogged the glass pane? It felt as if the sun would stop shining once she left.

The prep room door burst open. "Callum." Deirdre had been taking that overly concerned tone lately. It's what I got for allowing her to hug me.

I brandished an A/V plug with a pair of forceps. Deirdre recoiled, averting her eyes from the naked side-lying body. Orifices meant messes.

"Jaysus. You could've warned me."

"You could've knocked," I retorted.

"Quite a difference between knowing what goes on back here and watching you violate a body that looks disturbingly like my old headmaster with an oversize drywall anchor. Although Mr. Milton deserved far worse, if I'm honest."

"What do you need?"

"Have you talked to Lark?"

Silently, I redirected my attention. A leaky anus was preferable to this conversation. I shoved the A/V plug into place, effectively telling Deirdre where she could put her concern. She winced.

I dumped the forceps into a basin of disinfectant and rolled the man supine to shimmy a pair of plastic unionalls up his pelvis. Not–Mr. Milton was already a leaker and destined for burial in Dublin.

"I was preapproved for a few small loans. I've been trying to convince Pádraig to sell me his share in installments."

"You'd pay *him*? And go into debt?"

"He refused my offer, with O'Reilly and Sons circling like vultures. Pádraig wants to come all the way from Edinburgh to finalize this. He's itching to close the d-deal with O'Reilly before they lose interest, and willing to give me a small share if I let it go early."

"But you won't do that, right?"

"No. I won't. But if the offer still stands, you and I can get hitched."

"Of course. If you'll have an old lady like me." She smiled. "Desperate times."

"Desperate measures."

She chuckled lightly, then sobered. "I know this isn't what you wanted. Are you certain?"

"I hate to put your stability in peril. Maybe O'Reilly would keep you on staff."

"Think I want to work for that wanker?"

The thought of Deirdre and the rest of the team losing their jobs, on top of everything else, made me sick. She'd been loyal to my grandparents for years. Hell, she was willing to *marry* me out of that sense of loyalty and desire for career security. We'd discussed the logistics at length, and agreed I would offer her a stake in the company if we married to save it. If that didn't make her a contender for Employee of the Year, I didn't know what would.

The executor of my granda's will, the one who'd written up the document, had said exploration of any other avenue was futile if I couldn't afford to make a counteroffer.

The reception bell sounded, and Deirdre shuffled through the doorway, returning a moment later. "A young lady's asking after you."

She shook her head when she saw the hope in my eyes. It wasn't Lark. Of course it wasn't. I pulled off my protective gear and washed my hands, arriving at the reception desk to find a vaguely familiar woman with a brunette bob.

"Cielo?" I asked. Lark usually just called her Lo, but using the nickname myself didn't feel right.

She smiled. "Angel of Death."

The name must have been an inside joke with Lark.

"Is Lark with you?"

"She doesn't know I'm here, actually. She's at the studio to pack up her desk."

"Okay," I said carefully.

Cielo pressed a USB drive into my palm. "Watch this."

"I d-don't understand."

"She's been working on it for months."

"The movie?"

"Not the one you're thinking of."

Now I was even more confused. I handed the USB drive back to Cielo. "If I'm meant to have it, Lark can bring it herself. She's welcome here, you know. I'm not the one pushing her away."

Lark had specifically asked for space. So close, yet so far away. I ached for her with every breath. Out of respect—and fear of more rejection—I'd stopped myself from marching next door to talk to her. Soon an ocean would stretch between us. It sounded unbearable.

"But are you fighting for her?" Cielo asked.

"It blew up in my face when I tried."

"You didn't just propose for the sake of your inheritance?"

"I love her." My voice was firm. "I told her I'd walk away from all of it for her."

Deirdre's eyes bounced to me. Now she knew I was willing to sacrifice everything. Including *her* job. Expecting to find betrayal in her expression, I found nothing but empathy.

Cielo held my gaze. "Given her history, asking Lark to marry you for real was incredibly stupid. You know that, right?"

"Trust me, I know."

"Don't ask again."

"I won't." I sighed and stared at the floor. "I have an appointment tomorrow afternoon at the civil service office."

Her jaw hung open. "Seriously? With *who*?"

Deirdre coughed conspicuously, and Cielo blinked at the senior woman. "Believe it or not, I was the next best option," she said gently.

"Well, don't be rash just because Lark said no!"

"I'm out of time, and my father won't accept my counteroffer," I explained. "It's over. I have to file for a license now if I'm going to make the cutoff in July."

"Look. My cousin has been through hell and back, and she doesn't need a man to survive. But you're important to her. No matter what she told you at the beach, that's the truth."

"I don't have a choice."

Cielo didn't look convinced, though I'm sure Lark had explained it to her. "If you say so. Just take this." She stared hard at me until I pocketed the drive.

Deirdre slammed her fist down on the reception desk. The lampshade wobbled. "If you don't play that this instant, so help me, I will stuff you into an urn myself—"

"Whatever it is, I don't want to watch in front of an audience."

Cielo scrawled her number on a notepad on the reception desk. "In case you need it. I'll be in Ireland for a few more days."

I took the stairs two at a time to my room for privacy as Deirdre shouted a series of (mostly) encouraging curses after me. Not–Mr. Milton would just have to wait.

CHAPTER 46

Lark

THE NEXT MORNING, I carried a flash drive with my *Havarti & Plague Rat* short to work. Time-stamped proof that I'd begun it before Seán pitched his knockoff. For some reason, I couldn't find my original flash drive, so I made another copy, clutching it like a sacred talisman on the walk toward Mr. Sullivan's office. I took the long way, entering through a back door and winding through corridors instead of cutting through the animators' workspaces. Facing Seán immediately before this meeting could result in disaster; avoiding him was well worth the extra steps.

Mr. Sullivan's door swung open with a whine worthy of a suspenseful horror film. Or maybe I was just terrified Seán would get away with stealing my work.

Fingers tented, Sullivan sat with his signature indecipherable expression. The man was unavailable for weeks on end. Clearing his schedule to deal with plagiarism charges was a sign of how dire this situation was. Across from him sat Wendy. My knees threatened to liquefy. I pushed a palm against the wall to brace myself.

Unsure of the correct reaction but being positive that bolting for the door and hailing a taxi to the airport was inappropriate in this situation, I searched Sullivan's and Wendy's faces for a clue.

A mixture of indignation, desperation, and anxiety threatened to push tears from my eyes. If I attempted any words, I'd flood the room. Another emotional outburst in front of my boss was the last thing I needed.

Mr. Sullivan gestured to the sketchbook in my hand. I sat at the desk and handed Wendy the flash drive.

"This was a personal project. A gift for a friend, in fact. It was never meant to be pitched to the studio."

I opened to a drawing of the plucky heroine, Havarti.

Wendy found the file, and Mr. Sullivan's monitor displayed the corresponding unfinished animated clip. Tracked edits and dates proved my work on it predated the competition for the series. I'd used voice filters for all the dialogue myself, tweaking it higher for Havarti and lower for Plague Rat. Some of the character's lip-syncing was imperfect, as I hadn't had time to refine it yet, but it was unmistakably *my* creation—through and through.

"This muted palette works much better," Sullivan remarked as the clip played. Seán's version was hyperpigmented and clashed with the vintage-inspired illustration: his attempt to make it pass for his own, bolder style.

As they compared the originals to my competitor's facsimile, I recounted the afternoon Seán stole my art. Plagiarism was easier to prove than months of microaggression. My stomach twisted itself into a balloon animal ready to pop as they watched the short film.

Mr. Sullivan turned to me after the final scene. "That pitch was what tipped the scales in Seán's favor. It showed initiative and talent."

"He stole my ideas while he should've been pulling his own weight on the film. And I don't even understand. Seán's a great artist. Was it out of sheer laziness because he didn't want to develop his own idea?"

"I don't know, but I owe you an apology," Mr. Sullivan said. "This is clearly your work, and I praised someone else for it."

Sullivan? Apologizing to *me* after I'd swept into his studio like a tornado of drama?

"This isn't the kind of culture we support. Cutthroat is not what KinetiColor is about," Wendy elaborated.

I searched her freckled face and found sincerity. Along with a touch of embarrassment.

"You're not to blame for anything, sir. I wish I hadn't brought discord to your studio."

"I didn't realize Seán was responsible for so much strife in the office. That's my fault. I took him at his word because he's family."

Wendy adjusted her posture. "We conducted an anonymous survey about his behavior toward coworkers yesterday. Anvi said some people were afraid of retribution if they spoke up."

"Yes. I know about the previous art director."

Sullivan leaned forward curiously. "What about him?"

"Supposedly, Seán had a personal issue with him and got him fired."

"Fergus wasn't fired," Wendy said. "He left suddenly due to his wife's medical issues, so we didn't throw him a party."

"Oh. Everyone said Seán took credit for it."

Sullivan muttered something that sounded like a curse under his breath. "Evidently, our entire staff was living in fear of Seán. I only wish someone had brought this to my attention sooner."

"They were scared. They assumed you'd side with him," Wendy told him. Understandable. Seán had weaponized his relationship to the studio owner, even twisted the narrative around another man's retirement to serve his own agenda. Anything to reinforce the perception of his power.

"That survey was a wake-up call. I had no idea. And that was a failure on my part. I'm going to take a more active role in the studio going forward to make sure nothing like this happens again," Sullivan said. "Seán has already been terminated. We have a zero-tolerance policy for harassment. Or plagiarism."

To stay composed, I bit the inside of my cheek when my instinct was to hop up on the desktop and dance in jubilation. "If you'll give me another chance, I will resolve to do better by the team and by you, sir."

"Are you saying you still wish to be considered?"

Shoulders straightened, I said, "Yes, I am."

Ten minutes later, I walked out of Sullivan's office. No packing up my desk. No flight back to Austin. Just . . . a sense of relief. Hope. My pulse gradually settled as I weaved through the open workspace of the animation department. Anvi tore her attention from a half-finished storyboard for the new series and saw me grinning. She raised her brows and glanced toward Seán's desk.

He hadn't left yet.

An empty printer box sat atop the desk, stuffed full of the ephemera once littering his workspace. On a sharp inhalation, I met his fiery, resentful eyes. A defanged cobra whose instinct was to strike.

"Well, I hope you're satisfied," he spat as he shoved a framed snapshot of his children into the box. He angled it toward me for maximum guilt. Even with his parental responsibilities, he'd chosen to risk it all. To lie. To steal. *From me.* Father or not, I had a hard time cultivating sympathy for the freshly unemployed plagiarist.

The animators had paused their work to watch our confrontation. With how explosive the last one had been, who could blame them?

"Seán." My voice wobbled and I cleared my throat. "This was your doing, not mine. People have been walking on eggshells around you for years. I'm glad they won't have to deal with you anymore. I hope . . . I hope you reflect on that. We made something beautiful, and you were just hell-bent on ruining it for me. Why?"

He lifted the box with a jerk, its contents shifting violently inside. "Because I've earned it. I've paid my dues. And you don't belong here. I know it, and you know it."

"You still believe that?" A slow smile spread across my face. For once, I knew exactly what to say in retort. "God love you."

THE LAMBRETTA CAME to a stop at the curb of the office, not far from the impressive, green-domed Galway Cathedral. I peeled Lo's arms away from my abdomen.

"Good thing we're close to a church," she muttered. "I just promised I'd start going again if we arrived in one piece."

All right. So I had been speeding and weaving through traffic. "Sorry. They're already doing me a favor by getting me in on short notice."

My legs still vibrated with anxiety even after I'd shut off the engine. Lo had acted suspiciously after I got home the night before. It wasn't until late at night that she admitted she'd introduced herself to Callum and learned he had an important appointment the next day. Almost two weeks had passed since I last spoke to him, that fateful afternoon at Coral Beach. Now might be too late to relieve his pressure to marry for the sake of business. Even so, I had to try. Of all the regrets I had, not trying harder for Reese was my biggest. If I was going to open myself to Callum, it had to start with me fighting for him. Maybe I ought to send Lo to the cathedral to light a candle. I'd need all the help I could get.

A bell rang as we pushed inside.

"Aidan? Thanks for agreeing to see me today."

He rose to his feet from behind a desk, doing a double take at Cielo. "It's no trouble at all."

CHAPTER 47

Callum

I INCHED TOWARD the nondescript General Register Office like it was an iron maiden. A man condemned to a marriage without love. Not in the romantic sense, anyway. I swung the door open, and Deirdre preceded me inside.

A sign directed us to mute our mobiles, to respect the civil ceremonies performed in the building. My stomach knotted as I sat down with a stack of registration forms fixed to a clipboard.

This government building that smelled of fresh beige paint was the antithesis of romance, but a young couple hung all over each other across the waiting area, whispering and stealing kisses. Another older couple held hands and quietly exchanged reassuring glances. By contrast, Deirdre played Candy Crush on her phone to pass the time while I scribbled loops in the papers' margins to get their pen to work.

Lark. I wanted Lark. But time was up. If I was to make sure I still had a home, a job, and that my team—including the most loyal of all, my faithful receptionist, Deirdre—were still employed, I had to go through with this. Then Pádraig wouldn't have a leg to stand on.

"The bride needs to be present," the bored clerk said, once it was our turn for a license interview.

"I am." Deirdre stepped forward, and he cast another wide-eyed glance at me.

Yeah. There might've been about a thirty-year age difference between us.

He attempted to recover from his obvious double take. "Oh. I didn't realize. Only because it, uh, looks more like you're dressed for a funeral than a wedding."

"Sounds about right," she whispered out of the corner of her mouth.

Deirdre and I smiled wanly at each other. I was grateful to have her as a friend. In time, we could legally undo this, but it was the only way to save what my family had built. Ironically, to save it from one of its own members.

We handed over our IDs, and I continued signing the paperwork. This was wrong. When I had imagined my wedding day, it didn't look like a government office and my senior citizen receptionist. It looked like a blonde in a dress that made her look like one of those Disney princesses she loved so much. It smelled like a sun-warmed meadow on a summer day. And it tasted like Lark's kiss. But we didn't want the same things in the long term, even if we wanted each other.

After seeing what was on that flash drive, I didn't doubt that she cared. But she hadn't given it to me herself, and I couldn't bring myself to knock on her door last night to tell her I was applying to marry Deirdre.

I wouldn't pressure her again. She cared about me, enough to offer to sham marry me to save my business, but not enough for *forever*. She'd made that much crystal clear. Maybe Lark and I could figure something out one day in the future when circumstances were better, but at this moment, I needed to focus on my *own* future. And the future of those who depended on me.

Resigned, I handed the sheet to Deirdre for her signature.

Commotion from the hallway filtered through the door. Muffled voices. "Miss, you can't interrupt the interview. You'll have to wait your turn."

The door flew open.

"Cal! Deirdre! Wait—" Lark breathlessly tumbled into the room, all messy hair and wide gray eyes. Nearly two weeks had passed since I'd gotten more than a fleeting glimpse of her. It felt like a lifetime. "You don't have to do this."

Emotion surged inside me at the glorious sight and her overly loud, emotional plea. Relief and hope and . . . *wow*. Over the course of a few months, this woman had managed to turn me into an optimist. It would be disgusting if I didn't adore her for it.

"Oh, thank Mary, Joseph, and the wee donkey." Deirdre clasped her hands together in glee.

A security guard reached for Lark, and I jumped to my feet, instinctively putting my body between them. If he thought he was putting his hands on her, he was sorely mistaken.

"I'm sorry. She ran past me," the guard said to the bewildered clerk before he turned his attention back to her. "Miss, you have to leave this area if you're not serving as a witness to a ceremony or being interviewed yourself."

"She's welcome here," I assured them in a rush before turning back to her. "Lark?"

"Please tell me you haven't made it official."

"No, no. It's just an appointment for the license today."

A whoosh of air escaped her still-heaving chest and her shoulders dropped.

"Good. That's—" Her eyes shone in the fluorescent light, and she paused to swallow. "That's good."

Did she want to marry me after all? I took her hands in mine. Petite and soft, capable of such beautiful creations. Hands that had caressed me with heartbreaking tenderness. She squeezed back tightly.

"Because Aidan found a way. He found a way!"

Aidan? The singer with the tattoos? My whiplashed brain struggled to connect the dots.

"I brought him your grandpa's will," Lark continued, jerking her thumb toward the hallway where, sure enough, the man in question peeked his face through the doorframe. Cielo stood alongside him.

The exasperated guard narrowed his eyes. "Sir! Miss! If you're not an official witness or an employee, you can't be back here."

Aidan lifted his hands. "Okay, okay. We'll be in the waiting room." The guard cut Lark one last dirty look before escorting her companions out of sight, Aidan guiding Cielo with a hand at the small of her back.

"Lo was flirting with the guard as a diversion while I snuck past," she explained under her breath. "Only I'm not very sneaky."

Confusion must've still been splashed all over my face, because Lark's mouth lifted into a full, blinding grin. How I'd missed it.

"Aidan's a solicitor, remember? So I asked him for a consultation, and I think he found a way for you to keep Willow Haven without getting married."

Dare I believe it?

My granda's legal adviser of thirty years hadn't discovered such a loophole, and I trusted him implicitly.

Yes. I could believe it if Lark did.

Elation threatened to lift me off the drab industrial carpet. One moment, I was signing marital paperwork and swallowing down the bile in my throat. Next, I was holding the hand of the woman I loved. While she wasn't pledging herself to me, it meant something that she had come to disrupt my marrying someone else. It meant everything.

"You b-b-broke into my house?" was what I said instead. Not my most eloquent moment.

"Hell no. I learned my lesson the first time. I used the spare key you gave me, silly."

How could either of us forget her breaking into my prep room and being concussed via hurley? It was true, she wasn't sneaky. Nothing about Lark was subtle.

"I don't want you to be anyone else's husband. For any reason."

Time suspended as her declaration settled between us. I held my breath.

Lark's expression grew gentle as she stepped closer. "Because I love you."

My knees nearly buckled from the shock. "You love me?"

"So much, Cal. And I am so sorry for the way I've treated you. There's no excuse for what I did, and I—"

"God, I love you."

As her eyes filled with what I hoped were happy tears, she laughed. Even in a city brimming with music, her laugh was my favorite sound. Ever.

"Can I kiss you?" I asked. We could get back to the apology later.

Lark rose on her toes to grab my shirt collar. "You'd better."

Velvet-soft at first contact, the kiss started as demure. Then there was a detonation in my blood. I clutched her to my chest as her arms wrapped around my neck. Her mouth parted, desperately seeking more intimacy. We loved each other. Pure and elemental in its simplicity.

Deirdre interrupted us, wanting to make sure. "But how?"

Reluctantly, I set Lark back down. It took me a moment to recalibrate after disconnecting from the kiss. It didn't matter where we were. Or that I was still vaguely aware that we had an audience. My entire world whittled down to the need to connect with the woman who had turned it upside down with her arrival only six months earlier.

"Aidan can explain it better than I can, but, Cal, you'll need to call your father right away." Lark grabbed my arm and tugged me toward the door. We had a lot to sort out, but I'd follow her all the way back to Texas if that's what it took. I'd even face Pádraig. With her at my side, anything felt possible.

With an ear-to-ear grin, Deirdre ripped the paperwork in half and handed it back to the perplexed clerk. "Thank you for your time," she said, "but I think they'll be back another day."

THE NEXT DAY, my jaw tightened at the blurred outline visible through the door's stained glass window. Pádraig complained about his flight from Edinburgh as he pushed inside. No greeting, no questions about how I'd been running the parlor by myself.

Light green eyes, much like my own, fastened on a portrait of my grandparents in the hallway. Pádraig's pride had never allowed for a true reconciliation, despite my nan's many attempts to heal our family's rift. Pettiness was as much a motivation for his actions as greed. It wasn't enough to know his father was gone; Pádraig had to ensure his wishes went unrealized, even if that meant displacing me.

The worst part was knowing that he'd misled my granda in his dying days, promising to care for Willow Haven as had generations before. All to steal it out from under me. Pádraig had jumped on the first flight to Galway once I asked him to. Of course, that wasn't for my own benefit.

Aidan waited in the consultation room in a conservative suit.

After introductions, I offered my father a cup of tea, which he declined with a grunted no without the thanks. Out in the cemetery, nan Gráinne turbo-spun in her grave.

Fine, then. Let's get straight to the matter.

"I'm glad you're finally seeing reason, Callum. This should've happened months ago."

I sank into the antique leather office chair. "D'you have a notarized copy of O'Reilly's offer?"

Pádraig reached into a satchel and slid a stack of paper across the desk. "Your share would be twelve percent. It would've been higher, had you listened to me earlier."

How generous. Considering he stood to collect a small fortune off the company I'd helped build, it was woefully inadequate. Not that one could put a price on a family legacy and ancestral home. I was nothing more than collateral damage to him in his petty quest for vengeance against a dead man.

"We both knew you wouldn't find anyone by the deadline."

I *had* found someone. Lark was worth walking away from all of this, but she knew what it was like to live with remorse. Perhaps I would regret leaving the Flannelly family legacy, but I could never resent her. With her help, I'd learned to make space for both the light and the dark in my life. I wanted to bring the same sense of balance—of wholeness—to hers.

Aidan examined the figures and official notary's seal, then cleared his throat. "According to Tadhg's will, the trust will be transferred only to Pádraig if there's no reason to believe Callum would pass Willow Haven to the next generation."

"Right. And he hasn't married. So . . ."

The papers flopped in my grip as I waved them. "The same expectation applies to you. This is proof you don't intend to keep it in the family."

Pádraig's brow furrowed. Aidan's dark eyes cut to mine, and he nodded once.

"Granda Tadhg's wishes were simple," I said. "He'd rather let it wither on the last twig of the family tree than b-b-be auctioned off to the competition. Since you provided a good-faith offer of pending sale, you forfeit your claim."

Furious red colored his cheeks. "We had a deal. You had me fetch that paperwork under false pretenses!"

So the part about false pretenses was true, but I couldn't have gotten his cooperation any other way. According to Aidan, it had to be his name on the offer from O'Reilly for it to hold up in court. I wasn't taking any chances. A clause in the will stated that if neither Pádraig nor I intended to continue the legacy, then own-ership of Willow Haven would be transferred to Tadhg's brother, my distant great-uncle in County Mayo, presumably to be passed down to his adult daughters whom I barely knew. But I under-stood my granda better than that; he'd always wanted me to carry the mantle. He just didn't want me to do so alone, because he'd always had Nan to lean on for support on the difficult days. Thanks to Lark, I knew someone was there for me when burnout threat-ened to extinguish the sense of calling I felt.

"I said I'd consider the offer. I considered it. The answer is still no."

"Don't be daft, you can see the valuation!"

"I told you I'd never sell."

"The only reason I stepped foot in this godforsaken mauso-leum was to finally wash my hands of it," Pádraig barked. "You're telling me I came all the way from Scotland for nothing?"

Aidan and I exchanged a quick glance. He really was a damned fine solicitor, and the only estate planner I'd be referring my clients to from here on out.

"You didn't come for nothing. You came to grant Tadhg's greatest wish: that Willow Haven stays in the family. It's not per-sonal. Just business," I said. "Now get the fuck out of my home."

CHAPTER 48

Lark

WHILE CALLUM MET with his father and dealt with back-to-back services at work, Lo and I had spent the day in the Westend. I was finally being a decent host, treating her to all the boutiques, tourist sights, and Supermac's curry and cheese fries she could handle.

After we returned to my apartment, and I was awaiting a check-in from Cal, a knock sounded at the door. I opened it to find a set of killer dimples.

"Aidan?" I asked. Not who I was expecting.

Cielo jumped off the couch and ran to the door, smoothing her hair in place. "Hey!"

I knew that look on my cousin's face. My focus ping-ponged between them. Aidan couldn't tear his gaze away from her. I resisted the urge to slink back inside and avoid intruding.

I probably should've noticed this connection when they met, but I'd been more than a little preoccupied with Callum's future. Aidan was closer to my age than her twenty-two, but he'd been a gentleman during our date and had saved Callum's family legacy. The lawyer had my blessing. Turned out Aidan was the hero we didn't realize we needed until the eleventh hour.

Lo laughed awkwardly. "Guess who has a date with her own Irishman? Aidan asked me out for a late dinner and a drink. This little place called . . ."

"Let me guess: a little place called the Hare's Breath?"

He shrugged. "The finest pub in town, if I do say so."

I'd read that Galway boasted nearly five hundred pubs, and yet I still ended up only at the one in our neighborhood.

"Wanna come? For old time's sake?" she asked automatically. Her forehead crinkled in immediate regret.

I hadn't been on a group outing with Lo since Reese, but the memory didn't sting as much anymore. I felt . . . okay. Not without scars, but not shattered, either. New memories could be formed alongside the old ones.

"Yourself and Callum are welcome," Aidan added.

"No, Cal and I need time to talk."

So much was still unsaid that he needed to hear. My apology, most of all. I'd lose my mind if we couldn't have a deep conversation about where we stood tonight.

"I get it," Cielo insisted. "Don't wait up." I couldn't help but laugh as she waggled an eyebrow as the door closed. She and the lawyer were going to have plenty of fun.

Meanwhile, I hadn't seen Callum since the Hail Mary at the registry office yesterday. He'd had a late-night pickup that disrupted our plan to talk it out. All day, I'd fought the urge to call, not wanting to bother him when he was stressed about the arrival of his father and had back-to-back wakes and consultations scheduled. No rest for my wicked puffin.

As the sun began to set, I received a text.

> **Meet me in the garden?**

A murky, amethyst sky had begun to settle on the warm April evening.

Someone had drawn an open box in pink chalk on the sidewalk in front of my doorstep. An arrow sprung out of the top flaps. *Package thief* was written underneath in tidy, blocky letters. I gasped, thinking of the first time Callum and I met.

My head whipped around, but no one else was there.

The streetlight illuminated another chalk drawing of a familiar sight: a hearse.

I followed the trail toward Willow Haven, discovering another drawing on the sidewalk: a puffin. Then a mouse. Next to the hedgerows and wooden sign, a single roller skate. Then a Band-Aid. They were moments of our relationship. First meeting. First ride to work. First kiss.

A drawing of a chess piece graced his driveway. The first time we made love. Adrenaline spurred me faster at the memory of Callum's delicious mouth and desperate hands. His muscular arm hooked around my waist as he moaned into my ear. His yearning expression when our eyes locked. There was one more drawing along the path to his garden. Maeve's scooter. He'd laid them like bread crumbs, my heart pounded faster with every memory chronicled in chalk. Finally at the wooden gate, I raised my head to find the faint glow of lights among the willows and the rosebushes.

CHAPTER 49

Callum

I ADJUSTED MY shirt for the fifth time. I'd done my best to copy simple line-art images from my mobile. I was no artist, but hopefully Lark would recognize the elongated shape of my hearse and the Lambretta's curves. Or at least get a kick out of my idea to use mediocre skills to woo a professional artist.

The garden gate creaked open, and she appeared at last. Bright fabric hugged her curves, and her favorite cowboy boots peeked out from her jeans. Blond tendrils glowing in the twilight lifted in the late-spring breeze. She was the finest work of art I could imagine, more precious than anything in the *Book of Kells* or the National Gallery.

Lush willows draped in subtle fairy lights undulated in the breeze, lending the garden a magical atmosphere. Acoustic guitar played gently from a hidden wireless speaker. A quilt and inviting pillows covered the iron bench. A projector I usually used for memorial slideshows connected to my laptop and pointed to a sheet stretched across the fence. More fairy lights tangled in rosebushes framed the makeshift screen.

Lark took a step toward me. "Cal?"

God, I loved the way her perfect mouth formed my name. That one hopeful syllable meant everything.

"Hello, love." I cupped her soft cheek in my palm as her bottom lip trembled. Sweet citrus-vanilla filled my nose. "Sorry, I'm not much of an artist."

"It's . . . our story."

"It's also an apology for making you feel pressured to commit. And a thank-you for helping me keep the business even when you were cross with me. I'm not d-d—" I sucked in a breath. "I'm not done fighting for us."

"The thought of you with anyone else . . . it broke me, to think of you marrying someone else, for any reason." Emotion strained her voice as Lark squeezed my hand. "I've run hot and cold on you. Gave you mixed signals. I freaked out and abandoned you after you poured your heart out. Cal, I'm so sorry for hurting you. I've done a shitty job of showing it, but I love you. I really do."

"I know, my love. We're both figuring it out as we go along."

"I'm staying." Lark licked her lips. "I promise to do better by you. I fought for the job. For myself. For you. For us. You're looking at the art director for KinetiColor's first series."

"Lark! That's amazing!" I smoothed my hands along her face. She deserved to be as proud as she sounded. She'd championed for her own career. What she wanted in life. "I'm also sorry for jeopardizing your job. For all the stress it caused."

"No, you really don't need to apologize! I wanted to punch Seán myself. He was stealing my ideas. It's the reason he was chosen—he copied a concept of mine and presented it to his uncle as his own."

"He *what*?" This time, I really would put her nemesis six feet under.

"It's okay, it's over. Seán's fired."

I blew out a stream of breath. I felt as if I were on an emotional roller coaster. "Good riddance."

"And Lo convinced me to start seeing a therapist who specializes in grief. Losing Reese will always hurt, but you're right. I can't keep letting my past haunt our present. I'm going to keep working on myself. Just, be patient with me, okay?"

"We can go as slow as you need."

"And I know you want a family, but I don't know if I can—"

"It's you I want." A tear slid down the side of my nose. "I'm okay with not having kids if it means I get to have you."

Relief washed over her face. I only needed her beside me. Unable to contain the swell of emotion, I cupped her nape and brushed her lips with mine. A homecoming. A fecking miracle. Her tongue traced the seam of my lips, and I opened to her, enjoying the delicious intimacy.

"Cielo helped me arrange this private screening tonight," I admitted after we broke apart. I'd just kissed Lark for a good half minute, but it wasn't enough. It would never be enough. "And Deirdre, who I'm sending on a paid holiday for all her troubles. The woman ought to be canonized."

"But *The Pirate Queen* premiere isn't for another couple of months."

"While you were at work, Cielo brought me your short film. I thought it deserved a premiere of its own."

In a role reversal, it took a moment for Lark to respond. She formed a wobbly smile. "Lo did that?"

"I'm not the only one who loves you. Were you not going to show me?"

"It was supposed to be a goodbye present." Her mouth crumpled on the last two words.

"But you're not leaving anymore."

"No. I was worried naming my feelings would make them real, but they were real all along. All this time, I've been too wrapped up in my own morbid neurosis, too scared of hurting you to properly love you, and I hurt you anyway," Lark said.

"Callum . . . I'm sorry. I want to spend every day making it up to you."

"This whole time, on every feckless date I've endured, I've been yours. Completely, ridiculously, hopelessly yours." I crushed her to my chest as she let out a sobbing, relief-filled laugh.

"Wait. You set up a *bed*?" She quirked a brow at the bench loaded with pillows and the quilt.

"I heard about this thing called 'makeup sex.' Thought we might try it." It wasn't a bad idea, either, but not here. Well . . . maybe not. I wouldn't rule it out completely.

Lark laughed. "What will the neighbors think if they hear moans coming from the funeral home at night?"

Feck, I was mad about her. I couldn't help but lean down and kiss her again.

She broke away and sniffed the air. "Is that popcorn I smell?"

"Movie night isn't complete without our kitchen-sink mix."

"'Course not," Lark agreed with a smile.

Salted butter and caramel lilted on the breeze from the overflowing bowl I'd stashed under the bench. It was a beautiful night for an outdoor movie. Stars studded a velvet sky, and the willows danced in the periphery. With a few strokes of my laptop keyboard, the projector jolted to life. A title flickered on the white sheet stretched across the wooden fence. It resembled a black dialogue card from a silent movie, with an elegant white border and a serif font: *The Magical Adventures of Havarti & Plague Rat.*

"I can't b-b-believe you named my character Plague Rat."

"What can I say? You inspire me." She shrugged.

Stuffing myself into secondhand spandex and playing the Bee Gees had nothing on creating an entire short film from scratch by herself. "You're incredible. Know that?"

Lark tucked herself under my arm and nuzzled into my shoulder. She smelled divine. "Shhhh . . ."

A charming white mouse inspired by our beloved Houdini

appeared on the screen, tacking up *Help Wanted* ads around the forest. Only Plague Rat—a dashingly tall fellow who didn't believe in magic—responded. Recognition and awe had washed over me earlier as I realized what I was looking at. Us. An alternate, whiskered version, but us all the same.

"You'll be my assistant. All you need to do is listen to my instructions, stand there, and look handsome. And we'll split the Parmesan profits," she told him.

"I don't know," Plague Rat objected. "Isn't pretending magic is real telling a lie?"

"Illusions aren't *lies*. They're gifts. They give the audience something to believe in," she replied. "Help me put a little magic in the world."

Given that logic, Plague Rat agreed. Havarti promptly outfitted him in a sequined jumpsuit worthy of any Vegas show. Poor lad looked truly miserable in it. Beside me, Lark's expression filled with mirth. I chuckled and squeezed her closer.

A montage of rodents rehearsing illusions went by. Sawing a chunk of Swiss cheese in half as Plague Rat gulped and looked on warily. Pulling a cricket out of a hat. With each new trick, the fluffy white mouse and lanky black rat grew closer. We watched them fall in love. It had been only a few minutes long, but it packed an emotional punch.

"Houdini escaped, you know. The day we went to Coral Beach," Lark said. "And I felt so guilty because I hadn't noticed the latch on her cage was loose."

"Oh no."

"But I got her back. And once I did, I knew I had to get you back, too."

I swallowed, voice fragile. "You have me."

"I never meant for anyone to see this little film but you, but after Seán presented it as his own, Sullivan decided he wanted to expand *Havarti & Plague Rat* into a collection of shorts. So, now the world will get to see them when the series airs. You said I helped you find your voice, but . . . you also helped me find mine. Thank you."

"I can't believe you're staying."

"You made this place my home. I missed you so much over the past two weeks. I couldn't leave you permanently." Lark's lips grazed my neck. "Mo chuisle. Sorry I responded so weirdly to it before. It's beautiful."

"I meant it," I murmured. My pulse hammered under her soft kiss. Her love was the spark that promised to still ignite my soul long after my body departs.

"Will you teach me how to say 'I love you'?"

"I already did. 'Santaíonn mé thú' means to want and to love."

Lark gasped, then softly repeated the phrase back to me.

"'Tá mé i ngrá leat' is how to say 'I love you' on its own."

Her palms skimmed my biceps as she whispered, "But I want you, too."

"Only if you'll spend the night."

CHAPTER 50

Lark

THE BACK DOOR swung shut behind us, and Callum pushed me against it as he secured the lock. A jolt of excitement coursed through me.

"Take me to your room."

Callum scooped me up, surprising a laugh from my lips, and stomped up the stairs so fast I wondered if he was taking them two at a time.

He set me gently down on his bed. I'd never spent the night at Callum's; we'd never even kissed on his bed. But I felt immediately that this was where I belonged.

Sweet caramel still lingered on his tongue when he tilted my chin up for a deep, delicious kiss full of promise. My mind drifted to waking up here together, morning after morning. Going to sleep in his arms every night. I wanted every day, every night with Callum. I didn't just want a future together—I believed in it.

I eased his suspenders down over his shoulders first. The rise and fall of his chest deepened with each button undone. Wanting him to feel adored, I kissed his stomach while he watched me unzip his trousers. Callum's eyes were filled with what could only be described as veneration as he began to undress me. Unhurried and luxuriating in the sensation of every inch of exposed skin, after slipping off my jeans, he traced the inside of my knee, the hollow of my ankle, wrapped his hands around my calves. With every shallow breath, the tension grew until it became a palpable thing occupying every gap of space between our bare bodies. I removed his glasses and set them on the bedside table.

"You're absolutely gorgeous," he murmured.

"You say that after I take your glasses off?" I smiled.

"I don't need them to see you."

My heart swelled. He did see me, and it felt so *right*.

Callum pushed me back against the pillow. He was too much. The sheer size and power and earnestness of him. For the very first time, I could say he was mine and he had every part of me in return. Body, soul, heart.

He pressed his lips to my cheek where moisture pooled. "Lark, why are you crying?"

"I missed you. I missed us."

"D-d-don't hold back. Don't hide from me," he pleaded softly, kissing the tear away.

"I won't hold anything back."

To prove it, I sunk a hand into his hair and hauled him closer. Two weeks had passed since we'd been together like this, and I craved his touch. My lips ghosted over his thrumming pulse, my teeth tugged at his earlobe. A sensual hiss escaped his lips when I wrapped my other palm around his stiff length. His hands grew possessive stroking my curves, leaving nothing untouched.

With reverent eyes, he slid down my body until he was out of reach at the foot of the bed.

He rested my thighs on his muscular shoulders, then dragged his tongue across my clit in one torturous lick. His hot mouth soon had me melting and mindlessly tugging his hair. Callum was ravenous. Rumbling moans poured from his mouth and shook my core. His strong hands held me in place as my ragged breath gave way to cries of bliss. Legs quivering, I repeated his name again and again. Amazing as his tongue felt, I needed more. Needed him inside me. So I begged for it, spurring him on until the building pressure crested.

He gently placed my wobbly legs back on the bed.

Callum stalked over my body. Heat radiated off him, and his lips were swollen. "I need to hear you moan my name again."

My ankles hooked at his lower back. I wanted to revel in his pleasure, feed off it until it overcame us both. I reached down with one hand, lining him up against my drenched pussy. Anticipation ran between us like a pulsing current as our eyes met. This wasn't the first time we would make love with no barrier between our bodies, but it was the first time with no barrier between our hearts. I felt the difference. I felt whole. I placed a palm over his heart and felt my own beating in tandem.

"I love you." The words slipped from my mouth of their own volition. I wanted to tell him a thousand times more, and would, every day. "Callum, I love you."

He dropped his forehead to mine, his lips featherlight on my own as he murmured, "Mo chuisle mo chroí. Grá mo chroí." *Pulse of my heart. Love of my heart.* His forearms bracketed my head, and the delicious weight of his body cocooned me as he rocked his hips forward, the tip of his cock teasing my entrance.

He looked up and met my eyes as the resistance yielded and he slowly slid inside me. I dared not look away from his vulnerable face. No more hiding. I meant what I said. He pulled back and then thrust again, and again, somehow deeper, his hips picking up in tempo. My fingertips dug into his shoulders. In this position, all I could do was take in every inch of him. It rode on the edge of *too much*, but I couldn't get enough. He felt amazing. Callum glanced down, enjoying the sight of our fused bodies and the slap of our steamy skin forming a carnal rhythm. In this moment, there was no telling where I ended or where he began, because it didn't matter; we'd become one in every sense of the word.

Grasping my leg, he repositioned it until my ankle was resting on his shoulder, the underside of my thigh pulled taut. I gasped at his physicality. He straightened his arms to support his weight. "Is this okay?"

"Yes. *Please* don't tease me."

He entered me with one smooth motion. A moan tore from my throat, muffled by a messy, passionate kiss. Callum would make me forget my own name. Intensity burned in his eyes as he thrust slow and deep, with our foreheads pressed together. He was everywhere, in the thundering of my pulse and in my lungs when I pulled in his hot breath. He was between my legs and inextricably bound to my soul. He was where I belonged.

"That's it, love. Let me get you there."

"Finish in me," I cried, toes curling. "I need you."

His green eyes darkened. "Look at me."

Desperate for something to ground me as euphoria detonated like a bomb, I clung to his sweat-kissed shoulders. My vision faded out in pleasure. Rapt and relentless, Callum didn't let up until his brows knit and heat flooded the space between my legs. The sensation heightened everything. His groan in my ear was enough to make me whimper. I reached down, grabbing his muscular ass to keep him rutting into me until his hips finally stilled.

Eyes that crinkled in the corners gazed down at me. Rapid breath fanned against my dewy chest. Gently, he unpinned me from my captive position. Unwilling to lose the comforting weight of him just yet, I pulled him back down on top of me. Callum's five-o'clock shadow rasped against the soft skin of my breast as he settled in, and our breathing slowed. This was utter contentment. Total trust.

"Cal," I whispered. "I want this forever."

"That makes two of us."

Thanks to his patience and support, I felt like it was possible to honor the past and look toward the future. I didn't have to live only in the moment . . . but what a beautiful moment this was, being held by the man I loved.

EPILOGUE

Lark

Three Months Later

OVERHEAD, A BANNER reading *Galway Film Fleadh* waved in the humid July breeze. Flashbulbs popped like fireworks as photographers hollered at *The Pirate Queen*'s voice actors, who dutifully smiled and posed. Earlier, the same flashbulbs blinded Anvi, Rory, and me as photographers wrangled the KinetiColor crew. Spots still strobed in my eyes, but at least the gossamer overlay of my strapless gown looked opalescent under the lights.

Even though I'd been invited to the premiere of *Shoelace*, it hadn't felt right to enjoy that kind of fanfare when I'd blamed that project for so much personal strife. Now I could celebrate this achievement without guilt, and did so surrounded by people I cared about. People who cared about me.

My mom had called to wish me well and ask if I was bringing Callum home for the family's approval any time soon. Cielo was back home in Texas, but she'd been accepted into the University of Galway's foreign student program in the fall. I nearly blew out her eardrum when I screamed into my phone at the news. Our plan was for her to take over my apartment, and I'd move in with Callum.

My gaze wandered the gathered crowd in search of him but

instead snagged on a woman in a chic gown with expertly applied smoky eyeshadow. It had been over two years since our last interaction, but I'd recognize her anywhere. Even if I'd never imagined she'd show up in Galway.

Our eyes locked in recognition. Suddenly, it felt ten degrees hotter out there. She spoke something into a man's ear before breaking away from the group toward me. Canapés calcified in my anxious stomach. No more running. No more hiding.

Bracing myself, I made my way over. "Rachel. Hi."

She held her arms out for a hug for the briefest moment, then tucked them back in. "Lark. It's . . . been a while. I was hoping we could talk."

"Right now?" I couldn't exactly say I was hoping to be cornered by Rachel on the red carpet of a very public professional event. Distracted by preproduction on the series and celebrating Callum's recent birthday with a trip to Dublin—including a visit to the tomb of Saint Valentine—I hadn't noticed Blue Star's late addition to the lineup until two days earlier. The Galway festival was a big deal, but I hadn't expected the Texan indie company to spring for plane tickets all the way to Ireland.

"I saw Blue Star had a film, but I didn't think I'd see anyone."

Rachel looked over her shoulder and rattled off the names of a couple mutual colleagues in attendance. She drew in a shaky breath. "I'm really looking forward to your screening."

I curled my mouth into a facsimile of a smile. "Thanks. Your film as well. The concept is fascinating."

A server floated by with a tray of champagne. I snatched a flute and took a generous gulp. Rachel lifted her hand in a *No, thank you* gesture. It wasn't like her to turn down a complimentary drink, especially the good stuff. Instinctively, my eyes darted to her abdomen, where I found a modest swell under her gown. A massive engagement and wedding ring combo glinted as she placed a protective hand over the baby bump.

"You're married? Congratulations."

"Last June. And six months along. I take it you haven't read any of my emails."

My gaze darted away, and I took another sip.

"Okay. Yeah, I deserved that," Rachel said.

"Last time we spoke, you told me I was responsible. You told everyone."

"Lark, I made a mistake—"

"You ruined the one thing I still had after Reese, my work. I loved Blue Star."

"Look, I've been through a lot of therapy and . . . it made me realize how cruel I was. How I took it out on you because I couldn't scream at my brother. That's why I've been trying to contact you. To make amends. I can't take it back, but I needed to apologize."

She'd written to apologize? Every time I saw her name, it triggered memories of the worst period of my life. Out of cowardice and self-preservation, I'd shut down. If I had only mustered the courage to open them.

"I needed my best friend." My voice trembled. For so long, I'd avoided it, but today I would speak the truth. "I lost both of you."

Rachel's chin quivered. "I'm so sorry for everything. I've been thinking about family a lot since we found out we're expecting. How I wronged you. It wasn't your fault. Lark, I am sorry."

For so long, I imagined hearing those words from my accuser. Would they ring hollow or fill me with rage? It was surreal to hear them genuinely spoken—but what was more surprising was that it didn't matter to me like I thought it would. It turned out her apology didn't erase the mark her accusation had made on me. Three months of therapy had only just begun to help lighten my soul's burden, but I didn't need her permission to heal. I promised Lo and Callum I'd try. Facing those uncomfortable emotions head-on was challenging, but opening up was getting easier with each session.

"It breaks my heart that Reese will never get to meet his little nephew," she said. "Especially with how much he loved children."

Musical notes poured out of the speakers, and a smooth-voiced announcer declared the screening for *The Pirate Queen* was about to begin. Bubbles tickled my nose as I sipped champagne. Still no Callum.

"Do you need to go?"

"Not yet," I said. "I'm just . . . looking for someone."

Rachel gestured to a cluster of moviegoers. "*He* looks lost."

Beyond the string of photographers and journalists, Callum appeared. My heart could've burst at the sight. A tailored tweed suit wrapped around his strong frame, finished by a bow tie. Rich forest-green silk provided just enough color to complement his searching eyes. His sharply handsome, hard physique shielded the most patient, softest heart. I loved him. And I knew he loved me.

There had never been any point in trying to lie to Rachel; she knew me too well for that. And I didn't want to start now, because I wasn't ashamed. "Yes. That's him."

Wonderment lit Callum's face as he took in my glamorous appearance. Old Hollywood–style waves of hair fell over my bare shoulder, and my long gown's tulle shimmered in the summer sun. Unmoving, he drank in the details as I admired his polished look. I couldn't help but grin back. As he navigated the throng of filmmakers and tastemakers, a flicker of guilt dimmed my smile. At this rate, emotional whiplash would have my iridescent makeup ruined before the official group photo with the KinetiColor team.

Absently, Rachel rubbed her stomach. "Hey. It's okay. I never expected you to take an oath of celibacy. It's been two and a half years now."

"Sometimes it feels like two decades ago. Sometimes only two days," I admitted.

"For me, too. But it's not a sin to find light again after having been through so much darkness. That's what my mom told me after I met Javier. I felt guilty for being disgustingly content, in love and pregnant," Rachel said. "I've been concerned, knowing you're alone here."

"He's never let me feel alone."

Finally, Callum reached us. "The transport van got a flat on the way back from a pickup. I'm sorry we couldn't arrive together."

All that and he'd still managed to make it. I brushed my fingers against his fresh-shaven cheek when he bent down for a chaste kiss. "You're forgiven. Only because you clean up so well."

"You look exquisite."

My stomach butterflies fluttered to life. I'd stopped squashing them, and now the damn things were out of control, flapping enough to send me airborne anytime Callum unleashed that devastating smile. I wanted to be alone with him, but fate would rather give me an unbidden reunion than privacy. I hooked my arm under his and looked up adoringly.

Anvi and Rory walked up together, Rory in a slim white tuxedo, and Anvi in an embellished marigold sari that made her look like Bollywood royalty.

"Callum, this is Rachel. My sister-in-law," I said.

Shock crossed his face.

"Rachel, this is Callum. My boyfriend."

He softened, touched that I claimed him in front of the person closest to the love I'd lost. He looked to me with concern, a private check-in before he offered her a hand. I answered with a barely perceptible nod, and his expression toward her cautiously warmed.

"Hello."

Her diamond glinted under the lights as Rachel sized him up and shook his hand. "Nice to meet you."

Callum snaked a protective arm around my waist, pulling me closer. After the unexpected encounter, his touch was grounding. The steady source of strength I needed.

"Rachel? You have a lot of nerve," Anvi said.

We'd become even closer since I shared the full story of my

life back in Austin. Allowing my friends to truly know me felt freeing. Anvi was more than willing to put anyone in their place, but I'd learned I could stick up for myself. Only took thirty years, a crisis of the heart, and impending unemployment, but who's keeping track?

"Anvi. It's all right," I assured her. There was a lot to unpack, and now wasn't the time. "Rachel, these are my friends and colleagues at KinetiColor. Anvi, our storyboard artist. And Rory, our new senior lead animator."

"It's a pleasure. You're very fortunate to have Lark on your team."

"Well, then, this thing is starting in a minute. Let me know if you need *anything*. Champagne refill? Shovel? An alibi?" Anvi continued to plunge mental daggers into Rachel's chest. It was oddly heartwarming.

"Do you want to sit with us?" I asked cautiously, gesturing to Rachel.

To my relief, she declined with a headshake. "This is your moment. And the Blue Star team already has tickets. But I'll be rooting for you."

"Just save Cal and me a couple seats in the theater, please," I told Anvi. "I want to sit with you and Rory."

"Will do." Rory shot me a dorky salute, and dragged Anvi toward the refreshments before she could make a more overt threat.

"You work in the animation business, too?" Rachel asked Callum once they'd gone.

"No. I'm an undertaker."

Her jaw almost hit the red carpet. "For real?" Rachel turned to me. "Lark, you used to avoid Algodones Street because you hated driving past the old cemetery! You'd drive blocks out of your way just to avoid thinking about mortality."

I had. And that was *before* losing Reese.

Callum's eyes slid back to me. I'd come a long way, thanks to him. I still didn't want to dwell on the darker aspects of life, but I no longer avoided them with terror. Tragedy made me appreciate serendipity even more.

"Do you have a name picked out?" I asked to change the subject. "It's a boy, right?"

Rachel's smile made its first appearance. God, I'd missed it. "We're naming him Reese Wyatt."

Without thinking, I threw my arms around her and let out the sob I'd been fighting since the moment our eyes met.

"He'd want us to keep living," she mumbled into my shoulder. "He'd want you to. I'm sure of that. If you're finding a way to be happy again, then Reese would be pleased."

My gaze drifted back to Callum. "I am. I'm finally allowing myself to be happy again."

No more pretending. No more grinning through the pain. Genuine joy, found in the most unlikely person. If someone had told me nine months ago that a misdelivered package of body bags would lead me to a man I'd fall in love with, I'd have told them they had the wrong girl. But here he was. Patient. Kind. Sarcastic. Generous in bed, to boot. Falling in love was *not* on my Fresh Start In Ireland bingo card, but life would always have the last laugh.

Rory's wave caught my attention just as the chime went off again. The world premiere of *The Pirate Queen* would soon begin. Anvi smiled at me as Rory adjusted the lapels of their slim white tuxedo. Callum checked the time on his granda's vintage watch, only worn for special occasions.

"I'm glad you came," I told Rachel. And I actually meant it.

"Once I learned you had a film in the festival, I knew I had to apologize in person."

"Thank you. Good luck with your feature, as well."

Following the flow of people to rejoin the rest of the KinetiColor team, I took Callum's arm. He lowered his mouth to my ear, a reassuring hand resting on the small of my back. "Need to take a moment b-b-before we go in?"

I didn't even have to answer. We were in sync. Callum veered off from the crowd filtering into the theater and led me to the side of the building. Questioning arsenic-green eyes met mine as he gently tilted my chin up.

"I'm okay," I insisted. "That was a long time coming."

Callum kissed me on the forehead with so much tenderness, I could cry again. "I'm proud of how you handled that."

I knew we would talk about Rachel more later, that I needed to, but right now I was content.

His love had convinced me that I deserved to be genuinely happy, despite the regrets of my past. I could be a better person, a better partner. No taking him for granted or bottling up my feelings. In an interview, my animation hero Hayao Miyazaki once said that he strived to portray love as a relationship where two people mutually inspire each other to live. That was the kind of foundation Callum and I shared. His quiet strength inspired me, in every way, to live authentically.

"Having you there made it easier," I answered honestly.

"Mo chuisle, that was all you."

I curled my fingers around his lapel and tugged him down for a proper kiss. Slow and delectable. Pouring my gratitude into it, I stepped into his rain-scented embrace. Our noses brushed, and I lingered there, thinking of the look on Callum's face when I'd claimed him. "I'd never deny that we belong to each other, Cal. To anyone. I'm proud to be yours. You know that, right?"

"Just nice to hear, is all. Especially after I expected you to clobber me for arriving late."

I smiled and placed his hand over my sternum. "I'm yours. I always will be."

Callum's eyes roved over my face. For a moment, it didn't matter that the premiere was minutes away. It didn't matter who else was there in the audience. What mattered was that Callum knew I treasured him.

"We ought to head inside," he said, stealing one last kiss. "Don't want to miss your moment."

"You're right." I straightened his bow tie. He was so sophisticated in that suit. It would be delightful to muss his perfect hair and strip him piece by piece after we got home.

We stepped into the dim theater, shuffling into a row of reserved seating. Anvi sat on my left, Callum on my right. As the lights faded and excitement rippled through the audience, I squeezed their hands.

I loved my job and what our team created. I loved this vibrant, seaside city. And I loved Callum Flannelly. The last man I'd expected to fall for had sutured the hole in my heart. I'd helped animate the tale of an Irish folk hero, but he was my true-life hero. My safe port through life's storms. The wind in my sails. Life was unpredictable and magnificent, full of irony and happenstance. And I knew I wanted to spend the rest of mine making that brave, devoted, privately sentimental man smile.

Callum

PERHAPS GALWAY WAS a biased place to premiere the reinterpretation of a national legend, but Lark and her team did Grace O'Malley justice. Based on the standing ovation, the rest of the festival attendees agreed. My cheeks ached from smiling as the cheers and applause stretched beyond one minute. Lark looked positively incandescent taking a bow with her colleagues. I lifted her off her feet and wrapped her in a hug. A giddy laugh bubbled out of her.

I never knew another's happiness could bring me such joy.

She'd politely declined the invitation to the after-party at the Hare's Breath, knowing that my social battery was already drained. She held my hand during the drive home and opened the garden gate instead of the front door. The early-evening light caught the sheer layers of her gown, and she practically glowed. I followed.

Lark discarded her strappy heels on the stone path, sighing as she stepped onto the grass.

"Care to dance with me?"

I tilted my head. "A two-step to no music?"

With a challenging look, she pulled her phone from a jeweled clutch, and a soft song immediately played from the speaker. A smile spread across my face. I bent to unlace my wingtips and set them on the path. Cool blades of grass tickled the soles of my feet as I walked toward her.

"It's too people-y at the pub," she said. "But I still want to dance with you."

I took her hand in mine, brushing my lips against her knuckles before assuming the posture of the two-step. Lark looked up at me, adoring and tender.

"Tá mé i ngrá leat," she whispered as we began to move. *I love you.*

I watched her for a moment, speechless.

"What? Did I butcher it?"

"No, no. That was perfect." I'd caught her listening to language lessons more than once, but she'd never uttered those words to me in Irish before. She was determined to make Galway her home.

"I'm lucky to have a tutor who helps me get the tongue movements just right."

I hooked my arm around the small of her back and tugged her close. "Tá mé i ngrá leat."

My heart was more vulnerable than ever before. Beating outside my own body in another's. I knew firsthand how fragile each moment was, what a gift. Lark did, too.

We would cherish the light and honor the darkness, together. I would do everything in my power to build a beautiful, vibrant life for this woman who had splashed color into my monochrome existence. In this ivy-blanketed home where death was honored, we would create a life filled with honesty and love and joy.

IRISH / GAEILGE
PRONUNCIATION AND TRANSLATION GUIDE

gnéas béil / GNAYiss BAY-il / cunnilingus

ag bualadh craicinn / egg BOOLah krackin / sex (literally "slapping skin")

bod / bud / dick

tóin / TOH-in / ass

brollach / BRULL-okk / breasts

faighin / FY-in / pussy

púrsa te / POORsa cheh / wet pussy

áilíosach / AW-lee-OH-sokk / aroused (women)

féintruailligh / fayn-troo-ill-ig / touch yourself

le do thoil / le duh hul / please (literally "with your will")

tabhair póg dom / toor poge dum / kiss me

Santaíonn mé thú / son-TEE-un may hoo / I want you (with loving connotation)

braitheann sin go deas / BRAH-hin shin guh jass / this feels amazing

níos moille / NEE-us MWIL-yah / go slow

tá tú chomh tais / taw too kkoh tash / you're so wet for me

grá mo chroí / graw muh kkree / love of my heart

mo chuisle mo chroí / muh KKUSH-la muh kkree / pulse of my heart

ACKNOWLEDGMENTS

First, thank *you*, reader, for giving this odd little book a chance. I sincerely hope you enjoyed it.

I owe a massive debt to my fantastic critique group, authors Valerie Pepper, Alicia Wilder, and Kat Saturday. I'm so grateful for your honesty, your friendship, and your humor. Cheeto Dust Crew for life.

Shout-out to my kick-ass agents, Caitlin Mahony and Suzannah Ball at WME, for believing in this book. To my editors, Tara Singh Carlson at Putnam and Lara Stevenson at Transworld, for helping to bring it to a wider audience. Working with you to polish this manuscript was a pleasure. To Jill Bailin, who helped me develop this story. Credit also goes to the talented Epsilynn for the charming cover illustration.

Special thanks to Bre Brix for her insight into the mortuary profession. And to my wonderful friend Ashley, who answered many messages pertaining to embalming and dead-body butt plugs. Big thanks to Carolann, Emily, and Mollie, who graciously helped me with the nuances of Irish culture and language. And to my dear friend Krystina, who enabled this whole journey when I sent her an unhinged version of the meet-cute and she demanded the rest of Callum and Lark's story.

My deepest gratitude to the readers of the indie first edition, who uplifted it through reviews, recommendations, and social media posts. I'm still absolutely floored by your enthusiasm.

I want to thank Terry and my son, Eero, for their unwavering encouragement (even though he's not allowed to read this book until he's fifty). Lastly, thank you to my husband, Moy, for listening to my plot-hole rants and supporting my dream. I couldn't have done it without you, and I find inspiration in our own love story every day.

About the Author

Ivy Fairbanks is a shameless consumer of rom-com books, hazelnut coffee, and Hozier music. Not necessarily in that order. Living with Ehlers-Danlos Syndrome has made her a believer in the importance of representation in romance. Ivy writes stories where diverse and disabled characters find love, acceptance, and their happily-ever-afters. She lives in the Tampa Bay area with her husband and son. At any given moment, she is probably trapped under a sleeping tabby cat. *Morbidly Yours* is her debut novel.

Connect Online

IvyFairbanksBooks
IvyFairbanksBooks
ivyfairbanksbooks.com

Author of the Love in Galway series

Ivy Fairbanks

"Sweet and spicy and fabulous . . . Ivy Fairbanks is a terrific addition to the romance genre!"

—Abby Jimenez, #1 *New York Times* bestselling author of *Just for the Summer*

PUTNAM

SCAN ME

or visit
prh.com/ivyfairbanks

PRH collects and processes your personal information on scan. See prh.com/notice/